PRAISE FOR *TRUTH LIES BURIED*

'This hot new author's novel hits the ground digging, right in the middle of the action . . . Either well researched or owing something to insider knowledge, maybe both, this fast ride will keep you guessing all the way to the end.'
—Mark Ramsden, author of *Dread: The Art of Serial Killing*

'A gripping gangster novel with a fantastic protagonist. Like a cross between Cassavete's *Gloria* and *The Long Good Friday.*'
—Paul D. Brazill, author of *Guns of Brixton*

'A very British noir; dirty deeds and dirty minds described in some very clean prose. *Truth Lies Buried* is sharp, sexy and very smart. Its female characters are strong and seductive, its plot satisfyingly complex.'
—Geoff Nicholson, author of *Bleeding London*

TRUTH LIES
BURIED

TRUTH LIES
BURIED
LESLEY WELSH

THOMAS & MERCER

Published by Thomas & Mercer, Seattle

www.apub.com

Amazon, the Amazon logo, and Thomas & Mercer are trademarks of Amazon.com, Inc., or its affiliates.

ISBN-13: 9781503935785
ISBN-10: 1503935787

Cover design by Jason Anscomb

Printed in the United States of America

To Ian. Thank you for everything.

Chapter One
2 a.m., Friday, 11 April, 2003

Pitch-black and we'd been digging for an hour.

'This should be deep enough, eh?' Typical Joe, he never wants to do any physical work.

'Couple more feet, I reckon,' I said.

Headlights from the nearby road swept across the ground and he ducked for cover.

'Don't be stupid,' I said. 'Nobody can see anything through the trees.'

'Not taking any more chances. That's me done.' He chucked his shovel out of the hole.

'Me too, then.' I climbed out after him to pick up my end of the tarpaulin. 'Can you lift it?'

'It!' He snorted his displeasure at my blunt choice of words. '*Him*, you mean. Have a little respect.'

One, two, three and the tarpaulin-wrapped bundle landed with a thud in the makeshift grave. Joe let out a grunt and threw the gun in beside Benny Cohen's corpse. We worked in silence, filled in and levelled the ground. Finally, we chucked rocks and leaves on top to conceal the newly turned-over earth.

'Sorry to have upset your finer feelings,' I said after we'd finished and walked back to Joe's Land Rover. 'You haven't got religion, have you?'

I slung the shovels into the back of the car while Joe started the engine. I climbed into the passenger seat, keeping my gloves on. Joe took his off and threw them onto the back seat before he stuck a ridiculous plastic fag in his mouth. He drew on it hard as he backed the motor out onto the country road. 'That man,' he said, 'was a sentient being. He had thoughts, hopes, fears, a soul.'

'And children, a wife, a couple of mistresses, a dog that no doubt worshipped him, a puddy tat that purred on his lap.'

'Now you're taking the piss.'

'He was a stranger and you got paid. What do you care?'

Joe grunted. He'd been doing a lot of grunting on this job. I reckoned he was losing his bottle. We'd done a couple of jobs together in the north years ago and back then he was as cool as. But these days he'd got twitchy. A dangerous thing is twitchy.

'And what's with that?' I gestured towards the 'cigarette'.

'I'm trying to give up. This is a dummy. A mate of mine brought it back from Australia for me.'

'It'll never catch on.'

'Smoking real ones is bad for your health.'

'And you think you'll live long enough to feel the benefit, do you?'

'Nobody knows it was us.' Joe gripped the plastic thing between his teeth. We were heading away from the woods now but the road was still clear. 'Do they?'

'Only the person who paid us.'

'And we don't know who that is.'

'But we can hazard a guess,' I said.

'Guessing is bad for your health, too.'

'So is getting all cosmic about some dude you've just shot in the head.'

Joe's body stiffened as he glanced in the rear-view mirror. 'Jesus, Riley – there's a car behind us.'

'This is a road, Joe. We may even encounter one in front of us shortly.'

'I think it's following us.'

Joe put his foot down but the other car kept pace. He turned hard left into one of those upmarket residential estates, each of the houses different but somehow all out of the same brick mould. Medium-sized boxes, all with their standard-issue families sleeping the sleep of the contentedly mortgaged. We made another left then slowed to a crawl. The other car did not follow.

'Paranoia,' I said. Joe grinned, blew out his cheeks with relief and we drove full circle through the one-way estate back to the same road where we had entered.

'Bloody hell,' he said. 'How much must these houses cost? You'd think you'd get more than one road for your dosh.'

'It's social control,' I said. 'When the natives eventually get restless, there'll be fewer roads to block. That's what they taught me in the army, anyway.'

'Seriously?'

'Dead serious,' I said. 'But let's get back to the motorway. Get you home.'

'Yeah,' he agreed. 'Give me the frozen north any day. I hate unfamiliar places.'

We exited the one-way estate and I barely noticed the car parked on the other side of the road. Not until the driver hit the lights, started the engine and latched on to our tail once more.

'Do you think he knew that road went around in a circle?' Joe was agitated and chewing down hard on his faux fag.

'Yeah, must be a local.'

'Or a cop?'

'No, they'd have come mob-handed.' I turned around to check out the headlights. 'This is something else entirely.'

'Leave behind no witnesses, you mean?'

'Stop the car, Joe.' I opened the glove compartment and pulled out a handgun.

'Fuck me, Riley! I thought we'd got rid of those.'

'Insurance,' I said.

He pulled off the road onto a grass verge beside the remnants of a once proud forest. A Mercedes with tinted windows stopped a couple of hundred yards behind us. I took a deep breath and opened the passenger door.

'I'll come with you,' Joe said.

'No, you stay here. I'll go and talk to this geezer, see what's going on.' I held the gun by my side. 'If you hear shots and I'm not still standing, then take off.'

I moved towards the full-beam glare, conscious of the heft of the Glock in my right hand, blood pounding in my ears, and tried to get a look at the number plate. It had been muddied – that old trick – but even the numbers I could make out weren't familiar to me. The car's tinted windows revealed no interior shadows but I half expected a hand to emerge, shootered up, and my imagination revved into overdrive. *Bang!* I could almost feel the thud as the bullet hits, jerks me backwards, throws me off my feet. Then the screech of tyres as Joe drives away and I'm left on the ground with nothing but the full April moon reflected in my eyes.

But there was no stealthy hand and I could hear the thrum from the Land Rover's idling engine behind me, sense the faint purr of the black car ahead. The hundred yards I had to cover felt more like a marathon.

The driver's window was down. I peered into the dark interior. Nothing, nobody; it was the *Marie*-fucking-*Celeste*. Where was the bastard?

I looked back towards Joe's vehicle and spotted a shadow slither from between the trees. Sudden flashes in the Land Rover's cab and a muffled *pop, pop, pop*. I took cover beside the Merc, gun aimed two-handed across the bonnet at whoever might be about to try and take me down too. The shadowy figure straightened up, dressed all in black like a ninja. But it was a female silhouette that emerged from the darkness into the full beam of the headlights. A silenced gun was in her left hand and, in one fluid movement, she pulled the black balaclava from her head with the other. Monica! Her blonde mane fell loose to her shoulders and she screwed her eyes up against the harshness of the lights that made her look half-devil, half-angel. She smiled tentatively in my direction, dropped the gun on the ground and held out her arms to me.

'I had to do it, Sam,' she whispered. 'To keep us safe. You've got to understand.'

I stood and faced her. 'Joe didn't even know who Benny was, Monica. Joe was solid. He'd never grass on me.'

'Better this way.' She slid into the Merc's front passenger seat. 'So get over it. Get rid of the guns and take me home.'

Monica was the wife of Benny Cohen, a semi-retired gangster. He'd have had us both filleted if he'd cottoned on to our affair. She'd convinced me that was true. 'Benny will kill me. He'll never let me go,' she'd said. So we had to get rid of him, didn't we? Pretend it was a commission job by an out-of-towner. My old Manchester mate Joe Murphy was collateral damage. I felt stunned, but this was no time for regrets or recriminations. My hard-arsed, army-instilled professionalism and keenly honed sense of self-preservation kicked in. Man down. Move on. Survive. Sorry, Joe, I'll mourn you some other time. Right now, we had to get away from the scene – fast.

And Joe's simple plan had been so perfect. Benny Cohen and his distinctive gold Lexus would disappear on the way to Benny's late-night meeting. Police would be informed next day, by which time the Lexus would already be in a dockside crate headed for Nigeria, courtesy of Joe's steal-to-order 'specialist motor exporter' contact. The Lexus was already on its way to Southampton. But the final element of Joe's plan was now well and truly down the Swanee. Six months was supposed to go by; one phone call to Joe and what remained of Benny would be 'discovered' by people camping on that very spot. With Monica by then officially a widow, we'd hop it to Spain together and live happily ever after.

But now with Joe being whacked tonight, all our plans were screwed up, irrevocably. Come the morning, some nosy dog-walker would take a butcher's into the Land Rover and get a very nasty surprise. A gang hit and a missing villain on the same stretch of road would be too much of a coincidence for even the local plod to ignore. The cops' woof-woofs would sniff out Benny in no time.

Monica must be crazy. And I was in far too deep to back off now.

Chapter Two

10 a.m., Monday, 16 June, 2003

A sunny morning just five days to the summer solstice and two months after Benny Cohen's demise, and we were at the Liberal Jewish Cemetery in Willesden, North London. Monica looked sensational in black, like she was born to wear it. With her blonde hair swept up under a wide-brimmed hat, she was nothing short of angelic in my adoring eyes. She'd gone so far as to wear a veil – classy touch that, I thought. I watched her at the funeral, pale and tearful, leaning on the rabbi's arm. Her other hand was on the shoulder of her son Brando who was togged out like a mini-mobster. Reservoir Pup, all cropped hair and snarly mug, strutting around in his dark made-to-measure. Short for his age, it seemed to me that the kid already showed signs of small-man syndrome with his snide remarks and contemptuous manner. He growled like a dyspeptic bulldog whenever over-dressed and perfumed old tarts tottered up in stilettos and planted a smudgy kiss on his cheek.

'Shame Benny only had the one,' a skinny-arsed dowager in black Chanel chirped up, and Monica smiled ruefully. 'Such a handsome boy.' Hell, someone should tell the old girl she's in dire need of Specsavers.

Old lags and acquaintances clustered around Brando. 'Image of his dad,' they declared. 'Gonna be a big lad. Chip off the old block.'

Faces in deep mourning squeezed the kid's shoulder and tucked big notes into his pockets, like this was some kind of Mafia wedding. His grimace morphed into a grin. Yeah, chip off the old block. You said a mouthful there, pal – just eleven years old and already a greedy, heartless little tosser.

'What happens to us now?' That was Brando's first question when Monica told him they'd found his dad's body. What kind of a question is that for a kid to ask? Benny had always been a bit distant with the lad but he had given Brando everything he'd ever asked for. Except the posh education Monica wanted for him – to take place as far away as possible. 'No son of mine is being sent to one of them snotty boarding schools,' Benny had raged. Well that's where he'll be off to soon enough. She'll make sure of that.

'Any inside info, Sam?' Big Jim Carver asked me as we stood by the graveside.

'All I know is the cops found a Land Rover with an out-of-towner. And he wasn't talking. What with being dead and that.'

'Yeah. But who took care of the taker-carer?' Carver's voice always threw me, that high-pitched squeak emanating from his bulky body. Years before, a bullet in the throat had left him talking like a mouse on helium. But nobody laughed about it, not even behind his back – not anymore. Only Benny Cohen had called him Dog Toy, but what remained of Benny was in the casket being lowered to his final resting place.

I shrugged.

'Keep me in the loop,' Carver said. 'You got that?' I nodded my compliance to his thinly veiled threat. He walked away and my blood ran cold. Carver may be a squeaky-voiced fat guy but some of his heavies were enough to give SAS hard men nightmares. No way did I want to be on Big Jim's radar. The sooner I could get Monica to Spain the better.

This was my first Jewish funeral and I was uncomfortable with the tradition of mourners heaving a spadeful of dirt on the coffin. 'It's a sign of respect,' Monica had told me. But having already buried the guy once, I had no appetite for taking part in the rerun. So I was glad when she told me that it was not expected of the help. Could have felt insulted if I hadn't been so relieved. I watched dodgy characters of every stripe queue up for the privilege of chucking muck on their old rival, if only to make sure Benny Cohen was well and truly dead.

Monica sobbed decoratively. Should have been an actress, that woman. She hugged Brando close. For his part, his swinish eyes scanned the crowd. What's in this for me? his expression seemed to say. Fix your face, kid. Learn not to show what you're thinking. Though, no doubt, that would come given time. If he got his expensive boarding school education, he'd be the most ruthless operator that ever set foot in a boardroom.

Carver approached Monica, and Brando looked like he was about to cack himself. Big Jim's reputation as a kiddie fiddler had obviously filtered through to his young ears. Monica had the good sense not to clasp the boy to her heaving bosom; instead she pushed him forward to have his head patted and his pocket padded with a wedge of fifties. Brando's countenance brightened with avaricious delight and Monica's smile tightened. Yep, it's boarding school for you, matey – pretty sharpish. Even if the brat did turn out to be a bum bandit, at least it'd be through circle jerks with boys of his own age, not at the sweaty paws of Big Jim Carver and his pervy cohorts.

'Checking out the sexy widow?' Chinese Clive hissed in my ear.

'That's part of the job description.'

'Well, enjoy it while it lasts. No need for a guard dog when it's open house again.' Clive's weasel features contorted into what passed for a grin. 'Don't expect her to grieve for very long. Then it'll be back to bouncing for you, Sam. You're just not her type.'

Clive sniggered and slithered back to the East London guys surrounding Gerard Fowley, who was his usual sharp self in his navy Armani. Suited and booted he may have been but he was still Gerard Fowley – white junkie mother and Jamaican gangsta father, circa Railton Road. He'd started out by slapping hookers around, slashed and burned his way out of Brixton, used drug money to buy straight businesses and was now harbouring delusions of grandeur. Put a thug in an expensive suit and what do you get? A well-dressed thug is what. And he looked even paler than the last time I'd seen him. He nodded over to me. I raised a hand in acknowledgement and heard laughter and snide muttering from the group. Bunch of crossbred pricks! I had no idea why they were invited. Benny had never done much biz with that lot as far as I knew. He'd always laughed at Fowley and his attempts to emulate Michael Jackson's race hopper. 'Skin disease, my hairy arse!' was Benny's response to Fowley's gradual whitening. So maybe Monica was being diplomatic, trying to keep the peace while the territory was divvied up between the other members of the consortium.

Fowley shimmied over to me. 'Lookin' for a new job, Sam?'

'Not at the moment.'

'Well, I've always got a place for you.'

'Cheers, I'll keep it in mind.' Not at one of your nightclubs, thanks – full of Arabs and prozzies. I'd rather work Securicor.

Fowley patted me on the back and went back to his posse, leaving behind the stench of over-splashed aftershave and a queasy feeling in my stomach. I was barely on nodding terms with Gerard Fowley and suddenly he's all pally and offering me a job. And what was all that about Monica not grieving for long? What did Fowley and that nasty fucker Chinese Clive know that I didn't? My gut twisted with anxiety. Best we were gone, and fast.

The cops lurked around the trees making a total hash of appearing inconspicuous. Not Detective Inspector Morrison though. She stood with the immediate family ready to talk to the press once this was all done and dusted. It would be the usual old tosh about 'following up leads' but the truth was that two months on from the time Benny Cohen's body had been found, the police still appeared baffled. They didn't even know where he'd been killed. Not a bloody clue. Joe Murphy had been that good – an unfortunate loss to the disposal business.

DI Morrison was a redhead, almost six feet tall, yet she gazed around the throng of undesirables like a greedy little girl in a sweet shop. Oh, how she'd love to toss this lot into her goodie bag. Longing oozed out of her pores. There's only one thing more dangerous than a vicious villain and that's an over-ambitious copper. Keep my head down with this one. Stay well out of her firing line.

Over by the police-infested trees was an old lady in a wheelchair with a tartan blanket around her knees. Carver lumbered up to her and kissed her cheek. The notorious Lil Carver, power behind the Carver throne many moons ago. Old Man Carver had ended his days at Her Majesty's Pleasure and Lil had kept the family's nefarious business going with a legendary ruthless drive. Big Jim took a handkerchief out of his top pocket, handed it to his mother, and the frail old lady wiped away her tears. Clearly not a patch on her former formidable self – comes to us all, I suppose. Monica took Brando over to talk to Lil, and the woman clasped his hand while Monica raised her veil and bent down to have condolences whispered in her ear.

Monica looked up and raised her eyebrows at me. Cue to fetch the car. I walked across the flowerbeds to where the Bentley was parked. The odd face nodded to me but generally nobody took much notice. I was virtually invisible in their world and that was the way I needed it to stay.

Chapter Three
6 p.m., Monday, 16 June

Monica tossed her veiled hat onto the white leather sofa and kicked off her stilettos. She shook her head until her blonde hair once more fell in silky waves to her shoulders. My God, she was gorgeous.

'Go to your room, Brando,' she told the kid as he skulked in.

'I'm bored,' he said.

'Go on your computer, watch your TV, play a video game, play your guitar, or something.'

He slumped on the sofa, blank-faced. Monica swatted him with her hat.

'Shift your fucking arse,' she said. 'You've got a room full of stuff worth more than my mother's house. Use it. Get out of my sight.'

'Bit harsh, that,' I said. 'Give the lad a break. We *have* just buried his father.'

Brando looked up at me from beneath his usual scowl and I couldn't quite fathom what I glimpsed behind his eyes.

It was my turn to be hit with the hat. 'And you can butt out,' Monica snapped. 'What do you know about raising kids?'

Fair dos, I suppose. I'd worked for them for fifteen months and all the kid ever did was frown at me. When I dropped him off at school in the mornings, he'd hardly say a word to me. And when he wasn't at school he was holed up in his room like some kind of troglodyte. He was moody and seemed deeply unhappy, which was probably the reason why he didn't appear to have any friends.

Brando sighed and hauled himself off the sofa. 'You wouldn't talk to me like that if Dad was here.'

'Well, he's not, is he? He's dead and you're going to have to deal with me from now on.'

He walked towards the stairs and glared at me. 'Or you'll set your *guard dog* on me?'

'I don't need Sam to deal with you, young man.' She chucked a shoe at him and he stomped his way up the stairs, turning his head just once to cast a fleeting sidelong glance at me. I acknowledged him with a nod of my head. He nodded back and ran the rest of the way, disappeared into his room and slammed the door behind him.

Monica sat on the arm of the sofa. 'Come and rub my feet for me, Sam,' she said. 'They're killing me.'

I didn't make a move towards her. 'We've still got to be careful, Monica. What if he comes back down?'

'If Benny never guessed, then why should Brando?'

'Don't underestimate him. He's a bright lad. Kids suss out more than you think.'

'The sooner he's off at boarding school the better, then.' She massaged her feet and her red-painted toenails shimmered beneath the seven-denier stockings. I wanted to peel them off her legs with my teeth and suck those toes till she squirmed. 'But you're right.' She smiled over at me. 'We'd better cool it till he's safely tucked up in bed.'

I wandered into the kitchen with its stainless steel cupboards and worktops glistening like a sterilised operating theatre.

'I see Gloria's been in today.' The place was a tip when we left for the funeral but it had since been given a Gloria Kelso all-over special. I pounced on the pile of chicken sandwiches she'd left out for me. Okay for everyone else to eat at the funeral do but I was in attendance as security. No food and drink for the likes of me.

'Yeah, she's great. It'll be a shame to get rid of her,' Monica said.

'What? You planning on doing all your own cleaning and cooking from now on?'

She sashayed across to the giant Smeg fridge and poured herself a glass of Moët. 'Gloria was one of Benny's plants, brought in to keep an eye on me. Just like you were.' She emptied the glass in one go and poured another. 'So she has to go.'

I got myself a can of Diet Coke. 'But she still needs a job and with Benny gone . . .'

'A grass is always a grass.'

'You're the boss.'

'And don't you ever forget it.'

'Big Jim Carver was making noises about finding out who did for Benny and the shooter,' I told her as I carried a teetering pile of sandwiches on a plate back into the sitting room and placed it on the coffee table.

'Like he gives a toss.' She lay back on the sofa with her feet up. 'Once one of his offshore companies buys the nightclubs from me, he'll be one of the biggest players around. What with them, the takeaway pizza joints and launderettes, his money will be washed as clean as a baby's bum.'

'I thought Carver was into online gambling scams these days?'

'Yeah, but he's an old-fashioned sod at heart; likes the hard cash operations as well.'

'Gerard Fowley was all over you. So what's his angle?'

'Thought you never wanted to know the business side?'

'I don't. But he's a dangerous bastard.'

'He wants the nightclubs. He's offered more than Big Jim.'

'And you told him what?'

'I'd think about it,' she said.

'Dodgy ground, that. You don't want to make an enemy of Big Jim Carver.'

'I only said I'd think about it.'

'Is that wise?' Without Benny's protection, we were vulnerable. Things could easily turn very nasty if Monica set Carver and Fowley against each other. And we'd be bang smack in the middle. Not a situation to be relished.

'I've been playing this game for twelve fucking years, Sam. I know what I'm doing.'

Twelve years being pawed and petted by a big ugly bruiser more than twice her age. The thought of it still turned my stomach. Benny's fluffy eye-candy, all smiles and fluttery eyelashes, considered too dumb to understand the business they all talked about so openly in front of her. Little did they know she'd been listening to every word. Taking it all in.

'So mind your own fucking business. End of discussion.' She reached out her hand. 'Now give me one of those sandwiches, I'm famished.'

At the five-star hotel, after the funeral, she had pecked delicately at the food on offer, sipped her fizzy water and been the model of propriety. And now here she was, chucking back champagne and tucking into thick-cut chicken sarnies. The two faces of Monica Cohen. The third face was the one I'd seen when she killed Joe. It was an image I pushed to the back of my mind and didn't want to think about.

She was a selfish little animal in bed, too. But I didn't really mind; giving her pleasure almost always got me there. It was all very one-sided but I was sure that once the pressure was off, and with time and patience, things would improve. And she was so beautiful

I still couldn't believe she would have been interested in me in the first place. Right place, right time, I guess. But she'd made the first move and now she swore she loved me. That was good enough for me.

We had always been careful. I told Gloria that I made my own bed (army training, I'd said) so she rarely had any reason to enter my room above the garage. That way she didn't know I hadn't slept there when Benny was away. And it was true about the army, it had been my life for fifteen years. And now my life was Monica.

Brando was snoring when Monica took me by the hand and led me to her bedroom. It was so pink and girly I always found it hard to visualise Benny ever sleeping in there. Christ, I felt like a displaced person myself surrounded by the frou-frou décor, so I tried to ignore it. Monica sat me down in front of her gilt-edged dressing table mirror and stood behind me.

'You should let your hair grow.' She ran her fingers through my soldierly crop. 'It would really soften your face.'

'I thought you loved me as I am?' It was disconcerting to see my mug being reflected next to her face. It was a travesty, a crime against mirrors.

She slithered out of her black dress. 'I almost forgot to tell you,' she said. 'That Detective Inspector Morrison woman wants to interview you in the morning. Ten o'clock at the station.'

Oh, shit! I'd already made a statement to the local uniforms. They'd taken notes, nodded politely and left it at that. But Morrison was a very different prospect. I'd seen her type in the army: tough and ruthless bitches every one, mostly dykes. Always steered well clear of them. So an ambitious police inspector with her eye on the prize was the very last person I wanted to come face-to-face with.

'I told her you'd be there.' Monica paused for a moment before she stepped out of her black lacy panties. 'And Samantha, just for once, please wear a skirt.'

Chapter Four
10 a.m., Tuesday, 17 June

At ten on the dot, I was in an interview room at the police station. Detective Inspector Morrison flicked the tape on and stated in her husky voice that this was a recorded interview with Alice Samantha Riley. Also present were Detective Inspector Wendy Morrison and Detective Sergeant Trevor Jones.

Morrison was the first one to speak. 'Miss Riley, please state your occupation.'

'I'm a driver for Mrs Monica Cohen and her son, Brando. I maintain all the household vehicles and ensure Mrs Cohen and her son remain safe from harm.'

'Bodyguard?'

'Security.'

'Were you ever a bodyguard for Benjamin Cohen?'

'Only his wife and kid,' I replied.

'Never for Mr Cohen?'

'Mr Cohen drove himself everywhere. And if he'd needed muscle, it certainly wouldn't have been me. Always said he could take care of himself, anyway.'

'Until someone took care of him.'

I didn't respond.

'How did you meet Benjamin Cohen?'

'Straight out of the army. I got a temporary job working the door at one of his nightclubs, Legend. He was in one night and saw me defuse a potentially sticky situation. So he offered me a better job, good pay and with my own accommodation.'

A place of my own had been the main attraction of the job. I hadn't really fancied playing flunky to some spoilt woman and her brat, but I was sick of the messy cow I was sharing a house with. A place for everything and everything in its place, that was my motto. While hers was, take it off, drop it on the floor and bloody leave it there. She lived on takeaways, never did the dishes, stank the place out with cigarettes and left the butts burning in overflowing ashtrays. Insufferable.

'You live in the Cohen house?'

'I have a flat over the garage.' Plus the use of the gym Monica had insisted that Benny have set up in the basement. Though, as she had never raised a sweat in her life, she hadn't ever set foot down there and I was able to work out in peace. An hour or so a day on the cross-trainer did it for me, kept me fighting fit.

'Above the coach house that is attached to the Cohen house?' Morrison raised her eyebrows.

'I'm on call twenty-four hours a day, remember.'

Pretty convenient layout, too, through an interconnecting door. The key clicking in the lock from the other side was a signal that Benny was out of town and I was welcome in Monica's bed. Though it had remained locked most nights in the two months since Benny's death. We had to be cautious, Monica had said, until the funeral was over and all the legal matters out of the way.

'Mrs Cohen goes out a lot at night, does she?'

'She has a lot of friends. Goes to social gatherings, charity work and the like. And I drive her wherever.'

Morrison pointedly opened a file on the table between us, studied it for longer than I was comfortable with and changed tack.

'You came south after leaving the army. Why was that?'

'Everybody's got to be somewhere.' The fact was there were too many bad memories in the north.

'No family, friends in . . .' She looked down at the notes she had in front of her. 'Manchester, was it?'

'I joined up to get out of Manchester.'

'Why was that?'

'It was a dump. There were only three ways out for the likes of us with a duff education – football, rock 'n' roll or the armed forces. I'm the wrong sex for football and I'm tone deaf, so . . .'

'No boyfriends?' Morrison asked and Detective Sergeant Jones failed to hide a smirk. The DI gave him a withering glance that said 'knock it off' and he lowered his eyes. 'Girlfriends?' Morrison asked.

'When I joined up, all my friends from school were already pushing prams. Not my scene.'

'What *is* your scene?' Straight-faced, toneless voice.

Fuck you, lady, that's out of order. 'None of your business.'

'Mrs Cohen is an attractive woman.'

'So are you, if I may say so.'

'Let's just stick to the matter in hand, shall we, Alice?'

Got you! I grinned.

'Something funny?'

'Yeah. Only my granny ever called me Alice. Right before she beat me with a belt. From then on I only ever answered to Sam.'

The look in people's eyes – particularly those who are trying to take the piss – is priceless. Fact was, I never knew my granny. And if anyone had ever tried to beat me with anything, they would have swiftly regretted it. But the abused little girl story goes down a treat under certain circumstances.

Wendy Morrison's face remained composed. Sensitivity training, God bless it. In the old days, some sweaty Inspector with whisky breath and a crumpled suit would have pissed himself laughing. 'That what turned you into a raving lezzer, eh?' That was the type of cop I joined the army to avoid.

Morrison fixed me with a steady, blue-eyed stare. 'So why do you insist on playing the hard case, Samantha?'

Here we go. 'Because I don't know what this is all in aid of, do I? Tell me what you want and you will have my total cooperation, ma'am.'

I sat to attention and repeated the story I had told the police in my statement. Mr Cohen left that evening at eight. He drove away in his Lexus, leaving Mrs Cohen alone in the main house with Brando. I watched TV in my flat all evening until Mrs Cohen rang me just after midnight. She was distraught. It seemed that her husband had not arrived for his business meeting at Legend. Mr Cohen was a stickler for punctuality and had never been known to miss an appointment.

'Who called Mrs Cohen?'

'Mr Carver, I believe.'

'You know Big Jim Carver well?'

'He's one of Mr Cohen's business associates.'

'He was talking to you at the funeral yesterday.'

I had seen Morrison at the funeral, taking in the action, clocking the faces. She couldn't have failed to notice Carver lumber up to me at the graveside just before he went to shovel some dirt on old Benny's coffin. 'Mr Carver was just passing the time of day,' I said.

'And Gerard Fowley?'

Fowley gave me the creeps. All the designer label suits in the world couldn't disguise what he really was. Any more than his expensive cologne could dispel the distinct smell of pimp that shadowed him.

'Asked if I needed a new job,' I said.

'Your services are in demand, then?'

'Using female door security leads to fewer fights in nightclubs. Less police intervention means licenses aren't challenged every time they come up for renewal. Makes sense, really.'

'You writing a CV?' She rustled though that file again, searching for ammo, maybe.

'I don't need a job right now. I've already got one.'

'For the moment.' There was a significant pause before Morrison pushed a photograph across the table to me. 'Ever seen this man before?'

My heart almost jumped out of my chest. It was Joe Murphy, though thankfully not with his brains splattered all over his Land Rover. This was a police mug shot and, even with his head in one piece, he looked mighty rough.

'Face doesn't ring a bell,' I said, as flatly as I could manage, even though my stomach had suddenly developed a huge knot.

Morrison watched my response intently. She leaned forward. 'Sure?'

'Not a hundred per cent, no. God knows how many soldiers I met over the years. And I saw a lot of people in the club when I was working the doors.' I picked the picture up and studied it closely, my expression and voice in neutral. 'He's not very distinctive looking, is he? I mean, if he had a scar or something. Tattoo? An eye patch, maybe? Ring through his nose?'

'Yeah, well . . .' Her mouth pursed, no sense of humour this woman. She reached across the table and tapped the picture with her finger. 'Joseph Murphy, former petty criminal, recently moved up a few notches, it seems. He was the shooter. And he was from your neck of the woods.'

'Essex?'

'Manchester.' Her eyes bored into me. 'Sure you never bumped into him up there?'

'I've been away from that shithole for over sixteen years, Inspector. And last time I counted, Manchester had a population of over two million people.'

'He was the same age as you.'

'Early seventies baby boom. Big classes in school, hence the lousy education.'

'So you say you've never had any dealings with Joseph Murphy?'

'Not that I can recall.' Good thing I wasn't linked up to one of those lie detector machines – the reading would have zoomed off the chart.

A look passed between Jones and Morrison and the knot in my gut wound tighter. 'Why have you suddenly stopped cooperating, Samantha?'

'I'm just trying to be honest, is all. If I say unequivocally that I've never met him and you come up with some surveillance footage of me chucking him out of the club, then you'll accuse me of lying.'

'I was asking you about Manchester.' A note of impatience had crept into her voice.

'That was a long time ago and I didn't mix with any scallies. You're welcome to search for any juvenile record that I haven't got. I went into the army clean.'

Clean away, two steps ahead of old Whisky Breath. Joe and me on our third hit, back streets of Warrington, me in a fucking skirt and high heels, running like buggery, blue lights flashing all over the place. He'd grabbed my hand and hauled me along behind him. We ducked into some dirty, disused factory with water dripping down the walls, hiding, terrified. We were laughing like idiots high on adrenalin. This was one we wouldn't get paid for in full. Some bastard had tipped off our target.

We both knew that was the end. We'd pushed our luck to the precipice. Joe invested in a balaclava and went back to burglary; I cut my hair and joined the army. Nobody ever knew we'd been partners. The hits had been arranged via a contact of Joe's and I never met the guy. That way I was protected, Joe had said. Joe, my friend with benefits, one of the few men I'd ever had sex with. The last fling being the night we got away for the final time. Afterwards, we divvied up our money and went our separate ways. I made him burn the bunch of photographs we'd had taken together in one of those crappy photo booths. Four shots for a couple of quid – wonder how many fragments of how many lives have been recorded in those things? I had watched the little images burst into flames in an ashtray. 'Like it never even happened,' I told him. Joe said nothing. He just walked away.

Morrison's face remained unreadable but the tone of her voice altered slightly as she pushed another photo across the table towards me. 'How about this one?'

I let out a theatrical sigh, as though bored by the whole proceedings, and looked at the picture. A happy couple in palm tree paradise, standing on a sun-drenched terrace that overlooked a bright blue sea, only one little fluffy cloud to mar their idyllic sky. My heart almost stopped. The woman was Monica. Resplendent in one of her teeny bikinis with her blonde hair ruffled by the slight breeze, posed for the camera and smiling up at a man who had his arm around her waist. He stood a good head height above her and wore shorts with a flamboyant Hawaiian shirt. He was dark-haired, tanned and looked full of himself – reminded me of Tom Cruise before he had his ears pinned back.

'Ever seen this gentleman before?' Did I sense a note of triumph in the DI's voice? One that can't be disguised, that says, I know something you don't.

I kept my eyes on the photo, tried to keep control, not give away my rising anxiety. My mind reached out for a reassuring explanation: maybe this was an old flame of Monica's, someone she knew before she met Benny. But one glance at the bikini and I knew. She still had that item in her wardrobe and she never kept clothes for more than one season. This photo had been taken very recently. And the camera had captured a look on her face that unsettled me. A shiver crept outwards from my spine. My stomach was in revolt, about to throw up. I knew that whatever this was, it wouldn't be good news for me.

'No,' I said truthfully, 'I've never seen this man before.'

Chapter Five
2 p.m., Tuesday, 17 June

When I got back to the house, the gates to the Cohen estate stood open. What the hell was Monica doing leaving them unlocked? Without warning, a black Range Rover roared out. It almost took the wing mirror off my Honda Civic. The dark-haired man behind the wheel leaned out of his window, shouted something unintelligible and gave me the finger. For mere seconds I saw his face, but it was enough. It was the Tom Cruise lookalike. I entered the drive and killed the engine.

The gates closed automatically behind me. I watched them through my rear-view mirror, the giant custom-made B&M wrought-iron letters almost kissing as they met in the middle. Benny Cohen's final declaration of ownership over Monica, installed a year to the day before Joe Murphy pulled the trigger. What an ostentatious prick Benny had been with his twenty-two-carat gold jewellery. Monogrammed to the back teeth, shirts, dressing gowns, pillowcases, towels and rugs all with intertwined initials and, if that wasn't enough, those ludicrous gates. It was like something from the golden age of Hollywood.

I stared down the long driveway to the vast mock-Georgian mansion, replaying Benny's favourite anecdote about how he had been looking for a stately home. 'But I couldn't find one in Essex, could I?' He would pause and gaze knowingly around his assembled guests. 'So I thought, fuck it, I'll build me own!' Cue laughter, no matter how many times they'd heard the gag. When Benny Cohen said laugh, you chortled for all you were worth, if you didn't want to be left out in the cold, or worse.

Monica would swan about the place, regaling everyone with her most vacuous smile; her intelligence was on dimmer switch but her eyes took in the room. Who needs a personality when you're that beautiful? Her very presence lit up the place, and her pale skin shimmered as though it was silk. Men wanted to fuck her and women wanted to be her. I wanted to love her. At the first inkling of more than physical attraction I should have walked away. I'd backed off from emotional involvement with both men and women a few times before. Love leaves you vulnerable. It was something I had dodged ever since my youthful affair with Joe Murphy had ended. When I joined the army, I vowed never again to be dragged along in anyone else's destructive wake. And yet here I was again.

Along the driveway the coach house doors opened and Monica's red Porsche 911 drove out towards me. She was behind the wheel, her blonde hair haloed in the sunshine. She pulled up beside my car. 'I'm going out,' she said.

'Wait a minute and I'll drive you.'

'Those days are over, Sam.'

'That's what you pay me for.'

She smiled at me from behind her Dolce & Gabbana sunglasses. 'I fired Gloria this morning. You pick up Brando from school and give him some dinner. I'll see you later.'

'Where are you going?'

She ignored the question. 'And take the Mercedes when you collect Brando. Your piece of Jap shit embarrasses him.'

That was me put in my place.

The gates opened ahead of her, she gunned the Porsche's engine and was gone. I felt as though my world was being slowly flushed down the drain. Benny had trusted Monica and look where he ended up. I watched the mocking B&M close behind me and was trapped once more.

Chapter Six
3 p.m., Tuesday, 17 June

Gloria Kelso stood at the gates of her mother's house. Press the bell, swallow the pride, and get in there. But her hand was not responding to the electrical impulse from her brain. No matter how badly she'd been treated by Monica Cohen, she knew that being back in the direct orbit of her mother would be much worse.

Her family never had any respect for her. To them she was just some lackey to be bossed about. These days, even servants had the right to resign whereas she . . .

She looked down the long driveway and up to the window of the bedroom she had occupied during her childhood, if you could call it that. At least not after her eighth birthday when . . . She shuddered at the memory and consigned it once more to the dark recess at the back of her mind.

The one good thing was she'd heard that Bert was back in town. Maybe they could get together every now and again, like in the old days. He'd always been kind to her. She appreciated that. They'd always been careful, except for that one time. But she didn't want to think about that, either.

She hoped that Brando would be okay without her to pick him up from school every day, make sure he got to his guitar lessons on time. With Benny Cohen gone, the boy would be at the mercy of Monica, though Gloria suspected that he'd be sent away to boarding school any time soon. That was what Monica had always been angling for and now there was nothing to stop her. Brando wasn't a bad lad. Gloria had known enough nasty types in her time and Brando certainly didn't fit the bill. But you neglect a child, or worse, and they turn into monsters, just like her brother. Monica had been no kind of a mother to that boy – she hadn't even tried. And the language she used in front of the kid, now that was disgusting. Oh, Monica was a bad 'un, all right, just like her father had been.

There was nothing she could do to help Brando now. Perhaps Samantha Riley would help to curb Monica. Sam was okay. A bit dopey around Monica but otherwise she appeared to be straight up. Maybe she'd look out for Brando until he was safely away at boarding school.

Gloria took a deep breath and pressed the bell. The gates buzzed like a wasps' nest and opened for her. She got back into her car and drove towards the house to face whatever living hell Lil Carver had in store.

Chapter Seven
4 p.m., Tuesday, 17 June

Brando snarled when he saw me behind the wheel of the Mercedes. 'Where's Gloria?'

'Gone,' I said.

He lugged his heavy school bag into the back seat. 'Everyone fucks off on me.'

'Please don't swear, Brando,' I said. 'You know your mother doesn't like it.'

'She shouldn't swear at me then, should she?'

Point taken. 'What do you want for dinner?'

We pulled out into traffic and I could see his face in the wing mirror as he peered out of the window. Sulky or sad, it was hard to tell. 'Is Mum at home?'

'No. Just you and me, kid.'

'Bet she's gone to see that Felipe.'

That name was like a slap in the face. Felipe. Give a person a name and they become solid. No longer a face in a photo or a half-glimpsed figure leaning out of a Range Rover to give me the finger. No longer a vague someone to be dismissed as a lookalike and pushed to the back of my mind. A sense of impending doom crept over me. I shook it away. There had to be some other explanation. I calmed my pulse and resolved to confront Monica. But how did the lad know about Felipe? I didn't have to ask.

'Remember when she took me to the Canaries last year?'

Last year: when my brother finally fulfilled his ambition to drink himself into ultimate oblivion. David James Riley – loaded to the gills with the fatal combo of grief, guilt and whisky. 'Go and see to your family.' Benny Cohen had come over all Don Corleone on me. 'Family is the most important thing in the world.' He'd loaned me the Jaguar to drive to Manchester to get the funeral sorted. Then who should turn up at the crematorium but my old lover Joe Murphy? 'Jesus, Riley!' were his first words to me. 'You look like a bloke.'

While I was away, Benny had taken Monica and Brando to Spain to see how work was progressing on their 'dream' house. Monica had got bored, pouted and stamped her little foot, so Benny coughed for her to take Brando to the Canary Islands for a week while he dealt with the bolshie Spanish builders.

'She met up with Felipe there,' Brando said. 'Left me with some useless Spanish babysitter watching lame telly and went out on the town with *him* every night.' The lad snorted his disgust. 'It was a shit holiday and he's a total wanker.'

'Did your dad know about any of this?'

Brando laughed. 'How do you think I got my plasma TV?' Benny had refused that particular request but, amazingly, Monica had caved. Not like her at all.

'Sounds like a touch of blackmail or extortion to me, Brando.'

'No point having a slapper for a mother if you can't get something out of it.'

We sat in the kitchen sharing a pizza and I knocked up a salad to go with it. Brando's lip curled at the sight of it. 'I don't eat green stuff.'

'It's good for you.'

'Dad said salad is only for girls and nancy boys.' He stuffed his mouth with more pizza. 'Dad never ate salad and he would have lived to be really old if someone hadn't topped him.'

I chewed on the lettuce and said nothing.

'Do you think Felipe had Dad killed?'

'Why would he do that?'

'Mum will get all the money soon. Felipe will be made, won't he? She'll send me off to boarding school and I'll never see her again.'

For the first time, I recognised the vulnerable little boy beneath the snarly bluster. And he was right on the money. That had been *our* plan, Monica and me.

Brando pushed his plate to one side and fished a card out of his blazer pocket with greasy fingers. 'Do you think I should call Inspector Morrison? Tell her I think it was Felipe who put the hit out on my dad?'

'DI Morrison gave you her card?'

'She gave it to Mum.' He jumped down from his stool at the breakfast counter, leaving his pizza half-finished. 'Same thing.'

I imagined him rummaging through Monica's handbag, snaffling things he thought might be of use to him.

He pushed the card into my hand. 'Maybe you should do it. Tell the police what I think. Nobody takes any notice of what kids say. But they'd listen to you. You were a soldier.'

My mobile buzzed in my pocket. Maybe it was Monica. I flicked open the cover.

'Sam?' the husky voice said. 'DI Morrison here. We need to meet up again, and soon. Look, I'll buy you a drink. I've got something to show you. Off the record.'

Chapter Eight

2 p.m., Wednesday, 18 June

Just two days after Benny Cohen's funeral and I was at a second meeting with DI Morrison. This was 'off the record' she'd said, but my level of trust in the woman was less than zero. She was seated in the far corner of the small, out-of-the-way pub she had nominated for the meeting. I didn't know it at all and had almost got lost on the winding country roads. It was after lunchtime and the place was practically deserted. Apart from the landlord, who was deep in conversation with an obvious regular propping up the bar, there was a couple in their early thirties. They looked like the types who were both married to someone else. They gazed intently into each other's eyes and whispered sweet nothings. Their hands held fast together like they never wanted to let each other go – clandestine by their own design.

Morrison waved over to me and smiled broadly. She looked different today, her red hair fell in loose waves to her shoulders and she wore an informal jacket over a sweatshirt and jeans. To the casual observer we'd appear to be two women friends meeting for a quick drink. Casual it may have looked but she was all business.

'My colleagues in Manchester turned over Joseph Murphy's gaff,' she started in and fixed me with her blue eyes. 'And guess what they found, Sam?'

'Never my big forte, guessing.' I tried to sound disinterested, tried to tame my heartbeat.

She smiled but you could never have interpreted it as being friendly. 'This.' She slid a small photo across the beer-stained table.

It had started to get to me, all this sliding of photographs malarkey. I stared down at one of those damn photo booth pictures from years ago. There was Joe, pulling a stupid face, and me, all long hair and smoky-eye make-up, laughing. The brightness of the colour struck me as bizarre – how could that have been, when my memories of those times were always in mono? My young life spooled inside my head, like an old black-and-white movie. Joe and me, a multitude of captured moments. I wanted to look away from the taunting image but I couldn't. Christ, were we ever that young? Was Joe ever that stupid? He had burned them all, he'd told me. I had watched him do it, a little pile of ashes. That was what we had agreed and the idiot had gone and hung onto one of them for all this time.

'Seems he was a bit sweet on you, our shooter,' Morrison said.

'Is this where I say nothing till I see a lawyer?'

Morrison had me on tape saying I'd never set eyes on Joe Murphy. At that very moment some CSI-type nerd could be beavering away in a basement somewhere to find DNA that linked me to the Land Rover.

'I said off the record and I meant it.' Morrison gestured to the narky barman and he brought two glasses of Coke to the table. She paid him and he slouched back to his conversation. 'Sure, this links you to Murphy. We could get you on a conspiracy-to-murder charge. But that's not what I'm after.'

'What *do* you want?' My stomach seemed to squirm like a snake in a sack.

'Look, I don't give a shit who or why anyone bumped off Benjamin Cohen. He was no loss to the human race. And I have no real interest in who blew away your little playmate Joseph Murphy, either.' Morrison put her elbows on the table, folded her hands together, rested her chin on them and scanned my face with her baby blues. 'No,' she said. 'I'm after Big Jim Carver, for now. And I think you are ideally placed to pass on information to me.'

Oh, fuck! This was the kind of set-up you see in cop shows on the telly when some poor bastard is forced to grass. And what's the end result? One deceased informant, that's what. And here was I, sweating under the same spotlight.

'Inspector,' I told her as casually as I could manage, 'I'm just a glorified babysitter. Nobody tells me anything.'

But she was having none of that. She picked up the little sliver of my past life and slipped it into her pocket. 'Think about it, Sam,' she said.

I struggled to regain control of the situation. 'Why the sudden interest in Big Jim? He's well past his sell-by date.'

She eyed me suspiciously. 'That your expert assessment of the situation, is it? It has never occurred to you that the king is dead, long live the king?'

'I don't know what you mean.'

'Benny Cohen was semi-retired but he still ran a tight ship. He was a dodgy bastard but a relatively benign one.'

'And now he's gone . . .'

'Carver is next in line for the throne.' She took a sip of her drink. 'It's all rather Shakespearean, don't you think?'

'Get rid of him and there's only up-and-coming, less well-protected small fry to contend with. Plus, you get to prove your chops to your male colleagues and superiors. It's a bit like that in the army.'

'I'm so pleased you understand,' said the sarcastic bitch. 'You help me put Carver away and this piece of evidence gets lost.

Forever.' She reached across and patted my hand. 'And you and the delightful widow Cohen get to play house with all of Benny's ill-gotten gains without a stain on either character. How's that for a bargain?' She stood up to leave. 'I'll be in touch. And, Sam, when we meet up like this, it's Wendy . . . Much more convivial, don't you think?'

The canoodling couple at the other table looked at their watches in unison and followed Morrison out of the pub. Were they cops in disguise, or was I becoming paranoid?

My thoughts went into overdrive to try and keep pace with my pulse. The police knew about Monica and me. Or thought they did. Was it just guesswork on Morrison's part, testing some pet theory? I could almost see the snide headline. 'The Gangster, His Wife and The Lesbian.' It won't come to that. I won't allow it.

I shivered and my thoughts moved on. Right now there was only some old photo to link me to Joe. But dig deep enough and they'd find out we went to the same school, lived in the same street when we were kids. Then there were the hits Joe and I did together. Faces and places – all jammed behind a heavily bolted door in my mind – burst out to haunt me and I had no way to stop them. Some things may be easily overcome at the time, so much so that you hardly recognise them for what they are. But on a day such as this, confronted by a past I had run so hard to escape, I felt overwhelmed by guilt. My heart thundered and it was an effort to breathe normally. Keep control. Concentrate.

To cooperate with Morrison – to grass up Big Jim Carver – was a perilous game. I took a deep breath and a long slug of my drink. Okay, so I had known Joe Murphy. A smart brief would maybe get me out of that one. Ask why should I want to have my employer killed? Good question, if they didn't know about my relationship with Monica. Even so, knock off Benny Cohen simply to have his wife to myself? Well, I guess people have been murdered for less.

Then there was the money element. Monica would inherit all of Benny's dosh and then some. All of which would drag Monica into the frame. Once cornered, I hated to think how Monica would react in an attempt to save herself. Would I be the next one lying face down in a ditch? Or be stitched up for the murders of Benny Cohen *and* Joe Murphy? With this Felipe person on the scene, I was swiftly becoming expendable. So I had to try and protect myself *and* Monica – for my own safety.

Chapter Nine
4 p.m., Wednesday, 18 June

After my meet with Morrison, I went to collect Brando from school. He hated the place and all the snotty children who went there. Though it had certainly refined Brando's accent. So much so that, compared to Benny's cockney glottal-stop growl and Monica's slight northern twang, the kid sounded rather posh when he spoke with his normal voice. Sometimes, though, he tended to ape his dad's gorblimey accent to almost comical effect and I was never sure if he was joking or not. The other thing that had rubbed off on Brando from this over-hyped pile was the snobbery, though that was mainly to do with clothes and cars. Benny didn't go for designer clobber – 'made by a bunch of foreign poofs', as he had put it. He preferred a nice bit of schmutter measured up by some little Hackney tailor. But he did like his motors and every time he bought a new car, he'd take Brando out for a spin in it – just the two of them. 'Our little ritual,' Benny would say, leaving Monica to pout at home.

I hadn't the time to get back to the house and change vehicles, so my little piece of Jap shit would have to do for today. The ranks of Mercs, BMWs and Audis surrounding me made the cramped space seem like a Nazi officers' car pool. Yummy Mummies tapped their manicured nails impatiently on steering wheels while over-stressed nannies read trashy gossip magazines to pass the time until their spoilt little charges clambered into the back seat. Glorified babysitter, I had told Morrison, and I wasn't kidding. With Gloria gone, Monica would have me polishing the furniture next if I didn't watch my step.

Monica, what the hell was she up to? I had waited for her to come home the previous night. After I'd put Brando to bed I watched a movie in the main house. Couldn't leave the lad on his own in there. I was watching *About A Boy*, a bit of a weepy, but enjoyable nevertheless, when he appeared at the doorway dressed in his jimjams.

'I want popcorn,' he demanded.

'At this time of night?'

'I'm hungry.'

'Well, go and get yourself a chocolate biscuit and a glass of milk.'

He grunted and shuffled off into the kitchen, came back with a plateful and plonked himself down beside me on the sofa. 'Why are you watching this?' he asked. 'It's a girl's film.'

I looked at him and raised an eyebrow in response. He glanced back at me sheepishly. 'Sorry,' he said. 'I forgot.'

Gee, thanks, kid. I ran my hand through my cropped hair. Well, what did I expect?

'Why do people kill other people for money?' he piped up with his mouth full of chocolate digestive.

'Is that a serious question or are you just making conversation?'

'You killed people for money.'

'What?' My heart turned over in my chest.

'You were a soldier, weren't you?' He munched away, idly eyeing images of Rachel Weisz on the TV. 'So you killed people for money.'

Phew! 'I joined the army to help protect my country.'

'They paid you, though?'

'Of course they paid me.'

'So you did kill people for money.'

'No, I didn't kill anyone. I was a driver.'

'Tanks and stuff?' His eyes lit up.

'Nothing like that, just military transport.'

Brando yawned, bored by my apparent lack of cred. He put a cushion behind his head and closed his eyes. Moments later he had drifted off. I felt a tug of pity for the boy. Some twisted bitch of a fairy godmother had stood over his cradle and waved her malicious wand. Granted him all the toys and gadgets his materialistic little heart could desire but no real love, no affection. Not even from Benny who had appeared to see his role as a father to be little more than toughening the lad up.

Not wishing to wake Brando, I carried him up to bed and he clung to me for a few seconds before I put him down. That fleeting hug choked me up and I almost kissed him goodnight but restrained myself. I patted his head instead. My nephew Tom would be Brando's age now. I shook the thought away. Tom *would have been* Brando's age.

Kids disappear all the time, and most of them we know nothing about. But if they're very young, attractive and white, the story is splashed all over the newspapers. Then you turn the page, saddened, perhaps, but not permanently affected. Not until it's your own family and you watch the nuclear shockwave of loss devastate everything it touches. Nothing will ever be the same again – like my brother, for example, or me. I'd hardened my heart, tuned out my emotions, only to have them revived again by my feelings for Monica. I tucked Brando in and went back down to my movie.

Monica finally turned up just after two a.m. She breezed in and kissed me on the forehead. 'Sorry about that.' I could smell vodka on her breath. 'Business, you know.'

'You want to talk about it?'

'No.' She kicked her shoes off. 'And would you mind sleeping in your own bed tonight, Sam? I'm whacked out.'

The woman behind the wheel of a gleaming BMW parked next to me gunned her engine and brought me back to the present. She sneered as she pulled away, and I realised that all the other kids had gone. I was the last one in the school car park. There was still no sign of Brando. Not even at the main door where I had half-expected to see him sitting on the bench outside, eyes down and swinging his feet resentfully at the sight of my green Civic. But he wasn't there.

Pissed off with the little bugger for messing me about, I took the steps to the school entrance two at a time and collided with a severe-looking woman about to leave.

'Can I help you?' She glared at me.

'Brando,' I said. 'I'm here to collect Brando Cohen. Is he inside?'

She looked me up and down and suspicion darkened her already harsh features. 'And you are?'

'Riley,' I said. 'Samantha Riley. Mrs Cohen's driver.'

Her expression didn't change. 'Where's Gloria Kelso?'

'She doesn't work for Mrs Cohen anymore. Where's Brando?'

She stood firmly in my way. 'Stay here, Miss, er, Riley. I'll have to ring Mrs Cohen, if you have no objection.' She walked into an adjacent office and closed the door behind her.

Come on, woman, what sort of kidnapper asks you for the kid, shows you their face and gives you their name? I stared down the dark corridor, searching for any sign of Brando. The place was deathly quiet and a feeling of anxiety crept over me.

I could hear the woman talking on the phone in the office and moments later she came back to me, an apologetic look on her face.

'Sorry, Miss Riley, but we have to check these things. Security, you know.'

'And Brando?'

'Mrs Cohen tells me Brando was picked up by his uncle. She apologises for having caused you any concern and asks if you could call her straightaway.'

Uncle? What fucking uncle? I pulled out my mobile as I walked towards my car. 'Monica! You nearly gave me a heart attack. Why didn't you ring me?'

'Sam, I've just had a phone call.' I could hear the distress in her voice. 'Get back here now. Big Jim Carver's taken Brando.'

Chapter Ten
4.30 p.m., Wednesday, 18 June

When I got back to the house, Monica was perched by the phone in Benny's study. There was a thin dusting of white powder on the top of the desk. Snorting coke again when she'd sworn blind that she'd kicked the habit. She swiftly brushed it away as though it was nothing special. I said nothing. She lit a fag and her eyes narrowed, hardening her features as she looked up at me.

The third face of Monica Cohen emerged once more. Why had I dismissed it? Was I that bedazzled by her? Taken in just like everyone else? Before I could say anything the phone rang, she put it on speaker and held an index finger to her lips to shush me.

'Thought it over, have we, Monica?' Carver's instantly recognisable high-pitched whinny filled the room.

Monica put a big smile on her face. That old sales technique – all smiles on the blower and your punters think you sound sincere. 'I don't know why you're doing this to me, Jim,' she simpered. 'I was always going to sell the clubs to you.'

'You and your fancy man had dinner with Gerard Fowley last night, isn't that right? Or have I been seriously misinformed?'

Monica's smile never faltered, though I noticed her face flush slightly. 'Gerard invited me. He's an old friend. He was so kind to me when Benny passed. It would have been rude to say no. I took Felipe Garcia with me. He's my accountant.'

Accountant? I grasped eagerly at that particular straw.

Carver laughed. It was a bizarre noise, like a wasp trapped in a water pipe. 'Yeah, right, whatever you say, sweetheart. Now, be a good girl and send the dyke over to my office to get the papers. Sign on the dotted and get them straight back to me. She can pick up Brando once the deal's done. In the meantime, he's having a good time here with his Uncle Jim. Aren't you, son?'

The phone went dead.

'Do it!' Monica ordered. 'Get over there now.'

'You expect me to just collect the papers? To leave Brando with Jim Carver for another couple of hours?'

'He'll be all right.'

'With that old perv?'

'Some might say you're a bit of a perv yourself, Samantha.'

'Noted. But I've yet to meet a dyke who's a kiddie fiddler. You know Carver's reputation as well as I do.'

'Rent boys, Sam, not children. Brando's only eleven, he'll be safe enough.'

'I don't like it.' These young lads came in all sizes, from about twelve years old, or so I'd heard.

'Well, I'm his mother and I say different. And you do as you're fucking well told.'

⌣

It took me half an hour to get to Carver's office. The place was above a scuzzy kebab shop. People used to joke that if you crossed Big Jim you ended up on a skewer. Sweeney Todd for the twenty-first century. His door was adjacent to the shop and I noticed that it wasn't all that secure. One good boot and it would have been off its hinges. But it was ajar anyway, so I trudged up the stairs and knocked on the grimy door marked OFFICE.

It was a shabby place for someone with as much money as Carver was reputed to have stashed away. Maybe this shambles was an attempt to fool the taxman. Carver was parked behind one desk with his back to the window and Brando was in front of a laptop at another desk to the right. The kid's eyes lit up momentarily when he first saw me but he didn't move.

'Best get that door fixed,' I said when Carver looked up. 'Terrible neighbourhood, this. Lots of tealeaves about.'

He let out a witchy cackle. 'You know anybody who'd have the bare-faced bollocks to break in here?'

'True,' I said. Not if they wanted to keep breathing.

Carver heaved his bulk to his feet and came around the desk. He held out a large manila envelope to me. I took it from him and walked back towards the door, passing Brando on the way. The kid gave me a pleading look, he appeared scared and his bottom lip quivered.

'Come on, Brando.' I made the decision right there and then, not giving a flying fuck about the consequences. 'I'm taking you home.'

The lad leapt up, dashed round the desk, threw himself at me and clung on.

'Hey!' Carver pulled up to his full height and started towards me. 'That wasn't the agreement.'

I unwrapped Brando's arms from around my waist and faced Carver down. He was a big bloke, but old and badly out of shape. I stood for a moment and weighed him up. One punch to that lardy belly and it'd floor him, no problem. Probably literally bust a gut. No need for any unusual force, one jab to the throat could finish him off. I'd brought down much bigger and fitter in my time. Thanks to Her Majesty's Armed Forces extra curricular training. Want to learn how to kill some bastard twice your size with your bare hands? Then step right this way, ladies.

'Fair enough.' He caught on quick, he knew he was at a disadvantage here alone, so he slowly backed off and raised his hands in mock surrender. 'I'm a reasonable man. If the boy prefers to take his leave, then that's fine with me.'

'Cheers!' Like you have any fucking choice in the matter.

'And, of course, Brando can come back here any time.' Carver smiled with his mouth but his eyes were hard and threatening. 'Any time at all. Could be here or somewhere else. Makes no difference to me. You tell Monica that, Sam. I'm sure she'll get the message.'

Clear and understood, you cocksucker, but not on my watch.

I guided Brando down the narrow stairs in front of me and heard Carver shouting down his phone.

***

'You stupid cunt!' Monica raged at me when I walked in with Brando. 'What have you done?'

'The boy was frightened, Monica.'

She turned on him. 'Serves you right, you dim-witted, little shite.' She slapped the kid hard across the face and almost knocked him off his feet.

'Oi!' I grabbed her wrist before she could take another shot at him. Brando burst into tears, hurtled upstairs to his room and slammed the door behind him.

She lashed out at me with her other hand. I pushed it away and then released her. She ran to the sofa and threw herself onto it like a child in a tantrum. 'We're dead,' she ranted. 'Once I've signed those papers we are so fucking dead.'

'Cool it, will you? I understood you already had an agreement with Carver. And this is just stage one. Money has to be transferred and deeds handed over through lawyers for the whole transaction to be legal. The will hasn't even been read yet. All the legal shenanigans could take months. By which time we'll be well on our way to Spain, just like we planned.'

There was a portentous silence while she sat up and took deep breaths. 'I'll ring Gerard.' She was on her feet again, tight like a spring, ready to get stuck in. 'I'll do a deal to sell the clubs to him in return for protection.'

Bad idea. 'Fowley's a psycho, Monica,' I warned. 'And you should never, ever cross him. But even he can't rustle up anything like the amount of muscle Carver has to hand. Think about it. Carver recruited all of Benny's guys, didn't he? Nobody went over to Fowley, did they? And Benny's old crew are a bunch of evil bastards.'

'But Gerard wants the clubs and he'll pay more for them.'

'On a straight-up deal, yes, but is he likely to enter a turf war with Big Jim Carver over a few lousy nightclubs?' Take control here, reason this out. 'Sure, Fowley likes the prestige of owning clubs and all the easy pussy they pull, but his real money is elsewhere.'

I sat on a sofa while Monica frantically paced the room. Tried to appear calm in an effort to talk her down. 'Fowley's got his used car showroom, that builders' merchants and a garden centre,' I reasoned. 'He's all about moving up the social ladder. He wants to end up legit, rub shoulders with celebrities and all that bollocks. Once he's reached his desired Pantone shade, he'll be joining the fucking Freemasons.'

Monica stopped pacing and stood stock still in front of the window.

'So, don't think Gerard Fowley is your knight in shining Armani,' I said, 'because he isn't. Just do us all a favour and stick to your initial deal with Carver.'

She appeared to deflate in an instant. She sat back down, reflective for once. 'You know, even Benny was wary of Big Jim,' she said. 'He told me he once saw Carver kill the family of a business rival with a coal hammer. Little kids and everything. Benny was a hard man himself back then, but he said it was the worst thing he'd ever seen. There was blood and brains everywhere. Carver was covered in it, roaring like a lunatic, like he was drunk on all the gore.'

That was news to me and it chilled me to the marrow. Was the woman completely insane? 'So, why in Christ's name did you even contemplate crossing him?'

'I was badly advised.' She shivered, as though a realisation was suddenly upon her. 'I'm fucked all ways to Sunday.'

'Look,' I said. 'Sign the papers and get this over with. Placate Carver. If he thinks I dissed him by taking Brando, it will be me he comes after, not you. And I can take care of myself.'

'Yeah.' She was calmer now, almost dazed. 'That's what Benny always said. "Don't you worry about me, Monica, I can take care of myself".'

Not against Joe Murphy, he couldn't.

———◡———

It was around seven by the time I took the signed papers back to Carver's office. I didn't know what to expect when I got there. Carver had plenty of heavies on call if he wanted them. I walked up the narrow stairway to his office and could hear ominous sounds of low but intense conversation. Carver was there but not alone. I braced myself for a confrontation.

Seated in the chair that Brando had so swiftly vacated was a wiry, dour-faced guy I'd never seen before. He regarded me with steel grey eyes as cold as the grave. I nodded to the stranger as I walked in and Carver stood up.

'Thank you for getting these back so promptly.' He put the envelope down on his desk, didn't even check the contents. He indicated towards the other man. 'This is my colleague, Mr Swindley. You will be meeting up with him again. Very soon.'

Not if I see him first, I won't. 'Look forward to it.'

'My pleasure,' Swindley said in a broad Birmingham accent.

I walked back to my car with a sense of apprehension shadowing me. Whoever Swindley was, he certainly didn't have the look of any kind of accountant or lawyer I'd ever set eyes on. I recognised a cold-blooded hitman when I saw one.

Chapter Eleven
9 p.m., Wednesday, 18 June

When I got back from delivering the papers to Carver's office, Monica's Porsche was not in the driveway. She never put cars back in the garage after she'd used them. That, she tartly informed me, was my job. And as I hadn't moved it, it was clear she wasn't at home.

Once in the hallway, I could hear the *Star Wars* theme music blasting out from Brando's room. He'd become a big fan after Benny had taken him to see the premiere of *Attack of the Clones* in London. Since then, the kid had watched all the films over and over again. It drove Monica insane.

I went up to Brando's room to find him lying on the floor in front of his precious forty-two-inch plasma TV, scoffing down pizza and guzzling Fanta. The sound level was hiked up to intolerable and I had to shout over it to be heard. He looked around, hit the mute button and smiled at me.

'Your mum gone out?'

'Two minutes after you left.'

I sat down on the floor beside him. 'So, who cooked the pizza for you?'

'I can work the microwave,' he said between mouthfuls.

'That's more than your mother can do.'

'Gloria taught me. She used to go out at night sometimes and leave me to do my own dinner.' He grimaced. 'I never liked her. But you're all right.' He offered me a slice of pizza.

I hadn't eaten since breakfast, so I took it. 'Did your mother say when she'd be back?'

He looked at me askance. 'She banged out of here just after I watched you drive out of the gates. I thought she might come up here and whack me again when you'd gone. But she just slammed the door when she left. She never said anything to me.'

Wave goodbye to the Mother of the Year Award, then. 'So you don't know where she went?'

'I heard her on the phone.' His gaze was drawn once more to the silent images of flashing light sabres. 'You could try hitting redial if you want. That's how I find things out.'

'Maybe she used her mobile.'

Brando's eyes never left the TV screen but he grinned broadly. 'I dropped it on the floor yesterday and she doesn't know how to fix it.' Crafty little bastard! But maybe those were the tricks people resort to when you keep them in the dark.

'I'll be back in a minute,' I told him.

I picked up the phone in the room that had been Benny Cohen's office, hit redial and sure enough.

'Felipe Garcia's,' the female voice said.

I could hear people chattering in the background and music playing. It sounded more like a shop than an accountant's office.

'I'd like to make an appointment to have my miniature poodle clipped and shampooed, please.' It was the first ridiculous thing that popped into my head but was sure to get a response of some kind.

'Sorry, madam.' The girl sounded suitably flustered. 'This is a ladies' hair salon. We also do pedicures, manicures, tanning, facials and Botox procedures. But no pets.'

Accountant, my arse – Felipe was a hairdresser. 'Sorry, my mistake,' I said. 'But I might be interested in your tanning option. Where are you based?' I picked up a pen by the Post-its on the desk and made a note of the address.

———⌣———

I was tucking Brando up in bed when he asked me the question.

'What's the correct word for a man's thing? You know, his dick, his cock?'

'Penis,' I said. 'Why do you ask? You doing biology in school or something?'

'Uncle Jim showed me some pictures on his computer. They were of some fat old bloke waving his penis about.'

'In the photos?'

'It was a video. And there was this boy in it.'

'An old bloke and a boy, are you sure? Was he a big lad, maybe, more like a grown-up?' Carver, the dirty old bastard, did he get off on showing porno to a child? No wonder Brando had looked so uneasy.

'No. He was a kid, I think, a bit older than me. It was disgusting. I wouldn't watch it.'

Alarm bells were clanging like fuck in my head but I needed to sound cool, not frighten the boy. I took a breath. 'Did Uncle Jim touch you at all? Where he shouldn't have, I mean?'

Brando looked shocked at the suggestion. 'No, he just stared at me from behind the other desk. He had this weird look on his face.'

'Well, don't worry about it for now.' I patted him on the forehead and turned on his Luke Skywalker bedside nightlight. 'Get some sleep. It will all be alright in the morning.'

I slept in one of the guest rooms that night. Monica did not return.

Chapter Twelve

11.30 a.m., Thursday, 19 June

Detective Inspector Wendy Morrison fetched a couple of Diet Cokes from the bar and sat down beside me in the booth. These premises were brand new but decorated in the style of an old Irish alehouse, complete with reproductions of classic Guinness advertising, artificially distressed mirrors and suspect Gaelic bric-a-brac – ersatz to its tacky core.

'So you've decided to cooperate?' Down to business in a blink of her blue eyes.

We sat close so nobody could hear our conversation she had said – too damn close if you asked me – and she smelled of scented soap. She was playing me. I ignored it and went through the events of the previous day. She listened, but not as intently as I might have wished for.

'So all you've really got is that Carver and Fowley are both vying to buy Benny Cohen's nightclubs.' She took a swig of her drink. 'Tell me something I don't know.'

'I think Carver is in possession of kiddie porn.' I recounted what Brando had told me the night before about Carver showing him the video.

'Will Mrs Cohen allow the boy to make a statement?'

'I doubt it, even if I did know where to find her.'

'Even with it, I'd need more evidence than the say-so of an eleven-year-old to get a search warrant.'

'Would possession of kiddie porn nail Carver?'

'Depends what level it is.'

'There are levels?' Cut and dried, isn't it? Pictures of adults having sex with young kids – that equals child pornography, right?

'There are several levels,' Morrison said. 'Indecent photos of dressed, semi-naked or naked minors might get him just a slap on the wrist.'

'I've got a photo of my two-year-old nephew at bath time. It's the most innocent thing you could ever see.'

'You've got a nephew?'

'I did have. Once upon a time, a long time ago.' Too much information, Sam. Watch your step, this woman is no friend of yours.

Morrison scrutinised my face. 'Of course, it depends on who owns the images. But if this old guy was waving his dick about, it might be more like a level-five offence. And possession of grossly obscene child abuse images could land Carver with a sentence of nine years and up.' She sighed. 'But the age of the minor concerned and whether there is a distribution network involved can make all the difference to a judge and jury. It's a bloody minefield. I'd need to see this video, maybe pass it on to the Obscene Publications Squad.'

'What if I can get hold of it?' I jumped in with both feet.

She laughed. 'Should it just happen to come into your possession, Samantha, then do give me a call and I'll take it from there. But the video on its own is no good to me. It has to be the laptop.'

'But would a stolen computer be admissible evidence?' Was I digging myself into an even deeper hole for no end result? And could I trust Morrison to keep me out of the frame?

'I'll have it picked up from you by a tame fence of mine.' She smiled to herself as she thought it through. 'Then he gets to play the concerned citizen when he views the content. He hands it in to me and I get a search warrant for Carver's home.

'Ways and means, Sam, ways and means.' Morrison laughed, obviously pleased with her plan. 'Deal?'

'Deal!' I said.

This woman was every bit as ruthless as any villain I'd ever encountered. She'd bend any rule in the book to get what she wanted. I'd sensed it before and I'd been right. Set a thief to catch a thief and all that. My blood turned to iced water.

Chapter Thirteen
1 p.m., Thursday, 19 June

For all Big Jim Carver's bragging that nobody had the balls to turn his office over, even he wouldn't leave his laptop in there overnight. If this was to be done, it had to be in broad daylight. Anyway, with Monica doing a disappearing act, I couldn't leave Brando alone in the house at night.

My brother David and that slut Geraldine had gone down to the pub and left Tom, their four-year-old son, asleep in bed. I'd been on a tour of duty in Northern Ireland when I saw them on the television news, sobbing. 'Please let us have our little boy back.' I watched them shed tears of desperation and regret for the viewing public; too bloody emotional, too bloody late. The TV camera panned around Tom's room and focused in on the blue teddy bear I had bought for him on his first birthday. Tedders, his favourite bedtime companion, sticky from his kisses, now lay forlorn on Tom's little bed. I was devastated. Tom was gone. After months of appeals, accusations, press speculation and recriminations, the search had been called off.

I left Morrison, went back to the house and took the Mini out of the garage. A nondescript little number, it would blend in unobtrusively with Carver's seedy neighbourhood. It was the car Monica had learned to drive in and Benny had kept it for sentimental reasons. Monica would have scrapped it in a heartbeat, though she pretended to love it – a reflection of her feelings for Benny.

Carver's Audi Estate was parked outside the kebab shop. It was on a double yellow line but he appeared to get away with it. I watched a traffic warden skirt past the car and look sheepishly in the other direction – pay-offs, no doubt.

Various people came and went all afternoon. Some faces I knew; others I didn't recognise, but there was no sign of the enigmatic Mr Swindley.

The last person to exit the building had left the door to swing on its grotty hinges and I found myself with the depressing view of the dingy, threadbare stair carpet. I looked at my watch. One hour before I had to collect Brando from school and I was getting increasingly anxious. Then I saw Carver huffing and puffing as he heaved his bulk down the narrow staircase. He locked the door behind him. He wasn't carrying anything. The laptop must still be in the office. I ducked down in my seat when he got into his car, and was sure he hadn't seen me because he drove away without so much as a glance at the Mini.

I slipped a pair of latex gloves on, walked towards the office entrance and checked there was nobody watching. The lock on the outer door was pathetic. I could imagine Joe Murphy's jaw drop in amazement. 'Good grief, Riley,' he'd laugh, 'now this is one daft bugger who deserves to be robbed.' The security on the upstairs office was a bit trickier. Joe had been a true master, in and out in minutes with no trace left behind. I was clumsier but the knack came back to me faster than I could have imagined.

It would have been safer for me to take a portable hard disk with me and download the video but Morrison wanted the actual laptop. So I would have to snatch it and make this look like a break-in, mess the place up a bit. Mind you, one glance at that pigsty and I wasn't sure whether anybody would even notice.

A cash box in an unlocked drawer held a couple of hundred quid in walking-around money, so I pocketed that. I pulled filing cabinets open and threw papers about. Beside Carver's desk was a plastic carrier bag filled with the slowly mouldering remains of take-away lunches, beer cans and snack packets. No wonder he was such a fat fuck. I emptied the contents on top of the rest of the mess and tossed the carrier on the floor. I even considered taking a dump in the middle of the tatty rug, but then thought better of it.

When the phone rang, it echoed shrilly around the walls and the inside of my head. An old-fashioned answering machine kicked in and whirred its outgoing message before the caller spoke. 'Jim, it's me. Things are pretty stressful around here. Are you on your way?'

I knew that voice. Gloria Kelso. Monica had always been convinced that Benny had employed Gloria to keep an eye on her. But maybe Gloria had been Jim Carver's plant all along. Or working both ends against the middle. Perhaps that's why she left Brando on his own some evenings; she was probably reporting back to Carver. The message sounded like some kind of emergency. Which might explain why Carver had left in such a hurry. But who summons Big Jim?

I didn't have time to ponder and was about to get out of there when I heard footsteps on the stairs. 'Mister Carver!' The voice was unmistakably foreign. 'I think I see you go out, Mister Carver, then I hear noise up here.'

Keep quiet, maybe he'll go away, think he was mistaken. But he kept rattling the handle. 'Mister Carver!' His voice was a Middle

Eastern wail, swiftly increasing in volume and uncomfortably reminiscent of a siren. 'Mister Carver!' The last thing I needed was for him to skedaddle back to E. coli Express downstairs and call the police.

I grabbed the door handle, yanked it open and the scrawny kebab shop owner fell in. The first thing he saw as he tumbled into the room was my fist in his face. He was floored immediately and I rolled him onto his stomach so he couldn't get a good look at me. I kicked him in the ribs and he instinctively curled up. I seized the empty carrier bag I'd chucked on the floor and pulled it over his head. He gasped, and his panicked intake of breath moulded the plastic to his face as he clawed desperately to pull it off. I tucked the laptop under my arm and legged it down the stairs.

Chapter Fourteen
4 p.m., Thursday, 19 June

I picked up Brando from school and ignored his mocking grimaces about the Mini.

'Why did you bring *this* thing?'

'Just get in the front, Brando.'

He glanced at the back seat and spotted Carver's laptop. 'What have you got there, then?'

'What does it look like?'

He ignored my snipe, studiously stared out of his side window and didn't speak for the rest of the journey.

The gates to the estate were open and Monica's red Porsche was parked in the driveway, alongside a Daimler I didn't recognise.

Brando glowered at the sight of his mother's car. 'Mum's back,' he said. 'You won't let her hit me again, will you?'

'I'm sure she'll have calmed down by now.'

He clambered out of the Mini and walked towards the front door that stood, worryingly, ajar. I scooped Carver's laptop off the back seat and followed Brando inside.

The boy stood rooted to the spot in the living room doorway. He was staring at Gerard Fowley's gofer sprawled out on one of the white leather sofas. The TV was blasting out some MTV crap and Chinese Clive had both feet, shod in box-white trainers, on the coffee table.

'Mum doesn't allow feet on the furniture,' Brando reprimanded.

Clive sneered, his newly cultivated moustache making him look even more of a weasel than ever.

I walked up to Brando and placed my hand on his shoulder. 'You heard what the lad said.'

Clive leapt to his feet, every inch the lightweight boxer – nimble, strong and quick.

Best get the kid out of the way in case anything kicks off. 'Take this.' I handed Carver's laptop over to Brando. 'Now go and do your homework.'

He took it straight-faced and made a heavy-footed display of climbing the stairs.

'Fuck me, man,' Clive exclaimed in his cod Jamaican accent. 'Kids use laptops in school these days?'

'What can I tell you?' I shrugged and we stared each other down. 'So where's Mrs Cohen?'

'That's what Mr Fowley wants to know.' Clive nodded towards Benny's study. 'He's in there. He'll wanna talk to you.'

Fowley was sitting in Benny's swivel chair behind the desk while one of his goons rummaged through the filing cabinets.

'That's private property your friend's got his grubby paws on,' I said.

Fowley laughed. The goon, six-feet-four of coal-black muscle on legs, turned and growled.

Fowley held up his hand as though to restrain his employee from tearing me limb from limb. 'Where's Monica?'

'Search me.'

'That might be an option. But this is such a nice place.' He looked around at the overpriced reproduction furniture that Benny had bought by the truckload. 'Tasteful.' He smirked. 'We wouldn't want to make a mess in here, now, would we, Sam?'

'I have no idea where Monica is. In fact, I thought she might be with you. The two of you being so tight and all. Anyway, isn't that her car in the driveway?'

'It was parked on my showroom lot this morning. She'd left her house keys in there. Thought I'd be a gentleman and return them to their rightful owner.' He tossed a set of keys to me and I caught them.

'Look, Sam.' Fowley leaned forward on the desk. 'I'm a reasonable man.'

I almost laughed. That was the second time I'd heard that phrase in two days and both from the mouths of a couple of the most vicious characters this side of Watford.

'Yeah, I'd heard that,' I said. 'So what's with all this?'

'We had a deal, that's all.'

'You and Monica?'

'Me and Benny – or rather, me, Big Jim Carver and Benny – and a deal is a deal. The clubs to be split between me and Big Jim, for a fair price.'

'Mr Cohen was going to hand over his nightclubs to you two? I don't believe it for a second.'

Fowley's face split into a grin. 'You didn't know?' He laughed out loud. 'Get this, Clive!' Clive scurried into the room in response to his master's voice. 'Seems Monica's piece of lesbo pussy here didn't know Cohen was a goner.'

Clive chortled and I had rarely felt so tempted to floor someone in my entire life, but I kept it together. What else didn't I know?

'Benny had terminal cancer,' Fowley said. 'Wanted to spend his last few months in the sun, in the bosom of his family. He was coming to the meeting to sign the papers the night some fucker blew him away.'

A wave of shock almost sucked me under and I struggled to stay afloat. If Benny Cohen's days were numbered, then why would Monica have wanted him dispatched in such a hurry? Now I was coming out of my befuddled stupor, I recognised it for what it really was. She'd wanted Benny murdered to stop the deal with Fowley and Carver from going through.

'But these things happen,' Fowley said. I could see his lips move but the words seemed to echo in the distance. 'Old scores get settled.' He shook his head sagely like he was contemplating this almost inevitable state of affairs. 'That's the life we've chosen, man.' He sighed. 'So I try to explain the deal to Monica. And she's her usual sweet, ditzy self at first. Then she turns up with Felipe Garcia and he gets all arsey. And to think I introduced her to that dago prick.' Ironic, how those so sensitive to racial epithets are always ready to use them themselves.

'What's his business cover, Clive?' Fowley threw the question to his vile little henchman.

'He's got that poncy hairdressing and beauty salon. Bankrolled by Benny Cohen, the stupid old fuck. Hair dos at the front of the shop and Garcia shafting Benny's missus in the back room.' Clive's grin widened and I really wanted to tear his head off. He leered at me and affected a camp voice. 'Give us a Brazilian while you're down there, will you, Felipe.'

'Sorry to be the bearer of such bad news, Sam.' Fowley made a feeble attempt to sound sympathetic. 'Looks like you've been left holding the baby. Literally.'

Clive laughed.

The revelation that I'd been used was a punch in the guts and I mentally reeled under the impact. I felt sick, conned and fucking angry.

I struggled to regain control of myself.

Fowley's face locked back in to its hard-man persona. 'So, where is she?'

'She signed some papers for Carver.' Fuck you, Monica! I'm not protecting you any longer. Game over. 'Then she did a runner. I haven't seen her since.'

'Carver?' Fowley's bleached features momentarily registered surprise that he swiftly disguised. 'When was this?'

'Yesterday.'

He weighed me up. 'You'd better not be telling me any porkies, Sam. Cos, Winston here' – he indicated to the hulking figure standing behind him – 'his missus ran off with a carpet muncher. Didn't she, son?'

Winston glowered at me.

'And he's the vengeful type.'

Chapter Fifteen
6 p.m., Thursday, 19 June

After Fowley and his crew had left the house, Brando came downstairs, went into the kitchen and came back with a packet of Jaffa Cakes.

'We should try to find Mum.' He opened the box and started to tuck in.

'And where do you think we should start?'

'Felipe Garcia's place.'

'You know about that?'

'Mum persuaded Dad to back Garcia and his sister in the business.'

'I thought your dad didn't know about Garcia?'

'He didn't know Mum was shagging him.'

The words landed in the pit of my stomach and marched about in hobnail boots. What else was the lad aware of – Monica and me, maybe? Still, if he did know, he didn't seem fazed by it. Maybe he was waiting to use that knowledge to his own advantage. I looked at the smug look on his face and forced myself to remember that he was just a kid.

'The Garcia family runs drugs out of the Canaries and Spain,' Brando said. 'They wanted to expand and needed a legitimate business in the UK as a front. Dad put up the money.'

'Why would drug dealers need someone else's money?'

Brando raised his eyebrows. 'You're such an innocent,' he said. 'Because Dad's money was clean. That's how it works. He was investing in the salon for a share of the profits – or as a tax write-off. In return, Felipe got access to the punters in the nightclubs. Dad would get his cut and not get his hands dirty. Everyone's a winner.' Brando wiped his chocolate-covered mouth on his sleeve. 'It was a business deal.'

Reason enough for Felipe to want the deal with Carver and Fowley to be nipped in the bud. Fowley was heavily in with Jamaican drug dealers and, no doubt, Carver had his own suppliers. They, in turn, wouldn't take kindly to a Spaniard gumming up the works.

'You're eleven,' I said. 'How come you know about all this stuff?'

'You grow up quick in this house.'

'You spend all your time watching bloody *Star Wars*.'

'And listening at doors. Nobody takes any notice of a kid wandering in and out, so they keep on talking. Kids are invisible.' He gobbled another biscuit and grinned at me. 'Didn't you know that?'

I sat and watched Brando munch his way through the whole packet. I needed to get the laptop out of the house and pray that Carver hadn't cottoned on it was me who'd nicked it. Maybe I could find Monica and make her take responsibility for her son. She'd never shown any affection for the boy, but she was still his mother. If she'd take him off my hands, I might be able to wangle my way out of this mess. But with Brando in tow, I was stymied.

Brando smirked. 'By the way, I've put that laptop in Dad's secret safe.'

'I didn't know he had a secret safe.'

'That's because it's a secret.'

'Do you have the key?'

'Combination. That's a secret as well.'

'Let me have it, will you?' I felt uneasy; he was up to something. 'I need that laptop.'

He held me in his stare. This kid who knew things most adults had no clue about. He pulled stunts the average eleven-year-old wouldn't even dream of. 'Okay, Sam.' He nodded gravely. 'But only if you help me find Mum first.'

Great, add that to this particular shitstorm – being blackmailed by a kid.

By seven we were in the car on the way to Felipe Garcia's salon, me as chauffeur with Brando in the back, when he hit me with his plan.

'I'll go in,' he said.

'No,' I said. 'I'll go in and ask.'

'Right,' he scoffed. 'Going to pretend to be a customer, are you? Come on.'

I ignored the insult. 'But I can ask the whereabouts of my employer.'

'These people wouldn't answer any questions even if you put them in thumbscrews.'

'Thumbscrews? Bit medieval.'

'We're doing the Spanish Inquisition in history at school. It's cool.'

Yeah, he would think that was cool – murder, mayhem, treachery, torture – just another average day in the Cohen household. 'So, Mr Genius, what do you suggest?'

'Felipe's sister works in there. I go in and ask her where my mum is.'

'And she tells you straight away, does she? Or have you got a set of thumbscrews in your pocket?'

'I'm a kid and she's a woman – a Spanish woman. They're suckers for kids, the Spanish. I'll turn on the waterworks if I have to. Easy peasy!' The brat had more smarts and chutzpah than I'd ever given him credit for.

'And don't worry.' He scrambled out of the back seat. 'Nobody ever suspects kids of having ulterior motives.'

Then they hadn't met Brando Cohen!

I waited in the car and watched the door. A tall brunette came out of the salon, wearing nosebleed-inducing high heels and a geometric hairdo straight out of the 1960s. Must be back in fashion again. Ten minutes went by and I was about to go in there when the door opened and a petite woman with a cascade of shimmering black hair led Brando out by the hand. He was crying. I got out of the car, walked over to him and the woman gave me an apologetic smile.

'His mother will be back soon,' she said in a Spanish accent. 'She will call you when she comes back from *luna de miel*.'

She gave me a look I couldn't quite decipher when she hugged and kissed Brando. The sly smile was still on her face as she turned to walk away.

Brando climbed into the back seat. I glanced at him through the mirror and laughed. 'See you had to use the water torture method.' I started the engine. 'Where is this Luna place, anyway?'

He glared at me. 'Not a place, moron,' he snarled, 'it's a thing. She's on her honeymoon.'

Honeymoon! The ink was barely dry on Benny Cohen's death certificate.

'She's married that Garcia geezer.' Brando fished a hanky out of his pocket and blew his nose. 'They've gone to Spain. She's left us, Sam. She's left us.'

I manoeuvred the car into the traffic and steeled myself. Fool, you should have seen this coming. What the hell was I going to do now? I looked back at Brando who was staring blankly out of the side window. He was still crying.

Face it, Sam, it's just you and the kid now. Out on your own to deal with whatever comes down the pipeline. Morrison, Fowley, Carver or Swindley – the four horsemen of my all-too-personal apocalypse.

Chapter Sixteen
9 p.m., Thursday, 19 June

By the time we got back to the house, Brando's face was set, like he'd swallowed down all the pain. No more tears, no sign of anger, no emotion at all. I'd tried to talk to him on the journey but got only silence back from the rear seat, so I gave up. I didn't know exactly how to deal with this situation. What do you say to a kid whose mother runs off and remarries three days after laying his father to rest?

The lights were on in the house, on automatic timer to make the place look inhabited after dark. The gates were closed and there were no cars in the driveway. I'd put Monica's Porsche back in the garage after Fowley and his goons had left. There was no alarm system because Benny neither trusted them nor those who installed them. He reckoned every safe-jockey and burglar in the kingdom had gone into the home security business.

I opened up with some trepidation but was aware only of the silence of the building.

'I'll show you the secret safe,' Brando announced when we got through the door.

'Let's have something to eat first.'

'No,' he said. 'You helped me and I'll help you. A deal's a deal.' No sign of the tears he'd shed in the car. He was all business.

Brando's room was a mess – DVDs scattered all over the carpet, bed unmade and an Xbox on his pillow. In his en-suite bathroom I could see a wet towel that had been dropped on the floor. No Gloria meant no cleaning and I had no intention of picking up after him. He was going to have to learn to tidy after himself. The massive TV dominated one side of his room. An electric guitar was on a stand in one corner and an Apple computer on a desk alongside his phone extension. He had a separate dressing room and he led the way in there. He bent down, moved the rug to one side and lifted a small section of flooring beneath. And, cut into the floorboards, set in concrete, was a black textured safe with a brass-plated dial and handle. Brando dialled the combination, turned the knob and pulled open the lid. I reached in and lifted out Carver's laptop that was on top of files, papers and a metal box.

'Do you want to see what else is in here?'

'None of my business.'

'There's money.' He delved in and pulled out a wedge of fifties bound with those red rubber bands that postmen scatter along the streets.

'Not interested,' I said. 'That's not my money and it's not yours either.' I took it off him and dropped it back in the safe.

He stared at me open-mouthed. 'But we might need to buy stuff,' he said. 'Food and things.'

'I'll ring your father's solicitor and try to sort things out. We'll be okay. In the meantime, I've got money.'

'Look at all this!' He rummaged about in the safe, pulled out a brown envelope and tore it open. A photograph fell out. It was of Benny Cohen and a woman. It had obviously been taken at least twenty years previously because Benny had a lot more hair then and a lot less stomach. The woman was dark-haired, pleasant-looking rather than lovely, but she did have a dazzling smile. And Benny looked happier than I'd ever seen him.

'She looks Jewish,' Brando said. 'Maybe she's Dad's sister or something?'

I took the photograph from him. The kid could be right. 'We'll keep that out,' I said. 'I'll take it to the solicitor. Maybe you've got some relative you don't know about. Someone to take care of you until your mother gets back.'

Brando's face darkened. He slammed the safe shut, replaced the floor panels and pulled the rug back over it.

'What's wrong with you?'

'I won't go to someone I don't know!' He stormed out of the room.

I was about to follow him when my phone buzzed. Could it be Monica, full of remorse and wanting her son back? Fat chance. She'd abandoned us to our fate to save her own skin. Heartless bitch.

'Hello, Sam. Wendy here.' DI Morrison's dulcet tones sounded friendly for once. 'I wouldn't order a kebab for supper tonight if I were you. I hear they've had a break-in.' I imagined a smirk on her face and guessed that the kebab shop owner I bashed up had reported it to the police. There was no way Big Jim Carver would ever involve the cops. Carver had his own guys for sorting out that kind of trouble.

'Instead, can I suggest you order a takeaway pizza?' she said. 'They'll deliver right to your door.'

He turned up half an hour later on a motorbike, with a pizza. He wore black leathers and a full-face helmet. He held out a gloved hand.

'How much?' I asked.

'We're on the bartering system, these days.'

I handed over the laptop.

Brando sat and stared disconsolately at the food on the plate in front of him.

'Come on,' I said, 'eat up. It's your favourite.'

'I suppose you're going to dump me as well,' he said.

'I'm not dumping you.'

'I don't want to go to some old Jewish auntie. I want to stay with you.'

You could have knocked me over with the proverbial. 'Look, Brando. I've been in the army for years, I don't know anything about kids.'

'You're doing alright so far.'

I wasn't keen on where this conversation was heading. 'Right, by letting you eat pizza every day.'

'What about that picture in your bedroom drawer? Whose kid is that?'

'You've been snooping in my room, haven't you?'

He ignored the question as he probably deemed it rhetorical. He stared me down. 'So, who is it?'

Not wanting to have to talk about Tom with him but with a certain relief that he'd changed tack, I said, 'His name is Tom. He's my nephew.'

'Where is he now?'

'I don't know.'

'Why? What happened to him?'

What should I tell him? Put on the spot, I opted for the truth. 'It seems he was taken. Abducted. Nobody really knows where he is.'

'You should have asked Dad to find him. Dad could do anything.' Here was the child again, popping out from his hiding place behind the cynical little know-it-all facade.

'It was a long time ago,' I said.

'Maybe some nonce took him.'

'Nonce?'

73

'You know, like Uncle Jim. He's a nonce. I've heard people talking about him.'

'Listening at doors?'

He grinned and reached for a slice of pizza. 'It was Uncle Jim in that video.'

What was this? 'The video he showed you? The one on the laptop?'

'Yeah.'

This was the old Brando back again, releasing information only when it suited him. 'You said you only saw some fat old bloke with a kid.'

'I didn't see his face but I saw the tattoo on his bum. It's a dragon. I've seen it before.'

I tried to make light of this latest revelation. 'What, his bum?'

'No,' he giggled, 'the tattoo! When we all went swimming in Ibiza, I saw Uncle Jim pulling his shorts on. Dad made some joke about hot breath behind him. It was the same tattoo in the video. It was definitely him.'

He was eating heartily now, smiling at me, a smile that transformed his features. He wasn't such a bad kid after all.

'You won't leave me, will you, Sam?' And he gave me the puppy eyes.

'No, I won't leave you.' I said, with the slowly dawning realisation that I really meant it.

Chapter Seventeen
9 a.m., Friday, 20 June

Monica held up her left hand and wiggled it so her new engagement ring glittered in the early morning sunshine streaming in through the window of the plane. She loved it. Platinum with a one-carat diamond, this was more like it. When she'd fled the house in a panic and gone to see him, Felipe Garcia had told her not to worry. He would take care of everything. He had slipped the glittering diamond on her finger over the groove that had been made by her wedding ring.

She smiled across at Felipe – handsome face, good teeth, big dick and oh-so generous. And his consumption of the old Peruvian marching powder was almost as prodigious as her own, so she'd get no snide complaints about that little indulgence.

She was quite glad she'd put the dampeners on Felipe's rush to get married. It was always about ownership with these types. Though she needed him for protection, so agreeing to the engagement had been the pragmatic thing to do. She had to tread carefully because Benny had been a sly old bastard, so there was no knowing what clauses he might have had written into his will. She'd wait until she had complete control over all Benny's assets before she finally committed herself to Felipe.

Though, she mused, once she had her own money, perhaps she wouldn't have to bother after all. She'd think about that when the time came.

She settled back in her business class seat and sipped her champagne. This was the life. She'd never travelled in style with Benny, the old tightwad. But now she had Felipe, she could almost taste the sweet life to come.

Felipe's insistence on travelling to Spain straightaway to meet Miss Padres had her puzzled and not a little peeved. 'Who's she?' She'd pouted, all little girly. That usually got 'em going.

'*Mis padres.*' He'd laughed. 'My parents.'

That got her to wondering if he had two fathers, until he explained that *padres* was Spanish for mother and father.

She had a lot to learn, if she could be arsed, which she knew she probably couldn't. She opened her compact and applied a fresh layer of lipstick. Who needs to speak the language when you looked like this? She'd charm the pants off them. Now that was one thing she could do.

Duty done, they'd be back in England in nine days' time. Once the will was read and all the legal stuff set to rest, she'd have Benny's gelt in her back pocket. She'd be a rich woman in her own right. And when she signed the nightclubs over to the Garcia clan, they'd all be rolling in dosh. Now she was thinking straight, she realised that the document she'd signed for Carver wasn't legally binding. He must have known it too, and had forced her to sign it just to put the frighteners on. The evil old perv wanted to emphasise that, on her own, she had no way to stand up to him. Well, she had a new man now. See how Carver liked them apples.

Monica's mind was working overtime. When she and Felipe returned to England, she'd sack that stupid bitch Sam Riley. Monica could get Felipe to have Riley seen to later. Maybe a car accident or something like that – nothing that would raise anyone's suspicions.

In the meantime, she'd pack Brando off well out of the way. That school in Scotland, maybe. The one Prince Charles went to – all cold showers and twenty-mile hikes. That place would make a man of the little shit.

The Carvers were another matter. But if Benny had been so easy to do away with, how hard would it be to get at Big Jim and his crippled old crone of a mother?

Garcia took her left hand and lifted it to his lips. He kissed the engagement ring and she wondered if he might like to join the Mile High Club right there and then. But she resisted the temptation to ask. Didn't want him to think she was some kind of tart. She'd made him beg for it the first time. Had him drooling before she said yes. Best keep it at that level for now.

She smiled at him. Oh, yes, life was good.

Chapter Eighteen
8 a.m., Saturday, 21 June

Brando was getting ready for his weekly guitar lesson with some long-haired muso who was teaching him the 'Whole Lotta Love' riff. At least that's what it sounded like when the kid was practising. Could have been something else, but what do I know, I'm tone deaf. I'd seen the guy once, Mike somebody, all dyed black hair and leather jeans, pretty wife half his age and three small children young enough to be his grandkids. The guy's face was vaguely familiar, one of those used-to-bes who turn up in the 'Where Are They Now?' articles in music magazines complete with text that ran: 'Now working on his next project in a home studio at his converted Home Counties farmhouse and passing on his extensive musical knowledge to the next generation.' For which read: 'Desperately trying to get a new recording contract and using his over-hyped former glory to extort inflated tuition fees from the parents of wannabe guitar heroes.'

'Why don't you ring Dad's lawyer today?' Brando handed me a business card with the name Richard Bloom embossed on it.

'Solicitors don't work on Saturdays.'

'This one does. Ring him. He'll see you. Dad used to phone him at all hours.'

Correct again.

———————

I dropped Brando off, then made my way to Bloom's office. It was just a mile or so from the guitar tutor's farmhouse, situated down a narrow, leafy lane, beside a babbling stream and in a building that bore more resemblance to a country cottage than a solicitor's place of work. It was not the type of practice I would have immediately associated with the flashy Benny Cohen. I had expected some huge, glass building, glamorous receptionists, certainly something much more ostentatious than this rustic hideaway. But then, maybe this was some ever-so-discreet firm – for special, slightly iffy clients only.

I stopped outside, unsure I was at the right place even though the bossy voice on the satnav kept telling me that I had reached my destination. I drove into the adjacent car park where the only other motor was a Jag that I assumed belonged to the man himself. I got out and checked the name on the shingle attached to the door: Richard Bloom.

He was in his mid-forties, dark-haired, dressed in chinos and a polo shirt, the casual weekend uniform of the upper middle classes. I didn't recall seeing Bloom's face at Benny's funeral. There had been so many mourners there I might have overlooked him, but I doubted it. With the police making such a big show of their presence maybe he'd stayed away on purpose, as in what they don't see can't hurt him; discretion and valour and all that.

I apologised for calling him on Saturday but he smiled affably and invited me to sit. Once he too was seated, he flipped open a large file that was on his desk next to a computer.

'Mr Cohen was a client and a friend. I am only too pleased to be of service,' he said.

I explained about Monica absenting herself from the Cohen house, the news of her possible remarriage and Spanish honeymoon. He listened patiently, his face impassive.

'I find it a little implausible for a marriage to have taken place so soon' he said. 'One has to give fifteen days' notice to a registry office. I rather suspect the young woman you spoke to was mistaken.'

Or winding me up. That sly look on her face should have warned me of that possibility.

'When do you expect Mrs Cohen to return?'

'I don't know.'

Bloom hit a computer key and the machine bonged into life. 'She doesn't have to be in the country for the reading of the will, of course,' he said with his eyes on the screen. 'But I do need an address for her in order to inform her about her proportion of the estate.'

'Sorry, I have no idea where she is.'

'I'll have enquiries made.' He scribbled a quick note on a legal pad. 'The only other beneficiary is Mr Cohen's son, Brando.'

'What about this person?' I showed him the photograph of Benny and the dark-haired woman we had found in the secret safe.

Bloom looked perplexed, thrown almost. 'Where did you get this?'

'Brando found it amongst his father's papers.'

'Indeed.'

I tried to read his face but his expression had retreated to neutral. They say Orientals are inscrutable but they've got nothing on lawyers.

'I was wondering if she was a relative,' I ventured.

Bloom picked up the photograph and placed it in the file. 'I'd like to keep this if you don't have any objection.'

I was about to protest when he closed the file once more. 'I do know of the lady in the photograph. But, sadly, she is deceased.'

My heart sank. No nice Jewish auntie to fold Brando to her loving bosom, then. Bloom's manner told me that was all the information I was about to get from him on that subject.

'Brando has nobody in the world,' he said. 'Apart for Mrs Cohen and, of course, you.' He got up, crossed to the window and stared out as though deep in thought before continuing. 'Given the current circumstances, would you be prepared to sign a form of temporary guardianship over Brando, Miss Riley?' He returned to his desk, sat down and reopened the file. He flipped through it, finally settling on and scrutinising one particular page. 'You appear to be of good character.' He looked up at me. 'You were in the army for fifteen years, I believe. And you have no criminal record.' Did he sound impressed by that last bit or was it just my imagination?

'What exactly would this temporary guardianship entail?' I certainly hadn't expected this, neither did I relish the prospect. Having a child makes you vulnerable and I had never wanted to feel that way again, but I'd already promised the lad that I wouldn't leave him, and I knew that I couldn't bring myself to abandon him.

'No more than you are already doing, in reality,' Bloom was saying. 'The timescale would be for a maximum of ninety days during which time you would act *in loco parentis*. Your present salary will be tripled, effective immediately, in line with your added responsibilities.'

Without waiting for an answer he tapped the computer keyboard and a printer across the room began to spit out paper.

'It's a standard form to sign, if you are in agreement. You would be free to hire any staff you may require, as the Cohen house is quite a large property to maintain. All school fees and household bills are currently being paid via this office, so you have nothing to worry about on that score.'

It all happened so fast I felt like I'd been hustled by a double-glazing salesman and found myself signing the form, still warm from the printer. We shook hands afterwards.

'And Miss Riley,' Bloom said as I was leaving, 'should Mrs Cohen return to the house unexpectedly, please call me on my private number. Immediately. At any time, twenty-four hours a day.'

I felt dazed as I sat in the car – from driver-cum-dogsbody to guardian in the swoosh of a pen. A loud rap on my window made me jump and I looked up to see a looming presence. I opened the window, as it seemed unlikely that anybody was about to whack me in the car park of a solicitor's office, but I was wary.

'Gentleman would like to see you,' he said, leaning into the window. I recognised him as one of Benny Cohen's ex-employees, the type not to be messed with. He was known for being handy with a knife and a sawn-off. And was now on the payroll of Big Jim Carver.

How the hell did they know I was here? Had I been followed from the house? And, if so, why?

A black vehicle with tinted windows was positioned strategically across the car park entrance. No chance of making a run for it then, so I took a deep breath and accompanied the minder towards the car. The back window was down and when I heard a voice with a Birmingham accent say 'Get in!' it sent a shiver down my spine.

'My employer finds himself somewhat discommoded, Miss Riley,' Swindley said as I slid into the back seat beside him. The heavy sat in the front with the driver. 'Something to do with a purloined laptop computer, it seems. The police visited Mr Carver's home with a search warrant in the early hours of this morning. The whole incident was most unfortunate. Mr Carver's elderly mother was highly distressed.'

I had never actually met Lil Carver but her reputation was fearsome, so I concluded that it might have been the cops who were more flustered than that once-formidable matron.

'That's a shame,' I said.

'It certainly is, especially coming just a day after some ne'er-do-well broke into Mr Carver's office.'

'And I can help you how, exactly?' I felt sure that Carver hadn't seen me outside his office. Neither had the little kebab guy I'd clobbered. But you never knew for sure.

'Mr Carver recalls your warning him about the doors to his office being somewhat flimsy.'

'It was just a little friendly advice; I was trying to be helpful.'

'And a mere twelve hours later his office was burgled,' Swindley said.

'I'm sure I wasn't the only person to notice the lack of security, Mr Swindley. The timescale was purely coincidental.'

'My employer is not a man of superstition, Miss Riley. He doesn't believe in coincidences.'

'Don't you think this break-in has Gerard Fowley's signature all over it?' I was thinking as quickly as I could manage in an attempt to shift the blame onto someone better equipped to deal with any gathering storm.

Swindley surveyed me with his bleak grey eyes, but remained silent.

'In fact, I heard Fowley was mighty pissed off about your employer going behind his back to cut a deal with Mrs Cohen,' I said. 'Are you sure this present nastiness isn't some kind of spiteful retribution?' My nerves were clearly getting the better of me as I was starting to talk just like Swindley.

'That is by the by, Miss Riley.' With some people a Birmingham accent can often make them sound slow-witted, comical even, but with Swindley it had the effect of reinforcing the dark menace of the man. 'Today, it is merely my duty to pass on a message. Mr Carver wishes to inform you that, in order to disentangle himself from these current distasteful proceedings, he sincerely hopes a young man of your acquaintance will develop a certain degree of amnesia, shall we say.'

So that was it. Keep Brando quiet or else. 'Brando is just a kid,' I said. 'He has nothing to do with all of this.'

'You see, Miss Riley,' Swindley intoned, 'Mr Carver is convinced otherwise. And when he makes up his mind, he's a very difficult man to dissuade. Do I make myself clear?'

'As a bell, Mr Swindley. As a bell.' Keep schtum or be shut up. Permanently.

'Then I'll wish you good day, Miss Riley.'

The driver came around and opened the door for me. I got out.

'How did you know I was here?' I asked Swindley as the tinted back window began to rise.

'My employer has eyes and ears everywhere, Miss Riley. You'd be wise to remember that.'

Chapter Nineteen
10 a.m., Sunday, 22 June

'So where are we going?' Brando asked.

I was loading the breakfast plates into the dishwasher and had told him to go and get ready, to wear something casual and bring a sweater.

'Chessington,' I said. 'Surrey.'

'Why?'

'It will be good for you to get out of the house on a Sunday.'

'But is it seemly?'

'Seemly? Where'd you get a word like that?'

'I mean, Dad's funeral was only on Tuesday. Shouldn't we be wearing black or something?'

'I don't wish to sound insensitive, Brando, but your dad's been gone for a while.'

He grunted. I hated it when he grunted.

'Anyway, I'm sure he would have liked you to have some fun.'

'So what's at this Chessington place?'

'A World of Adventure,' I said. 'It'll be good.'

He grunted again.

We followed the site map to the Vampire Ride. The place was packed with parents and children. They were mainly the standard families but you could easily recognise the single mums counting the pennies and the Sunday fathers dishing out guilt money to hyperactive kids on a sugar-rush of candyfloss and ice cream.

I spotted her immediately: DI Wendy Morrison in tight blue jeans and a green T-shirt with her auburn hair tied back in a pony-tail. Beside her was DS Trevor Jones, also casually dressed. He held the hand of a pretty girl who was around Brando's age, though significantly taller than him. Maybe the boy would suddenly shoot up in a year or so but right now he was the size of the average eight-year-old. I was aware that being small annoyed him no end, and guessed his apparent lack of development might make him the butt of playground jokes. Was that one reason for his tendency towards isolation, for his snarling bluster and smart-arse behaviour? I'd never really thought much about it before but comparing Brando's height to that of the girl brought it all home to me.

Morrison dashed towards us and kissed me on both cheeks like we were old friends – a bit of street theatre for the benefit of the boy, no doubt.

'Sam,' she gushed, 'so lovely to see you.' She beamed and turned to Brando who moped sullenly by my side. 'And you must be Brando. I'm Wendy.' She ruffled his hair and he grimaced.

Introductions were made to Wendy's 'husband' Trev and daughter Amy. Trev took the kids off for a whirl on the rollercoaster.

'Rent a child?' I said.

'Amy *is* Trevor's daughter. He's a weekend father. Divorced. One of the many downsides of police work.' She waved to the kids just like a regular mother-type, then turned back to me and shifted gear. 'So what's with this emergency meeting?'

I told her of my encounter with creepy Swindley and described him.

'He's mid- to late-fifties, grey eyes, fair hair with flecks of white, receding slightly at the temples. Five feet six or seven, slim build but fit-looking. Smart suit and tie with well-polished shoes. Possibly ex-army. Broad Birmingham accent – talks like a character out of Dickens.'

'I'm surprised.'

'What, that I've read Dickens?'

'Your observational skills. You'd have made a good cop, Sam.'

'Yeah, well. Guess that army training comes in handy from time to time. I'm able to distinguish between uniforms and everything.'

She ignored my attempt at sarcasm.

'Anyway,' I said. 'He calls himself Swindley. Though it's probably not his real name.'

'No?' she gasped with mock surprise. 'Mr Swindley was the name of a TV character in the 1960s.'

'You're older than you look.'

'Pub quizzes.'

'With good old Trev, eh?'

'Good God, no!'

The sights and sounds of the theme park came from all sides, kids' laughter and screams from the rides. It was so very different from my own last time enjoying the fun of the fair. I'd forgotten about it until that moment. Twenty-odd years before, Joe and me in a muddy field, one of those scruffy travelling carnivals with precarious rides that look held together with spit and string. Punters swirling in huge teacups, spinning on waltzers, bumping in brightly painted cars. He'd tried to win a teddy bear for me but couldn't. Joe Murphy, who could shoot the eye out of a moggy at twenty paces, wasn't able to hit a target front and centre just a few feet away. 'It's a fix,' he'd shouted at the impassive stallholder. The man shrugged and gave me a plastic key ring as a consolation prize. I dragged Joe away before he caused any trouble. That was the night Joe kissed me for the first time, to the sound of 'Lay Lady Lay' booming out of the fairground speakers. In response, I shoved him into a puddle of water. But that was long ago and three hundred miles away.

'So, where have you got with Carver?' I asked Morrison.

'You know I can't discuss the case with you.'

'Hang on! I put my arse on the line for this. And now it's not just me in the frame, but Brando as well.'

Morrison' s expression instantly hardened. 'You stole that laptop for purely selfish reasons, Samantha. You want that photo of you and Joseph Murphy destroyed. Evidence of your link to the killer of that little boy's father.' She lifted her head and sniffed about dramatically. 'The air is thick with irony around here, don't you think?'

Trevor came back with the kids; the girl giggled away but Brando looked a bit green around the gills.

'Brando, are you alright?'

His eyes were wide with excitement. 'I've never been on one of those rides before.' He tugged at DS Jones's jacket. 'Can we go again, Trev?'

'Lots more rides to go on, son.' Trevor took each kid by the hand. 'See you later, ladies.' They disappeared together into the crowds.

Morrison leaned against the wall of the Pirates' Cove, hands in her jeans pockets, observing me. 'You're really quite fond of that boy, aren't you?'

'You get used to him.' I wasn't about to trust her with my feelings for Brando, just so she could use it against me whenever the fancy took her. 'He's not a particularly likeable child.'

'No wonder, growing up in that household.'

'At least tell me if you've arrested Jim Carver.'

She sighed, obviously aware I was not one to be fobbed off, and if she wanted my cooperation she would have to give me more. 'His brief is claiming the video was planted. Carver will get out on bail if nothing is found on his other computers.'

That was the very last thing I wanted to hear. I eyed her suspiciously. When had she intended passing on that nugget of information? When Big Jim Carver was standing over me with a hammer in his hand? With a sense of impending doom, I recalled Monica's story about Carver killing a whole family with a coal hammer. Blood and gore splattered everywhere, she had said. Granted, that had been when Carver was in his pomp. He was older and fatter now, but there was always the rest of his crew – and Swindley. My stomach clenched at the thought of that man and his Arctic stare. I was sure that Morrison hadn't been about to tell me anything about Carver being cut loose. She didn't give a toss about the kid and me. We were just a means of catching Big Jim Carver, one more tick in her promotion box. I remembered again Morrison at Benny Cohen's funeral, the determination on her face as she watched the assembled villains, her ambition to bag the lot of them flaring like an Olympic torch. Trust this woman? Never.

We wandered across to look at the sea lions. To any vaguely curious passer-by we were just two mothers waiting for our children to come back from their rides. The sign announced that feeding time was half an hour away, so we were the only ones by the enclosure.

'I've watched that video,' Morrison said. 'It's pretty gruesome. The violent rape of a minor by two grown men. One's a fat bastard and the other one, who holds the boy down, has arms like a gorilla. Can't see the faces, though.'

I gave an involuntary shudder.

'I know about your nephew, Sam. The disappearance.' Her voice softened.

'I might have guessed.' She'd checked my background. 'The police in Manchester were convinced my brother and his wife had killed Tom. Seemed to put most of their efforts into harassing them, digging up gardens and the like. By the time they'd finished screwing around, the person who'd taken Tom could have been in Timbuktu.' It had been seven years but the wound remained raw. 'Tom was never found.' I said. 'It destroyed my brother.'

'Well, back then, not much was known about the paedo rings.'

'Don't play me, Wendy.' Good cop, bad cop all wrapped up in one – quite a party piece. To mention the rape of the boy in the video and my nephew Tom in virtually the same breath, that was a low blow. But now, at least, I had the measure of her.

'I just wanted you to know—'

I wasn't about to fall for that one. 'Distinguishing marks?'

'What?'

'The men on the video – any distinguishing marks?'

'The fat guy's got a tattoo on his backside.'

'Then I suggest you pull Carver's keks down.'

She looked at me doubtfully. 'What are you *not* telling me?'

Oh no. No more info, lady. I give up only what is in my interests for you to know. No way was I about to let this lot question Brando, to allow them to drag him even deeper into this murky pit, only to use and abandon us both when it suited. Swindley had told me that Carver had eyes and ears everywhere. That would, no doubt, include a cooperative cop or two in his manor. The minute Brando walked through those doors he'd be a target for retribution. That was certainly what Swindley had intimated. No, Brando had to be kept out of this at all costs.

'What I *am* telling you is that it's Carver in that video. Go after him hard and be sure you get him.' I glanced up to see Trevor Jones approaching with the kids. 'You make doubly sure, Wendy. Or you might just end up with two dead bodies on your hands. Me and that little lad over there . . .'

'Lunch!' Trevor announced and we all headed over to the Greedy Goblin Inn.

'Did you have a good time?' I asked Brando when we were headed back to Essex.

'Great!' he said. He hugged the fluffy sea lion Trevor Jones had bought for him in the souvenir shop. After they'd seen the sea lions being fed, Brando and Amy had been clamouring for the toy, so Trevor had coughed up for both.

'They were cops,' Brando suddenly announced.

'You think so?'

'I *know* so.'

'Go on then, how'd you know?'

'I saw Wendy at Dad's funeral.'

And the sneaky little sod hadn't let on until now.

'Anyway, I can smell them,' he added.

'What do they smell like?'

'Marmalade.'

Chapter Twenty
Monday, 23 – Saturday, 28 June

With Monica gone and Morrison off my back for the moment, Brando and I settled into what passed for a normal routine. Any talk of Monica was off-limits. I didn't have any wish to upset him and he never mentioned her, so it was almost as though she had never existed. I liked the routine. Army life will do that to you. We were up at seven thirty, breakfast at eight and I'd drop him at school for eight forty-five. Back to the house for me, a two-hour workout in the basement gym, then food shopping, a bit of housework and suddenly it would be three thirty and I'd be heading back to the school again to collect the lad. He'd do his homework and practise his guitar until dinner. I'd cook whatever he fancied. 'You are the best cook . . . EVER!' he said after every meal. Not that he had much to compare my efforts with but I did love hearing him say it. Later we'd sit and discuss his day. He was mad about history and, as that had been my favourite subject at school, I could chip in an opinion from time to time.

'Why didn't we do this before?' he asked me. 'I never had cool talks like this with Gloria.'

He showed me his Xbox game, *Star Wars* of course, *Jedi Knight II,* and teased me when it was all a bit beyond me. We watched movies together before he went to bed and I'd tuck him in with Navy, his precious seal. 'Get it?' he asked me when he'd named the thing. 'Navy Seal?'

'Very clever,' I said.

At Brando's insistence, I slept in one of the guest rooms, just two doors from his bedroom, and he helped me move all my stuff from my previous accommodation above the garage. Not that I had much. Army life will do that for you too.

Brando was more relaxed than I had ever seen him. There were no more frowns, no more locking himself away in his room for hours on end and no more snarky comments.

'I like this,' he said as we watched Gwyneth Paltrow lumbering about in a fat suit for *Shallow Hal*. 'Just you and me.' He smiled at me. 'This is good.'

Six days of heaven, before all hell unleashed itself once more.

Sunday, 29 June

The circus was in town. I took Brando to the afternoon performance. He'd never been to the circus before and was disappointed that they had no animals.

'What kind of circus is this?' he grumped.

'It's not considered ethical to use animals as entertainment.'

'But it's fine to eat them?'

'Not lions and tigers, we don't.'

'But we keep them in cages in zoos.'

Unprepared to get into a conversation about the rights and wrongs of animal training, I pointed to the garishly painted folk tumbling into the arena. 'Look, here come the clowns.'

'Pathetic,' he said. Though he softened a bit after that and did like the fire-eaters and trapeze artists.

I promised to take him to the zoo soon and in the tacked-on shop I bought him a fluffy lion as compensation for the lack of lion-tamers.

We were heading home with Brando, and his lion, in the back seat. 'Do lions eat seals?' he asked.

'Don't think you get many seals in the jungle,' I said. 'So I think Navy Seal will be safe from your one. Have you got a name for him?

'Roary,' he said.

I laughed.

I was driving along listening to Brando chattering on about wanting to purchase another guitar.

'Don't worry,' he assured me. 'I've got money.'

'Not from the secret safe, I hope.'

'No. Dad opened a bank account for me. Richard Bloom's got all the details. I can use that money.'

'Let's discuss it when we get home,' I said as we turned into the private road that led to the Cohen estate.

Open gates and a black Range Rover in the driveway did not bode well. The car was similar to the one I had seen driven by Felipe Garcia.

'Maybe your mum's back,' I suggested.

'Like I should care.' Brando was stone-faced.

I parked next to the black car and Felipe Garcia was in the driving seat, reading. He nodded to me as we got out of the Mercedes.

'Mrs Cohen inside?' I asked him.

'My fiancée,' he said in a strong accent. He went back to flicking through his Spanish magazine with a smug look on his face – like he had a cock the size of a marrow stuffed down his pants. But that was interesting. Monica obviously hadn't married the slimy prick yet.

Brando hugged the lion close and trudged mournfully behind me. I had the house keys in my pocket but decided to ring the doorbell instead. Moments later, Monica opened it. She wore a pink suit. It was her colour. Just a few weeks ago the sight of her would have melted me, but now I saw only a hard-faced, gaudy tart. She barely looked at me but squatted down, teetering on her four-inch Jimmy Choos. She opened her arms wide to Brando and gave him one of her most glorious smiles.

'Mummy's home!'

'Fuck off!' He stood still beside me, rejecting her offered embrace.

Her smile disappeared, flicked off by an invisible switch. She stood up, smoothed down her cerise skirt and turned on her heel. 'Well, if that's how you feel, then you can go to your room and pack your stuff. We're leaving this fucking mausoleum today.'

'I'm not going anywhere with you.' He glared at her, almost crushing Roary in his folded arms.

We crossed the threshold in unison and stepped into the wide hallway where there were a dozen or so Gucci suitcases piled against the wall.

Monica turned on Brando, her face dark with anger. 'Go and pack, you little prick or I'll kick your arse for you.'

He looked up at me anxiously.

'I'll sort this out,' I said to him. 'You go upstairs for now.'

'What's going on?'

'It's alright, Brando. I'll deal with this.'

He was half way up the stairs, still clutching Roary, when she went for him. I raced after her, fearful she might try to hurt him. She lunged for the toy. 'What's this piece of crap you've got here?'

Brando held the lion tightly with one hand and hit out at Monica with the other. His small fist connected with her nose and she toppled backwards. I caught her.

'Get your hands off me, you filthy dyke!' She scrambled away from me and reached for the banister to regain her balance.

Brando ran upstairs and Monica went for me like a hellcat.

'You're fired,' she screamed. 'Get out of my house. Get out of my sight.'

She lashed out. I slapped her open-handed across the face. She spat at me and both hands flashed out to claw at me. I pushed her away, my fingers clenched around her throat with one hand, cutting off her breath, and I slammed her up against the wall. My left fist hovered just inches from her face.

'Don't push me,' I warned her. 'How'd your fiancé fancy you with a broken nose?'

She stared at me like a wounded animal. 'You wouldn't do that to me, Sam.'

'Oh, wouldn't I just.' I had both hands around her throat now. It would be so easy to squeeze the life out of her. Watch the light die in her eyes. It might almost be a pleasure. I pushed the thought away. 'You want to keep breathing?' Oh, Monica, you don't know how close you just came. 'Then back the fuck off.' Her expression was a mixture of shock and loathing. I'd just crossed the line between love and hate and she knew it. I could see it in her face.

I released my hold on her. Her knees almost buckled beneath her – she was winded but calmer now. She bent double with her hands on her knees and her anger appeared to collapse in on itself.

'You'll regret that,' she gasped.

'There's a lot of things I regret, Monica, but that will never be one of them.'

I turned and walked towards the office. 'I have to call Mr Bloom. Let him know you're back.'

She ran after me. She was breathing hard but rapidly regaining control of herself. 'I'll do that in my own good time. You are terminated as of this moment.'

She stood in the doorway, hands on hips, a trickle of blood at her nose. 'Get away from there,' she ordered. 'You don't know what you are dealing with here, Samantha.'

I picked up the phone and tapped in Bloom's private number.

'I'll call Felipe in here and he'll kill you.'

'Tell him to get in line,' I said. 'There's already a long queue.'

Bloom answered immediately. I told him Monica was back and he asked to speak to her. She refused. He insisted. She plastered that smile on her face and snatched the phone from my hand.

'Richard,' she simpered, 'always a pleasure.' She waved me away dismissively with elaborately manicured fingernails.

I went up to Brando's room. I had expected to see the boy lying on his bed, maybe even crying, but he was sitting at his desk, listening to the conversation on his phone extension. He had a big grin on his face. He handed the phone over to me. I could hear Monica speaking – her voice had a sharp, almost panicked, edge to it.

'This is bullshit,' she was saying. 'I saw Benny's will and he left everything to me.'

'If you would care to come to my office tomorrow morning at, shall we say, ten sharp, we can go over the details. In the meantime, please take nothing from the house apart from your own personal belongings. You are free to stay there, of course, with Brando.'

'Brando is coming to live with me and my fiancé.'

'I'm sorry, but that's not possible. The boy must remain in his home.'

'Well, he can't stay here alone, can he? I've just fired Samantha Riley.' Monica sounded triumphant.

'You can't do that either, Monica,' Bloom said. 'Miss Riley is Brando's legal guardian until such time as a court decides otherwise.'

'The woman's a lesbian!' Monica countered. 'She's unfit to look after a child.'

'The law does not discriminate on grounds of sexuality. And if you felt Miss Riley was perfectly capable of looking after Brando while you went away on holiday . . .'

'You can't do this to me, Richard.'

'Perhaps if you had contacted me sooner, some of this unfortunate confusion could have been avoided. These are the terms of Mr Cohen's will, Monica. I am merely following them to the letter.'

'We'll see about that,' she retorted.

'I also have to inform you that I will be calling Miss Riley in half an hour's time. And if she is not satisfied with the way things are developing – if either she or Brando have been upset or harassed in any way – then it will be my duty to call the police and to have you removed from the premises. I'm sure that neither you, nor Mr Garcia, would wish for any police involvement, now, would you?'

Monica remained silent.

'So ten on Monday it is, then.'

Brando and I looked on as Monica and Garcia threw her suitcases into the Range Rover. Monica didn't attempt to come upstairs. She didn't once look up to Brando's bedroom window, although she must have known we were watching her leave. But she did lean out of the window of the Range Rover to give us the finger as the car roared out of the gates.

The phone rang and I picked it up. 'Everything all right, Miss Riley?' It was Bloom.

'They've just left,' I said.

'A locksmith will be with you within the hour to change every lock in the house, including those for the gated entrance.'

That was a relief. I couldn't have kept Monica out for long when she had keys to everything.

'An alarm system will also be fitted and a private detective will be watching the house until it is fully secured.'

'Private detective?' That came as a surprise. 'Is that really necessary?'

'Oh, yes, Miss Riley, I do believe it is.'

Chapter Twenty-One
7 p.m., Sunday, 29 June

Once Monica had departed, Brando turned on his TV to watch *Star Wars* again.

I sat on the floor next to him. 'Everything will be alright, you know.'

He glared at me. 'No it won't. Mum's back and everything will change.'

'Let's wait and see what Richard Bloom has to say on Monday.'

'It doesn't matter what he says. She'll marry Felipe and send me to boarding school. And what can you do about it? Nothing. You're just an employee.'

I really couldn't argue that one. Despite what had just happened, Monica remained Brando's mother and legally entitled to decide the boy's future. My position was merely temporary. I couldn't promise him anything.

He turned up the sound on the TV. 'Go away.'

I got up to leave but stood by his door for a moment, watching him mentally rebuilding his protective armour. We were alike, the kid and me. We both carried an invisible shield. There were times that the weight of it became too exhausting and we allowed someone to slide in beside us. But when life chucked yet another bucket of shit at us, we were back where we started, hunkered down behind our defences and alone once more. I closed the door behind me and went to make dinner.

———⌣———

I was in the kitchen knocking up spag bol when the buzzer sounded from the entrance gates. Brando, who had finally emerged from his room to watch *Family Guy* in the sitting room, was on his feet in seconds.

'Check who it is before you let them in,' I called to him.

'Sorry,' he said. 'I've already pressed the button.'

'Oh, well, it will probably be the locksmith.'

He ran to the window for a look but quickly shrank back again. 'It's that Chinesey-looking bloke who works for Gerard Fowley.'

Clive was on the doorstep, bristling with testosterone. 'Mr Fowley has invited you both to dinner.' He pushed past me and strode directly into the house.

'It's not convenient.' I wiped my hands on my apron emblazoned with the legend 'Watch Out, Man Cooking'. Benny Cohen had been a big barbeque fan.

Clive looked me up and down and treated me to one of his mocking glares. 'He insists.'

'Why didn't he ring first?'

'Mr Fowley's a bit wary of phones. It's like, you know, a phobia.'

'He could hire a secretary.'

Clive ignored the remark. 'Me and Winston out there, we've been sent to bring you.' He indicated to the car parked in the driveway where I could see the intimidating outline of Winston in the passenger seat. 'So I suggest you come with us.' Clive looked unwilling to take no for an answer, he was under orders. 'Now!' he hissed.

I closed the door behind Clive, just to keep Winston at bay for at least a short time.

'Sorry,' I said, 'but tell Mr Fowley we have to decline his kind invitation, as we have other plans for this evening.' Try and keep this cool. I didn't know what Fowley had in mind but was certain it wouldn't be epicurean in nature.

I made a big show of taking off my apron while I weighed up the odds. I saw no sign of a weapon on Clive and guessed the car outside would be clean too. Fowley had his legitimate reputation to protect. He certainly wouldn't want his guys driving around all tooled up. Cops on fishing expeditions often stopped flash motors driven by dodgy-looking types like Clive and Winston. So I reckoned it was safe to assume this was a muscle-only job.

Clive was tough but only five feet-six, max – I could take him down. Maybe even Winston at one hell of a push – but not both at once. Certainly not with Brando in the picture, not when there was a possibility of him getting injured.

'Jesus, Riley,' Joe would have scoffed. 'You're getting soft, girl.' Why did I keep conjuring his voice? I wanted to forget him, not to have to recall my part in his demise, but he kept inveigling his way into my head. Joe Murphy, who had passed on all of his burglary techniques to me, taught me how to fight, handle a knife and play the role of honey-trap. Joe, the man I had once worshipped and, if I was being honest, loved. Joe Murphy, the only man who had ever loved me back. The man I had witnessed being executed by Monica. There would always be a hole in my tarnished soul about Joe.

All this was running through my mind while Clive sucked his teeth noisily and twitched his shoulders like he was itching to get stuck in. The gate buzzed once more. Brando rushed to hit the button.

'Locksmith.' A deep voice came from the speaker.

'Having the locks changed?' Clive asked.

'No flies on you, eh, Clive?' Everything must go – including you, chum.

'Who you trying to keep out?' An evil sneer etched itself across his ugly mug.

'Neighbourhood's gone to shit,' I said. 'We had a home invasion just the other day. Came back and found a bunch of mongrels rifling through Mr Cohen's office.'

Clive furrowed his brow, like he wasn't sure if he'd just been insulted or not.

'How'd you lot get in here anyway? Those keys your boss chucked at me didn't fit any of our doors.'

'Security,' Clive regaled me with a wolfish grin. 'It's just one of Mr Fowley's many business interests. He bought up the firm that kitted out this place.'

So Benny Cohen's apparent paranoia had been justified after all. No need to break in, when you can simply unlock everything.

'There's been a bit of chatter.' Clive inclined his head in the direction of Brando who was sitting motionless on the stairs. 'We hear the bitch is back.'

'Watch it in front of the kid, will you? That's his mother you're talking about.'

'Where I come from it's the fathers who walk out on the kids, not the mothers.'

'That why you're such a vicious little fuck-up, is it, Clive? Lack of a male role-model?'

'You've got some mouth on you.' He squared up to me. Perhaps he'd just worked out that 'mongrels' was derogatory.

'Well, as my granny always said', I adopted a Noo Yoyk accent, 'if you ain't got da looks, you gotta have da wit.'

He gave a snort, brought the physical aggression down a peg and replaced it with the sexual variety. He leered and looked me up and down. 'You wouldn't be half bad if you dressed like a woman.'

'I'll leave that kind of thing to you.' I paused for effect. 'Or so I've heard.'

His demeanour hardened once more. So I added a wee bit of levity. 'Of course, cross-dressing *is* a legitimate form of self-expression. Been doing it myself for years.'

The sound of the doorbell broke the tension. Brando jumped up from his place on the stairs and opened the front door. A black guy twice the size of Clive stood there beaming. 'Locksmith,' he said in a pukka Caribbean accent. Clive glowered but the locksmith stepped into the hallway and eyed him suspiciously. I took this as a cue, grabbed Clive by the arm and hustled our unwanted visitor towards the open door.

'You tell Mr Fowley that if he gets his secretary to phone ahead next time, we'd be only too happy to accept his invitation to dinner.'

'He won't like this,' Clive snarled. But even he knew better than to get physical in front of an unknown civilian.

I gave the nasty little bastard an almighty shove that sent him hurtling across the step and slammed the door behind him.

The big locksmith looked quizzical. 'Trouble?'

'Not anymore,' I said. 'Can I interest you in a plate of spaghetti bolognese?'

My phone buzzed, I answered it. 'Macdonald here. I work for Mr Bloom. Just arrived outside and I see a car exiting your premises at speed. Everything all right, Miss Riley?'

'Yes,' I said. 'We're fine. Are you hungry?'

Five-ten, same height as me, Macdonald was about fifty and, on the face of it, the epitome of the dour Scot. Reddish hair, broad-shouldered and bulky in a muscular way, he had the face of a sad bloodhound. But after a while, I noticed the quiet smile that made his eyes crinkle.

'Just call me Mac,' he said. 'Or Mr X. Ex-soldier, ex-policeman, ex-husband.' The third being the most recent, I surmised by the tone in which he announced it. So we settled for calling him Mac.

We all sat at the breakfast bar in the kitchen: me, Brando, Dwayne the locksmith and Mac the private dick, eating spaghetti.

'Best I've ever had,' Mac said. Dwayne nodded in agreement.

'Better than pizza,' Brando said.

'Italian connections?' Mac asked.

'Half-Jewish,' Brando chimed in.

Mac looked around the table.

'Trinidad,' Dwayne said.

'Manchester Irish,' I said.

Mac's eyes twinkled and he pointed to himself. 'Half-Scots, half-Italian – we're a right little United Nations.'

Brando went up to bed, Dwayne got on with the lock-changing and I sat with Mac in the kitchen. He'd already scouted the entire house, checking windows, access, all of the usual security routines.

'So what's the plan?' I asked.

'I'm here for all of tonight, until the place is fully secure via Dwayne out there,' he said. 'How you use my services is up to you. Mr Bloom told me you'd been in the army and security business yourself. I can stay outside the gates if you want. Or in the grounds, or on the premises, if you prefer.'

'Inside the house, I think.' For once I was glad of some adult company.

We settled down opposite each other on the two white leather sofas in the sitting room. 'I was a tad gobsmacked by those gates when I came in,' he said. 'Bit OTT.'

'Mr Cohen's final love note to his wife.'

'Bit of a coincidence, this,' Mac said. 'I was with the Met when I encountered Benny Cohen. Must have been about ten or so years ago. I was on the investigation into his wife's suicide. Charlotte, her name was. She hanged herself in the same room as the baby was sleeping. Can you believe that?'

The photo we had found in the secret safe of Benny and the woman I had assumed to be his sister flashed across my mind. Was that the first Mrs Cohen? If so, then why hadn't Bloom told me? Why be so secretive?

'The doctors put it down to post-natal depression,' Mac said. 'But there was a lot of suspicion down at the station. Especially when we found out Cohen was banging some little blonde piece at the time. But I interviewed him myself and I don't think I've ever seen a man more devastated.' His eyes strayed to the ornate rugs with their specially woven B&M motifs. 'Seems he got over it, though. And the lad looks fine.'

'Brando is Cohen's child by his second wife.' I was trying to process what I was being told. 'His widow.'

'No,' Mac shook his head. 'Brando Cohen – that was the name of the baby. When we searched the house we found loads of pictures of Marlon Brando, films, autographs, the lot. He was Charlotte Cohen's favourite actor. It seems she named her son after him.' He glanced across the room to the framed school photograph of Brando that stood on the windowsill. 'Anyway, he looks like her. There were pictures of her all over the house – from when she was younger. She was about forty when she gave birth to Brando. Everyone we interviewed said she'd been so happy to finally get to be a mother. Then the depression struck. Not helped by the fact that her old man was sticking it to one of his strippers.'

It transpired that Benny Cohen had owned strip joints in Soho back then, which had been where he had met his 'little blonde piece' and set her up in her own flat. After Charlotte Cohen's suicide the police had interviewed the girlfriend.

'Pretty girl,' Mac said. 'She was about eighteen or so, as I recall, but not very bright. Never did get what she saw in Cohen, apart from the money that is.'

'What was her name?' I asked the question but already knew the answer.

'Marlene, I think. Or it might have been Monica.' He looked back to the rugs and realisation dawned on his face. 'Is that the one he married? Is that what all this crap is about?'

'Seems that way,' I replied. 'And Brando doesn't know Monica's not his mother. So let's keep that between us for now, shall we?'

I shivered; it felt as though I'd been doused by a bucket of iced water. Stunned by my own stupidity at being taken in by that woman, I tried to pull myself together and reason it out. Monica would never have been satisfied as Benny's bit on the side, even if he had set her up in a flat. That could be snatched away as easily as it had been given, if he eventually got bored with her, or had an attack of conscience and became reconciled with his depressed wife. No, what Monica would have wanted was to go from stripper to queen of the castle in three easy moves. She would have had to get rid of Mrs Cohen, as she had eventually got rid of Mr Cohen himself. I knew only too well how she achieved the second one, but how did she manage the first?

'You said there were suspicions about Charlotte Cohen's suicide?'

Mac sighed and nodded gravely. 'The medical examination revealed she was heavily sedated at the time of her death. So there were questions as to how she'd managed to throw the rope over the wooden beam in the nursery. But she had no defence wounds on her body, no bruises, and there was no indication that anyone else had been present in the house at the time of her death. So it was all supposition on our part, we had no proof. And when the coroner came in with a suicide verdict, it was all over and we moved on. But I've always wondered.' Mac looked me in the eye. 'You know, it nags at me.'

'Who found the body?'

'The housekeeper. Gloria something. Yes, that's right, Gloria Kelso, if my memory serves.'

That bloody Gloria again. Gloria the housekeeper that Monica had fired, Gloria the plant that worked for Carver. I looked at Mac and wondered just why Bloom had chosen him to protect us. Was it to impart this information, off the record, or was it just a coincidence? It seemed to me there were too many of them floating about. And for once I was in agreement with Big Jim Carver. I didn't believe in coincidences.

Chapter Twenty-Two
8 a.m., Monday, 30 June

With all the locks changed plus an alarm system installed, I watched Mac leave. I dropped a morose Brando at school then headed off for my appointment at Bloom's office.

His receptionist was dark-haired and attractive in that I-spend-all-my-spare-time-in-a-tanning-booth way. She was buffing her long, elaborately decorated fingernails as I entered the office and her glitz-glam persona made me wonder if she was one of Felipe Garcia's clients.

Even though the door to Bloom's office was closed tight I could still hear his refined, calm voice, though not what was he was saying.

The receptionist smiled apologetically. 'His ten o'clock is running late. Can I get you a coffee while you wait?'

I watched her walk across to the coffee maker and wondered what was so familiar about her. Maybe I'd seen her when I was working the doors? She seemed the live-it-large clubber sort. But no, it was something else and I couldn't quite put my finger on it.

I looked at my watch. My appointment had been for eleven thirty and I had been bang on time but it was now eleven fifty-five. I flicked through a glossy fashion magazine and contemplated getting some highlights. Maybe letting my hair grow. That photo booth picture of my eighteen-year-old self with Joe had made me wonder if I could look more like that again – less butch, less the archetypal dyke. I stared at the images of perfect feminine beauty in the ads and felt an unfamiliar yearning.

'*You'll* be hearing from *my* lawyers!' Monica's screech came from behind Bloom's office door. Moments later it was thrown open and she marched out on the arm of Felipe. She was red-faced, furious and strode right past me, then she stopped and did a double take. 'You fucking evil bitch!' She flew at me but Garcia held her back. I leapt up, ready to defend myself. No backing off this time. Felipe must have clocked the look on my face because he lifted her off her feet and virtually carried her out of the room while she yelled, 'You'll pay for this!'

'Mrs Cohen was somewhat upset.' Bloom said dryly when I took a seat in front of his desk.

'Bad news?'

He smiled. 'For Mrs Cohen, most certainly, but the best thing all round in the interests of young Brando.' He buzzed out to the receptionist. 'More coffee in here please, Janine.'

That was when I remembered who she looked like.

'Your receptionist seems familiar to me.' I hoped I didn't sound like I fancied her or something.

'Janine was recommended to me by Mrs Cohen,' he said. 'She's the daughter of the Cohens' housekeeper, Mrs Kelso.'

'Oh, that's it,' I said. 'I can see the resemblance now.'

Gloria again. This set-up had Big Jim Carver's sweaty paw prints all over it. So that's how Swindley had known where to find me, how he'd been able to trap me in the car park. Young Janine had tipped him off.

'When I came to see you on Saturday, would Janine have known about my visit here?'

Bloom frowned. 'Yes, she would have booked the hours in.'

'On the day?'

'Why are you asking me this?'

I told him about being waylaid by Swindley in the car park and his comments about Carver having eyes and ears everywhere. Also that Gloria Kelso was now in Carver's employ and possibly had been for some time. And I immediately detected a sense of unease in Bloom's composure.

'I know you can't divulge who your clients are,' I said. 'But can you tell me those who are *not*?'

'James Carver is not a client,' Bloom replied emphatically. 'Most definitely not.'

'Then I think you may have a cuckoo in your nest.'

'I'll deal with that.' He didn't so much as glance in her direction when Janine brought in the coffee. But I knew from his expression that Janine Kelso was toast.

Monica's incandescent rage was explained by the fact that all she had been left in Benny's will was a fifty-one per cent share in Garcia's hairdressing emporium, a villa in Spain and twenty grand a month.

'However,' Bloom's eyes showed a sly satisfaction in what he was about to tell me. 'The monthly allowance is only payable until she remarries.'

It seemed that Benny had been aware of several of Monica's 'dalliances' as Bloom termed them, and had turned a blind eye. 'Old men and young women,' Bloom said. 'It always seems like such a good idea at the time.'

Had Benny known about Monica and me? Not that a smooth operator like Bloom would ever tell me anyway, unless it was to his advantage.

When Benny found out about Monica's affair with Felipe Garcia, he became concerned for Brando. He immediately contacted Bloom, changed his will and set in motion the sale of the nightclubs to Carver and Fowley. The news of Benny's imminent death from terminal cancer had been a closely guarded secret known only to Bloom, Monica, Carver and Fowley, it seemed.

'He intended his son to inherit only, shall we say, the more stable investments.'

Yeah, I get it. You mean legit, untainted. 'But who was to take care of Brando if Mr Cohen no longer trusted his wife?'

'I take it you had a conversation with Macdonald?'

'Yes, he said that Brando's mother committed suicide. But why didn't you tell me yourself when I showed you the photograph?'

'Client confidentiality, Miss Riley. It was Mr Cohen's express wish that Brando was not informed about his mother and the circumstances of her death until he was at an age when he was able to fully comprehend it all.'

'So, why the need to put me in the picture via Macdonald?'

'It will be your decision when the child should be informed.' Bloom looked me straight in the eyes. 'Because, Miss Riley, it was Mr Cohen who suggested that you should become Brando's legal guardian.'

I felt as though I'd been slugged. And I was still reeling while the solicitor went through the terms of Brando's inheritance. Bloom's practice would oversee all the investments until Brando Cohen reached the age of twenty-one. I would be his legal guardian until he was eighteen. The house was to be sold and I could choose a new property for us to live in – property that would revert to me when my guardianship of Brando came to an end. All expenses and holidays to be paid and my salary would be substantially increased to reflect my new status. It all made for a tasty financial package. I quelled any fear of reprisals and nodded my head in agreement.

'And the nightclubs?' I asked, when I got over the shock of the proposal and my own compliance.

'I believe that James Carver is currently in police custody,' Bloom replied. 'So we have to put that discussion on hold for a short while until we see how the situation unfolds.'

'What about those papers Monica signed for Carver?' I asked.

Bloom waved his hand dismissively. 'It was a Letter of Intent to Sell to one of Carver's offshore companies. I've seen it. Even if Mrs Cohen had been entitled to sign it – which she wasn't – the document was not legally binding in any way. Of course, Mrs Cohen was not aware that her husband's signature was a mere formality,' Bloom said. 'Everything else had already been set in motion. When he became ill, Mr Cohen put me in full control of his business affairs until Brando comes of age. The fact that Mr Cohen was murdered merely makes matters a little more complicated.'

Murdered. The impact of the word swept across me like a chill wind. It served as a sudden and stark reminder that Monica had so much on me. I didn't know what but I knew she'd do something. She wasn't going to settle for the shit end of the lollipop. Not Monica.

I was walking towards my car when my phone rang and DI Wendy Morrison's husky tones greeted me. She did not sound happy. 'Word to the wise,' she said. 'A certain gentleman will be hitting the streets tomorrow.'

'What?' Oh, fuck! Carver was being cut loose. 'Why so soon?'

'We need to find the boy in the video. The gentleman's lawyer claims the lad was a rather young-looking twenty-one and it was 'consensual play'. Swore black was white that it had been made for personal use only and not for distribution. Going after gays is a real no-no these days. We need a complainant.'

'So where does that leave me?'

'Maybe you should consider taking a holiday.'

Chapter Twenty-Three
1 p.m., Monday, 30 June

A dark blue van with blacked-out windows straddled the entrance to the Cohen estate. No other way into the property. One way in and out, easy to keep an eye on, just how Benny Cohen had liked it. Trouble was, I couldn't get past. It was a trap and I knew it. No point calling the cops. Take a holiday is what Morrison had said, so no protection expected from that quarter. Whatever this was I had to face it down alone. The van's door slid open as I pulled up beside it and Winston got out. Clive came round from the back. He had a gun. I sussed it was a Glock 17, the weapon of choice for drug dealers of every stripe.

'Bit early for a dinner invitation,' I said.

'Get in.' Clive indicated with the gun towards the open back door of the van. 'Don't do nothing stupid. Cos I'm itching to waste you.'

I turned towards him. Winston moved in from behind me and restrained my arms. Before I could react, Clive's fist came out of nowhere and my legs buckled beneath me. I felt another punch to my stomach, followed by a boot in the ribs. As I fell, I heard Clive laugh and felt a metallic blow to the head. The world went black.

I came to in a wooden chair in what appeared to be a small, scruffy warehouse. The place smelled of oily rags and diesel. My head felt like it had been stamped on and it hurt to breathe – cracked ribs for sure. Gerard Fowley was sitting behind a battered old desk with Clive standing on his right-hand side and Winston on his left.

'Tut tut. It is futile to resist,' Fowley said. All James Bond world-domination-plan bad guy. Very funny, should have been a fucking comedian.

Clive smirked but Winston remained deadpan.

I tried to sit up but my arms were gaffer-taped to the arms of the chair. A searing pain shot through my side. I felt sick. I could taste blood.

'Bit over the top, this, don't you think, Gerard?' I managed to say.

'I've tried to be nice to you, Sam.' He shook his head like the disappointed parent of an errant child. 'But you persist in distressing me.'

'What do you want?' Like I didn't know.

'Monica.'

'Nah,' I said. 'She's used goods, Gerard. Not your type at all. I thought you liked them much younger.'

'Why do you insist on pissing me off?' The avuncular tone turned to a tight-lipped hiss.

Clive flew out from around the desk and hit me across the face, open-handed.

'Where is she?' Fowley said.

'With her fiancé, I presume.' A trickle of blood dripped from my nose and I sniffed it back up.

'Felipe, the cunting hairdresser?' Clive snorted.

'That's the one.' My ears were ringing and my brain felt as though it was rattling around the inside of my skull.

'We had a deal before that fucking Spaniard double-crossed me,' Fowley said.

I tried to gather my thoughts. 'It seems Monica intended to sell the clubs elsewhere all along,' I said. 'And those papers she signed for Carver were worthless.'

'I had great plans for Legend.' Fowley sat back in his seat, arms folded across his chest, staring at the mucky ceiling as though visualising his dream. 'I wanted to do it up. It was a destination spot in its heyday, you know. Until Benny lost interest in the place, that is. Shame that. But nothing that couldn't be sorted with a wedge of dosh put into it. I wanted to take it upmarket again. VIP rooms, attract the celebs back. Make it a nice, discreet place where footballers and media guys can take their doxies, away from the lenses of the paps, out of sight of the prying tabloids. You know, a bit of class.'

'Sounds delightful.' A knocking shop, more like.

'Yeah,' he said without a hint of irony. 'You help me out and who knows what could occur. You could start your own agency, Sam. Get some fit-looking girlies on board to run the doors. We could get a little partnership going. Might be a good thing for both of us.'

I nodded, as though I was considering his proposal. With allies like Gerard Fowley, who needed enemies? On the other hand, a wee bit of back-up from the likes of man-mountain Winston wouldn't go amiss. Not with Carver back on the prowl on Tuesday and about to set Swindley on my case.

Fowley was in a schmoozy mood all of a sudden. 'So, you tell me where I can find Monica, we do the deal and put all this unfortunate nastiness behind us. What do you say?'

'Well, for starters . . .' I smiled though my jaw was resistant and it probably came out as a grimace. 'Monica can't sign anything because she inherited fuck-all.'

Fowley's face dropped like he'd just had a shot of novocaine. 'You're shitting me!'

'Look, Gerard. We've all been screwed over by Monica in one way or another. I'm not protecting her. She was in the solicitor's office this morning and Garcia had to drag her out of there, literally kicking and screaming. She'd intended to hand the clubs over to him.'

Fowley leaned forward on the desk, hands together as though in prayer, a high priest of sociopathy. 'Garcia came to me with a business proposition a couple of years ago but I had other commitments. So I introduced him to Monica because I knew she had Benny's ear. I tell you, Sam, an honourable man like myself finds it increasingly hard to fathom the depths of deception some people are willing to plumb.'

I almost laughed. For him to try to disguise the fact that Garcia was part of a Spanish drug cartel was laying it on far too thick. Did he really think I was that green? But if that was the little game he was playing, I'd go along with it, give him some info he already knew and see where it got me. 'My sources tell me that the Garcia family are medium-sized players in Spain, running blow to and from the Canaries.' I didn't say that my source was an eleven-year-old who got his info from covert surveillance on phone extensions and listening at keyholes. 'Wouldn't surprise me if Garcia had Benny knocked off to prevent the original deal with you and Jim Carver from going through.'

Clive snorted. 'You can't trust no spicks.'

'I think you'll find the word is "dago", Clive. Spicks are Italians.' I watched a slow-motion drop of nose-blood plop onto my T-shirt.

Fowley laughed.

Clive leaned over me, nose-to-nose, and bellowed in my face, showering me in spittle. 'I fucking hate you, I should take you for a little drive and blow your fucking smart-arse brains out.' He stood back and mimed shooting me. 'Two bangs and you'd never get home for Christmas.'

'Tell your ultra-sensitive little henchman to be gentle with me, Gerard,' I said. 'Because I might just hold the keys to your magic kingdom.'

I looked into the mirror above the sink in the grimy toilet. A bruise was emerging on the side of my face and my left eye was gradually closing up. My first thought was, what the hell am I going to tell Brando? I looked at my watch. The glass was cracked. I had half an hour to get from wherever this warehouse was to the school to collect the lad.

I dried my face on the filthy hand towel and went back into the main building. A grinning Fowley handed me a large Scotch. 'Misunderstandings,' he said, all pally. 'They happen all the time in business.' He held out his hand. 'No hard feelings.'

I shook it. 'No,' I replied. But I sure as hell didn't mean it.

I told him that the original deal had already been set up and that Benny Cohen's signature had been a formality. So there was no reason it shouldn't all go through as originally planned, fifty-fifty, after Carver got disentangled from the law. I looked across at Fowley. He wouldn't go for that, not now. I was sure of that.

'No fucking way,' he said. 'Not after Carver tried to do me over by flying solo with Monica.'

That was when it hit home. What if it had been Monica and Carver behind Benny's sudden demise – not Garcia? Why would Garcia need a northerner like Joe Murphy when he could fly his own *compadres* in from Spain to do the job? In and out of the country in a jiffy and no need for any messy double shooting.

It had to be Carver. He'd planned to cheat Fowley out of the clubs all along. So he'd got Monica to arrange the hit on Benny. To be done specifically by someone who couldn't be remotely connected with him.

I tried my theory out on Fowley, just to see if he bought it. 'Unless Benny's death was Carver's plan all the time,' I suggested. 'But, after Benny had been seen to, Monica double-crossed Big Jim.'

Fowley's face brightened. 'I wouldn't put anything past that dirty old bastard.' I could almost hear the cogs working. 'Or that slapper.'

'Of course,' I said, like it had just occurred to me, 'should Carver get banged up on this kiddie porn charge, then the nightclubs would be up for grabs by you, wouldn't they? What with Big Jim the paedophile not being a fit and proper person to be associated with licensed establishments.'

Fowley slapped me on the back, a big smile almost splitting his face. 'You know, Clive. I've always liked this girl. Haven't I always said that?'

Clive fumed.

Chapter Twenty-Four
4 p.m., Monday, 30 June

Brando said not a word about my wearing shades on a gloomy afternoon, the bruise on my face or even the blood splatter on my clothes. Nor anything about my driving the silver Rover I'd borrowed from Fowley's car lot. He did raise his eyebrows at the sight of my own vehicle parked outside of the gates of the house, but, without comment, he hopped out of the car as the wrought-iron B&M parted company. He walked along the drive towards the house lugging his heavy school bag. What is it with schoolchildren these days, carrying half a ton of stuff on their backs like little Sherpas? He'd slung his hefty backpack over his shoulder, weighed down on one side, almost limping but struggling manfully on. It was his way of showing me he didn't need me. I left the Rover in the street to be collected later by one of Fowley's crew, drove my Civic through the gates and was at the front door before Brando. I pulled the brown envelope given to me by Bloom out of the glove compartment and waited for the kid as he trudged towards me.

'Are you going to tell me what happened?' he asked morosely as I opened the door. 'Or leave me in the dark like every other grownup does?'

Settled in the kitchen with a biscuit and a glass of milk he was still scowling.

I told him I'd been in a scuffle with Fowley's mob and come out the worse for wear. However, it was all sorted now and there was no reason for him to be concerned. 'But you should see the other guy,' I joked.

He didn't even smile in response. 'Did they want to know where Mum is?' he said this in a very matter-of-fact manner.

'Initially, yes, but that's not important anymore, business-wise,' I said. 'Your dad left everything to you. Now it's for the lawyers to sort out.'

He took the news in quietly, nodding his head. No sign of any of the avarice I had previously noticed in his nature. Perhaps I'd been mistaken about him, misjudged the lad just as I had misread Monica. Too dazzled by her beauty to get past her attitude to him, seeing him through her eyes and not into his neglected little soul.

'So I don't have to go to boarding school if I don't want to?'

I looked at him with his dark hair beginning to curl as the thuggish crop grew out and wondered just how kids' minds work. Perhaps, when the world is such a frightening, complex and confusing place, the only way to survive is to concentrate solely on your own needs. Like a newborn wailing in the night with the pain of hunger in its belly and no experience to tell it that someone will come along to feed it. Naturally, it screams blue murder to get attention, in order to stay alive – the human animal at its most basic.

'You can go to any school you like,' I said. 'We can choose one together.'

'Are you going to stay with me?'

'I'm your legal guardian now,' I replied. 'Until you're eighteen.'

'And then you'll leave me?'

'No, Brando, I'll never leave you.'

'Promise?' He didn't even glance up at me.

'Promise.' I reached across the table to shake his hand. 'Not until the day you tell me to bugger off.'

He gave me a big grin and finished his milk in one glug, leaving a white moustache on his upper lip. I handed him a napkin.

'Was I adopted?' The question came out of nowhere.

'No.' What's coming next? 'Why do you ask?'

'There's a boy at school who's adopted.'

'And his parents told him. They were honest with him and that's good.'

'Couldn't not be,' he said. 'He's African or something and they're white.'

'Yes,' I said, 'people often adopt children from other countries to give them a better life.'

'What about me, though? I was wondering about me. I don't look like *her* and I don't look like my dad. So am I adopted too?'

This was it. The moment I had to tell him and it had come far sooner than I had hoped. Why me? But then maybe it was better coming from me than being told formally by some solicitor or having it screamed at him by that harpy Monica.

'Your dad was your real dad,' I started out. 'But your real mother died just after you were born.' I tried to read his facial expression but it was impassive. As though he'd expected me to say just that. Brando rarely asked questions he didn't know the answers to, or at least had already sensed. People talk, make snide comments, a dropped hint here, a half-heard conversation there; all would have been grist to the mill of an insular and mistrustful kid like Brando. It was also possible that finding the photograph in the secret safe had been a final clue. Something that slotted into suspicions he'd been mulling over for a while. As a wise man once said, 'How can you give love when you don't know what it is you're giving?' Love and empathy are learned responses and I hoped it wasn't too late for Brando.

'Everybody who knew her says you look just like her.'

'What did she die of?' He didn't appear upset, just curious.

'It was an accident,' I said. An image of a body swinging by the neck from beams close to a baby's crib flashed across my mind. Would Charlotte Cohen have killed herself in the same room as her child was sleeping? Depression and self-hatred – I'd seen its destructive power in my brother's rapid degeneration into alcoholism. But for Charlotte to end it all in the presence of her much-longed-for child seemed more malicious than desperate. A vengeful act intended to inflict maximum pain on those left behind.

'What kind of accident?'

'I'm not sure of the details,' I replied tentatively. 'It was an old house you all lived in, so maybe she fell down the stairs or something. Give me a little bit of time and I'll find out everything about her for you.' Was I being a coward or playing the sensitive adult here? I told myself it was the latter – one step at a time, for both of us.

I handed him the brown envelope Bloom had given me. Brando opened it and stared at the photograph of Benny and the woman with the dazzling smile and dark curly hair that we had discovered in the secret safe. Curly hair, just like his would be once it had grown out. The smile that lit up his face like a beacon in the dark every time he laughed. Maybe that was why Benny had been so distant with his son. Because Brando reminded him of his dead wife and all the pain her suicide had inflicted. Or perhaps Brando's all-too-real existence tormented Benny with his own guilt for playing around with another woman just when Charlotte had needed him the most. And Monica's insistence on Brando's hair being cropped so short was because Charlotte lived once more in Brando. Curls and a smile, that's not much to pass on to your baby. But perhaps it was something for him to cling on to.

'That person was your mother,' I said. 'Her name was Charlotte.' I watched his face for any sign of distress but saw nothing. So I ploughed on. 'I think your dad must have kept the photo to show you when you were older.'

Silently, he took it from me and slowly climbed the stairs to his bedroom.

Not sure what to do next – whether to allow the lad space or go after him to see if he was alright – I wandered from room to room, checking windows and doors. I was doing a security patrol more out of habit and the comfort of routine than of necessity.

The answering machine was flashing red when I entered Benny's study. I closed the door behind me and hit the button. Mutterings, music in the background maybe, whispers I couldn't make out and then *click*, nothing. The phone rang straight away and startled me. When I answered it, it took me a moment to recognise the voice I would have known instantly only days ago. But the sweet honey drip was gone, replaced by a venomous snarl. Monica.

'You're fucked, you ugly dyke.' She sounded drunk or high, or both. An excess of alcohol often caused her to become violent and abusive but drugs always made her hyper and paranoid. 'You'll rue the day you ever crossed me, you vile cunt.'

'Monica—'

'You always repulsed me. Do you know that?'

Did I know it? Was I so obsessed with her beautiful body writhing beneath me that I failed to recognise something like that? No chance. This was something else, a revenge of some kind, I could hear it in her tone, feel it crackling down the phone lines.

'Every time you touched me I shuddered,' her voice lowered, feeding poison into my ear. 'I couldn't stand the smell of your snatch or the sight of your wobbly arse.' Behind her vitriol, I could hear someone urging her on, a man's voice. 'I've got myself a real man now,' she slurred. 'A man with a great big cock.' She emphasised the last three words and there was the sound of a muffled snigger in the background. 'He doesn't need no stinking lesbo dildo. He's going to fuck me right now, stick his big dick right up me and make me come.'

'Oh, *querida*,' the voice said in the background. This was some twisted sex game she was playing with her new paramour and she wanted to make sure that I knew about it.

'Does that turn you on, Sam, imagining him bending me over the table and ramming his stiff dick right up me?'

'Monica,' I said as she paused for breath, 'there's no need for this shit.'

'Oh, yes there is.' Her voice hardened, rising in pitch, almost to the point of hysteria. 'Cos I'm gonna make sure you suffer for what you've done.' I heard her take a deep breath. 'And that bastard kid is going to get his comeuppance as well. Oh, isn't he just. You'll see. You think you can protect him? Well, you can't. Not from what I've got planned.' She paused for a split second. 'So you watch your back, Samantha, because we're coming for you and that little fucker. Guaranteed!' The line went dead.

I steeled my soul. Not on my watch, lady. I let you off the hook once but never again. Wherever you are and no matter who you're with, I will kill you.

Chapter Twenty-Five
Tuesday, 1 July

I found myself genuinely surprised by just how quickly Brando had inveigled his way into my affections. The snarly Reservoir Pup with his eye on the prize had mellowed, or had I been so caught up with Monica that I hadn't noticed this other side to him? Either way, I had come to care for Brando and was determined to protect him. He appeared to have taken in his stride the news that Monica was not his mother and had quickly got back into our established routine. The fact that I was now his official guardian had lightened his mood and his apparent trust in me was quite moving when I thought about it.

Even so, there were times when he remained incredibly annoying. He'd been pushing me in the direction of men lately, pointing out macho types in the DVDs we watched together after dinner. Apart from his *Star Wars* obsession, he was dismissive of kids' fare and hated Harry Potter and everything he stood for, as he put it. He solemnly declared animation to be a total waste of time, though cartoons like *The Simpsons* or *Family Guy* were acceptable. But he thought that adventure films were childish. So we were stuck with 12-certificate romantic comedies. And Brando fell in love with love, craving some dewy-eyed happy ending, all white dresses, confetti and Just Married signs.

'Why can't you do that?' That was his game plan, a happy-ever-after for Sam. Hence his fingerprints all over my back.

After we had eaten this evening it had been the turn of George Clooney.

'All the women like him, don't they?' he said in the innocent voice he used when his intentions were far from it. 'Do you think he's handsome?'

'Of course he is,' I said. 'What has that got to do with anything?'

'I was thinking that maybe you'd be happier if you had a husband.'

'Reckon I've got a chance with Gorgeous George, do you?' I laughed as I watched the man himself romancing Michelle Pfeiffer. 'This is not real life.'

'I know that,' he agreed. 'But you saw how happy my dad looked in the photo of him and my real mum.' He had placed the picture of his parents on his bedside table. 'I bet he loved her like in the movies.'

'I'm sure he did.' While bonking Monica in their little love nest – men, you can keep 'em. 'Anyway, can you imagine me all done up in a white veil?'

He looked doubtful for a moment, then brightened. 'Chinese Clive said you'd look good in a dress.'

Clive with his weasel features and sexist snarl, standing in this house, appraising me like a piece of meat – hardly the finest example of discerning masculinity to chuck at me. 'He was being sarcastic and you know it.'

'Anyway, *I* think you would.'

'What do you know, you're eleven years old?'

'I'm twelve in six months.'

'We've got to find a new school for you.' I tried to change the subject but Brando was nothing if not persistent.

'If you let your hair grow and wore a bit of make-up, I think you'd be *beautiful*.'

I gave him a hard look and he grinned. 'I was only saying . . .'

'Well, don't.'

'I bet you had boyfriends when you were young.'

'Oi! I'm not old yet.' Boyfriends. Only Joe Murphy and much good caring for me did him. I'd had a couple of one-night shagathons with soldiers in the army and a brief affair with Jill. I wondered whatever happened to her? Then Monica. The biggest mistake of my life, but then, love makes fools of us all. Brando was staring at me and I made an effort to sound more worldly wise than I actually was by saying, 'Anyway, it doesn't work like that. You can't help who you fall in love with. It's not really a choice you make.'

'I don't see why not.'

'You'll understand when you're older.' Dismissed by the cheesy old line that adults use on the young, he went into a sulk for a minute until the camera focused back on Ms Pfeiffer. Brando sat back with a faraway smile slowly spreading across his face. I looked across at him. He was moonstruck – a typical hetero male if ever there was one.

---

4 a.m., Wednesday, 2 July

'Sam, Sam!' Brando's voice came at me through a haze of sleep and I finally sat up fully awake. I saw his concerned little face at the end of my bed in the guestroom. He was dressed in his pyjamas and clutching Navy Seal and Roary close to his chest. 'You've been dreaming again, haven't you?' he said. 'You were moaning and crying out. You woke me up. I was scared.'

I dabbed my eyes on the corner of the top sheet, unsure if it was sweat or tears streaming down my face. The nightmare made its stealthy retreat and the all too vivid images of Monica hunting Brando down melted away without a trace. 'Always pay attention to your dreams,' my hopeless drunk of a mother used to tell me. 'They are whispers, warning you about things you already know but have yet to understand.' The only piece of advice I can remember her ever giving me.

I'd witnessed her death. I was sixteen years old, walking home from school in the rain when she staggered out of a pub. She had spotted me across the street, shouted my name and walked straight out into the road. I'd always heard that traumatic events happen in slow motion. But that's a lie. They happen in an instant and you are helpless to stop them. One moment my mother was headed towards me and I was cringing with embarrassment at her intoxicated state, hoping none of my schoolmates were around to see her. The sound of screeching tyres, the black taxi, the dull thud as it hit her and her body was tossed into the air. It was over in seconds. No time to say goodbye as my mother tumbled to final oblivion on that wet Manchester street.

'Are you all right?' Brando asked, and I could swear I saw his bottom lip quiver.

'Just a dream.'

'Can I get into bed with you?'

Appropriate. That repulsive PC word sprang into my mind. I'm his guardian but we're not related, so would it be 'appropriate' for an eleven-year-old boy to climb into the bed of a thirty-four-year-old woman? I loathe these people, the ones who have implanted these admonitory words in our brains. What kind of screwed-up Orwellian nightmare are we living in when a simple act of human kindness comes with cautionary, defensive and even reproachful strings attached? I looked blearily at my bedside clock and saw it was four twenty a.m. 'Hop in!' I shifted the sheet to one side. 'But just this one time.'

Chapter Twenty-Six
9 a.m., Wednesday, 2 July

Mac Macdonald was loading the remnants of his married life into a cardboard box. So far it contained a few photographs he never wanted to set eyes on again and the last of his ex-wife's extensive collection of Lladró ornaments. The house was on the market and he'd been clearing out the attic when he found them. He loathed those sentimental ornaments: cherubs, dancers and crap like that. He blew the dust off them, encased them in bubble wrap and placed them in the box. Her new husband would be picking this lot up in an hour. Good riddance, he was welcome to them and to her. Only nine months since the divorce, yet Mac found it hard to recall a time when his marriage to Nicola had been content.

He'd met her on a boozy night out in Colchester. She'd been a hairdresser back then. She was just eighteen, a glamorous wisp of a thing with a flirty smile and a dirty laugh. He'd been blootered, but by the time he'd sobered up he was enchanted by her. She had him hooked and she probably imagined that being a soldier's wife was an easy option. She soon found out otherwise. Army life swiftly transformed her from loving bride to dissatisfied whinger. 'I feel like a bloody parcel,' she'd say whenever they relocated to the married quarters on yet another base.

Nicola nagged him incessantly until he left the army and joined the Met. He'd hoped that once they'd settled down in one place, she'd change her mind about not having kids. Mac wanted to be a dad. Though, looking back, he realised that it was already too late for that. The rot was already eating away at their shaky foundations.

He closed the box, strapped it up with Sellotape and turned the radio on just for company. The second song up was David Bowie's 'A Better Future'. Irony filled the room.

Nicola had insisted he bought a bigger house than they could afford, that he paid for her tennis and golf lessons along with a brand new car. She filled her days with yoga and playing bridge with her snooty friends. She always seemed to be out bloody shopping yet she never cooked, not unless you included microwaved rubbish. He'd eaten better grub in the police canteen.

'Where's your ambition?' she'd screech at him. 'You're getting nowhere in the police force. Go private. There's tons of money to be made in close-protection work.'

Up to his eyes in her accumulated debts, but morally incapable of allowing himself to become involved in the corruption he saw all around him, he left the force and started up on his own.

By that time, their sex life was virtually non-existent. He'd strayed once or twice, he had to admit it, but the news that Nicola's golf coach was teaching her a lot more than how to improve her swing came as a blessed relief. The marriage was over now, done and dusted. Mac was single again, getting tubby around the middle and pushing fifty. Not much time left to start afresh – if anyone would have him.

The phone rang. Mac checked the caller ID. Richard Bloom. He was a reasonable bloke even though some of his clients were decidedly dodgy. The late and unlamented Mr Benjamin Cohen, for example. Mac thought about the huge house where he had spent the night protecting Alice Samantha Riley and Brando Cohen. The ostentatious B&M gates, the specially woven rugs, the expensive reproduction furniture. Whoever said crime doesn't pay had never been a copper.

'What can I do for you, Richard?'

He listened to his instructions. He was being ordered back to look after Samantha Riley and Brando Cohen. He'd seen the boy's type before, many times. Emotionally neglected rich kids with upper-middle class accents, protected by a silver spoon while trying to sound like a streetwise smart-arse. That had been his first impression of Brando. But that evening chez Cohen, when they were all eating the tasty spaghetti the woman had dished up, Mac had noticed the boy watching Samantha Riley with a look of guarded adoration in his eyes.

Mac had liked her too. He'd known what she looked like before he got there. He'd seen her army ID photo when Bloom had briefed him to check into her background a year or so back, for and on behalf of Benny Cohen. Even in the flesh, she was no great beauty but the photo he'd seen hadn't captured the intelligence in her light brown eyes or the sensuousness of her mouth. Her voice was mid-range and she'd either made an effort to rid herself of any traces of a Manchester accent or her years in the army had softened it. She was tall and fit-looking and he recalled watching her move with a swift grace around the kitchen, imagining that under her sensible unisex clothing was a hard yet curvy body.

Despite her somewhat mannish appearance and her air of self-contained dependability, he'd sensed something much more feminine about her. He spotted it first when he told her about the suspicious suicide of Brando's mother, just as Bloom had instructed him to do. She had been visibly shaken but quickly covered it up, like a true professional. That was army training for you. If the boy was being looked after by Samantha Riley, then he'd probably turn out all right in the end.

The thought crossed Mac's mind that, had he gone for someone like her in the first place, instead of wasting so many years of his life with the avaricious Nicola, he might have been a happier man today. It was all too late now, though.

He wrote down the details Bloom had given him. Mac had been handed far worse assignments than this. A few weeks in the countryside with those two might be just what he needed. And the woman could certainly cook. At least he'd get a decent meal out of this job.

Chapter Twenty-Seven
11 a.m., Wednesday, 2 July

Macdonald was standing on the doorstep. 'You rang?' He attempted a dodgy Lurch impression. An excited Brando had buzzed him through the main gates.

'Your detective's here,' Brando announced when he heard the deep Scots burr through the entry-phone speaker.

'He's not *my* detective.'

'Well, *he* likes *you*.' He scooted to open the front door.

'Don't suppose you've got any more of that spaghetti on the go?' Mac grinned as he stepped inside.

'Chilli con carne, tonight,' I said. 'Already made, it just needs heating up when we get there.'

'My favourite.' Mac ruffled Brando's hair. 'I do like a woman who can cook.'

Brando laughed and looked pointedly at me. 'See?'

'Cut it out and go and finish packing.'

Mac dumped a small suitcase on the floor.

'You didn't bring much,' I commented.

'I travel light and I'm not expecting to be invited to any hunt balls and the like. T-shirts, jeans, walking boots, socks and undies, everything the man-about-town needs for a spell in the country, or so they tell me.'

My early-morning phone call to Bloom had resulted in his offering us his three-bedroom weekend cottage for as long as we needed it, plus Mac as live-in security. I'd told him about Monica's threats, though not the more explicit sexual content of the phone call, and that had him swiftly making arrangements and getting back to me within half an hour.

'Monica has always been, shall we say, excitable. But just to be safe.' He used his best reassuring manner. 'Think of this as a little holiday. We could take out a restraining order but I doubt she would carry out any of these threats personally, if at all. But it might be better to stay away from the house until young Brando's legal matters have been completed. Dotted and crossed, as it were.'

Mac dangled the keys to the cottage in his hand and Brando was raring to go. He dragged his suitcase down the stairs and had his guitar slung over his shoulder.

'Do you play that?' Mac took the suitcase off the boy.

Brando nodded.

'Great!' Mac said. 'I've got mine in the car. We can jam.'

'Did you bring your *Star Wars* DVDs?' I hoped he hadn't but knew he'd be miserable without them.

'*Star Wars*!' Mac opened the door and dumped the cases outside. 'Fantastic. Which is your favourite?'

'I like the first one with Alec Guinness in it. Obi-Wan Kenobi, he was the best. The other guy, the younger one, he was rubbish.'

I set the alarms, locked the door and they chatted on about the movies. Mac was good with Brando, knew exactly what to say to keep him interested. I liked him for that alone.

Mac had parked his car out of plain sight in the garage. 'We'll be travelling in my Subaru,' he said and, for once, Brando did not pull a face about being chauffeured in anything less than top of the line. Instead, he happily climbed in while we piled the suitcases in the back. He kept his guitar, Navy Seal and Roary on the seat beside him.

'Here's a game for you Brando,' Mac said. 'You and Sam have to duck down until we are out of this road. And stay down until I say you can sit up again, got it?'

'What kind of game is that?' Brando had that tone in his voice, the one that means, don't try to fool me, man. Whatcha think I am, some kind of kid or something?

'I'll tell you later.'

'No,' Brando said. 'I know what's going on. You put the lights on the timer switch in the house so people will think we are still around. And you want us to duck down until you can see if we've got a tail of any kind. Is that right?'

Mac laughed. 'That's absolutely correct.'

I waited for Brando to ask more questions but he just unbuck-led his seat belt and lay across the back seat with a smug look on his mush. 'Thought so!'

I watched the gates close behind us and couldn't help but gloat. Some day soon those symbols of that counterfeit relationship would be just where they deserved to be, on the scrap heap.

On our two-hour journey through the countryside, I kept checking in the side mirror to see if we were being followed. A white van was behind us for a couple of miles but soon pulled off in another direction. For several miles a metallic blue hatchback stayed with us. I nudged Mac but by the time he looked, the hatchback had gone.

'Don't worry,' he said. 'I'm watching.'

After that, I relaxed a bit. We sped along to the heavy metal riffs of Led Zeppelin booming out the car speakers.

'Jimmy Page,' Brando raved. 'Greatest guitar player who ever lived.'

'You won't get any argument from me on that one, son,' Mac agreed.

Male bonding, don't you just love it.

The cottage was of the roses-round-the door variety but without the roses, though it did have a thatched roof. We reached it down a winding lane with one neighbouring property of similar vintage a couple of hundred yards away. Bloom obviously liked his privacy at work and at play. A barrier of unruly privets screened the cottage from the curiosity of passing foxes while the wooden five-bar gate led to a short driveway and a small, slightly overgrown front garden. Inside was a farmhouse-style kitchen complete with Aga and glistening copper pans. The comfy sitting room had wooden beams and, thankfully, a TV and a DVD player to keep Brando entertained. Off the narrow hallway was a small, neat office but there was no sign of a computer. No telephone either. Upstairs were three cosy bedrooms furnished with a classic, chintzy Home Counties look, just like the rest of the place.

I looked out of my bedroom window onto the large back garden with its tall surrounding hedges and wondered if coming here really had been the wisest move. The Cohen house had been a huge property to keep secure but I knew every inch of it. It had places where I could safely stash Brando if Mac and I had to deal with any trouble. But, in the confines of this small cottage, there was nowhere to run, nowhere to hide.

Only two houses in the whole street could be a good thing or not, depending on how you viewed it. It would be relatively simple for anyone to block the entrances to the lane, isolating us. However,

I could see open fields beyond the back fence and a small wooded area further on. Directly behind those woods, some two miles away, was the picturesque village we had driven through. The only pub, the King's Head, was set to one edge of a village green and a church with a small steeple stood on the opposite side. I'd noticed about a dozen houses scattered about and seen cars in the driveways, evidence that the village was inhabited and not just a place for weekend getaways.

A sudden movement in the hedge set my pulse racing and a small, furry animal bolted from it and went belting across the field. I breathed a sigh of relief as I realised I had just seen my first Norfolk hare. But it brought home to me just how alien a landscape this was. And I couldn't stop the gnawing feeling telling me something wasn't quite right. I resolved to talk it through with Mac once Brando had gone to bed.

The sound of guitars was coming from the sitting room, the promised jam session already in progress. So I wandered down to take a look at the kitchen and try to get my head around cooking on an Aga.

After dinner Brando watched the first *Star Wars* for the umpteenth time with both he and Mac giving a running commentary. 'This is the bit where . . .' 'Don't you love it when . . .' 'Darth Vader is cool . . .'

'I hate it when Obi-Wan gets killed.' I added my tuppence-worth.

They both looked at me as though I was a simpleton.

'You can't kill a Jedi,' they said in unison.

'Oh, okay.' That was me told.

Once Brando was in bed, I voiced my doubts about security to Mac and he sought to reassure me.

'I've done work for Bloom for a while now,' he said. 'And it's my opinion he's a straight shooter. He got rid of Janine Kelso the day you spoke to him, so there are no more leaks from his office. This place was his idea. My conversation with him was on the phone, mine is secure and he's had his office swept for bugs. Plus, even you didn't know exactly where we were going until we got here.'

I had to take his word for it. Besides, we were here now and I had no other options in mind.

Mac complimented me on my cooking and said he was surprised that someone who had been eating army grub for so many years had developed any culinary skills.

'I've been cooking since I was ten years old,' I said. 'My mother worked in the day and spent her nights in the pub. After a while you get heartily sick of eating from the local chippy. My brother was two years younger than me and hopeless in the kitchen, so I cooked for us both. Then, after my mother died when I was sixteen, I just carried on.'

We got around to talking about Brando and Mac said how much he liked the boy.

'He's a nice lad once he loosens up. But that poor kid craves affection.'

I agreed. 'He seems to have everything. But things are all he's ever had. You know, he'd never been to a fairground until I took him to Chessington. He's an outsider at his posh school because none of the other kids will have anything to do with him. I reckon their parents have warned them off because of his father's reputation. When I started working for the family, Brando spent most of his time in his room or in the company of the housekeeper, Gloria Kelso, and he didn't even like her. Monica treated him like a bloody nuisance and the one time that Benny took him anywhere was to a *Star Wars* premiere. That was it, just the one proper outing with his dad. No wonder the boy became obsessed with those movies; they were his only link to his father.'

'Kids need proper parents,' Mac agreed. 'And a lad needs a dad.'

Did I hear a note of regret in his voice? He'd told me he didn't have any children. Maybe it had been something he had wanted and his ex-wife didn't. He may not have had much experience with youngsters but he treated the boy like an equal. I liked that and so did Brando.

'I'm going to take him where nobody knows about Benny Cohen.' I took a sip of red wine. 'I want Brando to be a normal kid, have pets, playmates, birthday parties, that sort of thing. Put this entire gangster shit out of his mind.'

Mac raised his glass to me. 'Cohen got it right for once in his life, picking you as a guardian for his son.'

'If someone had told me a few weeks ago that I'd be going soppy over some little kid, I'd have laughed.'

'Seems Cohen knew you better than you know yourself.'

'Don't think so. I didn't have much to do with him in the time I worked there.'

'Yeah, but he had Bloom check you out before he offered you the job. I did some of the groundwork for Bloom myself. The file is this thick.' He measured out a brick size with his hands. 'Everything from your nephew disappearing, to your army record, which was exemplary.'

My stomach clenched. Joe Murphy. Did Bloom know about Joe? 'And before the army?'

'There was something about your mother being killed in an accident and you looking after your brother until he got married at sixteen on the wrong end of a shotgun.'

'His wife's name was Geraldine. She and David were just naïve teenagers when they had Tom, but . . . well you know what happened there.'

Mac nodded. 'That's why the police gave them such a hard time. I've seen the reports. What with David Riley's background, a drunken mother, no father that anyone knew of and the only respectable and responsible family member signed up with the forces for the foreseeable future.' He smiled across at me.

I sprang to my dead brother's defence. 'David was a bit of a no-mark, but I know in my heart that he would never hurt his son. The police looked no further for whatever the reason and whoever took Tom was home free before they realised the truth. I was in the army, so what could I do? But it still haunts me, Mac.'

'Look, you've got the money now to start a search for Tom if you want to,' he said. 'A lot of things have changed in the seven years since he was abducted. If you've got a photo of him, it could be digitally aged so we'd have an idea of what he might look like now. I've got a lot of contacts on the force and elsewhere that might be able to help.'

'You said you'd seen the reports about the abduction. How did you get those?'

'Same way I got all the info on you, because I'm good at my job. That's what I meant about contacts, Sam. If you decide you want to search for Tom, then I'm your man.'

And I believed him.

I went to bed that night and had a dream about a funfair. 'Lay Lady Lay' blasted out from one of the rides and Joe was trying to win a blue teddy bear for me, Tom's blue teddy. Joe kept missing, handing more money over to the sluggish stallholder and missing again. He whooped for joy when he finally hit the target and the teddy bear was thrust into my arms. I hugged it close to me and turned to kiss Joe as a thank you. But it wasn't Joe beside me holding the fairground rifle and beaming with masculine pride. It was Mac.

Chapter Twenty-Eight

It was eggs and bacon for breakfast with Brando chattering nineteen to the dozen.

'Let's watch *Star Wars* again,' he suggested.

'How about going for a walk instead?' Mac said.

Brando pulled a face. He was used to being ferried about like Little Lord what's-his-face but never going out to play. There had been nothing for a kid to play on in the meticulously manicured gardens of the Cohen house. There was plenty of room out at the back for a slide, a swing and suchlike, but Monica had loathed stuff like that. Even footballs were banned. 'That's what parks and playgrounds are for,' I'd heard her say on several occasions. Not that she ever took the boy anywhere near any of them. I recalled, on one of the rare occasions he'd been in the car with us, Brando had spotted a poster for a circus in a nearby town and begged to be taken.

'I'm busy that evening,' she had told him.

'Can't Gloria take me?'

'I'm not paying her extra to go gallivanting with you,' Monica snapped. The boy had fallen silent and that had been the end of the matter. Why hadn't I seen the spiteful cruelty of the woman then? Just how blind is love?

'What do you call those things between your bottom and your feet?' Mac asked Brando.

'My legs,' Brando said.

'And what are they for?'

'Walking.'

'Right, so let's put them to good use.'

Once outside, sullen and reluctant to venture into the countryside, Brando dragged his feet behind us. But Mac was having none of that nonsense. He play-chased the boy, made him laugh with funny walks and silly voices, told him tales of adventures he'd had when he was a kid on camping trips. And, after a while, once he got over the shock of being out in the fresh air, Brando was like a puppy let off the leash for the first time. He ran ahead of us, hurled himself over stiles, climbed trees, threw stones into streams and we played hide-and-seek when we reached the woods behind the house. Brando held his nose as we trekked past a pig farm but was delighted when the farmer came over and showed him some pink, wriggly piglets.

'I'm never eating bacon again,' he declared with all the solemnity and determination he could muster. 'Or sausages.'

This was a new kid, excited by everything he saw, thrilled by watching squirrels leap from branch to branch. He became fascinated by the birds and listened intently as Mac told him what type they were and how you could distinguish their calls. I was interested, too. As a city girl I could recognise a blackbird and a sparrow and that was about the lot. Caged budgies were more common than magpies where I came from. Mainly, though, it was the laughter I loved, and Brando's face alive with newfound joy. I had never seen him like that before. Reservoir Pup had been transformed into a normal eleven-year-old.

But it was the horse that made the day memorable. We had stopped at a pub for lunch. We sat on the wooden benches in the garden and in the adjacent field stood an old grey mare quietly cropping the grass. Brando spotted her and approached the fence with some trepidation. The creature whinnied and ambled over. He reached out his hand and she nuzzled it.

Our lunch arrived and Brando ate with gusto but kept one eye firmly on the mare in the field, as though she might disappear again if he took his eyes off her.

'Some boys at my school have riding lessons,' he said.

'Maybe you should try.' Mac was tucking into his Ploughman's.

'I asked,' Brando said glumly. 'But Mum . . .' He paused, clearly still coming to terms with the idea that the woman he had thought of as his mother for all of his young life was nothing of the sort. 'She . . .' He readjusted the word once and then again. 'Monica said horses were dirty and dangerous and she hated the smell of them.'

'And what do you think?' Mac asked.

'That one smells lovely,' Brando said. 'And it feels like velvet.'

'We'll bring some carrots for her tomorrow,' I said. 'And you can feed her.'

'Can we come back?' Excitement seemed to ripple through him. 'Really?'

'Of course, and if you still want to learn to ride,' I said, 'then we can make arrangements for that too.'

He flashed his own version of Charlotte Cohen's glorious smile at me. And my heart felt like it was about to burst.

———

Mac opened the cottage door and held it for me. I must have looked surprised.

'I'm a gentleman,' he said.

'A Scotsman and a gentleman.' I laughed. 'Not a combination that automatically springs to mind.'

'Och, lassie,' he said, 'you don't know what you've been missing.'

'Oh, I think I do.'

'O would some power the giftie gie us, to see ourselves as others see us.'

'Robbie Burns.' Brando sauntered through door behind me. 'Isn't that right?'

Mac laughed, chased him into the kitchen whooping like a Red Indian and they play wrestled. 'Victuals, woman!' Mac shouted to me. 'Your menfolk need feeding.'

Gentleman, huh! Just another hairy-arsed geezer if you asked me. Though he did have a certain appeal.

———

'You'd make a great mother,' Mac said, once Brando had gone to bed.

'I've got Brando to look after.'

'I know, but I mean children of your own.'

'That's not going to happen.'

'Why not, you're still young?'

'I'm never going to get married.'

'Don't see why not. You're a good-looking woman, you can cook, you're funny, good company, great with kids. What more could any man want?'

'I prefer women,' I said.

He chuckled. Didn't he get it? Some detective he was. Though, it was a pleasant sound, that chuckle. Had any other man responded like that I would have been incensed. But somehow, with Mac, I wasn't.

'As that rich guy said at the end of *Some Like It Hot*.' Mac raised his glass of wine by way of a toast. 'Nobody's perfect.'

'It was Joe E Brown,' I said. 'And that's my favourite film.'

'Mine too.' He laughed. 'Bet *you* fancied Marilyn.'

'Who didn't?' I smiled back. 'Though I've gone off blondes lately.'

'Something else we have in common, then,' he said. 'Fancying Marilyn, that is.'

'But then,' I played along, 'Tony Curtis did look quite tasty in a dress.'

'Maybe you swing both ways,' he said. 'I could wear a dress for you. If you ask me to.'

'Mr Macdonald!' I did my best Jean Brodie impression. 'Are you flirting with me?'

He was and we both knew it and I realised that, for the first time in a very long time, I was enjoying myself. Maybe we could stay here forever. Brando would go to a good school in Norwich. I'd bake cakes for Women's Institute bazaars, make jam, brew our own beer and forget everything that had gone before.

'I really like you, Samantha Riley,' Mac said. 'I want to get to know you better.'

Our conversation was nipped in the bud by my mobile sounding off. And my illusive dreams went up the chimney, evaporating into the dark reality of the night.

'Thought you didn't like phones,' I said to my late-night caller – Gerard Fowley.

'For you, I make an exception.'

'Any news?' I ran my fingers over my bruised cheek. My ribs still ached and I was sure that one of my teeth had wobbled when I'd brushed them. But any ally, no matter how mercurial, was a boon at times like this. After our troubled 'meeting', Fowley and I had come to an arrangement. He'd agreed to put out feelers in the seedier parts of London about any of Jim Carver's young rent boys. Try to find out if anyone would talk about any sexual encounters with the old pervert. Fowley wanted Carver out of the picture as much as I did, though for very different reasons. With Big Jim in the nick, the nightclubs could be Fowley's and he had been more than enthusiastic about playing his part in making that particular scenario come to pass.

'Nothing I'm going to talk about on the phone,' Fowley said. 'We need a meet. Are you at the house?'

'No,' I said.

'Can you meet me at my car showroom tomorrow evening?'

'Agreed. If it's that important.'

I must have sounded unsure. 'This is kosher, Sam,' Fowley said. 'I'm on your side.'

Chapter Twenty-Nine
9 a.m., Friday, 4 July

It was a breakfast of eggs only for Brando. After yesterday's pig-let encounter he was off the bacon option. Mac was busy scoffing down three rashers and Brando looked at him with disdain. 'How can you eat that? You saw those little pigs, they were alive – they had a mummy.'

Another conversation flashed across my mind, from what seemed a lifetime ago. Joe Murphy walking away from where we had just buried Benny Cohen; Joe brushing dirt from his hands with an expression on his face I had found hard to decipher. 'That man was a sentient being.' And his words, echoed now in Benny's son's defence of animals, made me feel queasy. Leaving my breakfast untouched, I leapt up from the table, ran to the bathroom and was violently sick.

Mac was at the door. 'Sam, are you alright, lassie?'

Lassie! Where did he get off calling me that? What right had he to care about me? I had no right for a good man like him to want to get to know me. Tears welled up in my eyes. I didn't deserve to be happy. I deserved to be punished. How many Hail Marys would the priests of my childhood have demanded for that kind of confession?

Forgive me Father for I have sinned. I took part in the deaths of four men: two for money and two more for the misguided love of a woman. 'God is watching you,' my mother used to yell at me whenever I did anything wrong. 'You'll go to Hell for that.' Well, she'd descended into her own kind of booze-fuelled hell, as had my brother David. Maybe all three of us shared a similar fate.

'Is she ill?' I heard Brando's voice from outside the bathroom door. He sounded upset. Mac spoke quietly, in an effort to reassure him. I washed my face and took a deep breath. Pull yourself together, Samantha, you've got a job to do. Forget your airy-fairy fantasies about being the perfect mother. You're in deep shit and coming over all girly isn't going to get you out of it. Toughen up. Bite the bullet, soldier.

'It's okay,' I called to them both. 'Must be something I hadn't eaten.'

A black Audi with tinted windows was barrelling down the motorway.

'Keep the speed down, will you,' Bob warned.

He hated Stan driving, no caution, that was his problem. The last thing they needed was to be pulled over by the cops. He wouldn't have been so concerned had he been driving alone. To any nosy police he'd be just another businessman in a suit, so they'd just give him a warning or a speeding ticket at worst and see no need to search the car.

Apart from his erratic driving, Bob wasn't too happy about Stan's appearance, either – what with the shaved head and all. Even when Stan was suited and booted, it still made him look like a hard case. Bob didn't see anything wrong with going a bit thin on top, it could make a man look just like any other middle-aged dad, blending in was no bad thing in their profession. But to shave it all off was a bit drastic. Especially when you had a fizzog like Stan. Bob had had better-looking shits.

He glanced across at Stan. He'd been acting a bit strange since his missus had left him; working out in the gym, giving up the fags, no more beer, no more red meat. What did he think, that he was going to live forever? Catch himself some fit babe? No chance.

Bob didn't like the fact that the motor had tinted windows, either. That was another way to get yourself stopped. Tinted windows spelled out *Gangsta* to the cops in this neck of the woods. But this was the car the boss had told them to take, and he'd been in no mood to hear any arguments to the contrary.

They drove down the lane and spotted the Subaru in the driveway but passed right by and on to the only other cottage in the vicinity. Bob got out of the car and checked it over. The place was locked up tight.

'We could break in,' Stan suggested. 'Lay low and then bust in tonight.'

'It's all alarmed up. Too much hassle.' He looked back to the first house. 'Let's give Bloom's cottage the once over.'

'I'll knock at the door and ask for directions,' Stan said. 'The Riley woman doesn't know my face. But she might recognise you.'

They drove back down the lane and stopped outside the cottage. Stan got out. Bob pulled out a map and put his head down as though studying it, just in case she came to the door and clocked him.

Stan was back in just a minute. 'Nobody home.'

'Maybe they've gone for a walk. Let's cruise around and see if we can spot them.'

They were driving back towards the village they had passed through earlier, when the kid ran across the road a couple of hundred yards in front of them. To the right, just coming out of the field opposite, were the man and woman.

'Why not grab the target now?' Stan asked. 'There's nobody else around. We could pop the other two and be back home in a couple of hours.'

'Stick to the plan, Stan.' Bob laughed. 'Wasn't that a Paul Simon song?' He hummed the tune.

'I hate all this hanging about,' Stan complained.

'Don't know what's wrong with you these days, getting all antsy all the time. You on steroids, or something?'

Stan did not respond.

'They'll kill you faster than burgers and chips, mate. And they'll shrink your dick.'

'Rubbish!'

'Drive back to the village and let's get some lunch. We can mooch around there for a bit and then drive around until tonight.'

'Waste of bloody time.'

'Just part of the job, old son. We go in when they're all asleep. That's what the boss wants, so that's what the boss gets.'

We found a camping shop in a nearby town and Mac chose some walking boots for Brando. 'Designer trainers are no good for anything but posing on street corners,' Mac said. He selected practical jeans, sweaters and jackets and handed them to the kid to try on. And Brando, who had previously sneered at wearing anything other than designer gear, snapped it all up. I stood outside the shop while they got on with it

Becoming a country gentleman was Brando's new ambition. 'My guitar teacher lives on a farm,' he said. 'Maybe I can be a musician *and* a farmer. What do you think, Sam? Can we buy a house round here? Can we get some ducks and chickens? Can we get a sheep dog? I'd take it for walks, I promise.' He was full of plans for our future life together and was mentally collecting a little menagerie to go with it.

'And cats,' he added, after he spotted one jauntily cross the road in front of us, its ginger tail held aloft like a question mark. 'They're good for catching mice and rats and things.'

A small herd of reddish-brown cows mooed about in a field and he ran over to the fence that kept them in their place. Idly curious, they ambled over to him and he climbed on the wooden struts to pat their slobbery noses.

'Cats are fine,' I said. 'But no cows.'

'But I love milk,' he said.

'That's what supermarkets are for.'

We took carrots for the old grey mare and Brando was more interested in feeding her than he was in eating his own lunch. 'Can we buy her? I'd love to have my own horse. I could ride her.'

'I think she's a bit too old for that,' Mac reached across the table to nick some of my chips and gave me a cheeky wink. 'I think she's in retirement.'

'Then we could keep her safe in a nice warm stable and feed her carrots every day and have *another* horse for me to ride. We could get *lots* of horses. You could learn to ride too, Sam. We could ride around together. It'll be great.'

I loved seeing him so exuberant, but my forthcoming meeting with Gerard Fowley was on my mind, so I left it to Mac to keep the boy entertained.

'Can we go camping, Mac? Those tents were cool.'

'We can do anything you want, son.'

Mac wasn't too happy about my going to see Fowley alone but there was no alternative. 'I'll cook for us tonight,' he said. 'You come straight back. I'll keep your supper hot for you.'

We had only the one vehicle so I took the Subaru. They both stood at the door to wave me off. Just like in the movies.

I exited the gate. An unfamiliar dark car with tinted windows and two occupants turned into the lane as I drove towards the entrance. I watched it pass by through my rear-view mirror. It didn't stop by the cottage but kept going towards the house further along the lane. That house had been all locked up when I gave it the once over. I was aware that well-heeled types like Richard Bloom kept weekend places in areas like this, so I told myself these might be people from London arriving for a break. Mac had assured me we were safe here. I had to take his word for it. Couldn't be suspicious of everyone. That way lay total paranoia. But I waited anyway until I saw the dark vehicle stop at the gates of the only neighbouring house. I breathed a sigh of relief and drove away for my meeting with Fowley.

Chapter Thirty

8 p.m., Friday, 4 July

Two hours up the motorway and I was in Fowley's office at his car dealership. The showroom was closed for the night and he was alone for once. There was no sign of Clive or Winston. I presumed he'd sent them home in a bid to reassure me that he did not speak with forked tongue. He was his usual elegant self in an expensive suit but had opted for wearing specs with a green tint. I'd never seen him in glasses before, except for shades worn, I'd assumed, for effect.

'Gotta wear these,' he said when he saw me glance at them. 'But I do without most times. Specs are a sign of weakness.'

'I think you look good in them,' I said and he preened.

'The batty boys are running scared,' he said. Fowley and his crew were a homophobic bunch and I could imagine the distaste with which Clive had carried out his master's orders to go trawling for information in gay hangouts. 'A DI called Morrison has been showing photos around, asking if anyone knew some kid in a video. These youths are runaways.' Fowley mused. 'They get beat up, raped, killed and who gives a fuck about them? Not the cops, that's for sure.'

'Gerard, do I detect a note of empathy here?'

'Nah, I'm just saying they're like regular whores – they need someone to look after them or they get hurt.'

Guess he was speaking with some experience, considering his former profession as a pimp. 'I'll bet nobody would admit to knowing the kid in the photo, then?'

Fowley laughed. 'Not to the cops, no. But my boy Winston has quite a way with words when he wants to.'

Yeah, scaring the living shit out of folk. 'So someone talked?'

'One kid did. Damien, he's been on the streets for three years; clever lad, smart, streetwise. Doesn't come across like your average fairy.' Fowley steepled his hands, and looked at me over the top of his green-tinted specs like some kind of hip professor.

'Sometimes in life, we have to do things just to survive. I understand that more than most and would never hold it against anyone. So I've given Damien a proper job in my garden centre. If he stays the course, I'll introduce him to a couple of my naughty ladies. They'll straighten him out a bit.'

Gerard Fowley, philanthropic sociopath.

'By all accounts, Carver used to like the very young ones.' Fowley got back on track. 'He had this oppo the kids called Chimp, who'd choose the lad and take him off in a limo. Carver would have the kid to his house, feed him up, look after him for a bit. Kid would go back to Soho, suited and booted, flash watch, latest mobile and brag to his mates how great it was. After a time though, he'd fall off the radar. Then Chimp would come prowling around again, hunting for fresh young meat, saying how the last one was abroad, had gone back home or some such.'

I suppressed a shudder as I recalled Morrison's description of the other man in Carver's sex video – arms like a gorilla, she'd said. Or chimp? 'And they bought into this?'

'They're greedy little shits, every one of them. They all had a hard-on for the goodies they saw their mate with. So, yeah, most of them fell for it.'

'And what about your informant?' Sour grapes from one of the unchosen ones, perhaps?

'He was sixteen when he hit town, bit too old for Carver's rarefied tastes. Even so, he said the whole thing smelled iffy to him and he tried to warn the other lads but they weren't listening. But he did recognise the kid in the picture. Said he called himself Jason. This Jason told everyone he was fifteen but my boy reckons he was really about eleven or twelve.'

'Has he seen Jason since?'

'No. Jason's gone missing as well. Like all the others.'

'*All* the others?'

'About eight or nine of them, to this kid's knowledge.'

It made no sense. Even if Carver had used the boys until he was bored, surely at least one of them would have resurfaced in their old stomping grounds. I'd met a few prostitutes in my time – my area of Manchester had been teeming with them – and they tended to stick together for safety's sake if not for friendship. I doubted that rent boys would be any different. My mind was racing with the possibility of a more sinister explanation. 'Do you think Carver might have sold them on?'

'Suppose he could, always a market for young lads, I've been told. But Carver wouldn't want to risk any future comeback. He's a very cautious man in other respects.'

'You think he might have had them killed?' No comeback there. Only Carver and Chimp would ever know the truth.

'Or did it himself,' Fowley nodded. 'Wouldn't surprise me. He always was a fucking nutcase. Might even get off on it, for all I know. Could have a backyard full of bones.' His delivery was chillingly matter-of-fact. 'Have you seen that place he lives in with his mother? You could bury an army in those grounds.'

The temperature in the room seemed to plummet. We hadn't found a lead for the child pornography charge but instead possibly something far worse.

Chapter Thirty-One
11 p.m., Friday, 4 July

I phoned Mac to say I was on my way, and found the sound of his deep voice warm and reassuring. It stirred something inside me that had been buried for such a long time that it took me by surprise. At the pub that day, the waitress who brought us our lunch had smiled at us. 'What a lovely little boy you have there,' she'd said. Mac had a silly grin on his face all day after that, as though he hadn't noticed what a strange parody of a family unit we were. Parody or not, I was willing to give it a go and so I drove fast, wanting to get back as soon as I could and willing the miles away.

The streetlights ended where the lane began and I put the headlights on full beam to drive the couple of hundred yards back to the cottage.

The wooden five-bar gate that led to the driveway was open and I couldn't see a light on anywhere in the house. I looked at the dashboard clock: twelve fifty-five. The hairs on the back of my neck stood to attention and my pulse raced. Heart pounding and with a feeling of trepidation churning in my stomach, I got out of the car and walked cautiously to the front door. It was open. I nudged it wide and listened hard but heard no sound. I stepped into the darkness.

'Brando!' I shouted, but nothing came back. 'Mac!'

Silence.

I switched on the light. It blinded me for a second before I saw Mac sprawled on the floor, his shirt soaked with blood. He had a head wound too. I couldn't make out the extent of the damage but was relieved to see he was breathing. I pulled my phone out of my pocket and dialled 999.

'Which service do you require?' The voice came from my phone.

'Ambulance *and* police.' I gave her the address.

'Stay with me, Mac.' I was down on my knees beside him. 'Hang on in there.'

I'd done basic first-aid training in the army but knew that these wounds were far beyond my limited capabilities. His pulse was thready, probably due to shock. I checked for blood in his mouth but found none and pushed his tongue out of the way. I turned his head to one side and could see his chest rising and falling as he breathed. With so much blood, I couldn't determine immediately whether he'd been shot or stabbed, but I reckoned nothing had punctured his lung. I ran to the kitchen for a towel and padded it up on his chest to try and stem the blood flow. Mac murmured and I bent to hear, allowing my lips to brush his bloodied forehead.

As though in response to my touch, his eyes flickered. 'Carver,' he whispered. 'Go. Now.' His eyes closed and he lapsed back into unconsciousness.

I talked to the emergency operator while I took the stairs two at a time. But as soon as I saw the door to Brando's room standing ajar, I knew that he wouldn't be there. On my phone, I heard the operator tell me that the ambulance would be with me in five minutes but all I could focus on was Brando's empty bed. I took a deep breath and tried to keep myself together. His wardrobe door was almost off its hinges and his clothes were scattered on the floor as though the room had been ransacked. I almost stopped breathing in terror. I felt light-headed and it took a moment for me to register what was on his pillow. His fluffy seal was pinned to it, stabbed through with a kitchen knife. I approached it, willing myself not to touch it. Didn't want to mess up any fingerprints that might be on the handle.

My phone pinged. One text message.

Run!

I checked that Mac was still breathing before I got out of there. I could hear the ambulance and police sirens close by and exited the lane just in time. I stopped the Subaru a safe distance away and watched the flashing blue emergency lights heading towards the cottage. I'd left the place all lit up with the doors open so they'd know they were at the right house.

I looked at my phone again. The sender ID wasn't familiar. I called it and was informed that the number did not exist. Should have expected that. I forwarded the text to Morrison's private number and drove away.

The motorway café had just a lone truck driver scarfing down a greasy full English breakfast at three in the morning. I sat with a coffee and hoped against hope that Mac was still alive. Brando would be petrified. But I couldn't afford to dwell on any of that. I needed a plan of action. Leaving the scene made me look as guilty as hell but there was no way I could have stayed and got caught up in a lengthy police procedure. I had to get to Brando, and fast.

I rang Morrison. A sleepy voice answered.

'It's Sam. Did you get my text?'

'Wait a minute, I'll look.'

No way was I going to answer any awkward questions from her. 'There's been a shooting and it's connected to Carver. If you really want to nail him be at his house at ten in the morning with armed backup. If I don't call you by ten, bust the doors down.'

I ended the call and turned my phone off. The only way I could prove that Carver had Brando was to go in there myself. And I needed time to find out for sure. If I was wrong and Wendy Morrison turned up mob-handed on a wild goose chase, then I'd have to take the flak. But someone had taken Brando and Mac was sure it was Carver's crew, so I'd go with that. I had no idea if the Carver house was guarded by men or dogs, so my going into unknown territory unarmed in the middle of the night would have been a sucker move. I was considering another plan. For all I knew they'd think I was dead, so my making a phone call to Carver in the morning would set all their alarm bells ringing, which gave me a bit of an advantage. Love makes you vulnerable but there are times when love can make you strong. I was going to find Brando or die trying. I got myself another black coffee and waited for the dawn.

Chapter Thirty-Two
6 a.m., Saturday, 5 July

Monica scrutinised her face in her dressing table mirror. You've still got it, Mrs Cohen – strange how she still thought of herself that way. Benny hadn't been a bad old stick. And until he'd become ill, he'd always been up for it. Not like this one.

She glanced at the reflection of her sleeping fiancé in the king-sized bed behind her. Sure, he was great looking but, as her adoptive mother always used to say, 'Handsome is as handsome does.' Unless Felipe Garcia was drip-fed Viagra he was sodding useless. It hadn't been that way when she'd first met him in the Canaries. Then he couldn't get enough of her, had a stiffy every time he touched her. But now . . .

Flattering? She didn't think so.

She turned back to her own image. Even in the harsh early morning light and with a little help from Max Factor, she was a still a total knockout. She did another line of cocaine. That would give her a boost. After the buzz hit, she brushed her blonde hair, smiled at herself and added a touch more lippy.

Garcia stirred, let out a snort, farted like a bull elephant and turned over.

This was not working out. Garcia had to go. Not so easy though, now he was in so deep with Carver. All those whispered phone calls between them were beginning to piss her off. She really couldn't take being left out of the loop. And Mr can't-get-it-up Machismo had told her to mind her own business when she'd asked what was going on. He and his snarky sister yattered away in Spanish all the time – she'd bet he told *her* everything. And when Monica protested, that bitch had sneered at her: 'You must learn Spanish.'

'Screw you, you stunted little whore,' Monica had screamed back. 'You're in England now. Speak fucking English.'

Felipe had smacked her in the mouth for swearing at his sister. The impotent prick was going to pay for that. One day, very soon.

Benny had always told her not to go off half-cocked. Right now she was regretting not having listened to him. He hadn't been such an old fool after all. 'Do what you can legit,' he'd advised. 'Then, if all else fails, go after what you want the hard way.'

She looked back at the prone figure of Garcia. Getting involved with that cocksucker had fucked her life up, for sure. She'd had it made as the main beneficiary to Benny's will. Once the cancer had done for Benny she'd have been like a pig in shit, what with all of Benny's dosh to play with and Brando sent away so she didn't have to see his face ever again. The older he got, the more like his mother he looked. Like Charlotte was reaching out of the grave to torment her.

Belatedly she was taking Benny's advice. Do it legit. The solicitor she'd seen on the sly had told her that she had a good case to challenge Benny's will, get what was due to her for ten years of marriage, not just that poxy villa in Andalucía. Richard Bloom wouldn't want Benny's finances scrutinised by some strait-laced London law firm. He'd cave all right. Give her anything she wanted. And that was what she was going to do – challenge the will – once this crack-of-dawn meeting with the Carvers was out of the way.

She hated the way Lil Carver summoned everyone, like she was the fucking Queen or something. And everyone came running, even Big Jim. The sooner that old crone was in the ground, the better. Big Jim would be rudderless and Monica would wade in there and have his balls for breakfast. But, for now, she was going to bide her time.

Whatever they wanted to see her about at this unearthly hour on a Saturday morning, she'd go along with – for now. Then she'd see to the lot of them.

Chapter Thirty-Three
8 a.m., Saturday, 5 July

I stood outside the double gates of one of those houses often used as locations for BBC costume dramas: Queen Anne, red brick, long sweeping driveway leading to a house that looked like it should have a horse and carriage stationed outside. The whole ambience of the place was so at odds with Carver's scruffy office that I had to check the address twice before I approached the gates. This was probably what Benny Cohen had wanted to emulate when he had his ostentatious pile built. Isolated down a discreet lane with no immediate neighbours, this place would be the perfect spot for Carver and Chimp to indulge their murderous perversions, with plenty of room in the huge gardens to dispose of any unsightly, incriminating evidence. A backyard full of bones, as Gerard Fowley had so concisely put it.

Mac's whispered message had been a clear indicator of where I should go. Had it not been for Fowley calling me to the meeting at his showroom, I knew I would be dead by now.

Once buzzed in, I drove slowly down a gravelled driveway edged with ornate, white mock-Victorian streetlamps, a touch of the naff that would make even the most hardened estate agent wince. I glanced at the huge rose bushes growing suspiciously tall in a vast flowerbed and speculated about the fertiliser used.

Gloria Kelso opened the door to me before I had time to ring the bell. 'You're a fool! You should have run,' she said.

'You texted me?' Gobsmacked wasn't the word for my reaction to that sudden realisation.

Gloria said nothing, instead she threw me a look conveying bemused astonishment at my volunteering to put myself in harm's way and ushered me towards a room off the wide, wood-panelled hallway. Before opening the door, she frisked me. It was fast and efficient. She found my phone in my pocket, took it off me and placed it on a console table by the door.

'You've done this before,' I said.

'Just get in there.' She pushed the door open.

Stuffed into a high-backed chair behind a large, green-leather-topped antique desk was Carver. To his right side sat Monica, wound tight, like a rattlesnake in a designer dress.

She almost hissed when she saw me. 'You are one stupid dyke,' she said. 'You could have scarpered when you saw what happened to that prick Macdonald. But you've got used to playing Mummy, haven't you? You want to protect that little shit, so you come here like some fucking saviour. Idiot!'

'Calm down, Monica,' Carver reprimanded her. 'We can at least behave like civilised human beings.' He gestured to a wooden chair in front of his desk. 'Take the weight off, Sam. I'd like to hear what you have to say.'

Monica folded her arms, crossed her legs and turned her face away from me as I walked to the chair.

'By the way,' Carver said amiably, 'you already know Mr Swindley, I believe.'

The door closed behind me and Gloria Kelso retreated. I looked over my shoulder, and, standing in the corner with his back to the wall, was Swindley. He held me in his frozen stare. One glimpse of his jacket told me he was packing a gun in a shoulder holster and making no attempt to conceal it.

I sat down and glanced across at the floor-to-ceiling window to the hunched figure of an elderly woman in a wheelchair. She appeared to be concentrating on the garden outside and not taking any notice of what was happening around her. It was Lil Carver, clearly a shadow of her former inimitable self, last spotted at Benny Cohen's funeral, shedding a sympathetic tear.

'So, why the visit?' Carver asked. 'Thought you'd be long gone by now.'

'You shouldn't even be here,' Monica said and she turned on Carver. 'You told me she was at the cottage with Macdonald. You said you'd seen to the two of them.'

'How did you know we were there?' Bloom had told me he'd sacked Janine Kelso, so no more leaks from that source, and Mac was convinced we hadn't been followed.

'Simple. Tracking devices,' Carver said. 'Macdonald should have been more careful where he parked his motor.' He gave a disgusted snort. 'Now, say your say and let's be done with this.'

'Hand Brando over to me,' I said. 'And I'll persuade Bloom to arrange for you to have all of Benny's assets.'

Monica laughed. 'Is that it? Is that your bargaining tool?' She turned to Carver. 'Tell her.'

Carver grinned, never a pleasant sight but this conveyed so much malice it was tangible. 'They're not called solicitors for nothing, you know, Sam. Bloom is just a hooker with an education, charging by the hour to the punter with the biggest wallet. No honour, no scruples and absolutely no conscience. Deal's already been done. You've sacrificed yourself for nothing.'

'But if Brando disappears?'

'We've paid a ransom for Brando,' Carver replied. 'To you. You killed Macdonald, kidnapped the kid and we paid you a ransom. You go off with the money and the kid lives his little life in the bosom of his loving family.'

They thought that Mac was dead. The plan had clearly been to kill Mac and me. Mac gets found at the cottage but my body was to be disposed of elsewhere. 'Clever, yet satisfyingly simple.'

'*They* thought so.' Monica tossed an angry glare at Carver. 'Until your guys fucked up.'

'And what about Brando? How long will he survive all the love you'll shower on him?'

'For just as long as is necessary.' Monica replied levelly.

'And Garcia? Where is your new *señor*, Monica?'

'I'm packing him off to Spain,' Carver said. 'Slimy little dago shite.'

'Widowed and disengaged within a few months,' I said. 'That's going some, even for you, Monica.'

'You'll laugh on the other side of your face when Swindley's done with you,' Monica retorted with a malevolent stare.

'Now, now,' Carver said. 'That's no way to talk to guests, Monica. You may be a slut but that's no excuse for bad manners.'

Monica stood up, smoothed down her skirt and stalked across the room. She didn't so much as glance in my direction. I was already dead to her. 'Fuck you, Jim, you incompetent tosser. Without Benny around to hold your dick, you can't even piss straight.' She stood by the door, hands on hips, until Swindley opened it for her. She turned back to Carver, her eyes blazing with anger. 'Call me back in when you're ready to talk proper business.' She walked out and slammed the door behind her.

Carver looked across to the frail figure in the wheelchair. 'She always was a hot-headed little minx, eh, Ma?'

Lil Carver did not respond.

'So, regretfully, Sam. This is to be our final meeting.' Carver said.

The sound of a car on the gravelled driveway caught Carver's attention.

'What's that?' Carver was on edge. I could hear it in his voice – see it in his body language.

'Gloria, going shopping.' Lil Carver turned her head away from the window. 'Get lost, Jim.' It wasn't a request – it was a command. 'I'll deal with this.'

Carver heaved himself out of the chair and looked over to Swindley, who hadn't moved a muscle.

'He stays.' Lil Carver nodded towards Swindley. 'He's the only person on this earth I can trust not to screw everything up.'

Carver hauled his bulk out of the room. Lil Carver pressed a button on the arm of her motorised wheelchair and it glided over the parquet floor towards me. She stopped just a few feet away and indicated that I should turn my chair to face her and the still, silent Swindley. I complied and it enabled me to get a better look at this underworld legend. Her steel grey hair was up in a French pleat and her face fully made-up. Close up she looked like an aged film star from the 1950s, all pencilled eyebrows and red lipstick – Joan Crawford crossed with Ma Barker. I almost expected her to pull a Tommy gun out from beneath the tartan rug that covered her knees.

'Mr Swindley has worked for me for many years,' she said, like we were having some kind of cosy chat. 'He's my friend in the north, collecting gambling debts from toerags who skedaddle back to their grimy roots. They think they're safe from me north of Watford.' She gave a sour smile. 'Not so safe from you though, eh, Mr Swindley?'

He nodded his head but remained silent.

She turned her attention back to me and the look in her eyes chilled me. 'My son tells me you are responsible for bringing all this unwanted police attention to my home, Miss Riley.'

I sat still and kept quiet.

'I see you're not bothering to deny it. Good girl, because we know it was you. You were seen exiting the premises. You did a very efficient job on the Turkish kebab shop manager but his assistant saw you getting into the Mini.'

'You're very well informed,' I said. 'So you'll also know what was on the video?' Surely, even a woman as ruthless as this couldn't condone what happened to those young lads.

She moved the wheelchair further towards me and made the act itself seem like a threat. 'My children have always been a disappoint-ment to me, Miss Riley,' she said ruefully, as though she'd hoped they'd become rocket scientists and they'd decided on gardening as a career instead. 'Gloria got pregnant at twelve. Can you believe that? Twelve! Sucking dicks when she should have been sucking lol-lipops.' She pursed her blood-red lips in disgust. 'If only she'd stuck to sucking.' She gave a humourless sniff. 'If only she'd had the grace to give me a grandson, someone of use. But it was a girl, so I had it adopted out. But, like mother like daughter, she turns up on my doorstep at eighteen looking like a ten-bob tart. Bloody Monica, more trouble than she's worth.'

It hit me like a hammer. Gloria Kelso was Monica's mother. All I could think was that Monica's father must have been a good-look-ing individual because there was no resemblance that I'd spotted.

'So you sent her to work as a stripper for Benny Cohen.'

Lil Carver's thin red lips spread into a smile. 'You're a smart one, aren't you? What a waste.' She shook her head. 'I might have been able to use a person like you.'

I could almost hear Swindley breathing in his stock-still posi-tion in the corner. One word from Lil Carver and I was for the chop. I had to keep this conversation going, play for time.

'Benny didn't know Monica was related to me. Nobody knew, only family,' she said.

'But why make Monica work at Benny Cohen's club?'

'Charlotte Cohen,' she said with emphasis and I could see long-held hatred in her eyes. 'Jim and Benny were a good team for me years ago.' Lil drummed her long, manicured nails on the arm of her chair. 'Benny kept Jim's excesses in check. Then Benny meets that Yid bitch and gets ambition. Wants to set up his own firm, run his own clubs. There's fucking gratitude for you. I pulled that raggedy-arsed little Jew out of the gutter, took him into my family, nurtured his talents. Then Charlotte comes along and sticks her oar in.'

Poor Charlotte had signed her own death warrant.

'Dealt with her after the brat was born. Don't know what's wrong with women today. There was no such thing as post-natal depression when I had babies. You just got on with it.'

'Gloria worked as Charlotte's housekeeper?'

'That's all she's good for. Anyway Gloria had that birdbrain Janine by then and deadbeat Tommy Kelso as a husband.' She looked over to Swindley again. 'But you sorted him out, eh?'

A name and a face came back to me across the years. Tommy Kelso.

Lil Carver was speaking again. 'It came in handy in the end, though. Gloria worked on the wife and we sent Monica to work on the husband.'

'Drug Charlotte, string her up and make it look like suicide,' I said. The mother and daughter team making room for Monica in Benny Cohen's bed. 'Nice touch doing it in the baby's room, make Benny feel even more guilty.'

'It was Monica's idea. It's always the dramatic gesture with that one. Excessive, I thought,' she added. 'Made too many people ask too many questions. Your friend Macdonald made a real nuisance of himself.'

'Then Monica becomes the new Mrs Cohen and you have Benny back in the fold, so to speak. One big happy family.'

Lil Carver gave a wheezy chuckle. 'She catches on quick, this one, eh, Mr Swindley?'

Swindley nodded.

'But when Benny's days are numbered, Monica gets ideas above her station?'

Lil clapped her hands together and I stiffened. Was that the cue for Swindley to put a bullet in my brain? But she was slow handclapping me. 'That's what I meant about girls being fucking useless. Along comes some Spanish onion with an exotic accent and a big dick and her brains go straight to her fanny. Thinks she can double-cross me. Thinks I'm past it. Thinks Jim is too busy playing games with dirty little rent boys to notice he's being done over by his own niece—'

'Where's Brando?' I cut in.

'In the cellar with Jim's disgusting playmate.'

My stomach clenched. I swallowed my fear for Brando and struggled to keep my facial expression neutral. Stay in the zone, Sam. Keep her talking. 'Chimp?'

Lil chuckled. 'Is that what they call him? Well, it fits.'

'How can you sanction what your son does to those kids?'

She waved her hand dismissively. 'Those foul little shits. Who cares? Everyone has a weakness and smart people use them to control you.' She looked directly at me, her eyes sparked with animosity. 'Yours being Monica, of course. And the boy.'

She'd lost interest in me now and she nodded to Swindley. 'Get them back in here. Let's get this over with.'

Swindley opened the door and Carver almost fell in. He'd been earwigging at the door. It was like a scene from a farce, but this wasn't at all funny, at least not for me. Get it over with could mean only one thing: I would soon be fertilising the roses.

'Get this bitch out of here,' Lil Carver ordered. 'She's taken up enough of my time. We've got business to discuss.'

Swindley unholstered his gun and came over to me. 'Come on now,' he said, his Birmingham accent less pronounced than the last time I'd heard him speak. I guessed it was put on, part of some professional disguise. I stood up with my mind whirling. I was a good three inches taller than Swindley. Maybe I could get myself into a position to disarm him once we were out of the room. But he was a real pro; he stayed close behind me as we walked towards the open door.

Once in the hallway, Swindley closed the door behind him and tapped me on the shoulder. I flinched but looked back to see him put a finger to his lips. 'Shush,' he whispered. 'Come with me. Be quiet now.'

He placed his hand on my shoulder and we walked past the stairway towards the back of the house. 'In here,' he said. 'I want to talk to you. Trust me.'

That'll be the day! The hallway was too narrow to tackle him, I had to wait until I got to wherever he was taking me.

I did a quick scan of the kitchen as we entered. There was a doorway to a utility room that appeared to lead to the garden. If I could overpower Swindley then I might be able to get out that way. But with Brando still in the house there was no way I was leaving without him. Swindley closed the door behind us.

The safest thing, when confronted by an armed man, is to do as you're told. Fuck safety. This was it. Now or never. I turned fast, grabbed his hand and forced the gun inwards towards his body. Twisting to get maximum leverage, I drove my other elbow into his jaw. The gun hit the deck and Swindley followed it down, hard. I grabbed the gun off the floor, pointed it at his head and stood over him, three feet away, legs apart, two-handed, by the manual.

'Bloody hell!' Swindley's accent hurtled a hundred miles up the motorway: Birmingham to Manchester in five seconds flat. 'Didn't expect that.'

'Must be slipping. Old age,' I said. 'Comes to us all.'

'You caught me off-guard.'

'Bollocks!' Typical northern male – can't admit a woman has bested him.

'I just wanted to talk to you.'

'At gunpoint? Yeah, right.'

'I wasn't going to hurt you or the boy.'

'Prove it.'

'There's another gun in my waistband holster. I could have dropped you with that, if I'd wanted to.'

He rolled to one side. I put one foot on his back, bent down with the gun pressed against his temple, retrieved the Ruger and backed away.

'Now will you believe me?'

'I'll think about it.'

'While you ponder, can I get up? This stone floor is somewhat chilly.'

He got to his feet and leaned against the marble worktop – very casual for a man with a gun aimed directly at his gonads. Threaten to blow some guy's balls off and he becomes very cooperative, or so my comrades-in-arms always told me.

'Joe always said you had the killer instinct. As he found out, of course.'

'Who the hell are you?'

'Joe Murphy was my nephew.' Swindley's steely grey eyes searched my face. 'He always loved you, Sam.'

Fuck you, buster. 'Don't play mind games with the one holding the gun. First lesson in hitman college, I'd have thought.'

'Who killed Joe?' It was a serious question. This was no game.

'Monica.'

He nodded his head. 'Makes sense.'

'Not to me, it didn't.'

'You have to get the boy out of here,' he said. 'This ends today. Right now, you're just going to have to trust me.'

'Give me one good reason.'

'That last job you did with Joe all those years ago.' His eyes held me in a frozen stare. 'Tommy Kelso.'

The final hit, the one that got away.

'Gloria begged me not to do it, so I handed the job over to Joe,' Swindley said. 'It was Gloria who tipped off the police.'

He knew far too much about Joe and me for this to be some kind of trick. Nobody else knew about the hits we'd been involved in, except for Joe's contact, it seemed.

'I'm really sorry about Joe.' It was the first time I had actually voiced my regret. I had a lump in my throat and an aching hollow in my heart.

'Me too.'

Whatever Swindley was up to I clearly wasn't his target for tonight. I had to get to Brando. But to give this man his gun back was perilous.

'I don't take kindly to being fucked over,' I said.

'One false move, eh?' He held out his hand.

'Absolutely.' I gave him the Glock but kept the Ruger aimed at him. 'How do we handle the Carvers?'

'We? I like that word. Back me up,' he said. 'If I need it.' With his gun back in his hand, he walked towards the door. I was right behind him. Literally watching his back.

Chapter Thirty-Four
9 a.m., Saturday, 5 July

We stood outside the room where the Carver clan was in conference. Whatever was going down, I was now right in the middle of it. But I was prepared to go the distance to get Brando out of that house. Swindley gave me a curt nod, pushed the door open and strode in ahead of me.

'What the fuck!' I heard Lil Carver say, just before the shot got her in the centre of the forehead and blew the back of her head off.

Carver moved faster than I would have thought possible, reached into his desk drawer and was halfway out of his seat in seconds. He didn't have time to aim the small pistol he'd retrieved; he just fired blindly in Swindley's direction. My response was an ingrained reflex, instant. All I saw before me was an enemy target. *Bang!* in the chest. Carver's gun dropped on the desk. He stared down at the red stain spreading across his shirt then up at me with a stunned look plastered all over his mush. – Dead man standing. I fired again. *Bang!* A head shot. Big man, little gun! Carver's bulky body tipped backwards, sending him and his chair crashing to the floor.

I'd seen dead and wounded soldiers and been shot at many times. That was a few years back with the Royal Logistic Corps in Bosnia and Iraq. And even though I'd honey-trapped for Joe, I'd never killed anyone. Not until that moment.

Joe had chucked up after his first kill. He'd been just eighteen. I was almost sixteen. I'd lured the guy out of a pub and into an alleyway where Joe was waiting to pop him. Afterwards, I'd gone straight home to cook dinner for my brother. The death of that stranger had meant nothing to me. One second he was there, the next he was gone. And the world moved on.

I turned to Swindley. He was stone-faced. 'Cheers!' He held up his bloodied left hand; there was a hole right through it. Carver's wild shot had taken its toll.

'Shit!' I said. 'Bet that hurts?'

He grimaced. 'Smarts a bit.' He turned towards the door. 'Gloria! Get in here!'

What was this? When she'd heard the car leaving, Lil Carver had said Gloria had gone shopping.

Gloria rushed in with a towel and wrapped it around Swindley's hand.

'Monica?' I said.

Gloria looked up from tending to Swindley. 'She's gone. She was never here. Understand?'

Swindley was clearly in real pain now. He tried to hide it but his face had turned as grey as his eyes. 'Brando is downstairs,' he said. 'I'll come with you.'

'No, Bert,' Gloria protested, and held on to his arm.

But he shook her off, tightened the towel around his hand and walked out of the room ahead of me. 'You stay there,' he instructed Gloria, 'while we get the lad away from that sick fuck in the basement.'

Swindley had not been thrown by Gloria's sudden appearance even though I had. But her blurting out the name Bert had him rattled. He checked himself in seconds but I'd picked up on it. I suspected that this carnage had been a plot hatched between the two of them. Gloria was to have hopped it while Swindley bumped off the Carver clan. My turning up had put the kybosh on that one. And Monica tear-arsing out of there had screwed it up even further. Snafu. And when everything goes tits up, improvise, soldier. But my mind was on Brando and getting to him as soon as.

A discreet door beneath the curved staircase led to the cellar and Swindley indicated that he would follow me down. 'After you,' he said, 'and make like you're my prisoner.'

Not so fast, mate. Just because I've saved your miserable life doesn't mean I trust you not to top both Brando and me.

He must have read my thoughts. 'Help me with these, will you?'

I put both guns back into their holsters for him. With one dodgy mitt he'd be a piece of cake to overpower and he knew that as well as I did.

'Won't the bloke in the cellar have heard the shots?'

'Doubt it. It's totally soundproofed down there.

Of course it would be, Carver didn't want to disturb Mummy, did he? Couldn't let her hear the agonised screams of his victims. I shuddered at the thought and hoped that pervert down there had kept his hairy paws off Brando.

At the bottom of the concrete stairs was a metal door, closed tight. Swindley banged on it with this uninjured hand. 'Swindley here,' he shouted. 'Open up.'

I heard the scrape of a bolt and slowly the door swung open. Just a few feet inside the room, I saw Brando sitting on what looked like an army bed. His eyes were red and he had a snotty nose. He wore a pair of shorts and his knees were scraped raw. It looked as though he'd been sick down the front of his T-shirt. He jumped up when he saw me but I motioned with my hand for him to stay put.

The figure that had opened the door emerged from behind it and glared at me from beneath beetle brows. He was about five feet nothing and wore a pair of paint-spotted jeans. His filthy white shirt was open to the waist, revealing a mat of thick black hair that spread from his neck to below his navel. His feet were bare on the concrete floor. 'No cunts allowed in here,' he grumbled.

'Go into the back room, Arthur.' Swindley's Birmingham accent was back with a vengeance.

The beast scratched his chin with a hairy hand, clearly uncertain about what to do. He ran his thick red tongue across already wet lips. 'I'll take the boy with me.'

'Leave him here,' Swindley said. 'Seeing this will be a lesson to him. Teach him a bit of respect.'

But Chimp was not convinced. He looked down at Swindley's hand swathed in a bloody towel. 'What happened to you?'

'Cut myself shaving.'

Chimp, unnerved, backed away and made a sudden grab for Brando. He pulled the boy in front of him as a shield. 'He's mine.' He stroked Brando's neck with his long-nailed paw.

'Not a good idea, Arthur.' Swindley spoke gently, as though to a small child. 'Now you do as you're told.'

Chimp started towards the door at the rear of the cellar, dragging a terrified Brando with him. 'Big Jim gave him to me as a present. He's mine.'

Swindley faced down the retreating Chimp. 'Now, Arthur,' he said. 'Don't be silly.'

He continued to shuffle backwards with one arm around Brando's neck.

Brando gave me a pleading look. 'Sam,' he said, his eyes welling up with tears.

Chimp clamped his other hand across Brando's mouth. Brando bit him and he grunted but kept a firm grip. Brando struggled and kicked backwards. Chimp tightened his hold and left Brando struggling to breathe. I took off straight at him. Don't touch my kid, you vile piece of shit! He must have clocked the look on my face because he panicked, let go of Brando, pushed him towards me, turned and made for the door at the rear. I was going full tilt but Brando dodged out of my way and I threw myself at Chimp. I turned as I body-slammed him and got him in the back of the neck with my shoulder. He went down hard and we both crashed to the floor. He was winded and groggy but he was strong and trying to get up from beneath me. I sat on him with my full weight, grabbed his greasy hair and pounded his head against the concrete floor. Once, twice, three times. Consumed with anger, I was about to beat the bastard's brains out.

Swindley moved fast and dragged me off him. 'You need him alive,' he said. 'When the police get here, Arthur will blub like a baby. Without Carver, he's nothing. He'll tell them where the bodies are buried. He's a pervert and he's a cretin.'

We dragged the unconscious Chimp by his feet, dumped him into the back cell-like room and bolted the door. I turned back and saw Brando sitting on the bed; he was crying. I went over and sat beside him, put my arms around him and tried to comfort him but he was still quivering with fright. I looked at my watch. It was over an hour since I'd entered the lion's den. I hoped and prayed that Wendy Morrison would be champing at the bit beyond the gates at ten sharp with armed backup.

'The police will be here in a few minutes,' I said with some optimism.

Swindley smiled. It looked odd, like it was an alien expression. 'Good girl,' he said. 'I knew you'd have a contingency plan. Joe was a good teacher. Now, if you don't mind, I'll take my leave of you before the constabulary arrive. Got to see the quack about this hand.'

'What about Gloria?'

'She'll back you up,' he said. 'She's no fool.'

'How will you get out?'

'I have my ways,' he said. He made for the door then turned. 'And by all means, tell them it was the mysterious Mr Swindley who did for this lot. My missus is itching for me to retire to the sun.' Then he was gone.

I could hear Chimp moaning from behind the locked door. The red haze that had enveloped me had lifted. I'd let the police deal with him. His current pain was well deserved.

Brando was still shaking and crying. 'They killed Mac,' he said. 'I thought you were dead too.'

'I'm fine, Brando,' I reassured him. 'And Mac is in intensive care at the hospital.'

'He's not dead?' His eyes were wide with amazement.

'I do hope not. But he's in good hands and he's as tough as old boots, that one.'

Swindley had left the door to the cellar open and I heard banging, as the front door was smashed open. Gloria was screaming and I could hear voices in the house upstairs. Wendy Morrison shouted my name.

'We're down here,' I called up.

I heard footsteps on the concrete stairs as she came down, followed by two armed officers. 'Jesus Christ, Sam,' she said. 'What the hell's going on? It's a fucking massacre up there.'

Chapter Thirty-Five
11 a.m., Saturday, 5 July

I decided to take Brando out through the door that led to the garden. Didn't want him to catch a glimpse of the carnage. To get there, we had to walk through the kitchen where Gloria was sitting. She was white-faced with shock, in paroxysms of tears and being consoled by a policewoman. Now I knew where Monica had inherited her acting talent. If I hadn't been there to witness what went down, I'd have believed Gloria too. She put on quite a convincing show.

'It's a good thing Monica left early, eh, Sam?' Gloria snuffled into a paper hankie.

'Please don't speak to other witnesses, Mrs Kelso,' the police-woman advised her gently.

Gloria collapsed into sobs once more. 'Oh, I'm sorry,' she said, 'I don't know about these things.' She plucked another tissue from the box and proceeded to make it soggy with her despair.

'There, there, dear.' The policewoman patted Gloria's convulsing shoulders. 'Let me make you a nice cup of tea.'

And the Oscar goes to . . .

'What's wrong with Gloria?' Brando said as we exited the utility room. He seemed curious rather than concerned.

'She's had a terrible shock,' I said. 'Uncle Jim's been killed.'

'How did he die? Did somebody shoot him?'

'Yes.' There was no point in fudging the subject. This was going to cause one hell of a media circus. He'd find out sooner or later, so rather from me than anyone else. 'It's a terrible thing.'

'Good.' His expression showed a grim resolve. 'Dad always said some people don't deserve to live.' He looked up at me and grinned. 'Except for you and me, and Mac.'

'Your dad didn't say that, though.'

'He would do. If he was here.'

———

Brando was a real little trouper at the police station but only after he insisted that Wendy Morrison ring the hospital in Norwich for an update on Mac's progress. And he demanded to be told the whole truth and nothing but. The news was not great. Surgeons had removed the bullet and, though it had missed any major organs, Mac remained in a coma.

'People come out of comas all the time, don't they?' Brando looked hopeful.

'Sometimes they do,' I said, as truthfully as I could manage.

'They burst in when Mac was putting me to bed,' Brando told Morrison. 'He was trying to protect me, but they shot him. Then the big baldy guy kicked him in the head when he was on the floor.'

'Could you recognise these men again?' Morrison asked him.

'I can do better than that,' he said. 'I can tell you their names.'

Brando had seen both of Carver's heavies before. Nobody ever takes any notice of little kids, he had told me. They don't realise that they're listening, or watching, just in case you ever need to know.

The police picked up both men within a few hours and Brando identified them over a video link.

When asked, he said that Chimp hadn't touched him sexually but had stroked him. 'Like I was a pussycat or something. So I put my fingers down my throat and made myself sick all down my T-shirt. He pulled a face and told me I was stinking the place up but he didn't come too close after that.'

'That's quite a trick,' Morrison said. 'Where did you learn that one?'

'Gloria told me,' he said. 'She said some man had tried to rape her once, so she threw up on him and he just smacked her in the mouth instead.'

Morrison gave me a look that said, who the hell is this kid?

I shrugged. Grandmotherly advice from Gloria Kelso; doesn't it warm your cockles?

DS Trevor Jones took Brando upstairs to the police canteen for some grub while Morrison continued interviewing me. According to the word later circulating the nick, the boy got a standing ovation from the snacking cops for identifying the two heavies.

I made a statement about Swindley, but left out the bit about him being Joe Murphy's uncle. 'He didn't say much, just that it was personal.'

'Birmingham accent, you said?' Those azure eyes searched my face.

'Broad.' I hoped that Swindley had reverted to his everyday persona and departed for warmer climes with his ever-loving wife.

I was presented with what seemed like hundreds of police photos in an effort to identify Swindley. Each time I flicked over a page I wondered if my facial expression would give me away should I recognise him. But he wasn't in any of the pictures, possibly had no record of any kind, so I wasn't compromised. I helped compose a photo-fit with a police artist and it was a reasonably accurate likeness but, in truth, could have matched a quarter of the middle-aged male population.

'Carver told me that the Cohens' solicitor, Richard Bloom, was in on this,' I told Morrison.

'We're looking for him,' she said.

Her comment seemed odd at the time, after all, Richard should be easy to contact, but I dismissed it. Right now, my main concern was Brando.

The police doctor suggested a sedative for Brando but he refused to take it. 'My dad got stung by a jellyfish once,' he said. 'And he didn't take anything for the pain. And Chimp-man wasn't half as bad as any jellyfish.' So that was the end of that. The doc also suggested we stay in a hotel but I felt that the kid needed to be somewhere familiar.

'Look, the doctor said Brando is unharmed, so I'd like to take him home.'

Morrison seemed unsure but it was probably obvious that I'd given her everything I was going to right now. I was being treated as a victim rather than a suspect. 'Okay,' she said. 'Take the boy home, get some sleep and call me in the morning.'

'We'll be going to see Mac in the hospital tomorrow.'

'Then call me from Norwich. I've got to liaise with the force there anyway. The shooting and kidnap happened on their manor so I have to be diplomatic.'

'Any news on who sent me the text?' Maybe the police techies could find out.

'We're working on it. But it's not exactly a priority right now.'

'Did you pick up Monica?' If the police had been outside the gates when she drove out, surely they'd stopped her.

Gloria's improvised message to me in the kitchen, when she was playing the role of innocent bystander, told me that she'd heard something about that and wanted to get our stories in line with each other.

'Monica Cohen?' Morrison appeared unconcerned and shuffled through some papers on her desk. 'The uniforms stopped her. She said she'd been visiting the old lady.' Morrison was reading from a cop's notebook. 'She confirmed James Carver's presence in the house. As well as you, Gloria Kelso and Swindley.'

'And Brando?'

'She made no mention of either Brando or Arthur Caine.'

'Did she come to the station?'

'We had no reason to detain her.' Morrison flashed an accusatory look at me. 'If I'd known what was going down in there, then that would have been a very different matter. But, under the circumstances, she was allowed to go on her way.'

'She's Carver's niece,' I said. 'I think she knew about the kidnap.'

Morrison reached for her phone. 'Find the Cohen woman,' she said. 'Ask her to come in for questioning.'

Morrison offered me Trevor Jones as an escort home but I refused and she appeared to be relieved. In addition to attempting to find Monica, they had two murderous fish to fry, both of whom were in no-comment mode. No denials, no nothing. Those two were professional villains who might never break, even when presented with incontrovertible evidence. Turning over their respective gaffs would take time. As their boss was now gracing the morgue with his presence, he wasn't available for comment either. And Chimp was under armed guard at a hospital somewhere with suspected concussion.

But with Monica on the loose I had to get Brando to safety. I knew every inch of the Cohen house, so I decided to go back there.

Chapter Thirty-Six
10 p.m., Saturday, 5 July

Monica sat in the airport lounge and glanced at the plane ticket in her hand. Cut and run, Gloria had said to her in the kitchen of the Carver house. She'd handed her two sets of keys. 'That's for my car. Get out of here, now. That's the key to my flat. Stay there and don't budge until I come for you.'

When Monica had fled the Carver house and the uniformed cops flagged her down a few hundred yards along the road, she'd smiled her best smile, fluttered her false eyelashes and played the innocent to the hilt. At the time, all she'd seen was one police car but once out of their sight, she'd texted Gloria just in case.

You may have company. Be ready.

Kidnapping Brando had been the most stupid thing Lil Carver had ever signed off on. The old crone was losing it, for sure. And Monica had no idea why the Carvers had sent a car for her so early in the morning. She'd bet money that Garcia was involved, what with all those hushed phone calls between him and Big Jim. If Sam Riley hadn't turned up on the bounce, she was sure the Carvers would have put her in the picture. They'd never have involved her if they hadn't needed her to do something for them. That had always been the way of it. Be a stripper, seduce Benny, kill his missus. Blah-de-fuckin'-blah.

When she'd got to Gloria's place earlier that morning, it was as neat as she remembered it, though she'd not visited it very often. Gloria wasn't her idea of any kind of a mother, so why bother to try and pretend. Of course she could never let on about it, seeing as Benny had no inkling. Best to keep it on an employer-employee footing, Gloria had said. And that suited Monica down to the ground.

The day had dragged, so she'd paced the floor and smoked her way through two packs of fags. She didn't like this set-up one little bit but the urgency in Gloria's voice had tripped her sense of self-preservation to red alert. Go! It had screamed at her. Go, now!

Gloria had rung the doorbell at five. She looked like hell. 'You get yourself out of the country,' she warned. 'A landslide of shit is about to engulf us.'

'What the fucking hell is all this about?'

'You've got some mouth on you, girl.' Gloria tutted and opened the windows. 'And don't smoke in my place. It's a disgusting habit.' She turned on the TV. *Newsflash: Gangland Killings in Essex.*

'The less you know about that the better,' Gloria said. 'I'm trying to protect you, Monica.' She crossed the room to where her laptop sat on a desk in the corner. 'Book a flight to Spain and stay in that posh villa of yours. I'll let you know when it's safe to come back.'

'Who's dead?'

'My mother and brother. But Sam Riley and Brando got away okay.' Gloria stared at her. There was a hardness in her face that Monica had never spotted before. 'Not that you give a damn.'

'Am I in the clear?'

'Only if you do as you're told for once in your life.'

Gatwick airport, ten at night and they were calling the last flight for Murcia. Monica had purchased a small suitcase at the airport and filled it with clothes she'd bought from the various shops. They weren't up to her usual designer-label standard but she could splash out once she got to the Costa del Sol. She had a key to one of Benny's safety deposit boxes in a Spanish bank and that was bursting at the seams with readies.

She stood up to make her way through security, then stopped and sat down again. What the hell was she running from? This could be the opportunity of a lifetime. Lil and Big Jim Carver were pushing up the daisies and it had been none of her doing. With Sam Riley and Brando as witnesses, Swindley would have hoofed it, so she was safe from him. She could easily deal with Gloria on her own. Her best bet now would be to link up with Gerard Fowley. He was a bit of a nutjob but he was a businessman first and foremost. Yes, that's what she'd do. Fuck all this pissing off and hiding bullshit. That was not her style at all. Never had been, never would be. She'd rather stand and fight. Anyway she hated that bloody villa in Andalucía. What would she do there? Sunbathe and drink herself into oblivion? Get herself another Spanish lover? That was a game strictly for losers. She was never going to be under the thumb of any man, ever again.

She tore up the plane ticket and headed to the airport's five-star hotel. Spend the night there and think it out. Now, *that* was a plan.

Chapter Thirty-Seven
1 a.m., Sunday, 6 July

When we got to the Cohen place, Brando was asleep in the back of the car, tucked under a blanket. I glanced back at him. I was just two weeks into being his guardian and look what a mess we were in already. When we approached the gates, I could see the lights still on in the house. The automatic timer was due to switch them off at two, so I felt reassured that everything was okay. I pressed the remote in my pocket and the gates parted. I drove in and was about to open the garage doors when a shadow in the shrubbery alerted me that something was not as it should be. I looked at the front window of the house and spied a silhouette flit across it, briefly illuminated by the light within the room.

Full reverse at top whack jolted Brando from his dreams.

'Stay down and hang on,' I said, about to do a brake-turn to get us the hell out of there. 'Cover yourself with the blanket and stay still.'

Sudden whipcracks of sound were followed by two thuds that rocked the car as the back tyres were hit. A slightly built figure emerged from the tall bushes adjacent to the gates. One more suppressed shot and the offside front wheel collapsed. The car hurtled into the wrought-iron M and came to a sickening halt. Maria Garcia stepped out into the drive. She was holding a machine pistol and she indicated with the barrel that I should get out of the car. I wasn't about to argue as she wielded an HK MP5K, the short-barrelled darling of the SAS, used for close protection work. I dumped my keys on the front passenger seat. 'Stay calm,' I said to Brando, without turning my head in his direction. He had to stay hidden so she didn't suss he was in the car. With my mobile still being looked at by police forensics, he'd have to get indoors to call for help. 'Wait five minutes. Once I'm in the house, sneak down the drive, get into my flat and phone the police. Give DI Morrison's name.'

'Okay.' His muffled voice came from beneath the blanket.

'Stay put in the flat until the police arrive. No matter what you hear. Understand?'

I got out of the car with my hands raised and prayed that, for once, Brando would do as he was told.

Maria Garcia had the gun pointed directly at my mid-section. One twitch on the trigger and I'd be cut in half. Thankfully she didn't look inside the car but concentrated on dealing with me.

'In house,' she said.

Had I been on my own, I would have tried to get into a position to tackle her, but, with Brando hunkered down in the car, I couldn't risk it. Any accidental stray shots might hit him. I was stymied. I had to face whatever waited for me inside the house to give Brando a chance to get to my flat above the garage and phone the police.

This had all the hallmarks of another double-cross by Monica. Carver had told me Felipe Garcia was being packed off to Spain but the door to the house was now open and I could see the outline of Garcia haloed in the light from the hallway. If Monica was in there too then it might be Goodnight Vienna for me. But how had they got into the house? The only other set of keys was at Richard

Bloom's office. I silently cursed the man and wished all the torments of hell on the two-faced bastard.

Garcia gave me a sardonic grin as I approached the door. He stood nonchalantly with a sawn-off shotgun balanced in the crook of his arm. Jesus, these Spaniards didn't mess about. But something didn't smell right. If this was supposed to be just a meet with Monica, then why come all tooled up?

The lights were on in the sitting room and Richard Bloom was perched on one of the white leather sofas. He looked like shit. His shirt was out of his pants and he'd obviously been roughed up. His hands were bound in front of him with one of his own expensive silk ties.

'Sam!' The colour drained from his face, like someone had just walked across his grave. 'They told me you were dead.'

'Not yet,' I said. 'But no thanks to you.'

'Sit by him,' Garcia snarled. 'Keep quiet. We wait.'

There was no sign of Monica. That had to be who they were waiting for. But where was she?

'I had nothing to do with this,' Bloom whispered when I sat down beside him. 'They came to my office just after eleven this morning. They ransacked the place and threatened to kill me if I didn't cooperate. They took the house keys and finally brought me here at gunpoint.'

'How long have you been here?'

'Hours. They're waiting for someone.'

'My guess is Monica.' But where was she?

'Shut up!' Garcia pointed the gun towards us while his sister came into the room and spoke in his ear. My heart flew into my mouth. Had she spotted Brando? But Garcia's expression didn't change, he merely nodded and Maria walked calmly towards the kitchen. It was all I could do to stop myself from breathing a sigh of relief.

I looked sideways at Bloom. I'd rarely seen a man look more frightened. His cheek was bruised and he flinched when he reached up to touch it with his bound hands.

'Look, Felipe,' I said to Garcia. 'There's no call for this rough stuff. You need this man to get the papers signed once Monica gets here.'

'How you know this?' Garcia glared at me with suspicion etched all over his face.

'It's obvious. Monica wants to be Brando's guardian again. That way she gets her hands on Benny Cohen's money and you get the nightclubs. Am I right?'

'We no need you.' His stance told me he was about to take me outside and put an end to me.

'Well, maybe you do.' I tried to sound calm, as reasonable as I could manage while staring down the barrel of a shotgun. He looked doubtful but listened. 'I'm Brando's legal guardian. If you kill me, and I disappear, it may take months, years even, for Monica to get Brando back.' I turned to Bloom, hoping he'd catch on and back me up. 'Isn't that right Mr Bloom?'

'Yes,' he agreed shakily, but then he appeared to get a grip on his emotions once more, become more composed. 'You'll find English law very different from that of your home country, Señor Garcia.'

'Stupid,' Garcia said. 'Monica is *madre.*'

'Stepmother.' I corrected him.

'What is stepmother?' Garcia looked puzzled.

'*Madrastra,*' Bloom said, and he followed up with a stream of Spanish I didn't understand.

Garcia appeared gobsmacked momentarily, although he checked the surprise on his face quickly. The fact that Monica was not Brando's real mother was not something she had shared with her new paramour. Oh, Felipe, spider-trapped just like the rest of us.

Maria came back into the room and stood guard while Garcia went to the kitchen to eat whatever she had cooked for him. It smelt like eggs and ham.

'Can I untie him?' I asked her. 'His hands are turning blue.'

She nodded but raised the sawn-off higher, aiming it directly at me, as though I hadn't already got the message.

'What did you just say to him?' I made a big show of undoing the slippery knots in the silk tie that bound Bloom's wrists. I hadn't been kidding about the hands. They were a decidedly unhealthy colour.

'Your signing the forms makes it legal with no need for involvement of the courts,' Bloom explained.

'Good. He looked convinced for now.'

'But what happens when Monica gets here?'

That was the million-dollar question. She'd driven away from the Carver house around half nine this morning, long before the cops kicked the doors in. That had been over twelve hours ago, so where was she? Why had she run off when everything seemed to be going her way? And when she knew the police were on the prowl, why hadn't she contacted Garcia to pull the plug on this little caper?

'We'll deal with that when it happens,' I said.

'Keep quiet,' Maria said, 'or I gag you.'

Bloom rubbed his waxy-looking mitts together and blew on his swollen fingers.

'Look, Maria,' I said. 'I'm cooperating here. I sign the papers and go on my way and you get what you want. I don't care one way or the other. There's no need for any more unpleasantness. The boy means nothing to me.'

She held me in a dark-eyed stare. 'You are not woman.'

'That's as maybe,' I said, 'but there's no excuse for bad manners. You could at least give us something to drink. Water, maybe, and some food?'

'I am not servant.'

Felipe came back into the room and Maria took her eyes off us for a second. I took the opportunity to glance at my watch. It was almost two in the morning. Had Brando called the cops? Keep talking, engage this brother and sister act in conversation for as long as possible before Monica turns up. But then, when she does, both Bloom and I might be dead meat. Although the thought of getting embroiled in a hostage situation – with the cops at the gates and two desperate Spaniards thinking they maybe had nothing to lose by shooting us – held no appeal either.

'Give them food,' Garcia told Maria. She pouted and walked back into the kitchen with a petulant toss of her shiny black locks. She reminded me of Monica with her spoilt-bitch act but I no longer found it remotely attractive and knew that I never would again.

'What is that?' Garcia cocked his head as a door creaked somewhere on an upper floor.

I tried to keep the sudden panic off my face. Please, please, don't let it be Brando roaming about upstairs. I'd told him to stay put in my flat above the garage.

'Cat,' I grasped at a straw. 'It's just the cat.'

'Maria!' Garcia yelled a stream of Spanish and she came running from the kitchen. He handed her his shotgun and nodded towards the stairs. She protested and they argued at high-speed. He rolled his eyes and headed upstairs unarmed. She turned the gun towards us.

A shot rang out from the top of the stairs, Maria's head jerked in that direction and she let out a panicked screech. Garcia's body tumbled down the stairs. I took the opportunity and flung myself forward at her. I grabbed her by the hair, punched her in the face and wrestled the gun from her grasp. The gun went off. Richard Bloom yelped. The shot peppered the far wall and shattered the huge mirror on the far side of the room, launching shards of glass into the air. Bloom collapsed to the floor and curled up into a ball as Maria screamed and tried to pull away from me. I punched her again and felt a knuckle crack. She went down hard and hit her head on one of those hideous marble-topped side tables that Monica had thought were so classy. Maria was out for the count.

I engaged the safety catch and threw the shotgun to Bloom who was on his knees and staring at me open-mouthed. The gun just missed his head as he recoiled in horror. It landed on the sofa.

'Keep an eye on her,' I said. 'Use that if you need to.'

Bloom, white-faced with shock, winced and stared back at the shotgun as though he'd rather turn it on himself than on anyone else.

'Well, if you won't shoot her, hit her with it. Or sit on her if she comes to.'

He nodded and got shakily to his feet.

I glanced into the kitchen and saw the MP5K on the breakfast counter where Maria had left it. I ran in and snatched it up.

'Brando!' I called up the stairs. 'Are you hurt?'

Nothing came back. I crossed to the stairs where Garcia lay sprawled. He looked in a bad way. I checked the pulse in his neck and noted that he was still breathing. He'd been hit in the stomach and was bleeding profusely. He'd come round any time soon but would, hopefully, be in too much pain to be dangerous. But where was Brando? I stepped across Garcia.

'It's Sam,' I shouted. 'Don't shoot me. I'm coming up.'

At the top of the stairs I saw him. The gun he'd fired was on the top stair and he'd been knocked off his feet by the recoil. I picked it up and rushed to his side. His eyes flickered open.

'Did I get him?'

'Oh, you got him, all right,' I said. 'But where did you find the gun?'

'Secret safe,' he replied. And he smiled.

Chapter Thirty-Eight

11 a.m., Sunday, 6 July

Wendy Morrison looked around the room. 'So what's the body count now?'

'Give me a break,' I said. 'How was I to know the phones had been disconnected? I was waiting for you to arrive with the cavalry. When he couldn't make a call, Brando took the initiative. He was scared they were going to kill me.' She looked sceptical. 'I take it you're not considering prosecuting him?'

'He is above the age of criminal responsibility.'

'We were all in danger. Just ask our solicitor in there.' Bloom was giving a statement to Trevor Jones in Benny's office. I made an attempt to keep my anger under control. Threatening *me* was one thing, but this was beyond the pale. I stared her down, my mind screaming. You go after Brando, lady, and I'll hit you with everything I've got. I'll take you and your precious career down with me, if necessary.

Morrison appeared to get my silent message because she looked away, shamefaced for once in her life.

Before the police had arrived, Bloom had intimated that I should say nothing about Garcia climbing the stairs empty-handed or that Brando had any knowledge that the gun he had used was loaded. I'd left the machine pistol at the top of the stairs alongside the handgun from the secret safe. My fingerprints would be on it but then so would those of the Garcia clan.

'And my breaking Maria Garcia's jaw was hardly excessive force in the face of two guns,' I reminded her. 'You saw the state of the car. Have you any doubt they would have used those guns on all of us?'

The doctor came downstairs. 'He'll be fine,' he said. 'He'll just have a bump the head. Nothing broken. He's a tough little chap.'

'Are you sure?' I asked as he headed for the door. 'Shouldn't he have an X-ray or something?'

'If he gets dizzy or vomits in the next few hours then you should call me straightaway. Otherwise, he'll be fine. Don't worry.' And with that he left the house.

'Where did the handgun come from?' Morrison was back on track and gave me one of her hard blue stares. I was getting used to them by now and they didn't faze me one little bit.

'Benny Cohen kept it in a safe, ready loaded.'

'You knew about that?'

'Not until it went off in Brando's hands.' That was my story and I was sticking to it.

'You know it's illegal to keep a loaded gun in the house?'

'Then I suggest you dig up Benny Cohen and prosecute him instead of hassling us.'

Morrison snorted her displeasure.

'Though, personally,' I said, 'I'm rather pleased about it. Otherwise that blood on the carpet may well have been mine and Richard Bloom's – or Brando's for that matter.'

Once the police had arrived at gone two in the morning, broken through the gates and entered the house, Garcia had been carted off to hospital in the first ambulance to arrive. The paramedics did their stuff and, with Garcia strapped in, they left, going like the clappers, police escort – the works. Garcia's sister was in the second ambulance, conscious by then, screaming blue murder, her dark eyes full of lethal intent. Senior officers arrived at four-ish but we had to wait for the SOCO team to turn up. They arrived all kitted out just after six. Morrison was called and finally got to the scene just after nine. By this time the house and grounds were overrun with police and there were reporters milling around the busted gates with their photographers and cameramen, capturing images of anything that moved. The shot-up Subaru had been hauled away by a police recovery vehicle. And it wasn't even midday.

Morrison handed me a clear plastic bag with my mobile phone inside.

'Don't you need it?' I asked her.

'The data has already been downloaded,' she said. 'And I need you contactable.'

Her own phone rang and she answered it. 'Oh, shit. That's all I need.' And she was up on her feet. 'Do I look like hell?' she asked me. 'Because I feel like it.'

'Does it matter?'

'Sure it does. There's a BBC TV crew outside and I've just been ordered to give them a briefing.' She ran her fingers through her red hair, took a deep breath and headed down the driveway to face her public.

I went up to Brando's room. A uniformed policewoman was sitting by his bed. He was fast asleep, looking like butter wouldn't melt. The door to his dressing room stood open, the rug was pushed to one side. I could see the top of the secret safe and the metal box we'd spotted at the bottom when we first opened it. The gun must have been kept in there.

Had he known it was loaded? I thanked the God I no longer believed in that it had been there, and that the boy had had the guts to do what he did. But at the same time, my soul clenched with the thought of what might have happened had Garcia climbed those stairs with a loaded shotgun in his hands. I was supposed to protect Brando, not the other way around. No more guns for you, young man.

Though he'd be bound to give me hell for my not letting him have a mobile phone. 'Of course,' Brando would say. 'If I'd had my own phone, I'd have been able to ring the police . . .' Guess I'd have to relent on that one.

The midday sun streamed through the windows. I could see the media mêlée outside of the gates and imagined Morrison giving them the routine police run around about 'incidents' and 'further statements to be issued at a later date'.

I could hear Brando snoring and nodded to the policewoman when she glanced across the room to me. We had to get away from this place; somewhere we could try to put all the violence and bad experiences behind us. I had loved the way Brando had responded to the countryside, the animals and to Mac. I recalled the excitement in his eyes, his laughter as I watched the little boy emerge from behind the tough façade. That was how a kid should be – wide-eyed with the wonder of the natural world and not some wise-arse with far too much knowledge of low-life scum. Maybe I could never erase those memories for him, but I was going to give it a damn good try.

Chapter Thirty-Nine
Monday, 7 July

Brando and I were at the hospital in Norwich. Once Brando got over the initial shock of seeing Mac hooked up to the machines in the intensive care unit, he became fascinated and started asking questions of the nursing staff. It was his way of coping. The ICU nurses were charmed by him and quite happy to explain what all the monitors were for. He was impressed by the gown and mask he had to wear whereas, for me, they were symbols of just how touch-and-go it was for Mac.

'Maybe I could be a doctor,' Brando suggested while we sat in the hospital canteen.

'Not a farmer, then? Or a musician?'

'I could be a doctor who owns a farm. What do you think?'

'You can be anything you set your mind to. How about mixing up the lot and becoming a vet?'

He grinned at me and sucked on his banana milkshake. 'Brilliant!'

We had booked into a hotel not far from the hospital and started trawling the estate agents for a property to rent. Staying by Mac's bedside was something I wanted to do more than anything else, but I couldn't subject the boy to an ordeal like that. He needed a diversion. There was no way that Brando was ever going back to chez Cohen. Once the police had given the all clear, the house would be cleared out, cleaned down and eventually sold up. In the meantime, we would remain in Norfolk, search for a new school for Brando and a new home. He was still rambling on about finding a farm, though I hoped he'd change his mind once he was aware of other possibilities. But the final decision had to be his. It was time for him to have some control over his young life.

Tuesday, 8 July

Bright and early in the morning, the first rental house we saw had everything I had asked the estate agent for: three bedrooms, three bathrooms, garden, games room – the lot. It even had a paddock. Brando was not happy.

'Don't want to live here,' he said.

The estate agent gave me one of those looks that a mother throws you when your child is playing up and hers is being a bloody little angel. I ignored her.

'It's not a farm,' Brando said.

'Not many farms for short-term rental.' She looked peeved.

'We can look for the perfect place afterwards,' I said. 'This is just for now.'

'I don't like this one.'

I shrugged and turned back to the agent. 'Alright, what's next?'

'I thought this one would be perfect but . . .' She gave Brando a pained smile, all mouth and blank eyes. 'There is one by the river.'

'River?' Brando's face lit up. 'I like rivers.'

The house was on the banks of the River Ant, a tributary of the extensive free-flowing inland waterways that make up the Norfolk Broads. The Ant is a seventeen-mile river, of which only eight miles are navigable by small pleasure craft. The nearby bridge that separated the Ant from the rest of the broads had a low clearance and the river had a speed limit of just four miles per hour. I didn't know much about boats but I reckoned there wasn't much chance of any James Bond-style attacks, or getaways, by water. And I had spotted plenty of neighbouring houses, so at least this place wasn't isolated. It had three bedrooms, an acre of land, a mooring dock and its own boathouse. Brando was entranced.

'We'll take it,' he said after exploring the inside of the house. 'I like this one.'

'It's a half-hour drive to any schools,' I cautioned. With Monica on the prowl, I'd have preferred to be closer to the town. But I wasn't going to discuss my concerns about security with Brando.

'There is public transport into Norwich,' the estate agent countered.

Brando gave her a look that would turn your average person into a pillar of salt but she was made of sterner stuff. 'Maybe when you're a little older,' she said. 'Just to give your mother a break from driving you around.'

The old Brando would have sneered and informed the woman that I was, in fact, his chauffeur. I stiffened, waiting for this retort but he didn't say anything of the sort. Instead he turned on his heel and went outside to look at the river.

He was standing on the deck when I found him. He didn't look at me but gazed at a couple of ducks slowly paddling by, quacking to each other, deep in some diverting ducky conversation.

'She thought you were my mum,' he said finally.

'It's an assumption people will make, I suppose,' I said. 'In future, we'll have to make it clear that I'm just your guardian.'

'I wish you *were* my mum.' He threw a disconsolate pebble into the water. Then he brightened. 'Can we have this house, Sam? I really like it.'

I pushed any worries I had about security to the back of my mind. I'd deal with them when the time came. 'If this is where you want to live, then fine by me.'

House sorted, we headed back to the hotel with Brando in the front passenger seat. It had been his choice ever since we left Essex. No words had been spoken – he'd just hopped in the front of the Mercedes, fastened the seat belt and grinned at me. Sam Riley: from chauffeur to guardian to mother-substitute in just a few short weeks.

I swallowed the lump in my throat.

'Can we buy a boat?'

'There's a lot to be arranged before we can buy anything,' I said. 'Anyway, this house is just for now. It's a lot smaller than you've been used to. There's no posh dressing room for you, or games room.'

'But there's a river. I've never had a river before. And we don't need a big place, do we? We just need a house for you and me and Mac to live in.'

'Mac? What makes you think Mac will be with us?'

'He'll need someone to look after him when he comes out of hospital.'

'Maybe Mac has family he'd rather go to?'

'He told me he has nobody. He's on his own too, Sam. We should look after him.'

'Well, we can ask him. But even if he does say yes, he may not want to stay for long.'

'He'll stay.' Brando had all the supreme confidence that an eleven-year-old can muster.

Back at the hotel I made an appointment via the registrar to visit a school on Wednesday morning. It was one of those establishments steeped in tradition, close to the cathedral.

'Unless you want me to find a Jewish school for you,' I said, suddenly aware that the lad might not want to attend somewhere so closely linked to the Christian faith.

'What would I want to do that for?'

'Well, Jewish heritage and all that.'

'Dad always said that religion is for mugs,' he said. 'And if you think this is a good school, then I don't care. So long as I don't have to go back to the other one.'

Not in a million years. The summer holidays were just around the corner but that place would be alive with rumours. Everyone would know that the Cohen house had been at the centre of even more trouble. There may even be reporters buzzing around the school. Though I was hopeful that the shootings at the Carver residence would take the newshounds in that direction and that nobody would put two and two together. Some hope.

'Samantha Riley?' The call on my mobile was from a number I didn't recognise.

'Who's this?'

'Dave Wright from the *Globe* news desk, Miss Riley.'

Now there was an oxymoron if ever there was one. The *Globe* was the raggiest of tabloid rags. This was not a good sign. They must be short of bed-hopping love rats to wag the finger at, or running scared of wife-beating footballers and their High Court injunctions.

I ended the call immediately and used the hotel phone to ask reception if there was a mobile phone shop nearby.

The local shopping malls had loads of phone shops vying for our business. And of all the mobile companies in all the malls, I had to walk into *that* one. There she was: Jill, my only other same-sex amour. I had rescued Little Jill from the clammy grasp of Ann, a dyke with muscles that could put Sylvester Stallone to shame. Neither woman lasted long in the army. Ann went off to become Andy and probably didn't need huge doses of testosterone to switch gender. Jill took the more conventional way out. Shag a soldier – one with a penis. Up the stick and out the door in a few easy moves. 'Is that you, Sam?' Jill came around the counter and I noted that her blue corporate uniform stretched to bursting point over her now matronly figure. Little Jill had morphed into Big Jill.

Brando purposely placed himself between us as Jill smiled down at him. 'Is he yours?'

'Yes,' he said, forcefully. I didn't argue.

We got our new phones and Jill handed me a card with her home number on it. 'Keep in touch,' she said.

Brando and I sat at a coffee shop in the food court. He sucked noisily on his milkshake and glared at me.

'What's wrong with you?'

'Was that woman a friend of yours?'

'From the army,' I said.

'Was she a *friend* like Monica was a friend?'

'Don't know what you mean.' But I did.

'I'm not stupid,' he said. 'I know you slept in Monica's room. It's disgusting!'

Now he hit me with it, in public, in the middle of a shopping mall – the little shit, I could have wrung his neck. 'What do *you* know about anything?' I said. 'You don't even wank yet.'

The woman on the adjacent table tutted loudly and her expression was of the turn-to-stone variety. I stared back at her. Screw you, lady, with your cosy middle-class values. Fuck you, *and* the horse you rode in on. She quickly looked away.

'You'd be surprised,' Brando sulked.

'Shut up and suss out how these bloody new phones work, will you.'

Chapter Forty
4 p.m., Tuesday, 8 July

The man in the bed propped himself up on his elbow and gazed down at the woman beside him. In all the years he'd known her she'd never been a looker, but the last couple of days, she'd really smartened herself up. He'd always believed that their twice-yearly flings had been just that and no more. But this time, after she'd finally told him the whole truth, he'd seen her in a different light. She was stronger and more resilient than he would ever have imagined. He realised now that he must have loved her all along. His other women had been fun for a time but he had always returned to Gloria. If that's not love, what is?

The fact that Janine was his daughter was the biggest shock. But he'd done the maths and realised that it had to be true. And he knew what he'd have said if Gloria had told him she was pregnant all those years back: get an abortion. And she'd have known that too. She'd already had one baby dragged away from her and she wasn't going to lose another. So she'd taken up with that gobshite Tommy Kelso; a junkie so stupid that, once ensconced in the Carver inner circle, he'd stolen money from Lil Carver then legged it up north. Bad move. Even then, Gloria tried to protect her husband and had him arrested rather than murdered. But Lil's talons reached deep into the prison system in those days and Tommy Kelso had supposedly OD'd in his cell.

Gloria opened her eyes and smiled up at him. 'How's the hand?'

'I'll never play the fiddle again,' he said. 'But everything else is in working order.'

She laughed. 'Yeah, I noticed. Want to do it again?'

'Give me half an hour.'

'It's time you retired, Bert,' she said, adopting a more serious tone.

'Well, as one of my main sources of income is no more, then I have to agree with you.'

'I'll get our Janine set up nicely here and then we can go anywhere we like together. I've always fancied Rio.'

Rio sounded good to him, what with all those luscious samba queens . . . But maybe those days were over and he could finally settle down with a woman who knew him for who and what he was, rather than having to pretend all the time. It can wear a man out. Though, of course, there was still Monica to contend with.

'She can look after herself – always has, always will,' Gloria said.

'She might go back to Garcia, I suppose.'

'He's yesterday's news. She's done with him. She'll have another scheme going. She'll be all right.'

'I'm going to check out Garcia, anyway.'

'Why bother? The sister's already been nicked for kidnapping that Bloom character and Garcia will be facing the same charges once he's out of hospital.'

'Consequences, Gloria. Everything has consequences. I'd deem it best if Señor Garcia never recovers.'

She reached under the bedclothes and grabbed him. 'Oh, Mr Swindley,' she cooed. 'You are so thorough.'

'You bet your firm little arse, I am.'

Chapter Forty-One
7 p.m., Tuesday, 8 July

Since every stitch of clothing we owned was either at Bloom's cottage or the Cohen house, I bought new gear for us both and with those purchases and our new phones we returned to the hotel. Brando was putting all his stuff away, so I took the opportunity to ring Wendy Morrison but was told she was off-duty. I phoned Richard Bloom only to get an answering machine. I decided not to leave a message. Would he have put reporters on our case? I doubted it, not seeing any advantage for him in that, but I didn't want to take any chances.

We were alone again, just Brando and me. Out in the cold with the tabloids sniffing about. My heart sank. Had I really believed we could walk away from all the carnage unscathed? How stupid was that?

Brando was soon bored with his new phone and turned the television on in his room to watch cartoons. I tried Bloom again and got him at once.

'Where are you?' he asked. 'I've been trying to reach you.'

'I'm in a hotel with Brando. Being hassled by a hack from the *Globe*, so I've changed my phone.' I gave him the new number. 'I've got to call DI Morrison and let her have it too.'

'I wouldn't do that,' Bloom said. 'She's on extended leave.'

'What does that mean?'

'Don't know for sure, the police aren't very forthcoming. But it sounds like some kind of internal investigation to me. Either way, she's out of the picture. Best let the police deal with you and Brando through me. Come and see me tomorrow morning.'

'I have an appointment to see Brando's new school.'

'Change it. I think you have more pressing problems at this moment in time.'

'And this reporter?'

'Ring him back on your old number. Tell him you have no comment to make. If he persists, refer him to me. Give him my office number, not this one. And don't talk to anyone else unless I say so.'

I could hear *The Simpsons* coming from Brando's room and he was chortling away at the bloodbath antics of Itchy and Scratchy. Thankfully, that gave me time to think. Wendy Morrison being investigated? She had withheld evidence and she still had the photo of Joe and me. If that ever came to light, then all of my plans for Brando were in danger. What would happen to the lad if I ended up in prison? I had to do something but couldn't work out a plan at this point.

I turned my old mobile on. It held ten messages. Eight were from the tabloid reporter, all wanting 'my side of the story'. One was from Richard Bloom and the final one was Wendy Morrison. I rang Wright from the *Globe* first.

'Ah, Miss Riley. We understand you were present during the gangland shootings at the house of Big Jim Carver.'

'No comment.'

'We know you worked for Monica Cohen.'

'No comment.'

'Oh, come on, Miss Riley. This is common knowledge. We're not asking you to talk about the shootings, we're just looking for a bit of background here.'

My brother and his wife had cooperated with the newspapers when Tom had disappeared. They'd been well and truly stitched up by the media, portrayed to look as guilty as sin. Give the tabloids something and they start digging the dirt; give them nothing and they swiftly move on. That was the lesson I had learned.

I gave him Richard Bloom's office number, ended the call and made the decision to ring Wendy Morrison. It was all very well for Bloom to warn me off her, because to him she was just the investigating officer. But for me, she might very well be my lifeline. I had to speak to her.

She did not sound her usual cool self. 'We need to meet,' she said. 'How about tomorrow afternoon at our first meeting place?'

'One,' I suggested.

'Fine.'

So I had to meet Bloom in the morning and Morrison at one, but what to do with Brando? I couldn't drag him along with me. I could take him with me to Bloom maybe but not to see Morrison.

I made one more call, this time to his guitar tutor.

'Hey,' the lazy voice said. 'Is Brando okay? There's been a lot of talk about the filth rampaging through the kid's house. I've heard that the Carver clan have been murdered. Heavy stuff, man.'

'Troubled times,' I said. 'Can Brando come to you for a few hours tomorrow? I need to sort stuff out and don't want to drag him around with me.'

'Sure he can. We can jam. And my kids are off school right now so they can keep him company.'

'This has to be discreet, Mr Watts. There might be tabloid reporters on the prowl.'

'Hey, it's Mike. And that scum don't get anywhere near my family, or me!' He sounded vehement. I seemed to recall some lurid drug-related stories about him in the newspapers in the past. So I hoped he was as belligerent towards the press as he sounded and that I could believe him. But any port in a storm.

'Sam!' Brando's voice came from his room and he sounded agitated.

I rushed through the interconnecting door to see him white-faced, staring at the TV screen. A newsreader was jabbering away and the banner beneath her screamed *Gangland Killings*. But it was the photo flashed up behind her that was the most disturbing. It had been taken from just behind my viewpoint at Benny Cohen's funeral. It was grainy but clearly showed Lil Carver in her wheelchair with Monica bending down to speak to her and Big Jim Carver handing his mother a handkerchief. Brando was in the shot, too, but his back was to the camera. I hadn't seen this photo before in the news coverage of the funeral. At the time, the media had been kept in check with promises of a press conference. It was possible that some freelance paparazzo had been standing on a ladder behind the high fence that surrounded the cemetery taking photos with a telephoto lens. But if so, then why hadn't the images appeared in the tabloids at the time? This photograph was grainy and out of focus but it packed more punch than the heads-down images of the family or the formal photos of Morrison's press conference that the papers had on tap during the coverage on the day.

I mentally retraced my steps at the funeral, placed myself back there and took up my position once more. The cops had been in front of me, the assembled villainous types in various groups all around. But right behind me, in a direct line to take this photo, had been Gerard Fowley and his henchmen.

Chapter Forty-Two

10 a.m., Wednesday, 9 July

We set off from Norwich early and I dropped Brando at Mike's farm. Mike Watts had told Brando the history of the place and the kid, always fascinated by that sort of stuff, had related it to me. Apparently parts of the house were over 400 years old. I wondered what the ghosts of generations of previous inhabitants made of the raucous rock music that emanated from the converted barn. The poor lost souls probably went around with their fingers in their ears. The squall of electric guitars stopped suddenly and I could hear the sound of young voices arguing. Must be the kids of Mike's rock school practising for yet another small club gig where parents stood around smiling proudly while regular punters made a beeline for the exit sign.

Mike swaggered out to greet us, wearing black leather jeans and a white shirt, every inch the Byronic rock star.

'The kid's welcome to stay with us for as long as you need,' he offered. 'Any press come knocking and I'll set the dogs on them. Or my wife – she's Russian, you know. She scares the shit out of me.'

'I haven't got my guitar,' Brando said. It was still at Bloom's cottage and we were waiting for the Norfolk police to allow us back in to collect our stuff.

'That's cool,' Mike said, 'you can borrow one of mine.'

'Can I use the Strat?'

'Sure, or the Les Paul if you like.'

Brando could hardly contain his excitement but he gave me a goodbye hug before he and Mike walked towards the house, nattering about guitars. I watched Brando go, astonished by his resilience. Everything that had happened: Mac being injured, the kidnap and Brando's encounter with Chimp would be enough to turn most kids into a gibbering wreck or a catatonic recluse. Add to that, Brando putting a bullet into Felipe Garcia and I'd have thought he'd be in dire need of counselling. But it seemed nothing had touched him at all. Maybe one day I'd have to deal with the fall-out but, for now, he seemed on a fairly even keel. And all I could do in the meantime was care for him and try to protect him.

Bloom was apologetic and grateful. He gave me a black American Express card – I'd never seen one before. Even Monica didn't have one of those – hers had been platinum and she'd flashed it about like she was the Queen of Sheba. If she ever found out about this she'd be seething with envy.

'In case you need anything,' Bloom suggested. 'You're free to use it as you see fit. Pay the first six months' rent on the house in Norfolk up front. School fees, anything Brando needs or wants. No limit.'

That was not a message I was about to pass on to Brando with all his talk about horses and boats and farms. He was going to learn the value of money.

I also got the impression that Bloom would bend over backwards to try and protect us from both the journalists and the police.

'Detective Chief Inspector,' he looked at his notes, 'Evans, that's his name. He wants an interview with you and Brando. He'll do it here, in this office sometime next week, at your convenience.'

'I thought the police would want to see us before then.' Wendy Morrison and her team had taken statements from us both on the day of Garcia's shooting. Bloom had been with us and, on his discreet advice, we'd limited the information we gave to the bare minimum. But I knew that wouldn't be the end of the matter.

'The police have got their hands full digging up the Carvers' gardens and that could take weeks. Arthur Caine is being highly cooperative, it seems.'

Swindley had assured me that Chimp would confess all. He'd obviously been right.

'I'm still concerned that the police may try to prosecute Brando for firing the gun.'

'Given the circumstances, it's highly unlikely. But if the CPS does want to have a go, I have an MP friend who is currently lobbying Parliament to have the age of criminal responsibility raised to twelve. It doesn't stand much chance at the moment, but the CPS would have to tread carefully. Especially considering the traumatic events the boy has so recently suffered. They'd also be aware we could bring enough expert witnesses to blow any proposed prosecution out of the water.'

Bloom would be the one to make this point most forcibly, I guessed.

He appeared confident. 'For who is to say that the gun didn't go off accidentally?' He raised his eyebrows and gave me a knowing look. 'Or, indeed, that a child of Brando's age could have been sure that the gun was loaded?'

Accidents speak louder than words. Bloom had done his homework.

'What about the newspapers?'

'They've been warned off. All those rumours about corpses buried on the Carver estate have them falling all over each other to get *that* story.'

Was it possible that Bloom had done some kind of deal with the press, as in 'Leave my clients alone and I'll give you a juicier story'? Nothing would surprise me.

'Wise to keep your head down, though,' he advised. 'Stay well out of the picture.'

'Talking about pictures – have you seen that photo on the TV news? The one from the Benny Cohen funeral.'

He nodded his head. 'That was unfortunate but it can't be helped now. I have no idea where it came from. Do you?'

'I have my suspicions.'

'Then I suggest you keep them to yourself.' The intimation being that making a fuss would result in even more media attention. Say nothing and it will quickly be forgotten.

'Any news on Monica's whereabouts?'

'It would seem that she has gone to ground.'

I didn't ask about Wendy Morrison. We left it that Bloom would call me to make arrangements for the interview with the Chief Inspector and I went to collect my car.

Outside in the car park was a Daimler I recognised. Gerard Fowley got out of the driver's seat. He must have driven himself because there was no sign of Clive or Winston. He'd probably decided that being accompanied by that pair only reinforced his wide-boy appearance. He was clearly in a jovial mood.

'Sam!' He greeted me. 'Just the lady I wanted to see. I've got a present for you. Come and see me at the warehouse in about . . .' He glanced at his Patek Philippe watch. 'Three hours? Give me a chance to get this business meeting with Richard Bloom out of the way.'

'Not sure I can make it, Gerard.' That warehouse was not somewhere I wanted to set foot in ever again.

His smile tightened. 'I insist. Now don't disappoint me, will you? You know how I hate to be disappointed.'

Dear God, what now? 'Since you insist. I'll be there at four.'

'You'll like the present, I promise.' And he headed towards Bloom's building.

Wendy Morrison was sitting in the far corner of the country pub where we had first met on the QT – the very place she had confronted me with the photo booth picture of Joe Murphy and me. She didn't seem half as cocky today. In fact, she looked worn out. She glanced up at me, her face set.

'I hear you're on leave,' I began.

'Personal time.'

'Did you know that some Chief Inspector wants to interview me?'

'I've been sidelined by some macho bastard. Typical.'

That didn't sound like good news for me. If she felt threatened professionally then she could easily try and get back into play by delivering me to the slaughter.

'Gerard Fowley?' She swiftly changed the subject. 'What's he up to?'

So that was why she wanted to see me. He was the next one on her hit list. She hadn't been able to nail Carver – Swindley had dashed all her hopes of that. Her investigation into the rent-boy murders had been snatched away from her. So now she wanted me to help her get Fowley.

'Don't really know him,' I replied. 'I have no idea what's going on in those circles anymore.'

'You're in thick with that dodgy solicitor Richard Bloom, though. What with you being his saviour and all. *And* he's handling the Cohen estate. *And* Fowley's in line to buy Cohen's nightclubs. Ergo.'

'Can't help, I'm afraid. I've got Brando to look after.'

'Playing nursemaid to some little rich boy,' she sneered. 'You've got it cushy.'

'What do you mean by that?'

'You've landed in a pot of jam, haven't you, Sam? It'll be the easy life for you from now on.' Her eyes darkened, baby blue to navy in seconds. 'But don't you ever forget what I've got on you.'

That was it. I lost it. 'I could have walked away from Brando at any time and left him to the tender mercies of Monica,' I reminded her. 'I could have called the ambulance from Bloom's cottage and done a runner. But I didn't, did I? I put my life on the line to help Brando.' I drew a breath, tried to calm down, but it was a real struggle. 'And it wasn't for the sake of any poxy little picture, either.'

'But if that evidence of your connection with the shooter ever suddenly turns up in all of the junk we received from Joseph Murphy's place in Manchester, what then?'

'If you want to save your own skinny arse by putting me in jail, then you go right ahead. I'm done with you.'

Morrison's eyes narrowed. 'Prepared to leave that little boy with Monica Cohen, are you? You'll never see him again once the truth is out, will you? Hardly be in a position to play Mummy again once he knows who set his daddy up for the chop.'

'You are one cold fucking bitch!' But she was telling it like it was. She had me bang to rights.

'Just doing my job.'

'Let me tell you right now: I did not murder Benny Cohen.' I tried to keep my voice steady. 'And it was Swindley who killed the Carvers.'

She wasn't fazed at all by my outburst. 'Why did the mysterious Mr Swindley leave *you* alive to tell the tale?'

'You'd have to ask him – if you can find him. Or you could question Monica Cohen about him. Have you found *her* yet?' I'd lay even money that she'd grass up Swindley and Gloria. And me, come to that. She'd play the innocent put-upon widow whose beloved stepchild had been snatched away from her. I could almost hear it.

'She's done a runner,' Morrison admitted.

'So you let Swindley slip through your net and now Monica Cohen gets away, too! My confidence in the police force has been severely dented, I do hope you know that.'

She didn't find that in the least bit amusing. 'Let's get back to Gerard Fowley.'

'He's a nasty piece of work. But I hardly know the man.'

'That's your problem. I want Fowley and you're going to help me get him. Do I make myself clear?' She paused just to make sure I got the message. 'Let's not forget that photograph of you and Joseph Murphy.'

But if Bloom was right about an internal police investigation, maybe I had something on Morrison. Out of sheer desperation, I gave it a try.

'Your withholding evidence to blackmail me into informing won't go down so well with your superiors, now, will it?' I watched for her reaction but she gave nothing away. 'Nor will your allowing me to go into a dangerous situation at the Carver house. Not exactly approved police procedure, was it?' Still nothing. So I played my final card. 'How would all that look now you're being investigated?' Touch for that, lady.

She gave a pained smile. 'Investigated? Who told you that fairy tale?'

'Don't try and fool me, Wendy. Why the sudden leave-taking right in the middle of your finest hour?' You're not the only one who can play hardball.

She sat back in her chair and pursed her lips. 'I told you, it's personal.'

'Bullshit!' An ambitious cop like Morrison would never take time off when she has the goal in her sights.

'My girlfriend is in the final stages of breast cancer.' She spoke quietly and I could have sworn she was suddenly close to tears. 'She was in remission, but now . . .'

Playing for sympathy, as in, we're all women together here. Anyway, did I believe her? Did I care? The answers were possibly and absolutely not.

She looked at her watch. 'I have to get back to the hospital.' She stood to leave but put her hand on my shoulder as she passed. 'Make sure you get me some gen on Gerard Fowley, Sam. Or prepare to wave goodbye to Brando Cohen and your comfortable new life. Forever.'

Chapter Forty-Three
2 p.m., Wednesday, 9 July

Monica walked into the reception area of Holloway Prison.

The visitors were predominantly female, all colours, some with wriggling toddlers on their knees. There was a brightly-lit children's play area at the back of the room and Monica hoped that they'd dump the brats in there. She didn't want their sticky paws all over the chair she was about to sit on. She'd had to leave her handbag in a locker, so she had just the key in her hand, even though a cheery volunteer-type had told her she could take enough money with her for a cup of coffee or a sandwich at the snack bar. Right, like she was about to eat in this place! She barely glanced at her fellow visitors and noted with disgust that it was like a United Nations sin bin. Prison gave Monica the creeps. The place was full of losers such as drug mules too poor and stupid to realise they'd be chucked to the wolves the minute a major consignment was on the horizon. It was standard business practice in the narcotics game to sacrifice these idiot women as a little taster for the authorities and draw attention away from the larger deliveries creeping in through the back door.

People want drugs, then let them have fucking drugs. It was all as pointless as the Yanks in the 1920s trying to ban alcohol. Monica liked the odd toot herself – nothing wrong with that. And hadn't Benny, Big Jim and Gerard Fowley all done nicely out of the cocaine business, thank you very much. That's why Garcia had been so eager to muscle in on the club game. Give the punters what they crave. Drink, drugs and sex, always bound to be bestsellers.

A few of the other women locked up in this hideous place had probably topped the old man after being slapped around one too many times. Fools. Pack your bags and leave the bastard with just his dick in his hand. Don't spend the rest of your life getting fingered by some lesbo just cos you didn't have the guts to fuck off when he first raised a hand to you. Monica shivered. She'd do a *Thelma and Louise* before she'd be banged up behind bars.

When Maria appeared in the visiting area, she looked like hell on skates. Her usually glossy hair was in tatters, her face bruised and swollen, and her jaw wired up. Even so she looked as though she'd happily slit Monica's throat without hesitation.

'I think you dead,' she mumbled.

'What the fuck were you and Felipe up to? Kidnapping that lawyer was stupid.' Best form of defence is always attack – that was Monica's motto. Hit them hard and leave 'em reeling. Then go in for the kill.

'Carver tell Felipe you come to house to sign papers. That Riley woman would be dead and you get the child back.' Saliva escaped from the corner of Maria's puffy, cracked lips and trickled down her chin. She patted at her mouth with a tissue.

Monica stifled a laugh. Or leave 'em drooling. She'd heard that this was Sam Riley's handiwork. Gotcha, you ugly cunt! The worse it will be for you when I get my way. 'Carver got himself killed before he could tell me the plan.'

'My brother is dead too. Why you not in black?

Oversight. Maybe the pale blue suit was a mistake. 'Disguise,' Monica improvised. 'Didn't want to make it too obvious and draw attention to myself.'

Maria raised her eyebrow, sat back in her chair and studied Monica sceptically. 'So why you here?'

'We can maybe work together.'

'In prison I can do nothing'

'But you have contacts. And I'm on the outside, so I can reach out to them for you.'

'Why you do this?'

'Revenge,' Monica smiled. 'Can you think of a better reason?'

Chapter Forty-Four
4 p.m., Wednesday, 9 July

Fowley's warehouse was situated in the middle of a trading estate that had seen better days, many years ago. His car showroom and one of his nightclubs were well within walking distance but might have been on another planet, the contrast was so great. If I hadn't known this estate was there, I'd never have guessed it even existed. Most of the businesses had long since departed to more salubrious neighbourhoods. Even the graffiti was out of date. What remained had a distinct feel of a war zone about it. Rubbish flew about like tattered birds and the only other business left, at one end of the thirty or so locked-down premises, was an old guy who was busy fixing a clapped-out car. He didn't even look up when I drove past. Probably knew better.

Fowley's place was at the other end of this depressing site and I could see a maroon Mini and a dark blue van parked outside. The van was the one I had taken my unconscious journey in when Chinese Clive and Winston set on me outside the Cohen residence. I felt queasy at the thought, but Fowley was an ally now, wasn't he?

I knocked at the side door and could hear bolts being thrown. A menacing Jamaican opened the door. He had two gold front teeth that were niftily accessorised by a heavyweight gold chain around his neck. He wasn't one of Fowley's usual crew, so I guessed he was one of his drug connections. Fowley's Daimler was parked inside and the door to the office where I had been beaten was closed. Outside the office was a bench where a young blonde girl was sitting. She looked scared and dishevelled. She had a large white dressing taped to the left side of her face and her left eye was blackened and puffy.

'Stay there and wait,' the Jamaican said. The girl didn't look at me when I sat next to her. Didn't even acknowledge my presence. I guess what you don't see won't get you into even more trouble. She nervously chipped at her nail polish.

The office door opened and the girl flinched. Gerard Fowley walked out, all smiles. 'Sam,' he said amiably, 'come and see what I've got for you.'

The room was as I remembered, with a large desk and a chair directly in front of it. Though in place of me gaffer taped, it was Chinese Clive. At least I thought it was him. His face was a pulpy mess, his once box-fresh trainers were splattered with blood and there was a pool of urine rolling slowly towards the corner of the uneven floor. Winston stood with his back to the wall. He was stripped to the waist and I shuddered at the thought of the obvious reason why. He wouldn't want any blood on his nice shirt, would he? He gave a slight nod of his head when he saw me and rippled his impressive muscles. I thanked heaven that I'd never been forced to face him down.

Fowley left me standing in the space between the chair and the desk and took his seat behind it.

'Thought you might like to see how I treat those who upset my friends,' Fowley said.

Clive moaned and Fowley raised his hand to quiet him.

'This is the toerag who sold those pictures to the press, Sam. Went sneaking around with his phone camera like the slimy little shit he is.'

I didn't speak. Keep your gob shut, Sam. See how this plays out.

'You know my rules, don't you, Clive?' Fowley said. 'No feelee, no squealee, no wheelee.'

Clive moaned again.

'Now, dipping your wick in one of my naughty ladies was a minor infraction I may have been inclined to overlook. But you hurt her, Clive.' Fowley tutted. 'I'm a gentleman. You know how I feel about anyone hurting my ladies. For that alone you'd be due a severe beating.'

That must have been the girl outside that he'd worked over.

'And upsetting my friend Sam here and her little boy – well, a broken leg may have sufficed.'

There was a reason he wanted me here for this. Otherwise he could have just told me about it. This was a warning to me as well as to Clive. Play ball, or else.

'And you used the money you got from that grubby reporter to pay off gambling debts, didn't you?' Fowley let out an exaggerated sigh. 'Roulette, Clive – rule number three smashed to smithereens. No wheelee.' He shook his head as though disappointed by his unruly child. 'It's the Chink in you, Clive. That's the problem. No restraint when it comes to gambling.'

Fowley opened his desk drawer, pulled out a thick brown envelope and laid it on the desktop, along with a Browning 9mm pistol. The pool of urine surrounding Clive's chair, spread substantially. Fowley got out of his chair and came over to me. He cocked the gun and offered it to me. 'Would you like to do the honours?' Fowley stared me down. 'He'd have killed *you* without blinking an eye. You know that, don't you?'

I stood stock still and said nothing, my mind racing. A refusal could mean anything might happen here. Fowley was a total psycho. But I was not about to pull that trigger. Not that I would have any regrets about topping the evil little fuck but to play into the hands of Gerard Fowley would not be a wise move. I held my ground.

Fowley nodded his head sagely. 'But you've got that little lad to think of, haven't you? You're a mother now. I respect that.'

He raised the gun and pointed it at Clive. 'Disloyalty, Clive,' he said. 'That is the one thing I cannot abide. I always told you . . .'

Clive let out a terrified yelp.

'Don't!' The first shot echoed around the walls. 'Break!' Fowley fired again. Clive's body jerked violently and the chair he was taped to toppled over. Fowley walked over to the chair to put a shot into Clive's head. 'The!' And another. 'Rules!' Blood and grey matter spurted across the floor. Who'd have thought a scumbag like Chinese Clive had so many brains.

Fowley tossed the gun to the impassive Winston who caught it in his huge paw. 'Clean up this mess and dump that piece of crap,' he said.

Winston growled his response. Fowley took my arm and ushered me out of the door, just like the gentleman he purported to be.

The terrified girl seated on the bench was on her feet immediately.

'It's cool, Kaylee.' He handed her the envelope. 'Here's some money, dear. Now you go and get your face fixed.'

She took it with trembling hands.

'You be back at work as soon as. Alright, darlin'?' It was an order rather than a request.

Kaylee nodded her head, turned and ran for the door. The Jamaican opened it for her and she fled.

'That's the thing with whores,' Fowley said. 'They're a valuable commodity like no other: you got it, you sell it, you still got it.' He laughed at his own joke. 'Whereas shitbags like our Chinky friend in there are two-a-fuckin'-penny.'

He walked me to the door and put his arm around my shoulders. 'Tit for tat, Sam. I do something nice for you and you do something for me in return.' The hand that had held the gun to despatch Clive squeezed my shoulder hard. 'You make sure the clubs deal goes through with no interference from your friend Detective Inspector Morrison. Understand?' He kissed me on the cheek and I repressed a shudder of revulsion. 'I never forget who my friends are, Sam. Or my enemies.' He released me and the Jamaican opened the door.

'I never forget,' Fowley called after me. 'I never, ever forget.'

Chapter Forty-Five
7 p.m., Wednesday, 9 July

I drove back to Mike's farmhouse, not sure which way was up. One simple solution would be to report the murder of Chinese Clive to Wendy Morrison. On the face of it, Gerard Fowley had served himself up on a silver platter. But the more I thought about it the worse that plan appeared.

I mentally ticked off the main players. The terrified Kaylee must have heard the shots but she hadn't seen anything. When questioned she might suddenly turn into the world's deafest dumb blonde. The Jamaican: nothing scared the boys from Trenchtown. Threaten to shoot 'em and they'd piss on your shoes, spit in your eye and say fuck you. The Jamaican police were renowned for their brutality, but even they rarely got Yardies to talk. PC Plod had no chance. Winston had been prepared to beat the crap out of his former colleague on Gerard Fowley's say-so. Not much chance of him spilling the beans. And Gerard himself was sure to be alibied up to the back teeth. I'd lay odds that it would be down to me to give the one and only eyewitness account.

Unless they'd crammed Clive's body in a conveniently accessible freezer, chances were he'd be deep in concrete and helping to support a flyover by now, or slowly floating away to sea as fish food. No body and everyone else in deep denial landed me as finger-pointer. DNA evidence from the no doubt already well-scrubbed premises would probably turn up dozens of other blood samples, mine included. It could all turn into a bizarre game of Who's the Dead Guy? Which left me looking over my shoulder for the rest of my days – because, as he'd been at pains to tell me, Gerard Fowley never forgets.

Plus, even if I did do my civic duty by reporting the murder, could I be sure that Morrison wouldn't screw me over again? She'd got Carver, one way or another, but I didn't get even a sniff of that photo of Joe and me. There was no guarantee that she'd hand it over – even if I gave her Gerard Fowley tied up in red ribbons.

I needed more time to think it all through. What I had to do now was collect Brando and get us both back to Norwich, sharpish.

I pulled up by the farm gates and spotted a red Toyota parked outside in the lane. I drove up to the house. Mike and his wife Lenka were in the kitchen.

'Where's Brando?'

'Playing Guitar Hero with the kids in the den.' Mike grimaced. 'None of my children are very musical, I'm afraid.'

'There's a car outside,' I said. 'Could be the press.'

Mike was on his feet in seconds. 'I'll set the fucking dogs on them.'

Lenka laughed and stood up. She was tall and willowy with shiny, natural blonde hair, bright green eyes and high cheekbones. 'I take dog.' She had a strong Russian accent.

'I'll go with you.' I followed her outside.

She collected a huge slavering Rottweiler from a dog run behind the house. 'You were in army?' she said while she put a lead on the excited beast. 'I too, in Russia – it was shit job, yes?' And we headed off down the drive towards the gates.

Lenka put the dog on a short leash like she was about to cross the road and walked in front of the vehicle. Then she stopped in her tracks and faced towards the driver. The dog reared up on its hind legs, massive paws on the bonnet, and barked fit to beat the band, spraying the windscreen in doggy saliva. I crept across to the driver's side, tapped on the glass and the only occupant in the Toyota turned to face me. Gloria Kelso.

———⌣———

I was used to seeing Gloria in scruffy slacks with her dark hair scraped back from her world-weary face. But the woman now sitting in front of me in Mike and Lenka's spacious sitting room was elegantly dressed in a stylish navy suit, light make-up and her hair looked like she'd visited a salon for once in her life. With her long slim nose and thin lips, she was a mirror image of Lil Carver, though more up-to-date.

'How did you know where to find me?'

'I didn't. Swindley wants to see you. I used to bring Brando here every week so I drove by on the off-chance. I saw him playing in the garden with Mike's kids. Didn't recognise him at first, laughing and running about. I've never seen him like that before. He seems so happy.' Her lips spread into a tight smile. 'Looks just like his mother.'

'Charlotte?'

Gloria didn't seem at all surprised that I knew about Brando's mother. 'She was a lovely lady, Charlotte Cohen. Very kind to me, she was. It was a shame what happened to her.' She sounded genuinely saddened though I thought 'shame' was an understatement. Surely Charlotte being drugged and lynched in her own home called for a stronger response. But at least it was a small sign of humanity from this bloodless woman.

'I thought Swindley would be long gone.' He'd told me he was off to the sun with his missus. But then he would say that, wouldn't he? Just in case I cracked under police questioning. Get them checking out all the ports and airports while he's holed up somewhere in Blighty, laughing up his sleeve. 'What does he want with me?'

'Business to settle.' She handed me a card with a phone number written on it in meticulous copperplate. 'Don't worry, he just wants to talk to you.'

'Where's Monica?'

'Gone.'

'As in . . .?'

'Skipped the country.'

'I take it you know about the trouble at the Cohen house?'

'Who doesn't? It's all over the news.'

'Garcia and his sister were waiting for Monica at the house. But she didn't turn up.'

'Did they say that?'

'Not in so many words, but . . .'

'And they won't.' Gloria held me in a hard stare. She was Lil Carver in more than looks. 'So I'd be careful what *you* say, if I were you.'

'Why are you protecting Monica?'

'Shall we just say she was dissuaded and leave it at that.'

Dissuaded by Swindley, most likely.

'We went to the station with a lawyer in tow. We saw some policeman, a Welsh guy, Evans was his name – that's it, Chief Inspector Evans,' she continued.

The same one Bloom had said wanted to interview Brando and me. So Morrison had lied about Monica not being interviewed. What else had she lied about – a soon-to-be-deceased girlfriend?

Perhaps she was being investigated after all. But to believe Gloria, sitting opposite me with not a feather out of her when she'd set up her own mother and brother to be killed, that was a step too far. Did these people have no feelings? And I'd thought my own family was dysfunctional. Either Morrison was lying or Gloria was bluffing. And right at that moment my money was on Gloria.

'So Monica walked away?'

'Monica always walks away.' The tone of her voice was ice cold. 'I took her to the airport. She's gone. And she won't be back.'

That didn't sound like the Monica I knew.

'Swindley did me a favour,' Gloria said. 'That lot always treated me like dirt. Well, I showed them. It's just me and my Janine now and she's a good girl.'

Perma-tanned Janine – birdbrain, Lil Carver had called her, just another useless girl to be used. But what was all this about Swindley doing Gloria a favour? Of course, there was always the money. With both the Carvers out of the picture, there was only Gloria left to inherit that enormous house and all of Big Jim's various enterprises. No wonder she was already tarted up to the nines; I was looking at a newly minted woman. It'd be a facelift and a boob job next.

'What did you tell the police?'

Gloria appeared nonchalant. 'I told them the truth, of course. I'd been the Cohens' housekeeper for years. Then my mother got ill and wanted me with her. I'd only been back there for a short time when Monica came to see me. Then you turned up later. I told them who was at the house on the day and that was all I knew. I loaned my car to Monica and went to do some gardening. When I got back to the house everyone was dead.' She smiled. 'Best back me up on that one, Sam.' She didn't add 'if you know what's good for you', but that's what she implied.

'You mentioned Arthur Caine, I suppose.' Chimp in the basement, he'd be pretty hard to ignore.

'The minute I saw that freak sneaking about, I knew Jim was up to his old tricks. I've stood for some things in my time but that was beyond the pale.'

Shagging rent boys was one thing whereas killing them might be seen as taking things too far, even by Gloria Kelso's flexible standards.

She got up to leave. 'That's all I'm going to say.' She picked up her Chanel handbag and made for the door. 'Ring Swindley in the morning,' she told me once more. 'He doesn't like being forced to find people. Makes him angry. And you really don't want to do that.'

Lenka and the dog escorted Gloria back to her car while I remained indoors. I looked at the card Gloria had given me. Contact Swindley? He'd told me he was Joe Murphy's uncle, but that might have been just a bit of old flannel to cover the fact that he'd killed the Carvers as a favour to Gloria and not as revenge for Joe's murder. He might have considered it an ideal way to get me on his side. On the other hand, why leave me alive? But then Gloria's husband *had* been the one that got away. The final hit gone wrong that compelled Joe and me to go our separate ways. Maybe we'd been working for Lil Carver all along. And I had a gut feeling that Monica, wherever she was hiding, would not stay away for long. There was only one way to find out. I had to chance a meet with Swindley.

Lenka walked into the room. 'You have trouble?'

'More than you can even imagine.'

'You want my help?'

'I'll be fine.'

'I am here for you,' she said.

'Why? You hardly know me?'

'To be a soldier is shit,' she said, 'but to be a mother is boring.'

'I thought you'd been a model.'

'In sex films, yes. Long time ago.'

A porn star – I'd never have guessed that. I looked at her, silhouetted in the light from the window. *Vogue* didn't know what they'd missed out on. She was older than I'd first thought, maybe forty, but still a good twenty years younger than her husband Mike. And she had three young children to consider. I couldn't get her involved in this mess.

'You could help a lot by looking after Brando for a little while longer.'

'Fine.' She sounded disappointed. 'But I have guns – shotguns for farm. Legal. We have a licence.'

'I don't think I need guns.'

'If you want, I have.' She walked out, leaving me alone in the room with its huge period fireplace and the walls covered in framed gold records.

Chapter Forty-Six
6 p.m., Thursday, 10 July

I sat on a bench at Thorndon Country Park and waited. Brando and I had stayed the night at the Watts' farm while I got in touch with Swindley. He had designated the time and place. I didn't argue. He'd given me very precise directions and I was sure I was in the right place. I gazed across the calm waters of Childerditch Pond. It was peaceful here and I could almost forget the anxiety that gripped me like a vice. I looked at my watch – the glass was cracked after my run-in with Fowley's mob and I decided that I really should buy a new one. I'd been there for over an hour. There was a plaque displayed on a wooden lectern beside the pond and I'd read it three times. Apparently, the pond had been man-made, created hundreds of years ago by monks from a nearby Cistercian abbey. I imagined them with their habits tucked into their belts, sweating away, shouting to each other in Latin. German POWs had been given the task of redigging it during the First World War – a more agreeable option than squatting in muddy trenches and being bombarded by artillery, I suppose.

The only sound was the occasional birdcall and the wind swishing through the branches of the oak trees overhead. A couple of hardy walkers had passed by but there was no sign of Swindley. Had the bastard stood me up? A jogger went past twice – oldish man, white hair, head down, muscular legs flashing. It was coming up to closing time, and I'd decided to give it another half hour when my phone rang.

'Car park in ten minutes,' Swindley said.

'Which one?' There were two, miles apart on either side of this vast country park.

'Blue Golf, parked next to you.' He rang off.

It took me all of the ten minutes to get back there. Sure enough, there was a dark blue car parked next to mine but no sign of an occupant. I sat in my car and waited. The sun was going down and the gardens would be closing soon, with only our two motors remaining.

The jogger I had seen earlier came towards me through the trees. It was like that scene from *Lawrence of Arabia* where Peter O'Toole sees Omar Sharif for the first time. The figure was just a spot in the distance gradually drawing nearer, but without the heat haze – or the camel.

He was thirty feet away from me before I recognised him. The fair hair was now white – the previous shade probably as phoney as his Birmingham accent. But when he raised his head there was no doubt that it was him. Those steely grey eyes were a dead giveaway. And his left hand was bandaged. I realised that he had already run past me twice while I was at the pond, probably to make sure that I was actually alone. A cautious man was our Mr Swindley.

He stopped by my car and I got out. He wasn't out of breath, even though he'd been haring around the park for the past hour. Cautious and fit, it seemed.

'Gloria came to see me,' I said.

'Gloria and I go back a long way.'

I was about to speak when he put his finger to his lips to shush me.

'Ask no questions and you'll be told no lies.' It was clear that he wasn't going to tell me any more than that about his links to Gloria Kelso.

'There's a new Spanish Armada on the way, or so I've heard.' He was a deadpan Mancunian to the very core. 'Seems Monica's ex is now expired.'

'Garcia's dead? But the ambulance arrived at the Cohen house within minutes of my call and he looked like a robust bloke.'

'Nope, he a goner,' Swindley said. 'Not from the gunshot wound, though – the doctors were patching him up and found some kind of heart disease. If young Brando hadn't got him, then his own body would have. And pretty soon, by the sound of it. He croaked from complications a couple of hours after they removed the bullet.' He let out a guarded laugh. 'Don't suppose all the Viagra they found in his bloodstream helped any. She's one hot little number, our Monica. Garcia probably couldn't keep up with her.' He held me in his frozen gaze but there was a shade of gallows humour in his tone. 'Or keep it up.' A mocking look flitted across his face. 'Sorry!' But it was obvious that he wasn't anything of the kind.

'Don't be.' And don't play mind games with me either, pal. I've got your number. 'Is that what you wanted to tell me?'

He fished his car keys out of the pocket of his shorts. 'I'm just passing on the information by way of a warning,' he said. 'Seems Garcia's sister is on the warpath, out for revenge. They're a temperamental lot, these Latin-types. I shacked up with a Spanish girl once. Wild woman, she was. Barely got away with my nuts intact.'

'Is that supposed to reassure me?'

'You're a big girl, Sam. You could deal with Maria, especially now her jaw's all wired up.'

'Maria's on remand awaiting trial on the kidnapping and gun charges – hardly a threat.'

Swindley stared me down. 'Just thought you'd like to know. I hear she's had a visit. And she's got two of her dago "cousins" heading your way. Short of stature, ugly as shite and mean as hell.' He paused for a moment as though to make sure I had taken in the gravity of the situation. 'She's connected, Sam. Those two are bad news.'

'You think Maria has put out some kind of hit on me?'

'I'd guess you and the kid, both.' Swindley walked over to his car and opened the boot. 'So I thought this may be of some use to you.'

I peered inside at an Uzi sub-machine gun.

'Spray and pray, eh?'

'You're a good shot; as Carver could attest, if he was here to tell the tale. You can handle it. Just don't use it on automatic.'

'Fuck me! Are you serious?'

'Untraceable,' he assured me. 'Just like that number you rang me on.'

Point taken.

'I could get fifteen years in the slammer just for being in possession of that. And if I ever used it, they'd throw the fucking key away.'

'Better than the alternative, I'd say.' He was apparently amused by my lack of enthusiasm for his gift. 'Please yourself,' he said, like he couldn't care either way. 'But believe me, you're going to need something. They *will* be coming after you and the boy.'

'You seem sure about that?'

'Oh, I'm sure, sweetheart.' Swindley's cold grey eyes conveyed a truth I didn't want to even contemplate. 'Dead sure,' he added. 'Now, do you want my little offering, or not?'

I could hear Joe Murphy's laughter in my head. 'Bloody hell, Riley. Get your arse in gear, girl. Take the Uzi and kill the bastards.'

Chapter Forty-Seven
8 p.m., Thursday, 10 July

The sun cast a lurid blood-red stain that stretched across the horizon. I've never been one for omens but if this was one, it was a humdinger. By the time I got back to the farmhouse, Mike and Lenka were in an intense head-to-head conference.

'We've been talking,' Mike said. 'We think you should stay here until you get sorted. You don't know anyone in Norfolk and it's a pain in the arse having to drive up and down the motorway all the time.'

'That's very kind of you but we can't impose on you like that. You've looked after Brando for me for two days and that's plenty.'

'You have big trouble. We want to help,' Lenka said.

'The news is full of all the shit going on at the Carver house,' Mike said. 'And I've heard the filth is still crawling all over the Cohen place.'

'You already knew that.'

'Yeah, but then you get a surprise visit from Gloria Kelso last evening and today you take off like the devil himself is after you . . .'

Lenka nodded. 'Big trouble.'

'Something's going down and you and the kid are slap bang in the middle of it.' Mike raised his hand as though to stop me from telling him about it – which I most certainly wasn't about to. 'Don't need to know, don't want to know. But we'd like to help out.'

'I can't land you in the middle of all this, Mike. You've got children to think about.'

'Brando is child,' Lenka said.

'I know, but all this is our problem and not yours. But thank you for the offer.'

'We've got a proposition for you,' Mike began. 'I'm going to a pal's house tomorrow to finish off our new album. He's got this fuck-off chateau in France with a big recording studio. My old band will be there with their wives and kids. Stu's got six of the little buggers and Danny's got five. We were going to go as a family, give the kids a holiday.'

'You want us to house-sit?' Maybe a few days here wouldn't be such a bad idea. We couldn't move into the new house for a couple of weeks yet and Brando was already getting antsy in the hotel.

'Not really, we were thinking that Brando could come with us,' Mike offered. 'One more kid won't make any difference. You'll have Brando safely out of the way and can get on with whatever it is you need to do.'

Maybe this was the break I needed. Get Brando out of the country and then find a way to deal with Morrison, Fowley and the two Spaniards that Swindley had given me heads-up about.

'I'd have to ask Brando—'

'You not *ask* children,' Lenka said. 'You *tell*.'

Mike gave me an apologetic look that said, 'She's Russian, you know.'

'Well, if he agrees, how long will you be gone?'

'Three weeks max – going by private jet from Biggin Hill. This will be well discreet.'

'Let me think about it.'

'But tonight, you stay here,' Lenka said, and I had no wish to argue.

Brando was excited about the idea of flying to France to see how pro musicians go about putting the final touches to their album. And he got on well with Mike's three children. I couldn't help but feel that being with all the other kids would be good for him. Nobody would even know he was out of the country.

'But why can't you come with us?' Brando insisted.

'I'll be visiting Mac at the hospital and getting our new house ready. Plus, I've got to see Richard Bloom and deal with all kinds of other tedious stuff.'

He looked unconvinced.

'You'd be bored being dragged around,' I said. 'This is a great opportunity for you. And you get to fly in a private plane. How good is that?'

'I don't want to go without you.'

'Look, if I can get things sorted before you get back, then I'll come out and join you. How about it?'

'Deal!' He spat on his hand and held it out. I shook it, saliva and all.

I just had to talk to Bloom and get his go-ahead. He'd said the police wanted to interview Brando and I didn't want that to muck up this plan. I rang him.

'I'll speak to Chief Inspector Evans,' Bloom said. 'They've already got Brando's initial statement so that should be sufficient for now. They'll want him to take part in a video identification parade of his kidnappers eventually but I'll remind Evans that the boy has been through a traumatic experience and he needs time to recuperate. The police won't want to be seen to be harassing a child who has recently lost his father. Just as long as you're here to be interviewed, they should be satisfied with that.'

'I'll be around.' At least I hoped I would.

'I'll need a passport for Brando.' I said as the thought struck me.

'I have all of the boy's documents in his file. I'll have the passport biked over to you in the morning.'

A bit odd that, I thought, most people have these things close to hand.

'That's good,' I said. 'I didn't fancy having to go back to the house for the passport while the police are swarming all over it.'

'Mr Cohen was a cautious man,' Bloom said, confirming my suspicion that Benny had been making sure Monica couldn't take Brando out of the country without Bloom's say so. Despite his apparent coldness towards the boy, Benny Cohen had really loved his son. We promptly got the okay from Chief Inspector Evans but he insisted on bringing my interview forward. I agreed.

11 a.m., Friday, 11 July

Brando and I were driving to Biggin Hill. The airport is located in Kent but less than twenty miles from central London. All manner of small to medium-sized aircraft fly to and from there. It has its own customs desk and hangars where the super-rich park their jets. Brando and I drove together in the Merc while Lenka piled their kids, Mike, luggage and several guitars into a Mazda people carrier. Brando was buzzing with excitement and chattering away. As we were approaching the airport I saw signs for a number of flying schools. Brando clocked them too and came up with his latest ambition – to be a pilot.

'I could be a flying doctor, or a flying vet. We could fly all over the world together. We could buy a plane.' Right, try putting a

Dassault Falcon 2000 on a black American Express card. But then, maybe you could.

Though all of our fine plans for the future would come to nothing if I couldn't get that photo off Wendy Morrison. My part in the death of Brando's father was a secret I had to keep from him, no matter what. Brando might be resilient, but I didn't want to even contemplate the repercussions should he discover that particular truth.

———

The band had chartered a plane for the short haul to their destination in France. Not being a music fan, I hadn't known what to expect. I'd thought the other guys would be like Mike with the dyed hair and leather jeans, but I was way off. One resembled a white-haired banker in his sharp but sober suit while the other sported tattoos and a shaved head. The wives were more like I had envisaged. Very WAG with designer togs and just-out-of-the-salon hairdos. Their offspring ranged from a rake-thin, sulky-faced girl of thirteen or so, to tiny tykes who presented their passports to the customs guys with an air of seen-it-all-before nonchalance.

This was all as new to Brando as it was for me. Benny Cohen had the dosh for sure but had always insisted on flying cattle class. 'Them airline tossers can go and whistle for my hard-earned gelt,' he'd storm when Monica even suggested travelling business class. 'I'm not paying *that* for a seat on some fuckin' flying bus!' So no matter how much she'd wheedled or cajoled, Monica never got her way on that one and the very notion of first class was enough to have Benny frothing at the mouth. So this private charter had Brando well impressed, though he quickly fixed his face to fit in with his new companions and strutted about the place as though he did this every day of the week. Brando Cohen, chameleon extraordinaire.

He said goodbye, without a hug this time as he probably deemed it uncool in present company, though he did elicit a promise that I would join them later if I could. I watched them all troop out to the plane on the tarmac. Brando didn't look back and I was momentarily overcome by a deep sense of loss. Swallow it, girl. Get on with what you have to do.

I turned away and prepared myself to drive back to the farmhouse alone when Lenka came out of the ladies' room.

'You're going to miss the flight,' I said.

'I not go,' she announced emphatically.

'Get on the plane, Lenka. You really don't want to get tangled up in my problems.'

'I stay.'

'I'm not sure that's a good idea as I really don't know what might happen next.'

She shrugged. 'That is story of my life.'

'An exotic break in a French chateau or the same old in England. I know what choice I'd make. If I could.'

'Exotic? You think? Music people are boring,' she declared. 'Every day they play, argue, fight and be best friends again. The women they sit, drink coffee, talk about children. Or get drunk and tell stories about famous men they fuck. Boring, boring, boring.'

'Who will look after your children and Brando?'

'Nannies look after – mothers sit and talk.'

'Please go with them, Lenka. You don't know what you might be letting yourself in for.'

'You tell me at house.'

246

Lenka sat in the kitchen and told me a story that started out as a cliché but moved swiftly along. She'd been raised on a farm, dirt poor and was the eldest of six children.

'My father was brute,' she said. 'He beat my mother all the time. I kill him with axe.'

'You're kidding me?'

'No. I kill.' Matter-of-fact, no drama – this was Russian understatement at its most convincing.

'Jesus! How old were you?'

'Sixteen. Good for my mother and brothers. He was a very bad man.'

She and her brother, Timor, had buried their father's body in the woods and she'd legged it pretty sharpish to join the army. We had more in common than I would have expected: enlisting in the army to put a shadowy past behind us,

'Shit job,' was all she said about her military service. After two years of a lot of marching about and shooting things she'd deserted, paid some black marketeer for new identity papers and taken off for Poland. Her money got her as far as Krakow where she found a job in a bar. One night a man came in and offered her work in porn movies.

'Easy job. Good money. The men were fine.'

'How many?' I imagined them standing in line to have sex with a foxy babe like Lenka.

'Ten movies, five or six men, I think. Many men cannot do sex in movies. All think they can but . . .' She laughed. 'They try but cannot keep hard. It is very funny, yes.'

She'd met Mike at a party when he and the band were touring Eastern Europe. She'd told him she was a model and not let on about the porno.

'Men very sensitive about this. They not care if you fuck for pleasure but to fuck for money is not so good, they think.'

'Not something I know much about.'

'Now I have nice life, good man and good children.'

'But Mike still doesn't know about the porno movies?'

She shook her head and downed another shot of vodka.

'And if he ever saw one by accident?'

'I deny it. Lot of girls from Murmansk look like me. I am not very different. I was more fleshy then, have tits and hips and arse. I am thin now. Is funny, no? The more food you have in cupboard, the less you need to eat.' A cloud passed across her emerald eyes for a moment and I wondered if, like me, her head often filled with images she would rather forget – a past that wormed itself into everyday consciousness. Maybe we are all haunted in one way or another. But some of us have more persistent ghosts.

'But you're willing to tell me all this?'

'I trust you with story.' She gave a sly smile. 'Now your turn!'

There are only so many things you can divulge, even to a woman who whacked her own father with an axe and buried him in the woods. But I did tell her about Garcia, his sister and the fact that two Spanish hitmen might be on my tail. She listened impassively and appeared not at all ruffled by the news. It was almost as though she'd expected it.

'This man who warn you, he can help?'

'He offered me an Uzi.'

'Good gun. But Kalashnikov better.' Her eyes lit up. 'You have it?'

'I turned it down.'

She raised her eyebrows as if to say that every home should have one. 'In Russia and Poland, is very popular.'

'This is England, you can't go around toting submachine guns.'

'You rather be dead?' She didn't mince her words, this woman. Always blunt and to the point.

'No, of course not, but there has to be another way to handle it.'
'They kill you or you kill them. That is way to handle.'

———

In a locked cupboard at the back of Mike's music studio stood two metal cabinets, one tall and the other that of a medium-sized safe. Lenka opened up and showed me two pump-action, twelve-gauge, smooth-bore, twenty-four-inch barrel shotguns. The smaller cabinet held the shells.

'We teach children to shoot when they are older,' she said. 'We live in a dangerous world. Children must learn to defend themselves.'

Not a principle I would necessarily go along with but the times they are a-changin', as the man said. Maybe she was right. I examined the shotguns. They were in good nick, well maintained, and would do the job.

Lenka loaded both shotguns expertly – two in the magazine and one in the chamber – and picked up two boxes of shells.

'We take into house,' she said.

'These guys won't know I'm here.' But I couldn't hide out there forever.

'You wait for them to sneak up and kill you in street?'

She was right on the button. I could be ambushed at any time. This had to be done and dusted before Brando got back from France.

'I don't even know who they are.' Swindley's description of the two men – 'short of stature, ugly as shite and mean as hell,' – wouldn't help me pick them out in a crowd.

'They know you.' She shook her head. 'Is not good.' She handed me a shotgun and a box of shells. 'Come to the house. We drink and talk. I have a good idea. You will like, I think.'

10 p.m., Friday, 11 July

I stood in front of the full-length mirror in the guestroom and stared at my reflection. The blue dress was a bit on the tight side. It was Lenka's and she was slimmer than me. Her shoes fitted me though and I opted for three-inch heels, as I hadn't worn anything higher than that for donkey's years. Lenka had put highlights in my short hair and she hadn't let me see the make-up she'd applied for me until it was complete. Brando had said he thought I could be beautiful and I wouldn't go that far, but the face looking back at me wasn't bad at all.

Lenka was pleased with my magical makeover. 'Why you choose to look like a man when you can look like this?'

My satisfaction with the new me was swiftly put into perspective when Lenka swanned in, all dressed up in her own knock-'em-dead outfit. The black dress she wore was virtually see-through with strategically placed lace panels to stop her from being arrested for indecent exposure. And now, fully made-up, she looked ravishing. She made Monica seem like the trashy tart she had obviously always been – the twenty-twenty vision of hindsight can be quite a jolt. So, even in my borrowed glad rags, I was instantly reduced to the role of one of Cinderella's ugly sisters.

'I drive,' Lenka picked up her car keys.

I followed her out of the house, unsure if this crazy Russian's plan was a good idea at all. Not that I had an alternative of my own. Give it a go, as an Aussie friend of mine used to say.

We drove into the night with the CD player blasting out Shostakovich – at least that's what she told me it was.

'This real music,' she said. 'Rock music is crap, yes?'

'They won't be playing any classical stuff where we're going.'

'Tonight not for pleasure. Is for business.'

And we sped along the country roads, headed for the nightclub where this whole bloody mess had started almost two years ago.

Legend.

Chapter Forty-Eight
11 p.m., Friday, 11 July

Legend, the dodgy sign on the wall outside stuttered its neon presence. Nothing changed there, then. And inside it was just as I remembered. With its red and black interior and dim lighting the place had an intimate and sexy ambience if you didn't examine it too closely. It looked like shit in the cold light of day but at this time of night there was an element of sleazy glamour about it. Not sure I'd been that aware of it so much when I was on the door, but coming here as a punter, I totally got it. I nodded to a tall bouncer I had once worked alongside. He nodded back but his face showed not even a flicker of recognition. I glanced in the mirror on the wall behind the reception desk and a curvaceous stranger in a tight blue dress stared back at me. I raised my hand and she did too. Yep, it was me, all right. So I really couldn't blame my ex-colleague for the blank look in his eyes. I reckoned even my own mother wouldn't recognise me.

The receptionist wasn't anyone I knew but she smiled broadly at us and waved away the proffered membership card. 'Lenka,' she said. 'So nice to see you again after all this time. Is Mike not with you?'

'In France,' Lenka said. 'This is my friend, Samantha.'

'When the cat's away, eh?' The receptionist grinned knowingly.

The bouncer opened the door to the main club for us and I winked at him as we passed by. He looked startled and I laughed. I recalled all his snarky, sexist remarks about what he called the 'stuck-up slappers' that frequented the club. Probably never could get his leg over. And there was a very good reason for that. He really was an ugly sod.

'What she say about cats?' Lenka asked.

'It's a figure of speech,' I said. 'Means you're out on the razzle while Mike's out of town.'

'In Russia we say, without the cat there is freedom for mice.'

'Doesn't have quite the same ring to it, does it?'

Business-wise it was a so-so night. Smooth R&B oozed out from the club speakers. Frank, the no-talent DJ, was being a lazy bastard as usual and playing a compilation, too busy chatting up some under-age girl to do his job right. No way would she have got past me when I worked the door. But the other bouncer's brain always was in his cock.

There were half-a-dozen couples on the dance floor, lost in their own little world. Single girls, out on the pull, made a big show of dancing together while guys stood around the bar, eyed up the prospects and waited for the right moment to make their moves.

Lenka strode up to the bar and it was like the Red Sea parting to let her through. She had everyone's attention. She ignored the open-mouthed throng and ordered two straight vodkas.

'My pleasure!' Some short-arse in a cheap suit waved a fifty at the barman.

'I pay for my own drinks.' Lenka looked down at him and he shrank from her gaze.

'They're on the house.' A familiar voice came from directly behind me. Gerard Fowley.

'My, my, Sam,' he whispered in my ear, 'don't you scrub up nice?'

We sat in a booth with Fowley.

'Taken over already, Gerard?'

'Not exactly.' Fowley smirked. 'But with a little help from my friends, it's just a matter of time.'

'Free drinks already, though?'

'The manager knows which side his croissant's buttered.'

I remembered the manager – a slithering little French toad who was too shit-scared to be on the fiddle when Benny Cohen was the boss. He'd have been making hay while there was no senior management around. Fowley would have sussed that right off. By making it known that he was about to take over, the manager would be less tempted to dip his hand in the till.

'When the deal's done, you'll see some real changes in this place. Get some big name DJs in.' Fowley cast a scornful look at the useless DJ. 'That one'll get his marching orders.'

I followed his gaze and saw Frank copping a feel of some low-rent Beyoncé wannabe, all blonde hair extensions and false nails. The guy was so stupid he couldn't behave himself even when his prospective new boss was in the house. Yep, it's back to driving a taxi for you, old son – and not before time, either.

Fowley knew the club game by heart. Famous DJs meant big crowds, greedy for the latest designer drugs. His connections would have a field day and his own hefty percentage meant he'd be raking it in.

'We'll put a classy VIP room at the back.' Fowley turned to Lenka. 'Get your old man to bring his mates along.' She looked unimpressed but he was undeterred. 'Lots of great freebies, of course. How's that?'

Lenka sat there and looked beautiful, nodding politely, but I sensed she wasn't taken in by any of Fowley's bullshit grovelling, not for one second.

She stood up. 'We dance.'

Fowley seemed about to move, as he must have thought her invitation was for him. But she held out her hand to me so he just shifted in his seat. Gotcha, you prick!

I followed her. 'I'm not very good at this.'

'You stand and I dance.'

I was reminded of the dance floor scene in *Basic Instinct* where Sharon Stone goes into her lesbian routine with another girl and has Michael Douglas tripping over his lolling tongue. I felt very self-conscious shifting from foot to foot but nobody was looking at me. It was all about the six-feet-something of Lenka. She was the main attraction here and didn't she know it. All the men in the club were probably hoping that those black strips of lace on her dress would magically disappear, or at least slip out of place, with every grind of her slim hips.

The music segued into another track and she stopped abruptly. 'Go back to your friend,' she said. 'I need to pee.'

'He's no friend of mine.'

'He is a bad man, I think.' And she walked away towards the ladies' with every eye in the place on her.

'That's one hot number you've got for yourself, Sam,' Fowley said when I sat down next to him. 'Gone all lipstick lezzer, I see.'

'She's married.'

'Never stopped you before.' Seemed like my little tryst with Monica Cohen had been common knowledge after all, not that it mattered anymore.

'Things have changed, Gerard.'

'I can see that.' His shark-like eyes flicked down to my breasts. 'And don't think it's not appreciated.'

'So pleased to have your approval.'

He laughed – always quick on the uptake when it came to sarcasm.

'Any news about our lovely redhead?'

I'd wondered when we'd get around to Morrison. She obviously had him shitting bricks. The word must be out that she had him in her sights.

'I hear she's on leave.'

'Keep me informed. Understand? How's that little boy you're looking after?'

'Fine, thank you.'

'You just make sure he stays that way.' Another veiled threat from Mr Fowley.

People use your weaknesses to control you, Lil Carver had said. Fowley's own Achilles heel being his ambition to appear legitimate. I filed that away for future reference. You don't beat me, sunshine. One way or another, I will get you. Let people believe you're weak and sooner or later you are going to have to kill them.

He looked up as Lenka walked back towards the booth. 'Here comes your *über*-sexy new lady-friend. You certainly know how to pick 'em, girl – I'll give you that.'

'We leave now.' Lenka's emerald gaze alighted on Fowley for no more than a second. 'Thank you for drink.'

He was on his feet to follow us. 'I'll see you to your car.' Ever the gentleman – when he wasn't slaughtering his employees.

⌣

We emerged from the club into the dark street and a chubby geezer with a shaved head and cameras slung around his neck appeared out of nowhere.

'Lenka! Smile, darlin'!' She went straight into a model pose, hands on hips, pouty mouth, full-on stuff. *Flash.* 'You too, Gerard.' Fowley beamed, clearly chuffed that this paparazzo knew his name, and he grasped Lenka firmly around the waist. *Flash.* 'And your lovely friend.' Fowley hustled me into the photo.

'What's yer name, darlin'?' *Flash.*

'Samantha Riley,' Lenka said.

'Nice tits, Samantha. Show 'em off, love. One more!' *Flash.*

Nice tits? The fucking cheek of the man.

The photographer turned to Lenka. 'How's Mike's new album coming along?'

'Out soon, Harry.'

'Give me a heads-up, darlin'. Exclusive pics in your lovely farmhouse, eh? Might get you into *Hello!* magazine. How's about it? Nice big splash, good for album sales. Whatcha say? Keep me in mind.'

'I will call you.' She walked away and I was right behind her.

The photographer handed Fowley a card. 'Anyone else in tonight?'

'Just regular punters,' I heard Fowley say.

'Well, you bell me when you get anyone good in and I'll be here in a flash – with a flash. Geddit? They don't call me Flash Harry for nothing. These shots will be great publicity for you, Gerard. Put Legend back on the map, eh? Let me know if you want any copies for your club walls. Blow-ups would look great in your foyer. You lookin' suave with two lovely ladies on your arm, can't be beat, you know. Good for the image . . .'

'Got some big names lined up,' Fowley promised.

'You just let me know, boss, and I'll be here. Okay?'

Trapped in conversation with the gabby snapper, Fowley wasn't able to escort us any further but I could feel his eyes boring into my back as I got into Lenka's car.

'He is a *very* bad man.' Lenka started the engine. 'How you know a man like that?'

'It's a long story.'

She glanced across at me. 'You tell me?'

'No.'

She shrugged. 'That's fine.'

'Anyway, how about your mate the pap?'

'He likes your tits. That is not an insult.' She laughed. 'He talk back leg off mule, yes?'

'You could put it that way.'

We'd been back at the farmhouse for just half an hour when the phone rang. Lenka held the receiver away from her ear, a pained look on her face. She finally broke in on the excited gabble from the other end of the line. 'I already tell you, Harry. Samantha Riley . . . Yes, *that* Samantha Riley . . .'

Lenka was tickled that her plan was working out so well. 'Picture will be on front pages in the morning. We must rest now and be ready.'

Well, I'd done it now. I was about to sup with the devil. Bloom would go ballistic. He'd worked so hard to keep me out of the tabloids and here I was inviting them into my life. But media attention was the one sure way to let the two Spanish hitmen know my exact location.

Come to Momma, boys. Bring it on.

6 a.m., Saturday, 12 July

Six bells and it all kicked off. But half a dozen cars outside the gates, and the doorbell and phone ringing didn't ruffle Lenka one bit. She merely closed all the curtains and walked calmly to the kitchen to brew a pot of coffee.

'This happen before,' she said. 'Some stupid girl tell stories to newspapers about "coke-fuelled sex romp" with Mike. She think she get rich and famous because she fuck my husband. Very stupid girl.'

'And did she? Make a name for herself, I mean?'

'Only one name for girl like that.' The look on her face told me I shouldn't ask any more questions. I supposed it was easy for the wives of rock musicians to ignore their husbands' on-tour shenanigans. Out of sight and out of mind, and all that bollocks. But to have your face rubbed in it with lurid tabloid headlines was another thing altogether. I bet she'd made Mike suffer for that one. 'She scares the shit out of me,' he'd told me. And I could see why.

When we didn't respond to the doorbell, someone began to rattle the letterbox.

'Samantha Riley,' a voice came though the door. 'Dave Wright from the *Globe*. Give me an exclusive and I'll get everyone else off your back.'

'Go away,' Lenka shouted. 'I set the dogs on you.'

'Don't be like that, Lenka.' He opened the letterbox flap with his hands to try and get a butcher's into the kitchen.

She walked over to the door. 'I will be like this!' She gave the door a vicious kick and the metal snapped back on his fingers.

'Fucking hell! You are one crazy bitch.'

'You think letterbox bite bad. Dogs bite worse.'

I pushed the curtain to one side just a tad and watched him retreat down the driveway. Even from the back he looked mighty miffed and was blowing on his hands.

Newshounds on the other side of the gate were taking pictures of Dave Wright from *The Globe* and pissing themselves laughing. The upside was that nobody else was about to venture any further inside the gate. And even better was that pictures of the house in the next day's press were a sure thing. Result!

My mobile rang. 'What the hell are you doing?' Richard Bloom was spitting fire. 'I've just seen the newspapers.'

'I was on a night out with my friend.'

'I've done my damnedest to keep the press away from you and now—'

'Yeah, they're on the doorstep.'

'Don't speak to anyone. Be in my office at ten at the latest. Chief Inspector Evans is not at all happy about this publicity. He's insisting on interviewing you today. Your being out on the town in the company of Gerard Fowley hasn't done you any good at all.'

'I wasn't with Fowley. We just bumped into him at the club.'

'That's not what that photograph implies. My office, ten sharp.' And he was gone.

Chapter Forty-Nine
9 a.m., Saturday, 12 July

Janine Kelso opened the door. Monica had been leaning on the bell for five minutes and was well pissed off. She knew her half-sister was there because she could hear voices from inside.

Monica stared in disgust at the dishevelled figure in front of her. The heavy make-up, still on Janine's face from the night before and smudged from sleep, made her look like a slutty clown. She was wearing a long, stained T-shirt she'd obviously just pulled on over her head. She reeked of recent sex. What a mess.

'Mum said she drove you to the airport,' Janine said.

'Changed my mind.'

'Mum'll go mad when she finds out.'

Monica pushed past Janine and walked directly into the flat. 'And that is the difference between you and me, kid,' she said. 'You do Gloria's bidding. Whereas I do what the fuck I like.'

The room was a wreck and Monica could see a young bloke in the next room, hopping about on one leg trying to pull his jeans on. Long bouncy dick, nice arse, a tattoo on his back and no underwear; going commando – a club pick-up for sure. Monica shifted a cast-off dress and panties from the sofa and made room to sit down.

'Can't you see I've got company?' Janine complained.

'Giving away the goods too soon, as always, Janine. Will you never fucking learn?'

The guy slouched out of the bedroom and Monica gave him a disdainful look. He was just another scumbag, like all of the others. This girl really was as thick as pig shit.

'But Barry's my boyfriend.' Janine said.

'Get rid.'

'Hey, Jan,' Barry slurred, 'who's your foxy friend?'

'Fuck off, shithead.' Monica retorted.

Janine handed him his jacket. 'Best go, Barry.'

'Stupid fuckin' slapper,' Barry snarled as Janine hustled him out of the door.

'Romantic type. Good choice.' Monica glanced around the room. 'I see you didn't inherit Gloria's tidy gene.'

Janine shoved more junk off another chair and sat down. 'I don't know who you think you are, coming in here and ordering me about. I'm an independent person, me. This is my home.'

'And who paid for it?' Monica reached forward and swept the powder-smeared mirror off the coffee table and onto the carpet. 'Who supports your little habit so you can spend your pitiful salary on trashy clothes? Who pays for your beauty salon treatments? Who coughs up for you to go clubbing with tosspots like Barry? Me, that's fucking who.'

Janine sat to attention, looked down at her hands and bit her bottom lip.

'Spare me the little girl act. I had that one down pat when you were still pissing in your nappy.'

'What do you want, Monica?'

'For you to remember that I own you, Janine.'

'But what do you *really* want?'

Chapter Fifty
9 a.m., Saturday, 12 July

With a long blonde wig, D&G sunglasses and full make-up, I was in my new version of mufti. Lenka was satisfied with the look. 'Beautiful,' she said, 'like a celebrity.' Tight black jeans and a low-cut purple blouse added to the disguise.

I drove to the farm gates in her red Alfa Romeo hatchback and lowered the tinted window. The reporters dutifully opened the gates for me. They photographed me in the car and I smiled like I was happy with my two seconds of fame. I heard several voices clamouring, 'Is Samantha Riley in the house?' No, Samantha has left the building, suckers.

I drove out. 'Please shut the gates,' I said. 'You don't want to let the Rottweilers get out.' There was a panicked scrabble to close them again.

I drove away and in the mirror I saw the group of newshounds swiftly turning their attention back to the house. Home free. Then I spotted him. Motorbike, leather-clad rider in a full-face helmet, right behind me. I floored the accelerator, pleased that the little Alfa had a good bit of poke. He stayed with me. I slowed into a sharp bend then accelerated out, gunning it. He was still behind me. There was a hidden turn coming up, a shortcut that would take me in the direction of Bloom's office. I slammed on the anchors at the last moment and indicated left. There was plenty of room for the biker to overtake me on the main drag. If he followed me along this rarely used narrow country lane, then I'd know for certain that I wasn't letting paranoia get the better of me. He must have spotted my indicator and, instead of overtaking me on my right-hand side, he skidded to a halt a few feet behind me. I hit the accelerator and took off again straight ahead at speed. With no traffic in front, I wellied it like a good 'un and ran a red light at a junction. I looked in the mirror. No sign of him. I'd either just put the wind up an innocent biker or outrun a tail. Though, if he was tailing me, he wasn't exactly a pro.

Bloom's office was in the opposite direction and I realised that I was suddenly back in Carver's old stomping ground, just a hundred yards from his former office above the kebab shop. I took the first parking spot I could find and waited to see if the biker was trawling the road looking for me. Cars and vans passed by but no motorbike. I pulled out into the traffic and made the first right turn that would get me onto the side road to go full circle and back in the other direction. There was a Chinese restaurant on that block, the type with lanterns in the window, very seventies with a sign that read Lee Wok, alongside some oriental calligraphy. The place had definitely seen better days. I was about to drive past when I spotted Winston standing outside. Curious, I parked once more and watched. Gerard Fowley strode out of the restaurant in the company of a small, stooped woman. He kissed her on the cheek and got into the back seat of his Daimler with Winston now at the wheel. The woman waved to Fowley and went back into the building. Could this be Clive's mother? If I could discover Clive's full identity, then there might be a way to trap Fowley without his knowing I had anything to do with it.

I rang Bloom. 'Sorry, Richard,' I said. 'Just had a flat. I'll be about half an hour late by the time I've put a new wheel on.'

'Detective Chief Inspector Evans will be in my office in an hour.' He didn't sound pleased. 'We need to talk before he arrives. Get here as soon as you can.'

I told him that I would and headed over to the restaurant.

The Closed sign was up and the door locked but I could see the small figure sitting at one of the tables hunched over a set of account books. I knocked on the door. She looked up and pointed to the sign. Probably thought I was a customer with an unnatural craving for chicken fried rice at ten in the morning.

'I'm looking for Clive,' I shouted through the glass.

She stood up with some effort, walked to the door, unlocked it and opened up just a crack. 'He not here.'

'He was supposed to meet me,' I said. 'When he didn't turn up, I got worried. He's not answering his phone. I thought he might be ill.'

'You my son's friend?'

This was the right place, then. 'Yes.'

She opened the door. 'Come in.'

Inside was as traditional as the outside. Most Chinese restaurants had modernised with white walls and the pictures of old China either swept away or kept to a bare minimum. But here the rinky-dink paper lanterns and faded images of Hong Kong Harbour clung on.

The woman smiled but she seemed guarded. 'How you know Clive? You work for Mr Fowley?'

Good grief, did she think I was one of Fowley's working girls? 'No, I'm a croupier.' No wheelee, Fowley had said just before he sent Clive to the great casino in the sky, so I reckoned I was on the right track with that one.

She shook her head sadly. 'He gambling again.' She sighed and stared at me. 'You are Clive's girlfriend? You look like nice person. What your name?'

'Jean,' I grasped for the first name that came into my head.

From the back of the restaurant a figure approached and I almost did a double take because the guy who emerged from the kitchen dressed in chef's whites was the spitting image of Clive. 'What's up, Mum?'

'Tony. This Jean. She Clive friend. She want know where he gone.'

'He's gone to the States.' Tony spoke with Clive's voice, minus the fake Yardie patois. If his mother had seemed guarded, then he had a moat and machine gun nests surrounding him. He took me by the arm and ushered me towards the door. 'So we can't help you. Sorry.' And I was back on the pavement. Oh, well, it had been worth a try. But at least now I knew more than I'd known before. Clive's surname for a start and also that his family had swallowed Fowley's fairy tale whole.

I was about to get back in the car when a voice called across to me. 'Jean!'

Tony was crossing the road towards me. The resemblance to Clive was uncanny, though Tony lacked Clive's cocksure swagger and gym-fit muscular gait.

'Sorry to have been so abrupt,' he said. 'Have you got five minutes?' He indicated to the greasy spoon café opposite. 'I'll buy you a coffee.'

Behind the counter was a sullen guy wearing a wife-beater over a ten-barrel beer belly. He nodded to Tony as we walked in. The only other occupant was an old bloke sitting at a table by the window, chewing morosely on a toasted cheese sandwich. We went and sat at the far corner.

'I don't want Mum upset,' Tony explained. 'She's not well.'

'I didn't intend to worry her,' I said. 'I was concerned about Clive, that's all. But if he's gone to America . . .'

'Who are you, Jean?' He held me in his gaze and his expression told me he wasn't taken in by my story, not one jot. He'd obviously inherited the smarts in the family.

'Like I said, I'm a friend of Clive's.'

'I know my brother and you're not like any of the women of his that I've ever seen.'

This was getting too awkward for words. I back-pedalled like mad. 'Look, I'm sorry if my visit upset your mother. That wasn't my intention.' Get out of here, Sam, now.

'I've been in touch with my eldest brother in California and he hasn't heard from Clive for three years.' The café proprietor brought our coffees over and Tony paid him. 'So what do you know that you're not telling me?'

'I don't know anything . . .'

He raised his hand to stop me. 'I get it.'

I took a sip of my coffee. It tasted like dishwater.

'Our Clive's always been trouble.' Tony conceded. 'I've been running the business since our older brother went to the States. He's got three restaurants in San Francisco now. I only stick around because of Mum.'

He wasn't at all aggressive so if he wanted to chat then I was prepared to listen. 'And Clive?'

'He hates the business. When he was a kid he wouldn't even wait tables when we were short-handed. Kept getting into bother and ended up doing two years in the nick. When he got out, Mum hoped he'd come and work with us but he didn't want to know. Only Gerard Fowley would give him a job.' The look on his face told me he had little time for Fowley. 'And Mum's very grateful, you know.' So that was why he'd given me the bum's rush; he was trying to protect his mother.

'But I've been thinking. It's tricky getting a visa for the States these days – especially for someone with a bit of form. So Fowley's story didn't quite ring true, you know what I mean?'

'Maybe you should have a word with Winston.'

'Have a word?'

'With Winston.'

'Me and a few mates, maybe?' He caught on quick.

'That's up to you.'

'And I'm guessing you'd like your name kept out of this, er . . . Jean.'

Very quick. 'That's the idea.'

'Thanks.' He got up to leave. 'Clive's still my kid brother, after all. And we take care of our own.'

I watched him walk out. He was the good son who took responsibility for his mother and the family business. I hoped that whatever he had in mind wouldn't land him in too much bother. Though if he'd had his own doubts about this set-up already then all I'd done was confirm them. Winston would be a hard bastard to break but when Tony had said that 'we take care of our own', I guessed he meant the Chinese community and they were not the kind of folk that I would be in a hurry to tangle with.

Man-mountain Winston might well be in for a bit of a shock. Being waylaid and worked over by a bunch of pissed-off Chinese guys was not a prospect to be relished. As a wise man once said, don't fuck with anyone unless you know exactly who the fuck it is you're fucking with.

But I didn't have time to ponder, I had to get to Richard Bloom's office before DCI Evans turned up to interview me. I left the foul coffee and made a mental note not to enter that particular establishment again.

I drove to the end of the street, took a left, then a right and was back on the road I'd come along but in the opposite direction, now heading past the kebab shop once more. And there it was, a motorbike where Big Jim Carver used to park his Audi estate car. I couldn't be sure it was the one that had followed me from the farmhouse but if this was one of Carver's cronies or ex-employees out for revenge or scouting for info then I'd have to watch my back. With Gloria in charge now there might be a lot of resentment building up. These guys wouldn't be too keen on taking orders from a woman like Gloria.

When her old man had been stabbed to death in prison, Lil Carver had inherited his mantle and she'd ruled with a fist of iron. But that was back in the old days when she had a gang of really hard men to fight her corner. Now they were mostly dead or retired. Later, the young guns had been kept in check by Big Jim's reputation for being a total nutcase. But if Gloria had taken control, even if she did have Swindley to back her up, there could be some kind of power struggle going on. I'd been at the house when the Carver crew had been whacked and I'd walked away unscathed. At worst, that could very easily put me in the frame. Or, at best, be seen as a source of information for any dissenters itching to take Swindley down. What an idiot for not seeing that one coming. I'd been far too preoccupied with Brando and his needs to even think it through.

I looked at the dashboard clock. I had no time to stop again and check this out. But that motorbike was a wake-up call as loud as Big Ben.

Chapter Fifty-One
11 a.m., Saturday, 12 July

There was a car parked by Bloom's building. According to him it would be another half hour before the police arrived but I had a horrible feeling they were already there.

Bloom met me at the door and raised his eyebrows at my appearance.

'Disguise,' I said, 'to get past the media scrum.'

I went to the loo, removed the wig and ran my fingers through my hair. Well, I looked a bit more like me, but only just.

Detective Chief Inspector Evans was big and beefy and looked like the type who played rugby – a sport played by barbarians and watched by gentlemen, as they say. His minion, whose name I didn't catch, was also tall but considerably thinner. The image of a praying mantis popped into my mind.

Evans was Welsh with a voice way down in his boots. He gave me some old flannel about 'an informal interview' and I tried to appear relaxed, but I was wary.

'Would you agree to giving us a DNA sample, Miss Riley?' Evans asked. 'Just so we can eliminate you from our enquiries.'

Bloom was about to protest but I agreed. Nothing makes you look guiltier than not cooperating with cops, I always believed. I opened my mouth and the mantis did the honours.

Evans sat back and waited for me to talk.

I gave the cops the spiel – army for fifteen years, job at Legend, employment as driver for Monica and Brando. Then I briefly went over the story surrounding Benny Cohen's sudden demise, and so on. Evans listened politely while his oppo made the odd note.

'In your original interview, I believe that DI Morrison asked you about your links to Joseph Murphy, the man who shot Benjamin Cohen.' That was his opening approach.

'I cleared that up at the time,' I said. Sorry, Joe, I'm denying you for a third time.

Evans smiled. 'You said you didn't know him. Is that correct?'

Had Morrison shared the info about the photo of Joe and me with her sidekick Trevor Jones? If she had and he had subsequently sold her out, then I was well and truly screwed.

'That's right,' I replied. 'But I've been through all this before.'

Bloom jumped in. 'Chief Inspector, have you any evidence to connect my client with this man Murphy?'

'No.'

'Then I suggest we move on as my client has already answered.'

Evans nodded. 'What is your relationship with DI Morrison?'

'Relationship? I'm sorry, I don't understand.'

'There were several phone calls made and you met up with her and Detective Sergeant Jones at Chessington Park, I believe.'

It sounded like they were investigating Wendy Morrison, after all. And Trevor Jones had been cooperating. There might be a smidgen of honour among thieves, maybe, but clearly none among coppers.

'The Inspector asked me to pass on any information I had regarding her investigation into the activities of Big Jim Carver. I merely told her that he and Gerard Fowley were interested in buying Benny Cohen's nightclubs. I was behaving as would any concerned citizen in aiding a police enquiry.'

'You were photographed in the company of Gerard Fowley only last night.'

I could sense Richard Bloom bristling with anger in the seat beside me.

So I told him I'd gone to Legend with Lenka Watts and about our encounter with Fowley and the pap. The Inspector appeared sceptical. 'The photographer informed my colleague that he was contacted by Lenka Watts and told to be there. Did you know about that?'

I shrugged as though it was of no consequence to me either way. 'Maybe she was after the publicity. Her husband has a new album out soon. It's the first one for almost five years.'

'And having you in the photograph promised a front-page story?'

I was more than happy to let him and Bloom think that Lenka had used me as a cheap publicity stunt. 'I hadn't thought about it like that. But, yes, I suppose so.' What a clever man you are, Detective Chief Inspector.

He wanted to know why Brando was away.

'You can't watch television without seeing news stories about police digging up the gardens at the Carver house, or reports about gangland killings in the papers. Brando's only eleven so it's been very upsetting for him and I felt it wise for him to be shielded from it all for a while.'

More nodding, more scribbling and Bloom stepped in. 'Mr Cohen chose Miss Riley as Brando's guardian. He deemed her the most responsible person to take care of his son once he was gone. Mr Cohen had only a few months to live and he was aware of his wife's affair with Felipe Garcia. Who, I'm sure you know, was involved with a drug trafficking cartel in Spain.'

The intimation being, so let's not be too concerned about Garcia's sudden departure from this earth, seeing as he was a scumbag of the first water.

Evans didn't react either way. 'Why did you leave the scene of the shooting of Angus Macdonald?'

Angus! I hadn't known Mac's first name until that moment.

'Mac managed to tell me that Carver had taken Brando. I felt I had to find him as soon as I could.'

Evans looked me straight in the eye. He was a difficult man to read.

'So you thought you could handle the situation better than the police?'

I didn't care for the remark but didn't even flinch. 'Someone texted me with the message "*Run*". So I forwarded it to DI Morrison and told her to be at Carver's house at ten in the morning with armed officers.'

'And DI Morrison took your word for it?' He glanced across at his underling who made another note.

Dodgy ground here – step carefully, Sam. 'It would seem so because she was there.'

'Did you know who would be at the Carver residence?'

'I had no idea. I was looking for Brando.'

'So Mrs Cohen's presence there came as a surprise to you?'

Bloom chipped in again. 'Mrs Cohen had already verbally threatened my client and Brando. That was why they were at my cottage with Angus Macdonald. It was a precautionary measure. Mrs Cohen has always been rather volatile, shall we say.'

Evans ignored him. 'Did you expect this Mr Swindley to be there?'

'As I said, I had no idea who would be there. I was concerned for Brando's safety. I didn't really think about it.'

'Did you tell DI Morrison of the events at the cottage?'

'Not much. I told her there'd been a shooting and that it was connected to Carver.'

'You didn't mention the kidnap?'

I said nothing. It was clear that they already had Morrison's phone records.

Evans sat back and stared at me for a moment, maybe expecting me to speak. But I kept quiet. Work it out for yourself, pal.

'You thought you could deal with this alone. Without any police involvement?'

'I think my client has already answered that question,' Bloom reminded him.

'How tall are you, Miss Riley?'

'Five-ten.'

'And Swindley?'

'Five-six or maybe -seven.' It was pointless to lie as I had already described him in a statement. But I guessed what was coming next.

'There's a little mystery you can maybe help us clear up, Miss Riley. You said in the statement you gave to Inspector Morrison that Swindley took you out of the room at gunpoint. Is that correct?'

'I thought he was going to shoot me.'

'But instead he told you to stay in the hallway and he went back into the room alone?'

'Yes.'

'Then you heard four shots?'

'That's correct.' Here we go.

'What my colleagues and I can't understand – and perhaps you could enlighten us – is why James Carver was killed with a second gun?'

That was the question I had steeled myself for. This could be my undoing. I should have let Swindley see to Carver. But I had to come over all avenging angel. I imagined some CSI type measuring bullet trajectories and scratching his head. At least that's what I'd seen on all those telly programmes – hence the question about my height. Stick to your story, Sam. Don't get thrown by this.

Bloom rescued me. 'Chief Inspector, I don't see how my client can help you when she wasn't even in the room.'

Evans moved on. 'Did you catch sight of a second gun, Miss Riley?'

'When I first saw Swindley, I noticed that he had a shoulder holster.'

Don't elaborate. Keep information to a bare minimum. The cops often know far less than you imagine. They might suspect that I killed Carver but they had no solid evidence. The only eyewitness still standing was Swindley.

'So you heard four shots and you stayed where you were in the hallway?' I knew where this was leading so I kept quiet.

'Did you have your mobile phone on you, Miss Riley?'

'No. Gloria Kelso went through my pockets when I arrived and took it off me.'

'But you were in sight of the front door?'

'Yes.'

'And it didn't occur to you to run out and alert the police, when they were just beyond the gates.'

'The driveway to the Carver house is a good quarter-of-a-mile long and I wasn't about to leave Brando in the house with a gunman on the loose.'

Evans nodded his head and continued, 'According to your statement, Swindley then exited the room and took you to the basement
where you found Brando with Arthur Caine? At that point, did you
still fear for your life?'

'As I told Inspector Morrison, Swindley said he wasn't going to
harm Brando or me.'

'And you believed him?'

'I didn't have much choice.'

'Except to try and alert the police.'

'I was there to find Brando. He was my main concern. And the
arrangement I made with DI Morrison was for her to storm in at
ten if I hadn't phoned her.'

We moved on to the events at the Cohen house, but Bloom had
already given a very precise statement and Evans didn't appear concerned about Brando's part. Though he did say he'd like to interview
the boy when he got back from France.

Evans got to his feet and we all stood up. He shook my hand.

'Thank you for your cooperation, Miss Riley. We'll be in touch
if we need to question you further. I take it you are not planning to
leave the country?'

'Brando will be back in a couple of weeks. I have a lot to do
before then, what with a rented house to sort out and a new school
for him.'

'You take your guardianship very seriously, it seems – enough
to put yourself in harm's way for Brando. Very commendable, I'm
sure. You were in Bosnia and Iraq, I believe.'

'Royal Logistic Corps there and elsewhere.'

'So you are accustomed to life-threatening situations?'

'I was a driver, but yes, I have been shot at on a few occasions.'

I wasn't about to trade battle stories. These are things you prefer
to forget – all that fucking sand, the intense heat and the resentment in the eyes of the local people. With RPGs coming at you

from out of nowhere, sniper fire from tumbledown buildings; or the sight of the truck in front of yours getting blown to buggery by an IED. If you need to regale people with tales of that stuff, then you need your head examined.

'You do live an interesting life, Miss Riley.'

'Isn't that a Chinese curse? May you live in interesting times.'

Evans laughed. 'Indeed it is. *Nil sin labore*, eh?'

Nil sin labore – was the old motto for what is now the Royal Logistic Corps. As a man once said, not many people know that. Was Evans friend or foe? Don't even think that way, Sam. He's a cop and more savvy than he lets on.

⸻

After seeing both cops to the door, Bloom came back into his office. 'Did the police examine your shoes and clothing after the shootings at the Carver house?'

'No. Why should they? I was the victim, wasn't I?'

'Have you still got them?'

'I was wearing them when I saved your legal arse, remember.'

'Where are they now?'

'At the hotel in Norwich.'

'Best place for them.'

Not as good as the bonfire they'll be thrown on once I get back there.

'One more thing,' Bloom added. 'There's been a development in the matter of the potential sale of the nightclubs.'

'Has Gerard Fowley backed out?' That would stop him from breathing down my neck.

'No, Mrs Gloria Kelso has opted in. I've been informed that she wants to renegotiate the initial agreement that Mr Cohen had made with her brother and Mr Fowley.'

Fowley would go mental. There was no knowing what he'd do if he was tripped at the final hurdle. I hoped my new Chinese friend was serious about finding out about his brother and that Winston would crack. Otherwise, I'd have Fowley after me. I recalled his words as we sat in the booth at Legend. 'How's that little boy of yours?' That was Fowley's style all over, cloaking a threat in an innocent question. 'You make sure he stays that way.'

'However, the point is now moot,' Bloom said. 'I have also had a letter from a solicitor in London. Apparently Monica is challenging Mr Cohen's will.'

'Can she do that?'

'In this country people are allowed to leave their estate to whomever they please, of course. They can disinherit everyone and leave it to the local donkey sanctuary if they wish to.'

'So what's her angle?'

Bloom shook his head and sighed. 'Under the Inheritance Act of 1975, a will can be contested if an individual fails to make reasonable provision for a spouse. It seems as though Monica feels that her ten years as Mrs Cohen has not been as well rewarded as she may have anticipated.'

'And where does that leave Brando?'

'All assets will have to be frozen until the matter is settled. So I would hold fire on using that credit card I gave you for the moment.'

Monica couldn't get to Benny's money one way so she was trying another.

'But I've already paid the rent for the house in Norwich on it."

'Frozen from the date of the letter I received. So those charges still will go through. Don't worry about that.' Bloom smiled. 'Your basic salary is safe but I'm afraid you and Brando are going to have to make do with that for a while.'

Monica going legit, that was quite a turn-up for the books. Though I wouldn't hold my breath. I knew only too well that if she didn't get exactly what she considered her due, she'd turn nasty again soon enough. She might have Richard Bloom lulled but the Monica I knew was an all-or-nothing kind of a gal. This had all the hallmarks of a delaying tactic – or a smokescreen. I had a sudden image of Monica waving a white flag in one hand, with a grenade launcher hidden behind her back.

Chapter Fifty-Two
2 p.m., Saturday, 12 July

On the almost deserted road, the biker was behind me once more. All black gear, with a full-face helmet. Yep, it was him, all right. It was time for a little confrontation. I put my foot down and the Alfa growled its response. It had started to pour down and the dry road would become very slippery with this first torrential rainfall. I knew the road well and there was a blind right curve coming up with a grassed parking space on both sides. I accelerated into the curve and, as I hit the bend, I floored the brake and swerved onto the verge. The rider was right on my tail and as he hit his brakes the bike skidded sideways. He lost control and was thrown off into the middle of the road while the bike skittered to a stuttering halt yards in front. I was out of the car in seconds and standing over the prone figure. I couldn't see any sign of a weapon.

'Bloody hell!' a woman's voice came from inside the helmet. A car coming from the opposite direction approached and slowed down, the driver wound down his window. 'Need any help?'

'No,' I replied. 'I've got it.' I helped the leather-clad figure to her feet and took her to my side of the road.

'Damned rain,' the driver of the car cursed. 'Makes this road like a bloody skating rink. Sure you don't need an ambulance?'

'We're fine,' I called to him.

'Best get that motorbike off the road,' he said as he drove off.

Leaning against the Alfa and taking off her helmet, a white-faced Janine Kelso looked back at me.

'You could have killed me,' she gasped.

I took a bottle of water out of the car and handed it to her. 'Drink this.'

I dragged the bike over to the other grass verge and by the time I got back she'd regained some colour in her face. Without the false lashes and ladled-on makeup, she looked much younger than I remembered and she had the most striking pale grey eyes. Just like . . . surely not? Joe and I had been sent to pop Gloria's husband. Wasn't *he* supposed to be Janine's dad?

'Why were you following me?'

'I wanted to warn you. Monica is after you. She's out to get you and Brando. She's as mad as hell.'

I eyed her suspiciously. 'What's it to you?'

'I have my reasons,' she replied. She crossed the road to examine the motorbike. 'I wish I hadn't bothered now,' she shouted across to me. 'This bike is well fucked.'

I gave Janine a lift back to the farmhouse. The media circus appeared to have left town. The vagaries of fame, eh? I laughed as I recalled the old joke: Knock, knock! Who's there? Kylie. Kylie who? Ah, that's showbiz.

Indoors, Lenka was watching the television intently.

'When did the press leave?' I asked her.

'One minute here, next minute gone.' She gestured towards the TV screen. The gates of the Carver house were in view with cameras flashing and journos in a lather of visceral anticipation.

'Police find the first bodies,' Lenka explained. 'More to come, I think.'

Someone's brother, someone's son . . . I shivered.

Janine rang a mechanic she knew to collect the motorbike and pick her up. She was bruised but mostly her leathers had protected her. Lenka handed her a glass of Stolichnaya Elit vodka – the Russian cure-all, it seemed. Either that or after a couple of them you don't give a shit anymore.

'Fuck me,' Janine said. 'This is good stuff. We'll stock this in Legend when I take it over.'

Lenka raised her eyebrows at me.

'Gerard Fowley's set his sights on that one,' I pointed out.

Janine laughed. 'Not if Mum gets her way. And, believe me, Mum will get what she wants. With Lil and Big Jim gone, she's in charge now. Didn't Richard Bloom tell you? She's opened up negotiations for the clubs again. Fowley can have the crap ones if he still wants them.' She held the glass out to Lenka for another shot. 'But it's Legend I'm interested in.' She downed the vodka in one go. 'I know loads of top-notch people. I'll get the young crowd in. And we'll definitely be stocking this stuff.'

So that was Gloria's plan, to set Janine up in the club business. 'And Monica?'

'That bitch will get sod all.'

'She's contesting Benny's will, so I wouldn't count my chickens if I were you.'

Janine's face dropped. 'Can't you just pay her off?'

'What if it's the clubs she wants?'

The look on her face translated as, does not compute. 'I've got to talk to Mum right away,' she said.

The doorbell rang. 'My ride's here.' Janine jumped to her feet. 'I'm supposed to let Monica know where you're living,' she added. 'That's another reason I was following you. But I'll play dumb if you want.'

'The picture of house is in newspapers,' Lenka said.

Janine looked at her askance. 'Newspapers? Nobody reads them anymore, do they?' And she was out of the door in the company of the mechanic from the garage. 'Can you fix it?' I heard her say.

'Sure,' he said, 'but it'll cost you.'

'Don't worry about that. Just get it done. Mum'll pay.'

She climbed into the passenger seat of the truck and they drove off towards the gates.

Lenka gave me a querying look. 'You trust her?'

'Who? Janine?'

She nodded her head.

'Not as far as I could throw that tow truck.'

Lenka shook her head. 'Weak,' she commented. 'Weak people are most dangerous. Will do anything to save skin.'

'Won't we all?'

'To betray is crime worse than to kill, I think.'

'You reckon she was lying?'

'Too stupid to lie. Girl like that will blow with wind.'

Lenka held me in her emerald gaze. 'You tell me whole story now?'

So I did. Well, most of it anyway. My relationship with Joe Murphy was nobody's business but mine. But I told her about my affair with Monica. And I stayed with my story about Swindley killing both of the Carvers. She took it all on board and I wondered if she might tell me to pack my bags and leave.

'I do porno movie with other girl once. Not exciting. But that was movie for men.' Her green eyes searched my face. 'You still like women?'

'I thought I loved Monica.'

'You are a romantic, I think.' She laughed. 'You should try men. Much more . . . stimulating.'

'I haven't had much experience in either direction.'

'Tonight, I let dogs out to roam the gardens. They will warn. You sleep and I take first watch. You take second.'

'You're still in this with me?'

'But of course.' She got up to make some coffee. 'You are my friend.'

I watched her walk across the room. Lenka appeared to be with me all the way, prepared to put her own safety on the line in order to help me. But I couldn't understand why. The fact was, she hardly knew me. I needed to trust her and hoped that she had no ulterior motive. Not that I could imagine what that might possibly be. Only time would tell.

Chapter Fifty-Three
7 p.m., Saturday, 12 July

Gerard Fowley was behind the desk in the office of his car show-room. Winston stood nearby with his back to the wall, impassive as ever. Seated in a leather chair in front of Fowley's desk was Monica. She wore a black suit with a skirt that showed her legs to their best advantage and a cerise blouse that revealed just enough cleavage to be sexy yet remain sufficiently businesslike.

'I've got a proposition for you, Gerard,' she cooed. She sat back in the chair and crossed her legs so the swish of nylon stockings insinuated itself into the room.

Fowley grimaced. 'Sorry, Monica, but doing the old cock-and-snatch routine with you holds no interest for me, whatsoever.'

Monica slowly uncrossed her legs, smoothed her skirt down and sat up straight again.

'Nothing personal, darlin', it's just that I'm a little jaded, you know. I've developed more, erm, exotic tastes.' He gave a wolfish grin. 'For example, seeing you tied down and taken up the arse by my boy Winston over there. Now that might just arouse my inter-est. He's got a knob-end the size of my fist.' Fowley bunched his fingers to illustrate. 'You up for that?'

Monica stared him down. If this was his little game, she wasn't having any of it. Carry on, clever dick. And just you see where it gets you.

'Thought not.' Fowley's grin widened 'Now your old friend Sam Riley is another matter altogether. She's come on a bit, hasn't she? Gone all lipstick lezzer, I notice, all ripe tits and hips.' His hands made the universal hourglass gesture. 'Watching her going at it with that hot new lady friend of hers, now that might get the old chap up and running.' He laughed. 'Don't suppose you could arrange that for me?'

Monica remained silent. Play away, little boy. You don't get a rise out of me. Let's get to the point.

Her composed demeanour disconcerted him and his smile slowly subsided. 'So, as you have nothing to offer me of the carnal variety,' he said, 'shall we stop pissing around and you tell me why the fuck I should want to make any kind of a deal with you.'

'Because we're friends, Gerard.' She threw him her most dazzling smile but got a stone-faced response.

'You and that Spanish fucker tried to do me over, girly. You're lucky to still be breathing. So get on with it.'

'I hear you're still hot to trot for the nightclubs.'

'That's not news, that's a given.'

'Just thought you'd like to know that I've been advised by my lawyers to challenge Benny's will. Which means all his assets are frozen as of now.' Monica casually glanced down to pick a piece of non-existent fluff from the hem of her black skirt, then looked back up at him. 'The probate is now on hold, nothing can be bought and nothing can be sold – and that includes the clubs, of course. It could take months, years even, to get sorted.' Fowley's expression darkened and she felt a rising sense of satisfaction. 'How's that for news?'

'And you're telling me this to my face, why? How easy would it be for me to have you disappear? And, hey presto, no more legal challenge.'

'Because that's what a villain would do, Gerard. And you're not a villain, are you? You're a legitimate businessman.' Monica smiled. 'Anyway, that's not the best part.' She paused for effect. 'Gloria Kelso will inherit all of Carver's businesses and she's planning to revive the deal you all had prior to Benny being blasted off his perch.'

Fowley's face fell three feet and the sense of impending triumph gave Monica a buzz far more intense than any orgasm. *I'll teach you not to try and humiliate me, you rat-faced fuck!*

Fowley gestured for Winston to leave the room but Monica stood instead and strode towards the door.

'You apologise,' she insisted. 'Apologise to me in front of him. Now! Or I walk out of here and you don't get to hear about something to our mutual advantage.'

Fowley raised his hands in surrender. 'You know me, Monica. Didn't mean to offend. It was all in fun, darlin'.'

She opened the door. 'That doesn't count as an apology in my book.'

Fowley stood too. 'I'm sorry. I forgot my manners. We live in stressful times, Monica. It gets to me sometimes, you know.' He gestured towards the chair, inviting her to sit down again.

But she was not to be appeased. She opened the door wider as though to leave. Fowley showed more contrition. 'Look, please accept my most humble apologies.' Monica slowly closed the door. Fowley clicked his fingers. 'Winston,' he ordered. 'Please see the lady back to her seat. Then bugger off. This is private.'

Monica allowed herself a little smile. *These men are so pathetic. Everything is reduced to a pissing contest.* But she had Fowley where she wanted him and she'd make him regret every snide remark he'd ever made about her. She was going to get the better of the lot of them. *That was a fucking given.*

Chapter Fifty-Four
9 p.m., Saturday, 12 July

Winston didn't know what hit him. He was sauntering along, just a few yards from the stairs to his mother's council flat in Sage House. The car park was pitch dark and the only light filtering through the gloom came from the three tiers of open landings that stretched from one end of the building to the other. Half of those lights were broken, as usual.

His mother never went out at night because of the vandalism on the estate.

She'd be indoors now and his dinner would be in the oven. It was chicken, peas and rice tonight – his favourite – and he was looking forward to it. And for once it wouldn't be all dried up because Mr Fowley had let him go early to talk to that Cohen woman in private.

Winston had caught the bus for the five stops to his mother's home because it was raining so hard and he didn't want to get his suit drenched. Usually he walked it, though he did it on his own these days. He used to walk with Chinese Clive who had a mate living in Thyme House. That was where Clive stashed his motor so Mr Fowley couldn't see how flash it was. Winston couldn't fathom why, but that was the way it was. He had come to accept that there were things he didn't quite comprehend but nobody laughed at him these days.

Clive had been all mouth, and Winston wasn't much of a conversationalist so he'd just listened, when he could be bothered, and most of the time he didn't understand what Clive was on about anyway. But they'd got along alright. He couldn't really admit that he missed Clive because if the boss told him to deal with him, then that's what had to be done.

Though Clive really shouldn't have beaten up that girl. That wasn't nice. It wasn't necessary.

Dogs, cats and girls: they were special and he hated seeing them hurt.

He'd preferred it when he first worked for Mr Fowley in the garden centre. He liked the plants, watching them grow and stuff. He liked being the biggest and strongest, being able to lug all the bags of rocks and soil about when other employees struggled to even lift them. And the digging, he liked digging. He hadn't liked that last digging job he'd had to do. But that was different and he didn't work at the garden centre anymore.

Mr Fowley had told him that the job in the car showroom was a promotion. Mr Fowley had even paid for his driving lessons and Winston was proud to have passed his test on the sixth attempt. His mum had been mighty proud too. She'd never believed he could learn to drive. And when he came home in the smart suit Mr Fowley had bought for him, his mum burst into tears and hugged him.

He'd almost reached the stairway when a van pulled into the car park and he was caught in its headlights. Winston squinted at it and the driver dipped the beams. A Chinese guy leaned out of the van window and beckoned to him.

'Hey, mate! Know where I can find Rosemary House? I've got a delivery for number sixty.'

Winston grinned and walked over to the van. Parsley, Sage, Rosemary and Thyme – he knew all the names of the estate's houses off by heart. His mum had drummed them into his head when he was a kid, so he wouldn't get lost. 'Next block,' he told the driver, pointing to the first grey building along. 'Number sixty is on the third floor.'

The back of the van slid open.

Winston turned his head to see Clive emerge from behind the van with something in his hand. Winston blinked hard. It couldn't be Clive. He'd buried Clive himself. Maybe it was the ghost of Clive. Winston's mum believed in them. She said that all your bad deeds would come back to haunt you.

The object wielded by Clive's ghost looked like a gun but it had a yellow casing. Winston had seen one of those before but he couldn't remember where. He didn't like guns.

'Hello, Winston.' The ghost raised the yellow gun and pointed it in Winston's direction.

'But you're dead,' Winston stammered.

When the weapon fired, two darts attached to wires hit Winston in the shoulder, penetrating his suit jacket. The severe shock was instantaneous and the wires appeared to shimmer as Winston's body tensed into extreme cramp. His arms froze and he felt as though someone was tightening a chain connected to his forehead from the base of his neck, drawing his shoulders up to his ears. The pain was intense and constant and he felt paralysed even though every sinew strained to respond.

Someone shouted, 'He's a big bastard. Do him again!'

Winston's mind was fogging up and he had to struggle to keep his balance. Out of the corner of his eye he could see the darts in his shoulder as they delivered another blast of excruciating pain.

'Get the fucker on the ground!' a voice snarled.

A sudden hiss and a blast of acrid spray in Winston's face scalded his eyes and blinded him. The van driver's door slammed outwards and toppled the giant, knocking him to the ground. The darts kicked in again and the world tuned out. Winston would never be sure what had hit him.

Chapter Fifty-Five
2 a.m., Sunday, 13 July

My turn on watch and the house was in darkness with only moonlight filtering through the curtains. The farmhouse layout was traditional in style, but was now renovated and fully modernised with double-glazed French windows that provided a panoramic view of the garden. Swings, a trampoline, a climbing frame and a splash pool were in the play area to the right and the remainder was a large lawn for the kids to run about on. The garden stretched as far as a small wood beyond.

Brando had been so happy here. I missed him. But he was safe and that was all that mattered. He'd texted me when he arrived in France. *We R here. Great place. Come soon. Brando x.* The kiss had choked me up, but I couldn't afford to start getting soppy. We were a long way off from playing happy families. I was back in soldier mode and had to concentrate on the job in hand.

All the doors were bolted. Outside, the two Rottweilers had been released from their enclosure and allowed to stay on the mats by the door.

The floodlights had a motion-sensor option but that was never used as it was too easily tripped by wildlife such as badgers or foxes snuffling around the grounds. But at any sign of any trouble the lights could be switched on manually.

The only other building on the land was the barn that had been converted into a music studio and garage. Lenka had checked the doors there and declared them secure. I doubted that the two Spanish hired guns would break in there, as the stand-alone building didn't provide access to the house. I reckoned they'd want to be in and out as fast as possible. Though Lenka was worried that they might hide out there until daylight and ambush anyone entering in the morning. That was the reason she had wanted the dogs set loose.

I was never too happy around guard dogs unless they were expertly trained. They were far too fickle and easily distracted. I'd often seen them killed, too. Dogs, goats, sheep – drive-by target practice in desert countries. Bored soldiers did it all the time abroad.

I sat and tried to weigh up all the possibilities. The woods at the back were a good half-mile away but a trained marksman could hit any target, moving or not, from that distance in the daytime. Though, with the neighbours fairly close at hand, gunfire would be certain to bring unwanted attention. However, a gunman with a long-range rifle and suppressor could pick us off and be home free before our bodies were found. After dark, it would be more difficult without night sights. And that was a lot of kit to get your hands on at short notice.

Anyway, would Garcia's sister want that? I guessed what she'd demand would be something more up-close and personal. Being swiftly executed in our beds was probably more to her liking. So I reckoned that a sneak attack inside the house was far more likely.

Lenka was asleep upstairs with a loaded shotgun by her bed. I had completed a check on the other rooms and seen both dogs snoozing soundly outside the French windows. So I settled down in the kitchen and watched the front door.

The sudden sound of barking echoed in the silence of the night and I was instantly on my feet. I hit the floodlights and the grounds lit up like a football pitch.

'I have it!' Lenka shouted from upstairs. The master bedroom was above the kitchen and the plan was, if it all kicked off, she'd watch the front of the house from that window as it had an uninterrupted view of the drive and land. I picked up my shotgun and ran to the back room on high alert. I crept to the side of the windows, eased the curtain to one side and looked out. In the brightly illuminated garden, I saw the dogs tugging at a hapless rabbit that had strayed into their territory.

I called up to Lenka. 'Stay put while I check it out.' It might well be a decoy. Get the dogs all excited about a bunny, then sneak up when they were all of a lather about their prize. I stayed in position by the side of the window and scanned the garden. The dogs, eyes wild with excitement, were tearing the bloody corpse to pieces. I scanned the grounds for any sign of figures edging their way along the perimeter fences. But with the lights full on there was no cover.

A movement from within the trees caught my attention and I had aimed the shotgun at the branches when the muzzle of a fox appeared for a second before it ducked back in again. A call, like the cry of a small baby, got the dogs' attention and, out of nowhere, from behind a small bush by the kids play area, a smaller fox appeared. With light shining brightly in its eyes, it hesitated for a moment then made a sudden mad dash across the grass towards the trees. The dogs, bloody of snout and sated after their rabbit snack, lumbered after it but it was far too fast for them. They followed it as far as the woods, then gave up in disgust and padded back to the dismembered remains of their kill. Once the young fox had made its getaway, I watched for more movement within the trees but, without any wind, even the leaves were as still as the grave.

'All clear!' I shouted up to Lenka.

I remained in position for ten minutes longer and my pulse slowly returned to its resting rate. Once I was sure everything was secure, I left the stupid mutts to argue between themselves over the scraps of the rabbit, then returned to the kitchen and turned the floodlights off.

I was livid. *Tomorrow night you lock the fucking dogs up, Lenka, before I'm tempted to shoot them myself.*

At three thirty, the hum of a car engine at the end of the drive had me up at the kitchen window. The driver killed the sidelights. Why would anyone drive down a country road on sidelights? I waited, shotgun at the ready. The waning moon came from behind a cloud and momentarily highlighted a figure standing at the gates, before it was obscured once more. I opened the front door just enough to get through, slid out into the cold, early-morning air and crouched down behind the small potted conifer that stood on the porch. With the person in my sights, I waited for the gate to open. The moon was my friend once more and I could see that the figure looked like a woman. She reached down to open the latch.

'Bloody satnav!' an agitated man's voice came from within the car. 'This is the wrong place.' The woman turned away and the car's headlights lit up the road. The car door slammed and moments later, they drove off. I breathed a sigh of relief and went back into the house.

The rest of the night passed without incident and Lenka came downstairs at seven on the Sunday morning. We were having breakfast when my phone rang. It was the hospital in Norwich. Mac was out of the coma. Though still being monitored in the ICU unit, he had been asking about me. Did I wish to visit him? I texted Brando. *Mac awake. Love, Sam.*

Lenka was adamant. 'You must go.'

'I can't leave you here alone, Lenka.'

'My brother is in London for business.' She smiled across the table at me. 'I will call him to come and see me.'

'Are you sure we should we get other people involved?'

She laughed. 'We are Russian. We understand such things. If I call him, he will come. You must go and visit your friend.'

This was the first time she'd mentioned that one of her brothers was in the country. Was she being secretive or just forgetful? In my eagerness to get to visit Mac, I put it down to having slipped her mind.

Chapter Fifty-Six
2 p.m., Sunday, 13 July

Mac was awake. He was still in the ICU and the nurses had warned me that he might appear confused and disorientated. He remained hooked up to a bunch of monitors that blinked steadily like watchful guardians.

His first word to me was a softly whispered, 'Brando?'

'He's safe.'

'I remember hearing his voice and yours. But I thought it was a dream.'

'Can you remember what happened that night?'

'Not much. Carver's guys burst in. Then everything went black. I recall the pain, hearing Brando shouting and then nothing. It was all a blur until you came back.'

'You told me that Carver's guys had taken Brando.'

'You kissed me.' He smiled warmly.

'No, I didn't.' I felt my face colouring up. My memory was that my lips brushed his forehead just before he spoke to me. But if it made him feel better to think I'd kissed him, then so be it.

'You did. You kissed me and told me to hang on in there. And that's all I remember.'

I gave him a rundown of what had happened at Carver's place.

'Carver's dead? Couldn't have happened to a nicer person,' was his dry comment.

Then I explained about the kidnap of Bloom and the events at the Cohen house.

'Oh, that poor kid. I should have been there to protect you.'

'You certainly missed out on all the fun and games.' I tried to make light of it but Mac didn't look convinced. 'I should never have gone to see Fowley and left you and Brando alone. But it's over now,' I lied. 'Brando is in France and I'm staying at Mike Watts' house until he gets back. In the meantime, I've found a lovely house by the river just outside Norwich that we can move into in a couple of weeks. And I'm looking to secure a place at a new school for Brando. We can put all this behind us.' I'd keep Brando's suggestion of Mac coming to stay with us until a later date. Did I really need more complications in my life?

Mac's eyelids drooped momentarily and he struggled to keep them open. I reached out and touched his hand. He placed his other hand over mine and held it there. I was not about to tell him about the two Spanish killers on my trail. It would only delay his recovery if he were worrying about me. Right now, I was the one worrying about him.

'Nurse! Is he okay?'

A businesslike young nurse bustled over and checked the monitors. 'He's fine. He may drift in and out of consciousness for a while before he's totally alert. It's normal.' She smiled at me. 'Yours was the first name he mentioned when he came out of the coma. Did you know that?'

The warmth of Mac's hand on mine made me feel safe and stronger. I was determined to get out of this current mess and to grasp whatever life had in store for me. Mac was a good man who cared for Brando and, it seemed, for me too. I would do all within my power to create a proper family life for Brando. And maybe find some happiness for myself into the bargain.

Mac's eyes opened once more; he seemed to have trouble focusing for a moment but then he was back with me.

'You look different,' he said.

'Make-over courtesy of Lenka Watts.'

'It suits you.'

'Change of life, change of image. I'm glad you approve, Angus.'

He grimaced. 'Can we make that the first and last time you ever call me by that name?'

'You have a deal, Mr Macdonald.'

Mac's facial expression changed, as though he was trying to bring something to mind but it was eluding him. 'Did you say Lenka Watts?'

'Remember, she's the wife of Mike Watts, Brando's guitar teacher?'

He was fully focused now. 'I know who she is. But do you know who Lenka's *brother* is?'

The blank look on my face was a giveaway.

'Timor Koslov.'

'And he is . . .?'

'Not exactly in the oligarch league but he is a player. One of those types that made all their money in their home country and then scarpered to England to avoid scrutiny by the authorities. Take the money and run, leaving Mother Russia in the poorhouse.'

'A gangster?'

'Legal enough, at the time, but you have to wonder just how he accumulated so much money *before* the fall of the Soviet Union. And managed to hold on to it all.'

'So what is your take on it?'

'I'm just saying you should maybe watch your step with Lenka Watts.'

A doctor came in. He was about forty, dark-haired with an air of quiet concern. 'Sorry to disturb you, but may I speak to Mr Macdonald alone, please?'

As I moved away to give them some privacy, I spotted two men standing at the doorway to the ward.

Once he had spoken to the doctor, Mac called me back over to his bed. 'Police,' he said. 'They want to interview me. I'd make myself scarce, if I were you.'

'I have to get back to Lenka's place. Lots of things to do. But I'll be back as soon as I can.' I attempted to keep my tone light.

He reached out and held my hand. 'Don't I get a goodbye kiss?'

I leaned down and kissed him on the cheek.

'Get out of here, Sam.'

'I'll be back soon.'

'You take care.' There was a tone in his voice that told me he knew I was holding something back. 'I hope you'll still be around when I get out of here.'

'You just get yourself better. I'm not going anywhere.'

On my way out, I passed the doctor and the two plain-clothes cops. I wasn't sure if they were local or had been sent from DCI Evans's manor in Essex. But it didn't really matter, because Mac was an innocent party.

'I'll allow you ten minutes with him but no more than that,' the doctor told them as he led them towards Mac's bed.

I sat in the Merc in the car park and wondered about Lenka. Was she for real or was there something else going on that I hadn't figured out yet? The secrecy about her brother being in England had me worried. But if Mac was right, and if Timor Koslov had been some kind of Russian mobster, perhaps he could prove to be a strong ally in a tight situation. Either way, I had to get back to the farm before nightfall.

Chapter Fifty-Seven
2 p.m., Sunday, 13 July

Adelaide Johnson was on a mission. She was distraught with worry and exhausted from being awake all night. But she had steeled herself, put on her best Sunday coat and hat, then headed out. Staying at home and brooding was not her way. She was a woman of action and she'd take on the world to protect her son.

Winston always came home at night. No matter how late Gerard Fowley kept him at work, she'd wait up for him and he would eat the dinner she had cooked for him. He was a good boy. He'd been a slow learner and was teased and tormented at school, until he'd grown so big. She'd always suspected that he was borderline autistic but had never had him tested. Once the social services label a child it stays with them for the rest of their life and she had never wanted that for Winston. She knew what was best for him. He was the cross she had to bear, though she believed that God hands you only the burdens you are able to cope with.

She'd worried that her son might fall in with the wrong crowd if he was unemployed and was delighted when Fowley had given Winston the job in the garden centre straight out of school. And he'd loved it there, spending most of his first month's wages on colourful plants for the window boxes on their balcony.

She had to admit that Fowley had been good to Winston by employing him, paying for his driving lessons, buying him a nice new suit and all. But she'd lived in this area for thirty years and she knew of his reputation as a whoremaster.

Winston never said very much but she'd noticed a change in his usual affable demeanour lately. And when, in passing, she'd mentioned Clive Lee, he'd clammed up. The cuts on his hands had also bothered her. 'How'd you do that, son?' she'd asked him.

Winston shrugged. 'Don't know.' But she knew he was not being truthful. And Winston had never lied to her before.

This morning's phone call to Fowley had brought her no joy. He was a smarmy one. 'Winston left here at eight last night,' he told her when she'd asked anxious questions about the whereabouts of her son. 'Maybe he went out with his mates. Maybe he hooked up with a girl. I'll give you a call when he turns up for work.'

Fowley obviously didn't have a clue about her son. Winston didn't have any friends. He never went out except for work. And girls wouldn't give him the time of day. Unless they were the floozies that Fowley employed. And Adelaide had always warned him about them. 'You can catch nasty diseases from that kind of person.' Winston was scared of diseases.

Adelaide hopped on the number twelve bus. Mothers should stick together. Sons were a blessing but you have to be strong, especially when the good-for-nothing father runs off. Men, they were all the same. Desperate to have a son but not prepared to share the responsibility for one that wasn't perfect. Nevertheless, Winston was a good lad, in his own special way. She'd kept him safe for twenty-one years and she wasn't about to give up on him now.

Mrs Lee was the mother of sons, so she'd understand. Clive had been a bit of a tearaway in his time but the other one, Tony, had stuck by his mother through thick and thin. Adelaide was sure she could talk to Mrs Lee, and maybe even to Clive. If Winston had got mixed up in any trouble she would find out about it, one way or the other.

——— ———

Lee Wok was closed and Adelaide couldn't see anyone inside. She thought that odd as it was past lunchtime and the restaurant did a reasonable trade in takeaways at that time of day. She'd ordered them herself when she used to work at the doctor's surgery just around the corner.

Mrs Lee lived in the flat above, so Adelaide rang the bell of the door just to the side of the building. A window above her opened, a voice called out and a key was thrown down. Adelaide picked it up, opened the door and trudged up the narrow stairway. Mrs Lee was waiting at the top of the stairs.

'Who are you?' She peered down at Adelaide myopically.

'I'm Winston's mother, Mrs Lee. Don't you remember me?'

'I thought you Tony. He forget key sometime.' She held out her frail hand as though asking for help. 'You see Tony? He not come work last night. He not here now. Not possible open restaurant today. I very worried.'

Adelaide felt as though all the air had been sucked out of her body and she grasped the rickety banister to steady herself. Something was wrong, she felt it in her bones. Help me, Jesus. Help me to be strong.

'I think we need to talk, Mrs Lee,' she managed to say.

With a sense of rising dread, Adelaide sat and listened to Mrs Lee's tale of Clive's sudden and unannounced departure for America. Her hands tingled; they always did that just before she heard bad news. It was a sign, her grandmother had told her, a sign from God.

But Adelaide would have preferred it if he'd given her something more useful instead, like the ability to pick winning lottery numbers. Playing the lottery was her only vice and she comforted herself with the thought that some of the money went to the needy. And if God ever blessed her with a million-pound win then who was she to turn it down. Though, so far, He'd been rather quiet on that score.

'Mr Fowley, very kind. He give me money,' Mrs Lee confided. Adelaide thought she looked a little puzzled. 'I surprised. Clive not work in restaurant, he never give me money.'

The tingling slowly moved up Adelaide's arms. This was not a good omen. She had always suspected that Gerard Fowley only did things that were in his own interests.

'What did Tony say?'

'Nothing. But person name Jean say she looking for Clive.'

'Was she one of Fowley's girls?' Adelaide asked.

'Not prostitute.' Mrs Lee pursed her lips. 'She nice girl. A croupier. That good job.'

'Have you seen this Jean since?'

'Tony say her picture in newspaper. He show me but I say Jean have long blonde hair. This girl have short hair. But he say same person.'

'What was the story about? Can you remember?'

'No. But she with Mr Fowley. In newspaper.'

Adelaide tried to console Mrs Lee by telling her that Tony was a devoted son and she was sure that he'd be home soon. But she had an uneasy feeling about these developments. Next stop, Gerard Fowley. She knew exactly where she could find him because his showroom was open seven days a week. She was going to get to the bottom of this if it was the last thing she did.

There was a young white boy working in the showroom, giving the cars a polish. He was no more than eighteen or so, smartly dressed, with bleached blond hair. Adelaide didn't approve of young men dyeing their hair, she thought it made them look effeminate. There was a customer outside on the forecourt talking to the middle-aged Asian salesman. The blond lad looked up at her expectantly as she walked through the door, probably hoping to make a sale but, after weighing her up, he soon got back to his polishing.

Gerard Fowley walked out of his office. He grimaced momentarily when he saw her, then slapped on his broadest smile. She thought he looked paler than the last time she'd seen him. That was something else she found hard to swallow, black folks trying to be white. All those pop singers with their indecently short skirts and long, blonde wigs and hair extensions, it just wasn't right. 'God made you black,' she'd shout at them when they appeared on her television screen. 'Be proud of who you are.' The world was going to hell in a handcart.

'Where's my son?' she demanded of Fowley without preamble and the white boy turned to look at her.

Fowley gripped her by the elbow and ushered her into his office. He offered her a seat but she told him that she preferred to stand. Adelaide knew that her height and weight made her an imposing presence and she wasn't about to diminish that advantage by sitting down.

'I'm as concerned as you are, Mrs Johnson,' he tried to assure her. 'In all the years Winston has worked for me, he's never been even a minute late. And he's never taken a day off sick.' He sat down behind his desk, steepled his hands and stared her down. 'But boys will be boys. Maybe he's out there sowing some wild oats at long last.'

Adelaide stood in front of the desk, hands on hips. 'Do you even *know* my son?'

'Of course I do. He's a good worker.'

'Is that all he is to you, "a good worker"?'

'He does as he's told and gets on with his job. That's what I employ him for.'

'You're just like everyone else.' She shook her head in despair. 'All you see is a big, strong black man. But my son is vulnerable. He's trusting and easy to take advantage of.' She suddenly found herself close to tears. 'That's why I'm here. I'm worried about him. I'm *really* worried, Mr Fowley.'

Fowley gestured towards the seat in front of his desk and Adelaide, desperately trying to hold on to her dignity and resolve, reluctantly sat down.

'I employ a lot of young men from different backgrounds. I try to give them a decent job.' Fowley's voice had taken on a gentler tone. 'See that one out there, Damien.' He pointed to the window between the office and the showroom where Adelaide could see the blond lad talking to a customer. 'He's had it tough and I'm giving him a fresh start.'

She was regaining her composure now, thinking straight again and wasn't about to be taken in by this claim to philanthropy. What about all the working girls he was also known to employ? It was no kind of 'decent job' he gave to them.

'Was Clive Lee a good worker, too, Mr Fowley?' Adelaide thought she detected a slight tic at the corner of Fowley's eye – the sure sign of a liar, in her judgement. 'I've been to see Mrs Lee.' Now she had his attention.

'How is the good lady?' Fowley smiled with his mouth.

'She's worried about her Clive, now. Ever since that lady friend of yours visited her?'

Fowley looked stumped. 'I'm afraid I don't know who you mean.'

'Jean. The one who was with you in that newspaper photo.'

Adelaide noticed a look cross his face that caused a cold shiver to run down her well-padded spine. He quickly masked it but she felt her heart thumping in her chest.

'I tell you what,' he proposed. 'How's about I get Damien out there to ask around about Winston. You go home and I'll call you when I hear anything.' Fowley stood up and walked towards the office door, as though expecting her to follow.

Adelaide remained seated. 'Or how's about I go to the police and report Winston as a missing person?'

'You can do that, of course. But if you'd let me investigate on your behalf, Mrs Johnson, I'd be pleased to do so. And if Winston isn't back home by this evening, I'll accompany you to the police station myself. What do you say?'

Adelaide got out of the chair and Fowley opened the door for her.

'You look exhausted,' he crooned. 'Let me drive you home.'

'I can catch a bus just outside.'

'I insist,' he said. 'I'd be so disappointed if you said no. And who knows, Winston could be waiting for you at home right now, full of contrition.'

Adelaide was unsure at first but was finally persuaded to get into the car.

'You don't see many of those, these days,' she commented when she saw him pull on his driving gloves.

'Old habits die hard,' he replied.

Fowley, ever the gentleman, walked Adelaide to the door of her flat. She felt it would be impolite not to ask him in for a cup of tea. He graciously accepted, quickly checked that nobody had seen him enter, then closed the door behind him.

Chapter Fifty-Eight
7 p.m., Sunday, 13 July

I was in no doubt that he was Lenka's brother, tall and slim with almond-shaped green eyes and finely chiselled features. I felt an unexpected stir of attraction. He was almost as striking as his sister, yet I didn't fancy her. I liked Mac, and if he felt the same about me, then I could probably learn to love him given time, but the animal appeal of Timor Koslov threw me.

He held out his hand by way of a friendly introduction and flashed his almost too-perfect teeth. 'Call me Tim.' His voice was only slightly accented. 'My sister has been telling me of your predicament.'

I threw Lenka a look but she just grinned back at me.

'I'm afraid I can't stay.' Tim kissed Lenka on both cheeks then made for the door. He turned back and smiled at us. 'Viktor is not a bodyguard but he's very dependable. He'll help take care of you until I can arrange for something more professional.'

I'd clocked the Aston Martin Vanquish, parked in front of the house, its metallic burgundy paintwork shimmering in the late-afternoon sunlight. I'd guessed it belonged to Lenka's brother. It was improbable that two Spanish gunmen would go driving around in a vehicle like that. It was a brand-new model and you wouldn't get much change out of 200,000 smackers. They usually had a waiting list a mile long, but, if Mac was right about Timor Koslov being a player, then he probably had a way around such minor inconveniences. The man behind the wheel had glanced up at me as I walked towards the house. He appeared fairly ordinary, but then so did Swindley, and I'd seen *him* in action: one cold-blooded bastard.

'You must both be tired after last night,' Timor said. 'Viktor will stay with you. You can have his services around the clock until all this unfortunate business is sorted out.'

Lenka, still seated at the dining table, gave her brother a little wave, and he left.

'You like Timor? He is handsome, yes?'

'And very—'

'Educated,' Lenka pre-empted my remark. 'I work in movies so he can go to school and I pay for him to go to good university.'

He is grateful, I think.

She read my mind. 'So when I need help, I get. You see?'

Viktor knocked at the door before he entered. He and Lenka spoke to each other in what I presumed to be Russian then she threw him the keys to the studio. He nodded in my direction as he left.

'He will sleep in the studio for a few hours. Have dinner with us and then watch all night.'

'He's not a very—'

'Big man.' She'd developed this irritating habit of interrupting me.

'I was going to say, imposing figure. But big will do.'

With Viktor having crept off for a short kip, I told her about my visit to Mac, but she wasn't particularly interested. In fact, she appeared preoccupied. Family business, maybe. So I didn't ask. We'd developed an unspoken agreement. If we wanted to share information, we would. If not, we left well enough alone.

'Brando rang,' she told me. 'He is having a wonderful time and wanted to tell you all about it. But he will maybe call again tomorrow, he said.'

I felt a hollow ache deep inside. I would love to have heard his voice. Tomorrow, then, if we were all still around.

I cooked dinner and Viktor ate with us. The few words he knew in English seemed to amount to yes, no, please and thank you. Even when Lenka spoke to him in Russian his responses were monosyllabic. It didn't make for scintillating conversation and the evening dragged.

My phone pinged. Brando had texted me.

Having a great time. Mike let me play his guitar. When R U coming?

I replied. *Soon. Miss you.*

A one-line reply came back immediately.

Me too. Brando.

I felt a flutter of disappointment that there was no x this time. But I'd get over it. I had other things on my mind.

Lenka, easily bored, got steadily hammered. I raised my eyebrows as she opened another bottle of vodka, but she dismissed my look with a wave of her hand. 'We have no need to worry. We have Viktor.'

I looked across at the scrawny figure sitting in front of the TV, watching Aussie rules football on Sky with the sound turned down and munching his way through a family pack of crisps. He sure didn't look like the type to inspire much confidence. Lenka might be reassured, but I wasn't going to rely on him to save *my* arse.

The dogs were set loose in the garden again, against my better judgment. I argued with Lenka about it and she consulted Viktor. But he wasn't about to disagree with the sister of his boss, so he appeared to back her up. Lenka, staggered up to bed, totally out of it, while Viktor took up his position in the kitchen to watch the door. He had Lenka's shotgun at the ready. I had a gnawing feeling in my gut, so I took the other shotgun with me when I went up to my room. I peered out of my window onto the back lawn but could see no sign of the dogs in the darkness – they were probably asleep by the French windows again. I turned off the light and lay on the bed, still fully clothed.

I must have drifted off to sleep for a moment when I was woken by the sound of frenzied barking. I edged towards the side of the window and cautiously peered out. Light crept into the garden from the rear downstairs room. Viktor must have turned that one on instead of the floodlights. The only part of the grounds clearly visible was that closest to the house and I saw the useless mutts tearing at another rabbit. I was watching with annoyance when the hairs on the back of my neck stood to attention. It dawned on me that there was something different about this bunny. The one they'd caught the previous night had struggled but this one was already lifeless. Either the dogs had learned how to kill it quickly or . . . My blood ran cold. Our stalkers were out there. I could sense them. I ran through the possibilities. Last night might have been a dummy run, to judge just how the dogs, and we, reacted. This could be the real thing – perhaps with poisoned bait. Get the dogs out of the way and us on the back foot. I flicked the safety off the gun and took a deep breath. I was about to move away from the window and go downstairs when I heard the French doors open. Viktor was striding across the grass towards the dogs. Get back inside, put the floodlight on, you fucking idiot! He bent down to pull the dogs away from their kill. *Pop! Pop! Pop!* The distinct noise of suppressed gunfire making a sound like a phonebook hitting a concrete floor. Viktor's legs collapsed under him and he fell forward. The two dogs slumped onto their sides, as motionless as that rabbit.

I suspected Viktor would have left the French doors open and I had to get down there immediately to secure them. Holding the gun by my side, I slowly opened my door and slipped stealthily out towards the stairs, faintly lit by the light below. Suddenly the light went out and the house was cast into darkness. I wanted the advantage of the higher ground to blast whoever was coming after us, but, to my heightened senses, the footsteps on the stairs sounded like cannon fire. I couldn't be sure of hitting them both – if there were two of them – without taking a bullet myself. With my back to the wall I edged my way towards Lenka's room and waited. Without any more ammo I had just three shots.

A short, shadowy figure dressed in black appeared at the top of the stairs, turned left, and made directly for the room where I'd just been sleeping. He eased the door open and went inside. I waited. A second man followed but turned right towards where I was standing. He was just three feet away from me and I saw the look of shock on his face just before I fired. The blast virtually took his head off as fragments of skull and brain tissue splattered across the confined space. The door behind me opened; Lenka was standing there, swaying on her feet. She was naked. I pushed her back inside as the bullet hit the door beside my head. It missed by inches and I fired the shotgun blindly into the darkness peppering the wall at the end of the corridor. One more shot and I was out of ammo.

Another bullet whizzed by, he was firing around the doorway. I crouched down and crept towards my bedroom. The guy on the floor was well and truly dead, and with my eyes still on the open door to my bedroom, I reached for his gun. A hand emerged from the doorway. I saw the flash. If I hadn't leaned across for that handgun at that second he'd have got me. The slug penetrated Lenka's door and I heard her yelp.

I tucked the handgun into my pants and blasted at the semi-hidden figure with my final shot. The flame almost blinded me as the wall ahead virtually disintegrated from the force of the blast. The gunman moved fast, hurled himself out of the door and barged straight into me. Momentarily winded, I was thrown against the wall as he tried to make his escape down the stairs. I swung the shotgun like a club, hit him hard on the back of the head and he tumbled down the stairs. The world retreated into slow-mo. I drew the handgun from my waistband and fired. He was in mid-air as the bullet hit. I watched him go down like a bag of wet sand as his body hit the bottom stair with a sickening thud and he remained still.

I walked down the stairs cautiously with the gun pointed at the prone figure. I'd hit him in the shoulder with the handgun but he'd already been badly injured by the shotgun. Dead man running. When I couldn't detect a pulse, I stepped over the twisted corpse, turned the lights on and checked the downstairs area just in case Swindley's sums had been wrong and there was another killer lurking in the shadows. But the place was still. The French windows stood open and the bodies of Viktor and the dogs lay leaking blood onto the lawn. I turned the floodlights on and headed back upstairs to Lenka. She was on the landing, wearing a silk gown and staring at me, white-faced with shock yet still half-sloshed. Her leg was bleeding from the bullet intended for me that had gone straight through the door and grazed her.

Startled by the sound of the phone ringing, she seemed to surface from her stupor and hobbled into her bedroom to answer it.

'Everything is fine, Mr Bradley,' I heard her say. The man on the phone must be the nearest neighbour. Unless he was stone deaf, he must have heard the shooting. 'Foxes come into garden and I shot them.' She took a deep breath and listened for a moment. 'Yes, I know. I should not drink and handle guns.' She grimaced at me as the voice at the other end castigated her. 'I am sorry you were disturbed, Mr Bradley. Everything is fine. No need to call the police.'

I looked from the mangled face of the dead guy at my feet to the body at the bottom of the stairs. 'Right now, *we* should be calling the cops.'

But she was already dialling. 'I phone Timor. He will fix this.'

Right, this should prove interesting. I'd like to see how the hell anyone could sort this fiasco. We had three dead men on our hands, blood splattered all over the place and half-demolished walls. I'd have preferred Lenka to have agreed to see a doctor about the flesh wound on her leg, but she insisted that I patch her up. She was adamant. No doctors and no police. Timor would fix.

A truck pulling a twenty-foot container turned up just before dawn. 'Universal Overseas Haulage' was emblazoned on the side. A removals company, how very droll. Perhaps this passed for Russian black humour.

I opened the gates and the dodgy-looking geezer in the driver's seat gave me a wave. He pulled up right outside the house and a second man got out of the cab. He was straight from the Ugly Agency. Looking for an interesting character for a new film are you, Mr Spielberg? Want to frighten the living daylights out of the kiddies, do you? Then I know just the man for the part.

He opened the back door of the truck and two more blokes got out. It was impossible to see what they looked like because they wore white chemical-splash boiler suits with hoods and medical facemasks. They handed a matching set to the driver and his bruiser mate.

I stayed by the gate and looked back down the road. There was no sign of a car anywhere in the vicinity. I'd expected to see one, parked up and ready for a quick getaway after we'd been seen to. But there was nothing I could spot that was out of the ordinary. How the hell did those fuckers get here? The wooded area at the back of the farmhouse had off-road access a couple of miles away. They could have left a vehicle there and planned to trek back to it once they'd done the job. If so, it could be weeks before anyone reported it as abandoned and months before it was towed away. Chances were it was a rental and the company would be happy simply to have it returned. It was doubtful that anyone would bother to investigate any further. But I hated loose ends and it nagged at me.

Lenka had been guzzling down black coffee and looked like she was about to throw up. 'I need food.'

'I'm not cooking breakfast for that lot.'

She gave me a pitying look. 'They are here to do a job, not to eat. We will go out and leave them to get on with it.'

Without a word to the disposal crew, she left a set of house keys on the table and headed to the garage to get the car. She was upset about the dogs – 'Poor babies.' But Viktor didn't get so as much as a glance. She really was something else.

Chapter Fifty-Nine
10 a.m., Monday, 14 July

Lenka drove us to the local golf club, set up in the late eighties for the upwardly mobile who couldn't quite afford Surrey house prices and their matching club fees. So they'd settled for Essex and cut-price posh – an eighteen-hole country walk, a clubhouse, solarium and other diversions for glam golf widows.

I was surprised the Watts family had a membership, as I couldn't quite imagine Mike swinging a club. But Lenka explained it had a swimming pool and gym that she enjoyed using and a crèche for the kids so they wouldn't be under her feet while she relaxed with friends.

'Mike says he is too young to play golf.' She gave a sly grin that indicated she thought he was fooling himself. I looked around and thought that he was probably right. This place was far too staid.

We wandered into the café and ordered breakfast. The early-bird golfers were out in droves and Lenka raised her eyes to the heavens when she spotted a man in his seventies that she knew. He was with a couple of other old codgers, all togged up in their flamboyant gear. He waved over to her and she waved back.

'That is Felix Bradley,' she explained. 'The man who rang last night.' She put on her most radiant smile as he left his friends and came over to our table.

'Recovered, I see,' he said.

'I hate foxes,' she replied. 'And when they use my garden to fuck, I hate them more.'

I saw him wince at her language and assumed she was trying to embarrass him into leaving us alone, but it didn't work. Without asking permission, he pulled up a chair and joined us.

'You have to be careful around guns, my dear.' His voice was gentle, but his manner was irritatingly paternal. 'When I was on the force, I saw some terrible mishaps with shotguns. And most of them were drink-related, I might add.'

Her green eyes flashed with annoyance but the smile remained plastered to her face. 'My friend Samantha was with me,' she said. 'And she was in the British army.'

He threw me a look that said, then you should have known better, as his bright, intelligent eyes searched my face.

'I saw you in the newspaper,' he said. 'Weren't you involved in those incidents at the Carver and Cohen places?' He was very observant for an old guy – although the media mêlée outside the house might have been a bit of a clue.

'As an ex-policeman, Mr Bradley, you'll realise that I can't discuss that with anyone.'

'Of course, my dear. It was just an observation.' He turned back to Lenka. 'I do hope your visitor didn't drive home in an inebriated state last night.'

'Visitor? We didn't have any visitors.' My heart leapt into my mouth. Had he seen the two intruders sneaking around?

'The young blonde woman. I'm a very light sleeper and when I heard a car in the lane I got out of bed and looked out of my window. I saw her driving at high speed straight past my house. I believe she was in a dark blue Rover, but it was hard to be absolutely certain of the colour in the dark, of course. I was about to go back to bed when I heard the gunfire.'

Lenka looked across at me. I tried to keep my face in neutral but I had a really bad feeling about this. There had been no sign of a vehicle parked around by the farmhouse. I had presumed that our two Spanish friends had stashed it somewhere out of sight, maybe at the other side of the woods. But what if they'd had a driver who heard the shotgun fire and realised that everything had gone tits up? If he'd been a professional he'd have come into the house to finish the job. Or at least try to get his partners out in one piece. The dead don't talk but the wounded can be a liability. So I suspected an amateur who might well panic and take off. The kind of thing that Monica would do. My stomach churned at the prospect of Monica teamed up with Garcia's sister, with the two of them gunning for Brando and me.

Chapter Sixty
6 p.m., Monday, 14 July

We'd lounged about at the golf club spa for most of the day and I'd been prodded and pampered to within an inch of my life. On our return, the truck had gone and I assumed that the wetwork had been dealt with.

As we got out of the car, an elderly lady passed the gate and called out to Lenka. 'Oh, I'm so pleased to see you.'

We walked over to her and her little dog barked at us. It was one of those silly creatures that looks like a mop on a stick. How the hell did she know which end to feed?

'When I saw that removals company, I was concerned you were leaving us. That would be awful. You never know what terrible types might move in. It's so nice to have decent folk as neighbours.'

I almost laughed.

'Don't worry, Mrs Bradley, we're not going anywhere,' Lenka reassured her. 'We have furniture in storage and they deliver to us.'

'That early in the morning? You'd never have got that kind of service in the old days. The world is certainly moving on apace, isn't it?'

'You pay and you get.'

'Isn't that the truth?' The mop was pulling at the lead and Mrs Bradley laughed indulgently. 'Topsy wants walkies. Must go. So glad to know you'll be staying.' She toddled off with the dog.

'Your neighbours don't miss much,' I commented.

'Good, most of the time. But not so good right now.'

Inside, the house was spotless. The landing walls had been replastered and painted. Lenka's bedroom door replaced along with a new carpet that was a pretty close match to the previous one. Everything smelled fresh and clean. If I hadn't been in the thick of it the night before I would never have guessed anything had happened.

'Wow, these guys are good.'

'Were once KGB,' she said as though it explained their expertise in disposal of bodies and their decorating skills – which it probably did.

All that was missing were the dogs and Lenka sighed as she looked into the empty run.

'What are you going to tell the children?'

'Children?' She looked puzzled.

'About the dogs. You can't exactly say they've gone to live on a farm.'

She gave me a blank stare.

'That's what people usually tell kids when they've sent Rover to be put down. They say he's gone to live on a farm.'

'You should not lie to children.'

'I don't think you've got much choice in this case.'

'I will buy German shepherd puppies. Children will like them much better.'

I was making coffee when Brando rang. He was full of tales of rivers and tree climbing, playing the latest video games, and going to the beach, but he was most enthused about the music and being allowed to play a few chords on one album track. 'They might delete that take,' he said as though he'd been in the recording business for all of his eleven years. 'But I've got a copy of it and I can hear myself playing. It's fantastic.'

He wanted to know when I'd be joining them, but I said I'd be visiting Mac and might not be able to make it for a while yet.

'I told you he'd be okay,' he enthused. 'I knew it. When I get back we can all move into the new house, like a proper family.'

I almost cried. He was called for dinner and had to go but promised to ring again. When he had hung up I sat and looked at the phone for ages, not wanting to sever the link.

'There is a man at the gate.' Lenka was peering out of the kitchen window.

I picked up a shotgun and walked out of the door.

Tony Lee raised his hands in mock surrender as I approached.

'Hello, Jean,' he said, 'I've brought you some Chinese takeaway.'

———

The newspaper photos of the farmhouse now meant that every man and his whippet knew where I was staying but I had thought that the long blonde wig I had worn when I'd encountered Tony and his mother might have had them fooled. Clearly it hadn't. Lenka asked no questions but took the food containers from him. I led Tony into the gold record room and closed the door.

He looked around at the display of framed records lining the walls. 'Are these the real deal?'

'I have no idea. I don't suppose anyone ever played one. Could all be Bing Crosby singing "White Christmas", for all I know.'

'Should I call you Samantha?'

'Sam will do. Did you speak to Winston?'

He blanched at the name. 'It all went a bit too far. Let's just say he won't be giving evidence against Gerard Fowley.'

Winston was dead. That hadn't been my intention. I was hoping he could have been persuaded to . . . I don't know what I'd hoped, but I hadn't wished him dead.

Without his evidence I was back to square one with Wendy Morrison. She'd wanted to nab Fowley in exchange for the photo of Joe and me.

'I felt sorry for Winston,' Tony said. 'He came across as – I don't know how you say this nicely – he seemed a bit simple.'

Great, I'd been instrumental in the killing of a retard. I felt like shit.

'He said that Fowley had murdered Clive and then ordered Winston to bury the body. He took us to the place. And then it all turned . . .' He shook his head as if to erase the memory. 'I never want to see anything like that again as long as I live.'

'He'd have told you I was there.' No point in beating around the bush, if Winston had given Fowley up then he'd certainly have told them about me.

'He said you refused to shoot Clive.' His eyes were full of regret. 'I understand why you didn't report it to the police at the time. I might not have done a few days ago. But now I've seen first-hand what these guys are capable of . . .'

'What now?' Was I about to tuck in to poisoned Chinese food?

'It's all got way beyond me. I'm going to sell the restaurant and get Mum out of there.'

'What about Fowley? Is anything going to be done about him?'

'Like I said, it's all out of my control now. I've had nothing to do with the Triads until now. Once you owe them, they own you. You have to give them something in return. I gave them Fowley.' He gave me a sad smile. 'They will exact revenge for Clive, but not right away. That's not how they do things. It's a waiting game.'

Triad involvement meant that Fowley was in deep shit. Not that he didn't deserve it. But Tony had paid a heavy personal price and I felt bad about it. 'I'm sorry I got you involved, Tony.'

'Me, too. But at least I know what happened to Clive. So I thought I should warn you. I think Fowley might know it was you who visited us. Winston's mother came to see Mum to ask if Clive knew where Winston was. And Mum told her I thought it was you in the newspaper. After that Mrs Johnson went to see Fowley. I'm not saying she told him, but she might have.'

'Maybe I should ask her.'

'Haven't you heard the news?'

'I've been a bit preoccupied today. What news?'

'Mrs Johnson was stabbed to death in her flat.'

Chapter Sixty-One
10 a.m., Tuesday, 15 July

Wendy Morrison was back behind her desk. That's what DCI Evans had given her: a desk job. He'd nodded sympathetically and caressed her with his deep Welsh tones – the poor man's Richard Burton.

'Are you sure you don't want to wait until after the funeral?'

No, she told him. Everything had been arranged and she'd rather be back at work, if he had no objections. Thank goodness he hadn't intoned the routine 'Sorry for your loss' or she might have been tempted to thump him. She'd heard them laughing behind her back. They all paid lip service to equality, but when it came down to it, the police force was still a dick-swinging hetero cabal. Women could rise through the ranks as high as they might but that beer-swilling, all-male secret society ensured that few women could make it to the inner sanctum. It was a fact of life that she had learned to come to terms with, albeit grudgingly.

Trevor Jones was okay in his way and she'd tried to be sympathetic when his wife had shown him the door. But she knew that, had he tried harder to be a better husband and father instead of one of the lads, he might still be married.

As though her thoughts had summoned his presence, Jones was suddenly standing in front of her desk.

'I think you might like to hear this, guv,' he said. 'Afro-Caribbean woman, Adelaide Johnson, found stabbed to death in her flat on the Sage estate. Seems they like the son for it.'

'Domestic. Why should that interest me? Not my case.'

He placed a photograph down in front of her. 'Recognise him?'

It was one of those cheesy family portraits so beloved of high street photographers. A sturdy middle-aged black woman in her Sunday best seated on a gold-painted chair. Standing proudly behind her was a huge man that Morrison had spotted at Benny Cohen's funeral.

'He's one of Fowley's crew, isn't he?'

'Big bugger, one of Fowley's muscle. The other one's an ex-amateur boxer, Chinese Clive they call him. He's done time.'

'Johnson got any form?'

'Not much known about him, except he lives with his mum. Seems to have kept his nose clean until now.'

Morrison got to her feet. 'Is DCI Evans in charge of this?'

'Yep.' Trevor Jones grinned. 'So maybe . . .'

'Is he in his office? I'll go and have a word.'

'Thought you might.'

⸻

Evans glanced up at her as she entered his office. 'This manor is turning into the Wild bloody West.'

'The stabbing of the Johnson woman?'

'We're looking for the son, Winston.'

'He works for Gerard Fowley.'

'He of interest to you?' He looked at her quizzically. 'You want in on this?'

'Who's got it now?'

'Hodges. They're doing a door-to-door, but you know Sage and the rest of those estates. See no evil, hear no evil, because every last one of them is at it, one way or another.'

'Adelaide Johnson?'

'One of the older ones left behind. Why the council doesn't rehouse the decent families and just build a bloody big barricade around the rest of them, I'll never know.'

'Shall I interview Fowley, sir? See if he knows where his employee might be?'

'Go ahead. If you feel up to it.'

Morrison walked out of the office, seething. Condescending prick! It was her partner who was dead, not her. She was very much alive. And any excuse to interview Gerard Fowley was fine by her. But she wasn't about to tell that to Evans.

Hodges was glad of a hand, so she boned up on the notes of the Johnson case, nodded to Trevor Jones and they went off to pay Mr Fowley a visit.

'To what do I owe the pleasure?' Fowley was all smiles. 'Can I get Damien to make you a cup of coffee, Inspector? Sergeant?'

They declined. Fowley held a chair for Morrison to sit. She wasn't charmed.

'Winston Johnson,' she stated flatly.

'Has something happened to him?' Fowley took his seat behind his desk.

'Why do you ask?'

'He hasn't turned up for work for two days. That's not like him at all. He's worked for me since he left school and he's always been punctual, never taken a day off.'

326

'Have you tried to contact him?'

'He's never been good with mobile phones. Keeps losing them. But I spoke to his mother at home and she said she hadn't seen him either.'

'When did you speak to Mrs Johnson?' Morrison asked.

Fowley's face remained deadpan. 'The morning he didn't turn in for work.'

Morrison nodded.

'Is Winston in any trouble? I'd be more than happy to stand bail for him,' Fowley said.

'You value your employees, do you, Mr Fowley?' Trevor Jones asked.

'The good workers, I do. And Winston was always solid. He had a bit of a temper at times but he never caused me any grief.'

Morrison eyed him. Alright, she thought, I'll bite. 'Temper, you say?'

'Before I answer any personal questions about my employees, would you be kind enough to tell me what this is all about?'

'Winston's mother is dead, Mr Fowley, and we need to contact him.' Morrison watched for his reaction. Surprise, concern, the normal stuff, but what she got from him was a sneer.

'Isn't that something you usually leave to the uniforms?'

'I can't discuss the circumstances of her death with you, Mr Fowley, but we are seeking Adelaide Johnson's son to assist with our investigation.'

'Well, let me tell you, Inspector, I stand by my employees one hundred per cent and I can assure you that Winston would never hurt his mother.'

Big red lights flashed a warning in Morrison's brain but she just stared at Fowley.

'Do you know who his mates are?'

'Winston always kept to himself. I don't know what he got up to when he left here.'

'Is he friendly with your other employees? Maybe Damien out there?'

'Damien is new here. Started just a week ago.'

'You have another man working for you? Perhaps we can talk to him?'

'I have an older part-time salesman but they never spoke two words to each other. As I say, Winston was always a loner.'

'I seem to recall another associate of yours, a Chinese man. Is he around?'

'Ah, Clive,' Fowley's eyes shifted to the right. 'He left my employ some weeks ago. I've heard that he's gone abroad. So I'm afraid he can't help you either.'

Morrison stood up and handed him her card.

'If you hear from Winston, please get in touch with me immediately, Mr Fowley. Thank you for your time.'

Damien, the young blond lad who was busy polishing the cars, watched them leave.

'Didn't seem very surprised that she was dead, did he?' Jones observed. 'She could have had a heart attack, for all he knows. So why assume that Winston had killed her?'

'And why is he talking about Winston Johnson in the past tense?'

———

Fowley unlocked the door to the store cupboard at the back of his office. The small wooden box was in there. He had to get rid of it and soon. He'd take it home tonight and bury it in the garden. That would do for now.

He was sure there was no blood on the clothes he'd worn on Sunday but you could never tell, the odd spot here and there and you'd be done for. He could burn that gear on a bonfire. She was a big woman, but he'd spotted the baseball bat by the door as soon as he'd walked into her flat. He'd floored her with it the second she turned her back. The sharp chef's knife she'd kept in a block in the spotless kitchen had cut her throat as easy as. Apart from the crash when she was felled, she had made no noise at all. He'd wiped the handles of the baseball bat and the knife, even though he had been still wearing his driving gloves. You could never be too careful. He checked there was nobody on the landing to see him leave the flat and then he scarpered. It had been as simple as that.

But this box was different. It had been sent as a warning and he was sure that Winston must have blabbed. Who wouldn't? Cutting a man's cock off. What kind of savage does a thing like that? He just hoped that the rest of Winston didn't turn up any time soon.

The phone rang. 'Mr Fowley?' said the voice he didn't recognise. 'I take it you received our gift. We'd like to set up a meeting tonight.'

This was the call that Gerard Fowley had been both expecting and dreading.

Chapter Sixty-Two

2 p.m., Tuesday, 15 July

Monica watched the TV news, searched the Internet, even picked up all the newspapers and scoured every page. Nothing. She'd have thought that the press would be champing at the bit. Maybe the cops hadn't released any information yet? But someone must have picked up on it. Shootings at the house of a rock star didn't happen every day of the week. If Sam Riley and the kid were dead, then all her troubles would be over. If not . . . In prison, Maria Garcia would be as much in the dark as Monica, so there'd be no joy in visiting her. And returning to the scene of the crime was a mug's game, so she'd have to wait it out. Maybe tomorrow there'd be some news.

She was already resentful about that snotty London lawyer bleeding her dry. She was outraged by his bill – 500 fucking quid just to write one sodding standard letter to Bloom. And when he'd told her how much contesting the will might cost, she'd been gob-smacked. There had to be quicker, more efficient ways to get at Benny's assets, and taking down Sam Riley and the kid had been the answer. She screwed up the lawyer's bill and hurled it against the wall. She was surrounded by shysters and jokers.

Those two Spaniards had been a right pair of tossers, but she should have heard from them by now. 'Our best men,' Maria had told her. 'Have done this many times.' But the minute Monica clocked them, she knew she wouldn't trust them to organise a fuck-fest in a knocking-shop. She'd handed the shooters over to them and even driven them to the bloody house. They were supposed to go in, do the job then hide in the woods for the night, bury the guns, get a taxi or bus to the airport the next morning and ring her when they were back in Spain. But she hadn't heard a dicky bird from them. She had a bad feeling that everything had gone tits up. The bloody idiots had wanted to go storming in on the first night. Take out the dogs and go straight in there, guns blazing. But if there was anything she'd learned from Benny Cohen, it was planning and the element of surprise.

'Lull the other side into a false sense of security. Feint and bob, then come up from under and hit 'em right between the eyes.' Benny would do the boxing moves while he explained. 'Or in the bollocks.' The very thing that had got him disqualified from a junior championship fight in his youth. After the little demonstration of the art of pugilism, he'd go straight into the movie line: 'I coulda been a contender!'

And she'd laugh and pretend she didn't know that Marlon Brando had been Charlotte Cohen's all-time favourite actor. Pretend she'd never been to the old Cohen house, never seen the actor's photos in pride of place in Charlotte's dressing room, never watched with sat-isfaction while Lil Carver's crew had strung the bitch up in the nurs-ery. If only they'd killed the brat at the same time she wouldn't have all the hassle she had now. They could have made it look as though Charlotte had smothered the baby and then topped herself. Now that would have been a plan. Regrets, she'd had a few . . .

Monica paced the floor of her hotel room. And to top it all, Gloria now had her sights on the nightclubs. That much Monica had managed to wangle out of Janine. Along with the two grams of speed Janine had hidden in the freezer. It was shit gear but all that Monica could get her hands on for the moment. It felt like she was snorting soap powder, but it did the trick and would have to do for now.

As she paced, she considered her situation: on her own she could deal with Gloria, but Swindley was another kettle of *poisson*. He was a real motherfucker. The secret of his affair with Gloria had been news to Monica. Maybe she could use it to her advantage, get Swindley to back off, somehow. Nobody takes Monica Cohen for a fool. She'd find a way.

Fowley's phone call interrupted her train of thought. 'Gerard. I didn't expect to hear from you so soon.'

'I'd like to invite you for dinner,' he said. 'My house. How about eight o'clock?'

⌣

Monica had never been to Fowley's gaff before and was surprised to find it was a modest two-bed at the end of a new mid-market housing estate. Not really what she'd expected but she could understand his reasoning. Too flash and you've got the taxman on your arse asking awkward questions about your income. Fowley wasn't in Benny's league yet, so probably couldn't afford a Richard Bloom type to take care of business. One day, though, when their joint plan for the nightclubs came to fruition, they'd both be rolling in it. And she'd be on top of the heap once more.

Fowley greeted her at the door and, although he was putting on his best face, she sensed that something was wrong. And when she clocked the two Chinese guys, all suited up and sitting in the dining room, she knew her instinct for trouble hadn't deserted her.

'Our new business partners,' Fowley whispered.

'Over my dead body.'

'Don't fuck this up, Monica. Just sit there and look pretty.' He was wired – she could hear it in his voice. 'Compromise. Or our deal's off. Do you understand?'

Fowley introduced her, but the pair remained unnamed. Like a soap opera actress, Monica slipped seamlessly back into the role she'd played for all those years as Benny's wife, the blonde airhead. She smiled vacantly at the two men sitting across the table from her. It was difficult to tell if they bought into the façade. She didn't know anyone who'd had dealings with the Chinese. They usually confined their activities to exploiting their own people. Others shipped illegals in from the provinces of China to work for slave wages to pay off their debts back home. These two were Londoners who were polite and businesslike, but they obviously had something on Fowley. Something big enough to have him quaking in his Gucci loafers. What she wouldn't give to root out that juicy nugget of information.

A silent partnership was what they were after. Fowley was to be the front man while they supplied the goods, as they put it.

'The Jamaicans are out,' the fatter of the two said. 'They are far too violent and volatile. It's bad for business.'

'They won't be happy.' Fowley looked like he was about to shit himself. Cross the Yardies and you could kiss your arse goodbye.

'Any trouble and you can leave us to deal with them,' the thinner one assured him and when he grinned a diamond twinkled in his tooth.

They could sort the Jamaicans, could they? And presumably tackle any other obstacles in their way – Swindley for example. Monica smiled inwardly. Going into business with these Chinks might not be such a bad decision after all.

She drove her rented dark blue Rover back to the hotel. She was elated. Maybe things were finally going her way. Those Chinese guys had a lot of money and muscle behind them, enough to have caught Fowley with his keks down. A three-way split wasn't what she had originally envisaged. She'd wanted them to buy those dumps from her outright. But the Chinks were far cannier than that. Their plan was for the nightclubs to stay in her name, for Fowley to front them and they'd cough for the refurbishment through some offshore company. Cash businesses were the best way to get drug money laundered. These guys were moving outwards. Those rat-hole restaurants were all well and good but you could hardly promote designer drugs on your list of today's specials. But club-goers were another market altogether, gagging for all that stuff. It made good business sense.

Fowley hadn't appeared exactly chuffed by the prospect of a partnership with them, but he'd agreed and she'd gone along with it. What she needed now was to get her hands on the nightclubs. If the Spaniards had fucked up and Sam Riley and the kid had survived, then she had to go back down the legal route and pay that con-man lawyer his exorbitant fees. If she was forced to get her fair dues that way, then she'd bite the bullet.

Her room was on the top floor of the hotel; it was the most expensive and she liked the view. She was running out of cash but she could always skip without paying the bill. The credit card she'd used when she'd checked in was one Garcia had given her and that might be pulled any day now, what with him being dead. But she'd worry about it some other time. Worse case scenario: she could always hop it to Spain for a day or so and raid one of Benny's safety deposit boxes. She could even put the villa on the market. Then again, a bolthole was never a bad option to have.

Tomorrow she'd check the newspapers again, see if there was anything about the farmhouse shootings. She'd switch on the television news when she got back into her room, surely there should be something on the story by now. At one time, she could have called one of Benny's snitches at the police station for information but those days were over and she was on her own now. But then she'd always been on her own. That was her life.

She slotted the card in to open the door to her room. The lights came on and then instantly switched off again. Bugger! She hated these sodding cards. What was wrong with a key? You always know where you are with a key. She went inside and searched the darkened hallway to find the switch.

Strong hands grabbed her from behind and threw her up against the wall. She could smell him behind her and hear his steady breathing. He wasn't a big man but he forced his body against hers so she couldn't move. A rapist. She'd heard of lone women being attacked in hotel rooms late at night. Stay calm, try and talk your way out of this. The cold steel of a razor-sharp blade against her face made her gasp. He drew it down her cheek and she felt it nick her skin, then the trickle of blood.

'Now you be a good quiet girl and I'll let you go, Monica,' an unfamiliar voice said. 'Scream or try to run and I'll cut that pretty white throat from ear to ear. Understand?'

'I understand.'

He reached across, locked the door and switched on the light. It blinded her for a second. He took her by the shoulders and turned her around to face him. Swindley.

He sat in a leather armchair across the room from her while she examined the cut on her face in the mirror. She held a wet tissue to her cheek. Bastard! She could see his reflection as he watched her. His left hand was bandaged but by his right, on the arm of the chair, was the carpet-layer's knife he'd used to cut her, its blade still unsheathed from its grey casing and glinting in the light. She'd always loathed sharp objects and those weapons were legal and lethal. She'd heard reports of lads robbing a young mother by holding a Stanley knife to the baby's face and threatening to scar it for life unless her purse was handed over.

'It's just a nick,' Swindley said dismissively.

'It'll scar.' She dabbed her cheek with the bloodied tissue.

'A change of appearance is never a bad thing.'

'Fuck you!'

'Now, now. That's no way for a lady to talk. Be a nice girl and fetch me a whisky from the mini-bar.'

'I thought you were from Birmingham.' Having only ever heard him speak in a broad Brummie accent, she hadn't recognised his voice immediately.

'There are a lot of things you don't know.'

'I know that you're fucking Gloria.' She handed him the whisky and opened a small bottle of white wine for herself.

'Ah, Janine.' He held her in his baleful grey stare as she sat down on the sofa. 'I don't wish to speak ill of my own flesh and blood. Did you know that she's my daughter?' He watched her to gauge her reaction. 'No, neither did I until recently. She's a sweet kid, Janine, but not a very reliable ally.'

'She's a slapper with a coke habit.'

'Encouraged by you, I believe. Your mother will sort her out, though. There's more to Gloria than meets the eye, you know. You really shouldn't try to cross her.'

'She's never been any kind of mother to me.'

Swindley sat back and took a swig of his drink. 'I knew your father.'

'Gloria would never tell me who he was, so why should she tell you?'

'Pretty Boy Carver they used to call him.'

Monica laughed. Stupid old fool, Gloria's pulled a fast one on you. 'You've got that wrong. Pretty Boy was my grandfather.'

Swindley smiled. It didn't look right on him. 'Let me tell you a little story . . .'

'Is that what you're here for? Is this our Jackanory moment?'

'It's about a plain eight-year-old girl whose handsome daddy used to visit her in her bedroom at night. Started off with the easy stuff, like. He'd make her suck his dick, toss him off, that sort of thing. He was a proper gent and didn't start actually fucking her until she was ten.'

'You taken up social work, or something?' Monica tried to brazen it out but an uneasy feeling settled on her shoulders like a dark shroud and she couldn't shake it off.

'The little girl told her mummy when it all started but she was called a lying little bitch and beaten black and blue for her trouble.' His eyes were on her throughout.

'This has nothing to do with me.'

'Want me to continue? It gets better – or worse, depending on your viewpoint.'

He was enjoying this, she could tell. He was heating up the branding irons with relish like some medieval torturer.

'So the inevitable happened and, at the tender age of twelve, the girl ended up pregnant. Mummy called her a whore and Daddy, realising that screwing your own daughter can have consequences, moved on. He started fucking his son.'

'And the baby?' She needed him to say it but she didn't want to hear.

'Gloria kept her pregnancy a secret until it was too late for Lil to insist on an abortion. So Lil had you adopted.'

Monica's head was spinning, her heart thundering. She felt sick but tried to pull herself together. She drained her glass of wine in one go. In for a penny, might as well get the whole picture.

'What happened to my dear father, then?'

'Lil found out about him sticking it up the arse of her precious son, so she set Pretty Boy up. He was arrested, but when it looked like he might beat the charges, she had him stabbed to death when he was on remand. I arranged it myself. It's a heart-warming tale, don't you think?'

'You are one sick fuck.'

'Jim turned into a fat bastard with a taste for sodomy. Giving, of course, not taking, and we are seeing the results of that on the TV news every day. Lots of digging going on behind those white tents at the back of the Carver abode – ten bodies, so far, and counting.'

Monica was pole-axed. She stared at Swindley, unable to speak.

A look of quiet satisfaction spread across his face. 'Enough history for one night, I think. But here's one piece of free advice for you. Once you've found yourself another schmuck, I do hope you don't consider breeding. The world doesn't need any more like you, Monica.'

If he'd told her all this to hurt her, then he'd succeeded, but there had to be something else. There was always something else. Hit 'em hard and leave them reeling. Then go in for the kill.

'So you see, Monica. As the product of incest, you had no right being born in the first place. Therefore, it would be of no consequence to anyone if you stopped breathing right now. And that is what will happen, if you don't do exactly as I tell you to do.'

She shivered. Alone – she was always alone.

'You will stop contesting Benny Cohen's will. You will leave the country and not come back. Under no circumstances will you contact Janine. Comply, Monica, and you will never see my face again. Any deviation from this and I *will* find you. I'll find you and cut you a second smile that no plastic surgeon on earth would ever be able to fix.'

Chapter Sixty-Three
11 p.m., Tuesday, 15 July

Timor Koslov arrived on the doorstep with a dog basket. Two German shepherd puppies – little balls of black and tan fluff with bright, watchful eyes – peered out. Lenka rushed over, plied her brother with kisses, scooped up the pups and held them close. She seemed delighted but I knew her well enough to sense that she was a little disgruntled. I thought it might be a sibling thing. Maybe she'd wanted to choose her own dogs and not have these foisted upon her but she could hardly appear ungrateful, not after all he'd done for us.

Timor smelled of expensive cologne and, while his sister cooed and fussed over the dogs, his green eyes held mine. He had a way of making me feel I was the only woman in the room, like I had his total attention. Almost as though he'd come with this gift for Lenka as an excuse to see me.

Lenka cuddled the puppies and took them onto the patio through the French doors to play, leaving Timor and me together.

'I would like to speak to you,' he said.

I rustled up some coffee and, even with my back to him, I could feel his gaze on me, checking me out, watching every move. We sat by the table, opposite each other and he smiled at me in a way I found hard to decipher.

'I have many interests,' he said. 'But I wish now to invest in the entertainment business. Do you think that would be a wise move?'

'Not much of a business person, myself. Though I take it we are talking about Benny Cohen's nightclubs.'

'I'm sure you know a good price when you hear one.'

'The probate still has to be settled and any future business deals will be left to the Cohens' lawyer. Though I believe there are others in the running.'

'Mrs Kelso and Mr Fowley. Both of whom have a rather shady past, I've been told.'

The baboon was laughing at his brother's bottom.

Okay, pal, let's get down to brass tacks. 'What is it you wish me to do, in exchange for the help you provided?'

'Oh, Sam, why so formal? This is merely a request from one friend to another.' His voice was gentle, but I have rarely felt so intimidated. Moreover, I began to suspect that killers like Swindley and Fowley were pussycats compared to this guy. Someone who could arrange the disposal that I had just witnessed would be capable of anything. I hadn't been prepared for this. I'd been taken in by good looks once more. How shallow is that?

'What about a personal introduction to the lawyer?' I suggested.

His smile widened. 'That's not exactly how these business transactions are conducted. My name will not be mentioned, you understand. Another company will approach Mr Bloom. All you have to do is tell me what price Kelso and Fowley are willing to pay and I will top their offers. It's as simple as that.'

But if I'd learned one thing since this whole mess began, it was that nothing is ever simple.

Chapter Sixty-Four
10 a.m., Wednesday, 16 July

The Norfolk police phoned me to say I could collect all of the items not needed as evidence from Bloom's cottage. These included Mac and Brando's gear plus my clothes. But since I'd had a radical makeover and Brando had new togs too, I was really only concerned about his guitar. I had to go to the police station in Norwich to pick them up, so I thought I'd visit Mac in the hospital while I was in the vicinity.

He was out of ICU and in a side ward, I'd been told. I was looking forward to seeing him again. The two assassins Carver had sent to kill Mac and me and abduct Brando were currently on remand in Brixton prison with the list of charges ranging from kidnapping to attempted murder. They'd already been identified by Brando, and now by Mac, so even if they kept schtum, they wouldn't be seeing the light of day for a long time once it came to court.

I decided to take the Mercedes. The sun was shining and driving alone was a perfect way to chill out and consider my options in peace and quiet. Those puppies were sweet, but they'd whined all night and I'd been woken several times. I'd heard Lenka going downstairs to try to soothe them but I'd become tired and cranky, in no mood to play nursemaid to dogs, so was glad to get away for the day. I had reached the stretch of road where I'd got the drop on Janine Kelso and glanced across to where her motorbike had skidded to a halt. I might have taken my eyes off the road for a second because I didn't see the car come tear-arsing out of the side turning. He sped out in front of me and I just managed to hit the brakes. Moments later he slammed his anchors on and stopped dead in front of me.

'You fucking idiot!' I was out of the car in seconds. I leaned into the open passenger window, mad as hell and spitting fire. The driver was a young blond lad. He looked no more than eighteen. 'You could have killed us both. Who the fuck taught you to drive?'

I felt something poke into my spine. 'I did.' It was unmistakably Fowley behind me. 'Get in the car or I'll drop you where you stand.' He opened the rear passenger door. 'After you!'

I had to comply, and so I slid into the back seat. With the muzzle of the Browning 9mm he'd used to kill Chinese Clive pressed against my ribs, Fowley got in beside me.

'We really have to stop meeting like this, Gerard,' I said. 'People will begin to talk.'

'I'm beginning to understand why Clive hated your guts.'

The blond kid started the engine and we sped away, leaving the Mercedes with the keys still in the ignition on the bend of the road.

'You like to start them young, I see.' I indicated towards the lad behind the wheel.

'Shut the fuck up, Jean!' Fowley pressed the gun into my side. If he knew the name I'd used when I'd visited the Lee family, then Winston's mother must have told him. I wasn't sure I'd be able to talk my way out of this one. 'One more word and I'll shoot you right now. Get it?'

I sat back and kept quiet. I'd heard the clunk as the driver locked all the doors so there was no chance tackling Fowley and making a jump for it. Anyway, that's a boneheaded manoeuvre you only see in the movies. If the fall didn't kill me, a truck coming in the opposite direction very well might. And even if I did make it without breaking my neck, I'd be a sitting target, stunned in the middle of a country road. I'd have to wait until we got to our destination before trying to make a run for it.

The warehouse was locked tight. There was no sign of the Jamaican I'd seen there last time. With Clive and Winston probably sharing eternity together who knows where, Fowley had to do his own dirty work. The kid got out of the car and opened up the warehouse door. Once inside that building I was done for. Best to stay out in the open. I had to make a move now. Fowley slid out of the back seat with the gun pointed straight at me.

'End of the line,' he announced.

I got out and stood facing him; I didn't want him behind me again. He was a couple of feet away from me with the gun held at arm's length and pointed at my upper body. I edged closer to him. Fowley didn't back away, clearly certain that he held all the cards.

He cocked the gun. 'Hands up, higher.'

'Now, Gerard, don't do anything you'll regret.' I moved in closer, looking him in the eye to keep his attention on my face.

I lashed out with my right and, with the palm of my hand, knocked the gun sideways; bent my knees and dropped my weight downwards until my head was beneath Fowley's. As I came back up fast with my whole weight behind me, the top of my head connected with his jaw. Fowley's knees buckled and he went sprawling against the wall. Disorientated, he gasped and bent double. I disarmed him and clocked him one on the side of his head with the butt of the Browning. I cocked the pistol, aimed it double-handed at his head, then slowly backed away.

'Down on the ground. Now!'

Still groggy, he virtually collapsed onto his knees.

'On your belly. Hands behind your head.'

Fowley lay in the dirt. 'I wasn't going to kill you. We had a deal, remember.'

Yeah, and you threatened my kid, you psycho bastard. I should blow your brains out. I took a deep breath and counted to five. 'You know, Gerard, for all his many faults, Clive would never have made a basic mistake like that. You've gone soft, man.'

'He was . . .' The kid was staring at me, wide-eyed. 'He *was* going to kill you, just like he killed that black woman.'

'Shut it, Damien, you ungrateful poof!'

'I should put an end to you right now, Gerard.' I spoke to Damien without taking my eyes off Fowley. 'You got a mobile on you?'

Damien nodded.

'Then call the police before I change my mind.'

'Sam, be reasonable,' Fowley pleaded.

'This is the reasonable me, Gerard. But you move one inch and I will shoot. Not to kill, mind you. Just take off your kneecaps, maybe. Does that appeal?'

Fowley lay still. Damien rang the cops. The police station was close by and within a couple of minutes I could hear the sirens.

'If I give evidence against him, will you say I helped you?' Damien looked close to tears.

'You little shit!' Fowley kicked out sideways at Damien and the lad jumped back with fright.

I fired a warning shot an inch away from Fowley's extended leg. The bullet hit the tarmac and ricocheted into the car door.

'I told you to stay still. The next one won't miss.'

'You don't want to shoot me, Sam. I know you don't.'

I aimed the gun straight at his arse.

'Gerard, it's all I can do to stop from sticking this up your jacksy and pulling the trigger. Come on, give me just one excuse.'

He stayed where he was.

Three police cars came roaring up the road and screeched to a halt just feet away. The cops were out of the vehicles in seconds and I saw that two of them were armed.

'Lower the gun slowly, Sam.' Wendy Morrison shouted to me. 'Drop it and move away with your hands up.' Now that was a turn up for the books.

———

I sat in a police cell for five hours while they investigated my insistent claim to the desk sergeant that I was the innocent party. Eventually, I was ushered in to see Wendy Morrison. I'd expected to be led into an interview room but instead it was just the two of us in her office. She stared at me across her desk. 'We've found your vehicle where you said it would be. Frankly, I'm amazed it hadn't been nicked.'

'That's the luck of the Irish for you.'

'You've had a lot of that of late.' She stared up at me with an all too familiar look in her eyes. 'You didn't ask for your solicitor to be present when you made your statement. Why was that?'

'The minute I'd overpowered Fowley, I got the kid to phone the police. So I reckoned I didn't need a solicitor. All I did was defend myself.'

'You've been doing a lot of that lately, too. The last time we spoke you said you hardly knew our friend Fowley.'

Here we were, like a music hall double act, back in the old routine. 'And you asked me to get some info on him. People like Gerard Fowley don't take kindly to questions being asked.'

'You appeared to be very pally with him in that press photograph.'

'Just doing what I was asked to do to help the constabulary. I'm your model citizen, me. Ex-army, risked my life for Queen and country and all that.'

'Spare me the bullshit.'

'I'm sure you've asked young Damien what happened today. He was itching to give you the skinny on his boss.'

They'd put the kid in the back of another cop car to drive us to the police station and, as they'd tucked him in the back seat, he was already in full flow. If he had any solid evidence against Fowley, then he was already talking up a storm.

'Damien told me Fowley had murdered some black lady.' Poor Adelaide Johnson, just trying to find out about her son. The thought of what had happened to both of them gnawed at me.

Morrison raised her eyebrows. 'I can't discuss that with you.'

'Understood. But am I free to go?'

'We could charge you with discharging an illegal firearm.'

'Now who's full of bullshit? Think of all the unnecessary paperwork involved. Nobody was hurt and you've got yourself a suspect for the murder of Adelaide Johnson. A polite thank you would be sufficient.'

Morrison got up. 'I'll walk you to your car. It's outside.'

We stood together in the car park and she handed me the keys. There was a look on her face that I couldn't decipher. It was as if she wanted to tell me something, but couldn't bring herself to do it.

I broke the silence. 'How is your friend doing?'

She looked momentarily taken aback, but quickly covered it up. 'She died. The funeral is later this week.'

'I'm sorry.'

She cleared her throat. 'Me, too. It's time for a fresh start. I think you should know that I've applied for a transfer.'

'Where to?'

'Anywhere but here.'

'And our deal?' The photo of Joe Murphy and me, would she finally give it up?

'Are you still at the Watts' place?'

'For the time being.'

'Then look out for some post on its way to you.'

Did I believe her? I'd have to wait and see.

———

I was exhausted so headed back to the farm. The kitchen floor was covered with old newspapers just in case the puppies got caught short. I glanced down and saw that one of the pups had recently peed on the front-page photo of Fowley with Lenka and me outside Legend. The stain was gradually spreading like a virus that threatened to engulf us all.

'Where is Brando's guitar?' Lenka asked as I strode in empty-handed.

I told her about my encounter with Fowley and his subsequent arrest. I watched her grin spread from ear to ear. Not much sympathy there, then.

'You must tell Timor.' She laughed. 'One down and one to fall.'

'Can't help you with Gloria Kelso.'

She handed me the phone. 'He will say what to do.'

And he did.

Chapter Sixty-Five
11 a.m., Thursday, 17 July

Monica pulled up outside Fowley's car showroom. She'd get even with Swindley, because Monica Cohen didn't take threats lying down. She'd rationalised what he'd told her; she wasn't to blame for the circumstances of her birth. She recalled a line from some Shakespeare play she'd been forced to study at school: 'In the lusty stealth of nature . . .' Well, that was the way it was, she was here and there was fuck-all anyone could do about it. Gloria was weak. If some bloke had raped Monica night after night, she'd have gutted the bastard and stuffed his severed prick down his throat. All her adult life she'd exploited the reality that men in the throes of orgasm were at their most vulnerable. Give them what they want and get what you want. Whether it was money or their head on a stick.

She was sure she could persuade Fowley to set those Chinese guys on Swindley and on Gloria. Let's see how that wise-arse, twisted Mancunian liked them apples. Cut her a new smile, would he? Not if she got to him first.

The cars were parked at the front of the lot in neat polished rows but the showroom's glass doors were locked. She peered through the windows and saw a middle-aged, balding Asian man inside. She banged on the door. He looked up, walked across the showroom and opened up just a tad.

'I'm sorry, madam. We are closed until further notice.'

'I need to see Mr Fowley.'

'He is not available.'

'This is urgent. Where can I find him?'

'Mr Fowley is not available,' he insisted.

She didn't like his superior tone one little bit. Come on, you supercilious immigrant, play the white man.

'I have to see him immediately.'

'Then I suggest you try the police station, madam.'

She went straight into innocent mode. 'Oh, dear. Have you had a break-in?'

'Mr Fowley has been arrested.'

'What are the charges?' Pimping probably, the fucking idiot. Why he hadn't given up on that game she would never know. Drugs were the cash crop these days, not a fifty quid blow job from some skank with track-marks. These goddamn men, it was always about power. Bunch of arseholes.

'Murder, madam.' The man had a look of sly satisfaction on his face. He leaned forward, poked his head out of the door and spoke quietly. 'That Afro-Caribbean lady, you know, the one who was brutally murdered in her own home. It really was a terrible thing.'

'I saw something about that on the news.' And she'd been as mad as hell. If that had got onto the TV, then why was there not a peep about the shootings at the farmhouse? She'd made a detour past there for a quick shufti despite her memories of Benny's warnings. 'Never return to the scene, Mon. Only amateurs or idiots who want to be caught do stupid things like that.' All the good ignoring his advice had done her, though. There had been no way she was going to risk stopping in that quiet lane and with gate to the farm-house drive being closed, she could spot no sign of life at all. She couldn't figure it out. Unless no bugger had been left standing and the bodies hadn't been found yet. Maybe that would account for it. Let them all rot. She had bigger fish to fry. Taking Swindley down was her number one priority.

'I saw Mr Fowley leave this very showroom with the woman on the day she met that sad end. I've worked here for three years and I do have a certain amount of loyalty to Mr Fowley, but when the police asked me if I'd seen the lady, I had to tell the truth.' He looked around conspiratorially like a spy passing on top-secret information and his voice dropped to a whisper. 'The policeman told me they had CCTV footage from the bus the lady was on. It dropped her right there.' He pointed to the bus stop across the road. 'I was with a customer at the time. I'm sure she'd pardon me for say-ing this, but the lady was on the large side and rather hard to miss. And, a while later, I saw her get into Mr Fowley's car.' He shook his head, sadly. 'Mr Fowley didn't come back to work that day and I had to lock up. I still have the keys.'

And hanging on to them, she'd bet. He was sure to be the first one to hotfoot it into the witness box to have Fowley put away. Then he'd club together with a few of his extended family to make a bid for the business. That's what she'd do, if she were in his shoes. They'd probably pick it up for a song. This guy already had a proprietorial air about him as though envisaging himself in clover. Indians like him were moving into the area in droves and an Asian-owned car showroom would be their first port of call. That would be quite a result for him. But with Fowley cur-rently incommunicado, where did that leave her? Screwed over from here to Christmas.

She got into her car. Her only hope was to find out the names of those two Chinese guys and contact them directly herself. She could maybe go it alone on a deal. Even if Fowley was innocent, his reputation would be tarnished and those two Chinks would disappear, not wanting to be associated. She'd gleaned that much from meeting them.

She couldn't get into the showroom office but, anyway, she doubted that Fowley would leave that kind of info at work. She'd go to his house. She hadn't spotted an alarm of any kind; perhaps if she could break in and rifle through his stuff she'd find something sooner or later.

It was lunchtime by the time that Monica got to Fowley's place. The police were out in force and it looked like they were emptying the joint. Cursing her bad luck, she parked a little way down the cul-de-sac and watched them carrying out cardboard boxes filled to the brim. One of the cops was lugging computer gear and another had black bin bags, probably full of Fowley's belongings for forensic examination. They were going the whole hog on this one. But then riots had been sparked over far less. Some gangbanger gets topped and the black 'community' rises up as one, demands justice, starts setting fire to buildings and looting shops. A law-abiding woman, murdered in her own home, could have massive repercussions. The police needed a suspect, pronto. Though she couldn't figure out why Fowley would put all he'd worked for on the line to kill this woman. It just didn't make sense to her.

Neighbours stood around gawking and gossiping. Monica got out of her car, walked up to a gaggle of women and casually eavesdropped on their conversation.

'Those people are always up to no good,' one woman declared.

'I never liked the look of him with his Daimler. He was too flash by half. They try to look respectable, don't they? But they never can quite carry it off. And did you ever see that big black man, his driver? Now there was a brute if ever there was one.'

'They should stick to their own neighbourhoods, if you ask me. The minute he moved in, I said to my Jim, "Here comes trouble". I mean, you know me, I'm not racist or anything but . . .'

Monica walked back to her car. Oh, Gerard, you are well and truly fucked. And, without backup, so was she.

The thought of doing Swindley's bidding by retreating to Spain held no appeal whatsoever.

She sat and thought it through. She'd go and talk to Richard Bloom face-to-face. They'd never got on. He'd never been susceptible to her charms, not so much as a flicker. Consequently, she'd always suspected him of being a bit of a shirt-lifter, what with his hideaway cottages and all, but with clients like Benny, it would have been unwise for Bloom to be openly gay. Yet if she went in there and played it right, she might be able to gauge his reaction, see if he knew anything about the shootings at the farmhouse. She found his number in her phone.

'You shouldn't be speaking to me directly,' he said when she finally got through to him. 'All future communications should be through your solicitors.'

'I'm thinking about dropping the challenge to Benny's will, Richard. If we can come to some amicable arrangement then I'll ring my lawyers—'

'I'm sorry, Monica, but there's a conflict of interest here. I represent Brando and Miss Riley. If you have any problems or queries, then you should take legal advice elsewhere.'

'Richard, please. For old times' sake.'

He was adamant. She should have known. Before he hung up, Monica could have sworn she heard a voice in the background. She started her car and drove towards Bloom's office. If her suspicions were correct and Sam Riley was not only still in the land of the living but was with Bloom right now, then she had to find out what they were up to. It was only about five miles to Bloom's place. At this time of day, she could be there in ten minutes. She gunned the engine. Fuck it! Make that six.

Chapter Sixty-Six
1 p.m., Thursday, 17 July

Richard Bloom gave me an incredulous look. 'Did Gerard Fowley explain why he held you at gunpoint?'

What could I tell him? I was in this up to my neck. I didn't know much about the law but I did know that you have to handle lawyers with caution. Confession soothing the soul is all very well but lawyers can't unhear what you tell them. So I told him about my getting the better of Fowley.

'That was when Damien claimed Fowley had intended to kill me just like he'd killed that black lady – his words exactly.'

'This is a very bizarre turn of events, I must say.'

'I'm as disconcerted as you are.' I managed to say with a straight face.

'You made a statement to the police to this end?'

'To DI Morrison.'

'She's back on the case?' He sounded mildly surprised.

'She turned up at the warehouse and interviewed me later, so yes, she's back at work.'

'I suggest you go to Norwich tomorrow and see how this house move is progressing. And do make an effort to keep out of any more trouble.'

You don't know the half of it, mate.

His phone rang and his new receptionist spoke to him for a minute.

'I'm with a client,' he said but she carried on talking. 'Then put her through.' He looked at me. 'I'm going to have to take this.'

I nodded and stood up to hold the door for the receptionist as she brought in another pot of coffee.

I tried not to listen to Bloom's clipped conversation but when he mentioned Monica's name, my ears pricked up.

'Thanks for the coffee – and the biscuits,' I said to the woman as she retreated.

Bloom ended the call rather abruptly and sat back in his seat looking a little distracted. 'That was Monica Cohen. It appears she wishes to make a private arrangement rather than contesting the will. But I can't possibly see her without her legal representative present.' He shuffled through some papers on his desk. 'I'll contact the police regarding your latest escapade and get the lay of the land. In the meantime, go to Norfolk and keep your head down.'

I left his office and walked back to my car. It was far too late to make it to Norwich now; I'd have to return to the farmhouse to talk Timor's plan through with Lenka. Though with Fowley now out of the running for the nightclubs, that was one less competitor standing in the way of her brother's ambitions. I'd find out about Gloria's bid for the clubs some other time. I was tired and hungry and hoped those damned puppies would behave themselves tonight.

Though Monica's sudden U-turn regarding the will made me nervous. It sounded like desperation to me, and that made her dangerous. I had no real proof that she'd been the driver for the Spanish killers, but the suspicion was embedded in my brain.

I glanced up at the darkening sky and shivered. Black clouds scudding by and wind whipping at the branches of the trees; all the signs of an impending storm.

———

Monica had arrived at the end of the road that led to Bloom's office when she spotted Sam driving away. With her worst fears realised, the only thing a shaken Monica could think to do was follow at a safe distance. Two cars behind just as Benny had taught her. 'Who takes any notice of cars that far behind?' he'd say sagely. He loved passing on snippets of information to her, secure in the knowledge that she didn't fully understand what he was talking about. Monica smiled to herself. People see what you want them to see. The smile swiftly faded. Until the old bastard did her over by changing his will.

When Sam pulled into the farmhouse driveway, Monica parked on the verge beneath the overhanging branches of some trees that were in dire need of cutting back. They might be a danger to cyclists but were good cover for her while also allowing her a clear view of the farmhouse gates. Satisfied that her car was well camouflaged, she settled down to wait. Monica Cohen would get to the bottom of this and, if it meant staying put in her car all night, that's what she'd do.

She took this quiet time to reason it all out. Without a police presence and no news of the Spanish hitmen, she knew that evidence of the shootings had been swept away like nothing had ever happened. She'd witnessed a couple of such disappearances during her time with Benny. She remembered one minor villain, pissed out of his box, pulling a knife and carving up a business rival at one of the parties she and Benny hosted. Random violence was to be expected in their business but the rule was that you settled grievances on your own turf, or on neutral ground maybe, but certainly not while the boss was entertaining guests in his own home. It was disrespectful, that. So no matter who had won the argument that night, both men involved in the ruck were disposed of. When she'd complained about the bodies in the garden and blood on the rugs, Benny had reassured her: 'We'll call in the cleaning crew. Come morning, this place will be spotless.' And so it was.

But Sam Riley wasn't in that league; she was a civilian and didn't have access to that kind of specialist aid. The only way she could have knocked off those two Spaniards and got rid of the bodies was with Swindley's help, surely.

Monica stayed put in her car, determined not to move until Sam reappeared.

Chapter Sixty-Seven
11 a.m., Friday, 18 July

The dogs snoozed peacefully on Thursday night, and I got some sleep too. But after my second conversation with Timor, my trip to Norwich had to be postponed for yet another day. Lenka's wall calendar had a ring scrawled around the date.

'Birthday?' I asked her.

She gave me one of her inscrutable smiles. 'The day my father died,' she said. 'Every year it is a time for celebration.'

I sometimes wondered about the sanity of my new friend.

I left her to her own devices and drove to Carver's old office above the kebab shop. Gloria would steer well clear of the Carver house as the police had it cordoned off and the media crew remained huddled around the gates, smacking their chops in anticipation of the next gory find. I knew Gloria had a flat somewhere close by but didn't have the address, so I thought I'd give Carver's office a try.

Monica glanced at her reflection in the vanity mirror. It confirmed that she looked like hell. But it was nothing that couldn't be fixed when this was all done and dusted. She pulled out the vial of speed from her handbag and took a couple more hefty snorts. The powder momentarily scalded her sinuses just before the rush kicked in. Sorted!

The Mercedes drove down the driveway and stopped at the farmhouse gate. When Sam got out to open up, Monica ducked down in her seat. She was reasonably well hidden from view but not taking any chances. She waited until Sam was back in the car and on her way out. Monica started the engine and tailed her, close enough to be able to see where she was headed but at a sufficient distance not to be spotted.

The moment Sam parked in the high street, Monica knew exactly where she was going. Monica got out of her car and stood looking in the bicycle shop window opposite Carver's office. To anyone passing she would appear to be an ordinary, slightly dishevelled mother window-shopping for a kid's bike. But Monica's gaze was firmly fixed on the reflection of Sam Riley as she walked up to the door beside the gutted kebab shop and pressed the bell. The only person in that office would be Gloria Kelso. Sam's visit was further evidence that those two bitches were out to get her.

Monica walked back to her car and waited. She'd had little sleep and nothing to eat or drink for hours. She was running on speed, adrenalin and hate.

The first thing I noticed was that the grotty kebab shop had closed down and shopfitters were renovating the interior. The door to the right-hand side that Carver had left swinging on rusty hinges had been replaced and there was a security camera above the entrance. I pressed the bell.

'Yes?' Gloria's fuzzed-out voice came through the speaker.

'Sam Riley here,' I said.

'I can see that. What do you want?'

'Can I come up?'

'If you must.' She buzzed me in.

The walls of the stairway had been painted and the tatty carpet had been ditched. At the top of the stairs, the door I had busted open had also been replaced with something much sturdier, and kitted out with a formidable array of locks. I doubted that even Joe Murphy would have been able to get past those with ease.

Gloria opened the door to me. Her transformation was almost complete: her hair shone, and a stylish red suit enhanced her neat frame.

The room had been made over too. Carver's office had been a pigsty with scruffy rugs and battered desks, whereas everything in here now was modern and spotless, to the point of sterility. Typical Gloria.

'You're quick off the mark,' she accused as she seated herself behind the highly polished desk with her back to the window. 'The email only went out to Bloom last night. I suppose with Gerard Fowley out of the game you want me to change my mind. Well, I won't, so you needn't have bothered. You'll have to find another buyer. I'm out.'

Timor had asked me to find out if she might be open to some kind of deal and here she was already backing out of the bidding for the nightclubs. Not that I'd clearly understood why she'd wanted them in the first place. They'd need a lot of money pumped into them to make them viable again. I didn't doubt for a moment that she had the dosh but wasn't sure it was quite her style. Big Jim Carver had never owned clubs and had most likely only agreed to the initial deal with Benny to get one over on Fowley. I decided to wait and see what she might say, so I kept quiet. My silence appeared to disconcert her.

'I wanted the nightclubs for my Janine but I've decided that it's not the right environment for her. I'm sending her to business college instead.'

Evidently, she planned to hand over the legitimate operations to her daughter but first wanted to ensure that Janine had a rudimentary grasp of business.

Gloria ran her left hand through her hair with her manicured fingernails gleaming with a red shade that matched her suit, when I spotted a diamond glinting on her finger.

'Are congratulations in order?' I ventured, tapping my ring finger.

'Yes. Thank you.' She glanced at the ring momentarily and her thin lips spread into a smile. 'Bert reckoned it was time we got hitched.'

'You've certainly made some changes here,' I said. 'And what's happening downstairs?'

'I got rid of those dirty little Turks. I hope you never ate anything there. The kitchen was disgusting. I wouldn't have fed a dog on that muck. I'm turning it into a nice little gastro bar. It's about time this street went a bit more upmarket. There are a lot of people with money around here but they all go out of the area to eat. I'm planning to change all that. I've just bought that old Chinese restaurant around the corner. The woman who owned it was past it. Peruvian food is all the rage, I've heard. But me, I think that's a bit too poncy for round here, so I'm leaning towards organic vegetarian.'

I had a mental image of the soon-to-be Mrs Swindley stepping up on stage to accept a Business Woman of the Year award.

'So you see, Sam, I'll be leaving the club business to others. My family wants nothing to do with that game.'

'Where is Monica?'

'Bert went to see her. She'll be out of the country if she knows what's good for her.'

Where had I hear that before?

'Gloria Kelso doesn't want to do a deal,' I told Timor on the phone. 'She's no longer interested in buying the clubs.'

Everyone a winner, it seemed. Timor gets the nightclubs, Tony Lee sells the restaurant that had been the bane of his life and I had Fowley off my back. With Mac on the road to recovery and Brando home soon, all I had to do now was get the house in Norwich sorted. But where was Monica? Swindley was one scary bloke but was he really enough to put the wind up Monica?

Monica followed Sam back to the farmhouse and contemplated spending another day and night in her car beneath its canopy of branches. She needed a shower and a change of clothes but decided to wait a while longer and track Sam's movements. An elderly couple walked by with a little fluffy dog on a lead. The man stopped for a moment then ambled back towards her car. He tapped on the window. 'Are you lost?'

'I've been driving all day,' she said. 'I'm a bit tired, so I thought I'd take a break here before I continue my journey.'

'Best way, my dear, though I'm not sure that a country lane is the ideal place for a woman on her own.' His steady gaze discomforted her. 'I could have sworn I've seen you around here before. Aren't you a friend of Mrs Watts?' He indicated towards the farmhouse.

Monica put on her best blank face.

'My mistake.' He smiled benignly. 'You have a good rest before you drive off, dear. But I'd park a little further along the lane, if I were you. These branches are hazardous and any other vehicles using the road might not spot you. Better safe than sorry.'

Monica watched him in her wing mirror as he went back to his wife and the yapping dog but she was sure he had scrutinised her number plate. That was it. She'd take this one back to the hire company and trade it in for another model. As the old geezer had said, better safe than sorry.

⌣

Back at the farmhouse Lenka handed me an envelope. 'This came in post for you.'

I took it up to my room and opened it. It contained the photo of Joe Murphy and me in a folded sheet of blank paper. There was no note but it seemed that Wendy Morrison had kept her word.

The faces in the picture were of two youngsters, recognisable strangers from a lifetime ago. Joe had kept it all those years but I had to destroy it as it had almost destroyed me. I'm sorry, Joe. For getting you mixed up in this in the first place; for not loving you as you loved me; for standing by while Monica took your life. I tore the image in two, then into four pieces. I spread the pieces on the bed and put them back together like a jigsaw puzzle. Could Swindley have been Joe Murphy's uncle? Had Joe been working for Lil Carver all along?

I sifted through the conversation I'd had with Joe when I'd asked him to do the hit on Benny Cohen. 'I'm out of that game now,' he'd told me. 'But I owe you, so I'll do it.'

I'd never questioned it at the time. I'd been so bedazzled by Monica and our plans for the future that I'd just been grateful to have his agreement. 'I owe you.' The words echoed in my head. I picked up the pieces and shredded them into tiny fragments, wrapped them in a tissue, and flushed them down the loo. Perhaps 'I owe you' had meant he was filled with remorse for having involved me with Swindley and everything we had done when we were both so young. I resigned myself to the fact that I would never know.

'The police are on the telephone,' Lenka called up to me.

What now? I had so many secrets, so much to fear and so much to lose.

'Miss Riley,' said the deep Welsh voice. 'Would you mind coming down to the station?'

'Should I bring my lawyer?' It had to be about the Carver shootings. Some evidence to link me to the gun I had used to kill Carver. DCI Evans had been keen to ask about the height difference between Swindley and me. Maybe CSI-style hocus-pocus had brought something to light.

'No, this is another matter entirely.' His tone was soothing and my heart revved in my chest. 'But maybe you should consider being accompanied by a friend.'

'What is this about?' Cold dread crept over me.

'Your nephew, Miss Riley. We have reason to believe that one the bodies found at the Carver house may be that of your nephew.'

Chapter Sixty-Eight
3 p.m., Friday, 18 July

Monica spotted the Mercedes at the gate again. A tall blonde got out of the car and opened up. It had to be the Mrs Watts that the nosy neighbour had referred to. Sam was driving. Where the hell was Brando? He'd been stuck like glue to Sam. Maybe she and the Watts woman were going to pick him up from somewhere. And once they were all together, then she'd strike. When the Merc was a fair distance ahead, Monica set off behind them once more, and they led her straight to the police station.

Monica parked her rented car across the road from the cop shop, took a couple more speed hits and stewed in her juices. Sam Riley was behind all this grief. She realised that now. She'd been so obsessed with getting to Swindley that she'd failed to spot what was right in front of her nose. Sam had to be in league with Gloria and Swindley. Monica was convinced that they were all out to destroy her. That was why Swindley had let Sam and the brat get out of the Carver house alive. Not because the bastard had a conscience but because they were all in it together.

Monica had watched Sam swan out of Bloom's office, all done up like a proper woman rather than a bloody lesbo. Sam's previous look had been a disguise, that's what it was. All part of the plan to lull Monica into thinking she had the upper hand, while the three of them had been plotting to rob her of what was her due.

This was the final straw. Monica had gleaned from the BBC radio news that this station was where the cops were holding Gerard Fowley. If Sam Riley had something to do with Fowley's arrest, then the trap was closing. Though if they imagined that Monica Cohen was helpless without Fowley, they had another think coming. There was only one way out for her. She'd get back into the Cohen grounds and dig out Benny's stash of guns hidden under the gazebo in the garden. Nobody else knew they were there. Once she had her hands on the weapons she'd be able to take the lot of them down.

Benny had enrolled her in the local gun club as a twenty-fourth birthday present. She'd been enraged at the time; she'd wanted a diamond bracelet. But he'd laughed it off and told her that she should learn how to shoot. 'When push comes to shove you might need to defend yourself, my love.' The lessons came in handy when she killed that northern shitbag Sam had recruited to do for Benny. Monica had crept to the side of his Land Rover and *pop! pop! pop!* He didn't see that one coming, didn't know what had hit him. Some fucking professional he was.

She'd teach this lot not to underestimate her. Monica Cohen was a winner – always had been, always would be.

Chapter Sixty-Nine
6 p.m., Friday, 18 July

Lenka and I were asked to wait in Wendy Morrison's office. We were offered tea but both refused. I could hardly think, let alone drink tea. Please let there be some mistake, I prayed to the God of my youth. I'd been through the process of grieving for Tom years before and had tried to soothe my distress by imagining him safe, having been taken for a couple that couldn't have a child of their own. He'd be happy and growing up in a loving environment, I told myself.

While I entertained thoughts of the best possible scenario, there always came a time when the very worst intruded. He'd been taken and abused, crying out for his mother in his agony, his broken little body disposed of like so much garbage. My mind filled with so many horrific images I couldn't deal with that I had to shut them out to remain sane. I'd even harboured suspicions that my brother or his wife had killed Tom. That's what the police had suspected, that's what the tabloid newspapers had insinuated and what the neighbours speculated about. What sort of parents leave a four-year-old asleep in bed and go down to the pub? Why had there been no sign of a break-in when they'd both sworn the house was locked up tight? Round and round the doubts and questions went like a demonic carousel and, for a time, I felt I would go mad. The intervening seven years had dulled the pain but it was always there, that hollow ache, and the uncertainty.

The phone call from the police had sent me spiralling back down into the living hell of that first day; the impotent anguish I'd felt watching the television coverage of Tom's disappearance and seeing the cameras focusing on the blue teddy bear on his empty bed. My first thought had been that he'd be so upset without Tedders. After that day, I had switched off my emotions. I got used to not thinking about Tom as the lack of answers only tugged at my wounds. And it stayed that way until Brando. He revived my ability to love unconditionally and all my protective armour slowly fell away. Tom would be eleven now, the same age as Brando. Once, while I was waiting for Brando outside his school, I'd spotted a boy whose face reminded me of my brother at that age and I'd watched with a leaden heart as the lad clambered into the back seat of a posh 4x4.

My hopes were raised when I saw newspaper reports of adults who had been kidnapped as children discovering their true identity via websites. Maybe one day my nephew might do the same. And Mac offering to help me search for Tom had lightened my burden. I'd clung on to the slightest fragment of hope but right now the distress I was feeling as I waited was so intense that I felt exhausted and sick. Lenka sat beside me and held my hand in both of hers. She was living a mother's nightmare through me and was close to tears herself but putting on a brave face. Maybe people come into your life for a reason. All I knew at that moment was I was so glad she was with me and prepared to grant me the silence.

I didn't want to talk but nothing could block out the doubts that hammered at me. Who would kidnap a child from Manchester for Carver? A person who'd done his dirty work in the north of

England. Who would be capable of breaking into a house and leaving no trace of entry behind? The answer to that question filled me with dread. Joe Murphy knew my brother and his reputation, knew that he had a small son. The weight of that suspicion almost sank me but I gasped for air and fought my way back to the surface. Joe had turned up at my brother's funeral even though he wasn't a friend of his. I'd assumed Joe was there to give me moral support but he may well have attended to salve his own conscience.

I scoured my memory in a desperate attempt to believe I was in the grip of hysterical paranoia. Joe had kept that photograph of us both for all those years. Swindley had told me that Joe had always loved me. You don't take a child from someone you love. Joe was my friend, had once been my lover. But he was also a hired killer. Murder for money, kidnap for money, was there any real difference? Deny the bad thing, make an argument against it and it will turn out not to be real. It was a standard defence reflex that I'd seen on the faces and heard in the voices of soldiers whose friends had been killed in battle.

Minutes ticked by, then half an hour. I felt like a condemned prisoner, counting off the seconds, listening for the footsteps in the corridor, taking the final walk that would put an end to my life.

The door opened and I withdrew my hand from Lenka's. Wendy Morrison walked in and the terror I felt almost stopped my heart. 'I'm sorry,' she said quietly.

Sorry for what? For having dragged me down here? Sorry for the massive error and for the body of the child to belong to someone else? That's what it was. But I guessed from the expression on her face that she'd drawn the short straw. She sat behind a desk, putting the barrier of officialdom between us.

'Arthur Caine gave us a list of names and dates,' she said. 'The moment I saw one of the names, I checked into it. I had the DNA sample you provided for DCI Evans analysed and . . .'

Before she told me, I knew what was coming and my heart seemed to stand still.

Morrison's face was grave. 'I genuinely regret having to tell you this but the comparison was positive. One of the bodies found was that of your nephew, Tom Riley.'

Chapter Seventy
8 p.m., Friday, 18 July

Monica surveyed the B&M gates. With the police investigations into the Garcia shootings out of the way, the house was now locked up until the legal matters were all signed off. She drove down the dead-end lane beside the high walls surrounding the Cohen estate and parked.

Just behind the gazebo within the grounds of the house was a ten-foot, ivy-coated wall. The gate was hidden beneath the foliage. 'Contingency plan, Monica,' Benny had told her. 'Nobody knows about this but you and me.'

Monica paced the ground along the outside barrier; the door was as invisible from here as it was from within. Once she was satisfied that she'd reached the right spot, she fished a pair of garden shears out of her holdall and set to work on the ivy. The clank against metal reassured her that she had found the entrance and she worked away until she reached the lock, breaking a fingernail in the process. She uncovered the lock and searched in the bag for the key. Try to keep her out of her own home, would they? She held up the key triumphantly. With some effort, she turned it in the rusted lock but had to chop aside more ivy and put her whole weight behind the final push before she was able to gain entrance. She closed the gate behind her and gave the grounds the once-over. The grass was in dire need of mowing but the days when she'd closely supervise that lazy bastard gardener were gone forever. Though once she'd seen to her enemies, she'd be back on top again – the Queen Bee would return to her hive.

Situated in the gazebo was a Victorian cast-iron bench like the ones that were once strategically placed in public parks. Benny had found this one in an antiques emporium and had it restored. It was fiendishly heavy and it took all her strength to move it just a few feet. Two more fingernails went the way of the first one, but she didn't give a damn anymore. She brushed away three inches of gravel and found the board that covered the buried box. It wasn't locked. Quick getaways require easy access, Benny had always said. The guns were wrapped in grey, synthetic-fleece bags. There was a rifle and two handguns plus ammunition in plastic containers. She chose a Glock 19 and a fifteen-round magazine. Self-defence ammunition, they deemed it. They were having a laugh. She put the gun and ammo into her holdall, closed the box, then redistributed the gravel and pushed the heavy bench back over it. Moments later she was out of the door behind the gazebo, locking the gate and pulling the ivy back into place to camouflage her tracks.

She returned to her replacement rented car. It was a silver-grey Volvo – the typical housewives' choice. Lots of space inside for the kids and the shopping – or a bag packed with lethal intent. She started the engine and drove away. Lady Luck was back on her side. Try to screw Monica Cohen over, would they? Right then, get ready for the shitstorm.

Chapter Seventy-One
4 p.m., Saturday, 19 July

I could hear Lenka on the telephone. When she was upset, she was loud. 'I don't care if you have not finished recording. I want children back here with me.' There was a short gap in the conversation. 'You stay and do what you want.' The next gap was even shorter. 'I will not argue. My children and Brando must come home. You make sure they are on plane tomorrow.'

The police doctor had given me a sedative and I hardly remembered the trip back to the farmhouse. Lenka drove. The roads and the trees whizzed by in swirling soft focus. My world was wrapped in cotton wool and I didn't like it one little bit. I disliked too much alcohol for the same reason; you have to retain control or you're doomed. When we arrived, Lenka insisted that I went to bed. I fought sleep but had finally succumbed. I must have slept for the rest of Friday night and most of Saturday, and I may well have slept on had I not been woken by Lenka's voice berating Mike on the other end of the line.

I sat up, still groggy but with my heart pounding. I remembered being told that the police were trying to contact Tom's mother to break the news to her. I'd been too distraught to take in all I'd been told at the station but seemed to recall that it would take a while to ascertain the cause of death. Arthur 'Chimp' Caine was spilling his guts and a number of other people would be in a similar position to me. Their kids were dead too and there was little any of us could do about it but grieve.

But I could do something. There were too many unanswered questions tormenting me. If anyone would know whether Joe Murphy had taken Tom, it would be Swindley. I quickly dressed and went downstairs. Lenka was sitting in the lounge, looking tearful. Maybe it takes something as drastic as the death of another child to bring home to you just how precious your own children are. Now she wanted her kids back home where she could keep a watchful eye on them.

'You should sleep,' she said. 'Brando will be back tomorrow. It is organised.'

I picked up my car keys from the kitchen table. 'I'll sleep when I'm dead.'

'You must not drive.' She was on her feet to stop me, but the look on my face halted her in her tracks. 'I go with you.'

'No. You stay here. The less you know about this the better.'

The shopfitters working on what used to be the kebab shop were packing up for the day. One of them was standing outside, having a crafty fag while supervising a young apprentice as he hauled a heavy bag of tools out to the van. 'Don't you drop those, Billy,' he warned as the young lad struggled.

'You could give me a hand,' the kid complained. 'What's up? You got a bone in your arm?'

The older guy flicked his cigarette butt in Billy's direction. 'Fuck off!' He was laughing, but remained leaning against the wall and nodded to me as I approached the adjacent door to the office above.

Gloria reluctantly let me in.

'I need to see Swindley,' I told her.

'That's not possible.'

'I'm not leaving here until you contact him.'

'Are you drunk?'

'I'm in no mood to play silly games. You tell Swindley to meet me.'

Gloria reached down to her handbag beside her desk, fished around in it and took out a set of keys. 'I'm off home now. You can stay here if you want to but I'm not ringing him and that's that.'

I lunged at her, grabbed her by the shoulders and shook her violently. 'Get him on the phone, now!'

She glared at me. 'Take your hands off me. Hurt me and you'll regret it.'

I released her, picked up the telephone and handed it to her. 'Ring him.'

She punched in the number. 'Bert. It's me. Sam Riley is here, demanding to see you . . . Are you sure? All right, I'll come with her . . . If you're sure than I'll wait here for another half hour, then.'

She looked puzzled. 'Fifty-five Victoria Street, top flat. The name on the bell is O'Connor.'

I walked towards the door.

Gloria had regained her composure. 'You ever lay another hand on me and I'll have you filleted. Understood?'

———————

The shopfitters had buggered off home by the time I got out of there. As I stepped into my car, I saw a silver-grey Volvo had parked right up to my rear bumper. It took quite a few turns to manoeuvre out of the tight space.

The address in Victoria Street was a two-storey Edwardian house that had been converted into flats during the housing boom of the 1980s. I rang the top bell and heard someone coming down the stairs. Swindley opened the door, nodded his head, and I followed him up to the flat.

'The police have identified one of the bodies from the Carver house,' I said.

'This is not a conversation I ever wanted to have with you.' He indicated to the sofa and I sat down. 'Your nephew.' It wasn't a question; it was a statement of fact.

'You knew about it all along?'

'Not at the time.' His face took on a look of grim resignation. 'You sure you want to hear this?'

I nodded, but my gut was squirming. Be careful what you wish for.

'Alright. But it's not pretty.' Swindley sat opposite me. 'When you joined up, Joe fell apart. He started doing a lot of speed. He was so wired and angry he was no good to me anymore, so I dumped him. I wasn't sure what he was up to after that, not until he got nabbed on a burglary charge and ended up doing six months. I went to see him in prison, but he was still all messed up and as bitter as hell. All he could talk about was you and getting even.'

'But I never did anything to Joe.' We'd agreed to part company. Though thinking back to the look on his face when I forced him to burn the photographs. Had it been pain or anger? The very thought of him as a procurer for a child molester repulsed me and I made a vain attempt to wipe his image from my memory.

'Look, all I can do is tell you what I know. Joe was obsessed.'

'Joe kidnapped Tom and handed him over to Carver as a way to hurt me? I don't buy it. For leaving him and for not loving him? What kind of twisted, sadistic logic is that?'

'Or for money. He was really screwed up at the time.' Swindley held up his hand, palm forward. 'Not that I'm making any excuses, you understand.' He paused to light a cigarette. 'I hadn't seen Joe for years when I heard he was in rehab and so I visited him in there. I hoped that he'd finally sorted himself out. But I hardly recognised him. He was rake-thin and jumpy, clinically depressed and riddled with guilt. The minute I walked in, he broke down and confessed like I was his priest.'

Those cold, grey eyes held me in their gaze but there was a softening in his tone. This was a side of the man I had never seen before. 'Your nephew wasn't the only child Joe snatched for Carver, you know. There'd been a couple of boys from Scotland and another one in the Midlands, as far as I could make out.'

I felt gutted. What had I expected Swindley to say? That Joe would never do such a thing. 'I can't understand how anyone could kidnap children and hand them over to a monster like Carver.'

'Me neither. You know how I make my living. But kids . . .' Swindley shook his head. 'That's something else. We were all aware of Carver's particular indulgences but none of us ever imagined—'

'You still worked for Carver, though. Even after Joe confessed?'

Swindley shrugged. 'It's complicated. The Carvers weren't people you could just walk away from. I could disappear on my own but there was Gloria. I've always tried to look out for her. Leaving wasn't an option for her, so we bided our time. Then I heard that Joe had been killed in this neck of the woods so I came here. When I first saw you in Carver's office and realised you were working for the Cohen family, I thought you'd found out about your nephew somehow, lured Joe here and seen to him yourself. And I reckoned fair dos, I'd have done the same in your position. It was nothing more than he deserved.'

'Lil Carver must have known what was going on in that house.'

'You had a cosy little chat to her. What do you think?' The cynical Swindley resurfaced.

'That Lil Carver was evil. And that monsters breed monsters.'

Swindley scrutinised me. 'Gloria wasn't aware of all this until she saw Arthur Caine at the house, you know. So don't try to place any blame at her doorstep.'

'Joe and Carver are both dead and Chimp is in police custody. He'll never be set free again. So there's nobody left to hold accountable. I just needed to know the truth about Joe.'

'And does that knowledge make you feel any better?'

'I don't know what I feel anymore.'

Chapter Seventy-Two
5 p.m., Saturday, 19 July

'I've come to say goodbye, Gloria.'

'Get out of here, Monica. Get on a plane and leave. I can't be held responsible for what happens to you if you don't go.'

'Swindley told me the whole sordid truth, Mother.'

'If you'd gone when I first told you to then you'd have been none the wiser. If you'd just stayed with that couple that adopted you and never asked any questions, you could have lived a normal life. That's what I wanted for you. It would have been the best all round. But now you do know, you should go to Spain and start again. What's done is done.'

'You want to wipe me out of your life again. Try to destroy me.'

'I'm trying to protect you.'

'You're a liar.'

'I always loved you, Monica. But I look at your face and I see his. Can you imagine what that's like for me?'

'You let him fuck you.'

'I was a child at the time.'

'I was *your* child.'

Monica pulled the gun from her bag and levelled it at Gloria's heart.

'Don't do this, Monica. I beg you.'

'Beg away, bitch. It's over.'

Chapter Seventy-Three
11 a.m., Sunday, 20 July

'I am sorry.' Lenka's eyes were firmly fixed on the road. We were on our way to Gatwick Airport.

'Sorry for what?'

'I have not been a good friend.'

'That's ridiculous. Without your help, I'd probably be dead in a ditch somewhere.'

'But Timor . . .'

'Same thing. But he's a businessman. He wanted the nightclubs and I was a way to get to them. I understand and I'm still grateful. So, forget it.'

'He did not want them until I told him about them. To betray is worse than to kill.'

'You didn't betray me. You are a really very good friend.'

'When you begin life like we did, you learn to take every opportunity.'

'Same with me.'

'You will tell me your story one day?'

'Maybe, one day.'

'Many people do bad things for money or for power. But you do them for good reasons: for love, to protect child, to save friends. Some people have clean hands but dirty soul. You have dirty hands but clean soul, I think.'

———— ————

Gatwick Airport. Brando and the kids were coming back business class on a scheduled flight. One of the nannies was accompanying them. Lenka had insisted on that. Poor Mike was getting it in the neck. 'Children will not fly alone. You send someone with them or you come. You choose.'

The young nanny pushing the trolley piled high with luggage into the arrivals area did not appear too pleased to be back on her home turf. She'd landed herself a tasty gig in France and being sent back early was clearly not something she had welcomed.

Lenka's three rushed over and threw their arms around her in a huddle whilst Brando helped the nanny push the trolley. He had his sulky face on.

'I don't see why I had to come back with *them*,' he grumbled.

'Don't be like that, Brando. We'll go to see Mac and prepare to move into the new house. It'll be great.'

'Yeah. But what's the big rush?'

Because I need you around, kid. Because I need to focus on the future so I'm not plagued by the past. 'I missed you.'

He sullenly unloaded his luggage from the trolley so the nanny could get to hers. She dragged it off, and Lenka handed her some notes for cab fare. With a petulant toss of her brown curls, the girl left without a word to the kids.

'She was a right cow,' Brando said as he watched her walk away and Lenka laughed.

'So you're glad to be back?' I asked him.

He flashed me his best big grin. 'Yeah.' He hugged me and I wrapped my arms around him tight. I didn't want to ever let him go again.

⸺

The silver grey Volvo drove slowly down the suburban street. The white-haired man carrying a suitcase in his right hand was lost in his thoughts so he didn't take much notice as it crept along in his direction.

The phone call from Janine had shaken him to the core but professionalism immediately took over. He had to leave; he had no other option. The indulgence of playing the grieving lover was not for him. I'm sorry, Gloria, my dear, he thought, but my weeping over your grave isn't going to do me any favours. He was too closely associated with the Carver family. If the cops found out his real name, they wouldn't have to dig too deep to establish his links to Joe Murphy. Those two bozos Carver had sent to snatch Brando could identify him and they were both behind bars. If one of them turned Queen's Evidence against him in exchange for a lighter sentence, then that would be him banged-up for the rest of his natural.

When Janine had told him the news about Gloria, he'd immediately suspected Sam Riley. She'd been in a right state when she visited him at the flat. Though, when he thought about it rationally, Sam killing Gloria just didn't seem in character. But you never really know how people will react. He would find out who had murdered Gloria and he would exact his revenge, but for now he had to disappear. A woman walked by him with a baby in a pram. She smiled at him but he didn't acknowledge her.

'Then there was a loud bang,' she told the police later. 'It sounded like a firework or a car backfiring. I was startled and looked back. That was when I saw the man lying on the ground. I pushed the pram into a neighbour's garden, banged on the door and told them to call an ambulance. Then I ran back out to see if I could help the man. But he wasn't moving. He'd been shot in the chest. I was sure he was dead. You hear about these drive-by shootings, don't you? But you never expect to actually see it happen. Not in a nice neighbourhood like this.'

'The car you saw driving away?' the uniformed policeman asked her gently. 'Did you see the number plate?'

'No, I'm sorry. But it was a silver grey Volvo. I've got one just like it.'

The housewives' choice.

---

9 a.m., Monday, 21 July

We had decided to stay the night at the farmhouse and go to Norwich the next morning. Brando was up and about first, excited about seeing Mac again.

'You're an eager one,' I said as I came downstairs and saw him sitting impatiently by the kitchen table. I made breakfast.

'You're the best cook, ever,' he said as he tucked into his eggs. 'Have you asked Mac to come and stay with us?'

'Not yet.' I recalled Brando's telephone call and his talk about the three of us being 'like a real family'. It had been a nice pipe dream at the time but now that it appeared a real possibility, it had me a bit spooked. Mac moving in with us would take all our relationships to another level and I wasn't sure I could cope with that. He was a good man, but maybe he was too good.

'Why not? Don't you want him to live with us? Because I do.'

'I was waiting for the right moment.' On the other hand, what harm could it do? Brando's heart was set on it. Maybe I should just play it by ear.

The doorbell rang and I opened up. DI Wendy Morrison, DC Trevor Jones and a uniformed policeman were standing outside. Morrison's face was fixed. 'Alice Samantha Riley, I am arresting you on suspicion of the murder of Gloria Kelso. You do not have to say anything, but it may harm your defence if you do not mention when questioned something which you later rely on in court. Anything you do say may be given in evidence.'

Chapter Seventy-Four
11 a.m., Monday, 21 July

It was the same police cell I had been in before. I recognised the graffiti on the walls. My one phone call was to Bloom and he'd assured me he was already on his way. Brando had phoned him the minute I was accompanied to the police station following my arrest. The lad's presence of mind was astonishing. He'd come home hoping for a bright new future only to witness me getting hauled off by the cops.

'You know I'm not a criminal lawyer,' Bloom had pointed out to me. 'But I'll stay with you until someone more qualified can take over. Mrs Watts tells me she has already arranged that. Don't say anything until I get there.'

In view of the fact that I had chosen to remain silent, I was left to stew in a cell, with no information other than that Gloria had been killed and I was in the frame. I could only assume she had been murdered at her office and that the shopfitter guys had identified me as her visitor. As they'd been gone by the time I left her, right now the finger was pointed at me.

My first instinct had been to deny it, to say I didn't do anything to Gloria, but that would have left me open to questioning. Why had I gone to see her? Where had I gone after I left her? To see Swindley, the man I had accused of killing the Carvers. I knew the whereabouts of a wanted criminal; that smacked of conspiracy and I'd be looking at a long stretch in prison for that alone. I'd gone to see Swindley because he was the uncle of Joe Murphy, a man I had denied having any knowledge of. What the hell could I say? I was well and truly stuffed.

Look for Monica Cohen, I wanted to tell them, she's the one behind this. She plotted to have her husband killed by the same Joe Murphy. But that was hardly something I could divulge to anyone. I was up against a brick wall. I was convinced that Monica had driven the hitmen to the farmhouse to kill me. But as far as the cops were concerned, that never even happened and Timor Koslov wouldn't take kindly to me making any mention of his and Lenka's part in it. If I coughed about the shootings and the clean-up, I probably wouldn't even make it into the witness box.

Unless this was a gang hit by someone else in the Carver organisation, the only person I could think of who might want Gloria out of the way was Monica. Maybe this was Monica's latest plan. Frame me for Gloria's death and go back to being Brando's stepmother. I couldn't let that happen. If the worst came to the worst, then I would confess my part in Benny Cohen's murder and drag Monica down with me. Brando would be left to fend for himself, but it was preferable to his being in her clutches again. Maybe Mac would step up to help the boy if I was behind bars. Surely Monica knew that I would sacrifice myself to keep Brando safe. Or maybe that was beyond her comprehension. All I could do now was wait and see how things developed.

The cell door opened and Bloom walked in, grim-faced. 'Tell me what happened.'

'I didn't do it.'

'That's good to know, but tell me what happened.'

DCI Evans cautioned me again in the interview room. Wendy Morrison wasn't present but DC Jones was. Richard Bloom sat beside me as we went through the introductions and all the other procedural rigmarole.

'You were seen entering the premises of Mrs Gloria Kelso,' Evans said.

'That's right. I visited Gloria on a private matter.'

'This is a murder investigation, Miss Riley. There can be no privacy here.'

I looked at Bloom and he nodded his head.

'I'd just been informed that the body of my nephew had been discovered at the Carver house. I was upset. I wanted to tell Gloria face-to-face.'

'Did Mrs Kelso know your nephew?'

'No. But I suspected she might know who had taken my nephew to her mother's house.'

'Did you hold Gloria Kelso responsible in any way?'

'Her brother and Arthur Caine murdered Tom and those other boys. Gloria had nothing to do with it. I just felt she might have some inside knowledge.'

'And did she?'

'No, but she told me that her fiancé might.'

'Fiancé? We understood that she was a widow?'

'She has recently become engaged.'

'And the name of this man?'

'I'm not sure. She called him Bert. But the name on the bell of their flat was O'Connor.'

'So your meeting with Gloria Kelso was amicable, would you say?'

Relatively speaking, apart from my shaking her by the shoulders and her threatening to have me filleted. 'Perfectly amicable. She rang her fiancé to tell him I was on my way and gave me the address.'

'And Gloria Kelso?'

'She told this Bert that she would be leaving the office in half an hour. And I assure you that she was in perfect health when I left.'

The fact that Gloria had a man in her life was evidently news to the police. I wondered if Swindley, or whatever his name was, would stay around or disappear into thin air. Not that his evidence would do me much good. I could have killed Gloria and then gone to see him. So I gave DCI Evans the address and, for the time being, my interview was terminated and I was taken back to my cell.

Bloom said that Lenka was taking care of Brando. 'Apparently Brando has been talking to Angus Macdonald. It would seem that he's discharged himself from hospital and he's on his way here.'

Bloom returned two hours later, accompanied by another man in his mid-forties who introduced himself as Quentin Stephens from a London firm I had never heard of. But if Lenka or Timor Koslov had arranged for him to represent me, then I reckoned he'd be a top-flight criminal lawyer. Bloom seemed relieved to hand over the reins to him. Stephens' manner was brusque and businesslike as we went through what had happened.

'It appears that the gentleman you mentioned to Detective Chief Inspector Evans – Albert O'Connor – has been shot.'

'When did that happen?' If whoever had killed Gloria had subsequently seen to Swindley, then I had no backup for my story. It might even look as though I'd done for both of them in a fit of revenge.

Stephens gave a wry smile. 'The incident took place while you and Mrs Watts were meeting arrivals at the airport. Of course, if the bullets that shot both Gloria Kelso and Albert O'Connor came from the same gun, then you are no longer a suspect. But the forensics will take a little time to confirm. So I'm afraid you may be in here for a short while. But, chin up! I'll try to get you out on your own recognisance first thing in the morning. And, if the police aren't in an amenable mood, then Mrs Watts has assured me that she will stand bail for you at the magistrates' court. You have some very valuable friends, Miss Riley.'

Chapter Seventy-Five
4 p.m., Monday, 21 July

Monica parked her car in a clearing on the far side of the woods. She knew this area; she'd recced it for those two incompetent Spaniards. It was a bit of a trek to the farmhouse from here and she'd decided against it at the time because the men would be going in at night and it might be a bit tricky for them to find their way back. But now she was planning a daytime approach. From the woods she'd have direct access to the garden and with those dogs out of the way, it would be a simple matter to just walk in there, do the job and leg it back to her car.

It was two down and two to go, along with anyone else that got in her way. The look on Gloria's face when she realised she was for the chop gave Monica a thrill of satisfaction that she would never tire of reliving. And Swindley, the stupid old fool. He'd looked up as she stopped the Volvo in the middle of the road. She hoped he had seen her face because it was the very last thing he would ever see. She'd shot him in the chest and he'd fallen backwards, drowning in his own blood. Gotcha, you bastard! She reached up and stroked the faint scar on her cheek he'd given her with that Stanley knife. They were wrong about revenge being a dish best served cold; it tasted sweetest when you were seething with rage.

She'd bought a sleeping bag so she could spend the night in the car and go in first thing in the morning. She'd have to make sure that Sam Riley and Brando were at the house – no point wasting bullets on strangers. Although that Watts woman looked like a stuck-up cunt, so popping her wouldn't be a hardship. These model-types marry rock musicians and get above themselves. Monica Cohen would take her down a peg or nine.

Monica pulled on her walking boots. She'd bought them at a camping shop in the local village, along with jeans, a pair of binoculars, a sweater, a small rucksack, gloves and a watch cap to cover her hair. She peered at her reflection in the vanity mirror; with no make-up and half an inch of dark roots coming through, she looked dreadful. Her hands were as bad. After breaking three nails she'd had to file them all back down. But it would all be worth it in the end. Kill the lot of them; make it look like a gang execution as there were still a few of Carver's mob the police would be only too happy to pin it on. A revenge hit for the death of their old boss. That might fly. With Gloria and Swindley gone, plus Fowley in the slammer, there could well be a godalmighty turf war on the horizon and it could get very messy. That stupid tart Janine would be bang in the middle of it all. She'd probably get her idiotic head blown off. Not that Monica gave a flying fuck. She'd have made her escape to the villa in Spain by then. She could stay there until the dust settled, then come back to claim her inheritance with tears in her eyes and a sob in her voice. 'What heartless person would murder my beloved stepson? I can't believe it.'

She took two long snorts of speed, guzzled down some water, put the binoculars in her rucksack, locked the gun in the boot of the car and set off through the woods towards the farmhouse. You never want any nasty surprises, so she'd check the lay of the land for now. But come tomorrow, all her troubles would be over.

The woods were denser than she remembered, with no pathways, and she had to fight her way past hanging branches and prickly bushes. She'd been right about the dozy Spaniards; they'd have certainly got lost.

Finally, she found her way to the back of the farmhouse and looked across the large swathe of garden. She held the binoculars in her gloved hands and scanned the scene. To the left was a building that looked like a converted barn, probably a garage. On her right was a brightly coloured climbing frame plus all the other shitty kids' stuff that she hated so much. Three blonde children were in the play area, but where was Brando? Then she spotted him, sitting alone beside the trees. The miserable sod, he never did know how to have a good time. He was reading a book. She'd never seen him do that before. That was Sam Riley's influence. Well, enjoy it while you can, you vile little turd – because your time will soon be up.

A sudden movement inside the house grabbed her attention and Monica forced herself to focus on the interior. The Watts woman was standing inside the French windows watching the kids play. There was no sign of Sam. Where was the bitch? Monica bit down hard on her bottom lip in frustration. She tasted blood but hardly felt a thing. Her fingers were itching to pop the lot of them NOW as speed-fuelled paranoia screamed inside her head. Though she still possessed enough self-awareness to know that had she been carrying the gun at this moment, she wouldn't have been able to stop herself from going in there, guns blazing, picking them off one at a time – screaming brats first with Brando shitting himself before she dropped him.

Monica took deep breaths and struggled to control herself. Walk away, stick with the plan and never go off half-cocked is what Benny had taught her. Keep your cool. Riley might not even be in the house. She may have gone out shopping, for all you know. But bide your time and come the morning, they will all be there. That's when you make your move on the farmhouse.

Chapter Seventy-Six
7 p.m., Monday, 21 July

I cooled my heels in the cell for another four hours, expecting to be there until the next morning, but Stephens was better than his word. Suddenly, to my astonishment, I was brought before DCI Evans and told I would be released immediately on police bail. I was not being charged at that time while further leads were investigated. Evans was polite but a bit shirty while Stephens remained very formal and quite impossible to read. Bloom was waiting for us outside the station. He shook hands with Stephens, who curtly nodded to me and left.

'Hop in, I'll drive you home,' Bloom offered.

'What just happened in there?'

'I'll tell you in the car.'

Swindley had survived and identified his assailant as Monica Cohen. If the bullet they'd dug out of him matched the one that had killed Gloria Kelso, then I was off the hook.

'You've done some idiotic things since I've known you,' Bloom said. 'But going to see Gloria Kelso and Albert O'Connor takes the bloody biscuit.'

No point in offering feeble excuses, so I didn't bother. 'Anyway, thank you for getting me out of there.'

'Don't thank me, thank Lenka Watts. She brought in the big guns.'

Which was pretty apt way of putting it.

Bloom dropped me off at the farmhouse and a guy in a suit opened the gate for us.

'Who's the welcoming committee?'

Bloom shrugged. 'Apparently Mrs Watts's brother feels you all might need security.'

Lenka was waiting at the door, beaming at me as I strolled up the driveway, then she ran out and hugged me. Brando was right behind her and he held on to me for dear life. 'Mac's here,' he announced.

I walked into the gold record room to see Mac reading a newspaper. He looked up, got slowly to his feet and opened his arms to me. 'Thank heaven,' he said. 'I thought I'd be visiting you in jail.'

'You can't get rid of me that easily,' I said, as I tentatively embraced him.

Timor Koslov had provided two security guys. Lenka was not best pleased. 'They have guns. They should not be around children,' she said. 'Mike will make Timor send them away when he gets back.'

Or when we leave. I was the one who had brought all the grief into Lenka's life, so could understand why Timor would want his sister and her children protected. Lenka might have been angry about the arrangement but I was relieved. Monica was still on the loose; we were bound to be next on her hit list, so until the police found her, we would be constantly looking over our shoulders.

I watched the guys doing the rounds during the evening and, unlike the luckless Viktor, they appeared to know the ropes. One was at the gate and the other was stationed in the garage-studio. They'd take turns on watch later. That was the usual procedure. Lenka's kids ignored the two silent strangers most of the time but Brando eyed them suspiciously.

'They're like the blokes who used to work for Dad.'

'They're more likely to be British ex-forces,' Mac countered.

'Well, I don't like them. Why do we need them?'

'Famous people often have minders,' I told Brando.

But he wasn't having any of that. 'Mike's always been famous and he never had bodyguards before. So why does he need them now?'

'Maybe because of the new album. He'll be back on top when that comes out. Lenka's brother is just taking precautions.'

Brando sniffed in disgust and fished a penknife out of his pocket.

'Where did you get that?' I asked.

'One of the guys in the band gave it to me as a present.' He held it up for me to admire. 'Look, it's got carvings on the case. I think it's cool.'

'I don't like you carrying that around.' If I'd had my way, he would still be safely in France but Lenka had taken that decision out of my hands.

Mac laughed. 'Let the lad have it. When I was a kid, we all had penknives. It's a boy thing.' He winked at Brando.

Brando grinned at me triumphantly. 'Lenka said she'd teach me how to use a shotgun.'

Over my dead body.

Mac tired easily and went to bed early. He was pale and it remained painful for him to move about. Plus, he was medicated up to the eyeballs. I was amazed that he'd made it but he told me he'd been out of bed for a couple of days already. 'They get you up and about as quickly as possible, these days.' Though the journey was bound to have taken it out of him. But Lenka said she'd make an appointment for Mac to visit her private doctor for a check-up the next day, so I felt marginally reassured. Though I wished he'd stayed in hospital instead of signing himself out and getting a taxi all the way from Norwich.

'Three hundred quid for taxi fare?' Brando's eyes widened.

'It was worth it.' Mac had said as he climbed the stairs to bed.

Once Mac was out of earshot, Brando gave me one of his sly looks. 'He must *really* love you.'

'Behave. He was worried about both of us.'

'Well, I think he loves you best.' He was smiling like some Bond villain whose master plan for world domination was finally falling into place. 'And I don't mind sharing you,' he said.

Brando's ambitions aside, ultimately we all slept easier in our beds knowing that Timor's men were keeping vigil outside.

8 a.m., Tuesday, 22 July

Lenka decided to spend the day at the golf club gym. Her three kids clamoured to go with her but Brando chose to stay with us. The security guys advised against it but she was not to be stopped. As she prepared to leave, one of them was adamant that he should be driving her.

'I take my own car,' she stormed. 'I don't need a driver.'

'Orders, ma'am,' he said forcefully and she had to relent. They drove away in her Mazda people carrier while the second bloke, having been on the early-morning watch, asked permission to take a brief nap. Lenka's insistence on leaving the house had obviously screwed up their schedule.

After breakfast, Mac and I sat by the table in the kitchen while Brando headed off into the garden to play with the puppies.

'I accept your kind offer,' Mac said.

'Brando asked you to come and stay with us in Norwich?'

'And I said yes. If that's what you'd like.'

He reached out and took my hand in his.

'Of course I would.' I felt the warming glow of his skin on mine, like a tingle of electricity. Was this a real and intense physical attraction?

'Then it's settled.'

Chapter Seventy-Seven
9 a.m., Tuesday, 22 July

For Monica, that night cooped up in her motor had been night-marish: every minute was like an hour, every movement in the trees triggered drug-fuelled hallucinations, setting off cold sweats and palpitations so intense she felt her heart might burst. She was forced to shift from lying on the back seat to sitting up when over-whelmed by the spectres invading her peripheral vision. She had barely slept with all the speed and adrenalin surging through her system. Time enough for resting when this was all over, she rea-soned, as she fought to stop grinding her teeth. Concentrate on the details. The gun had a fifteen-round magazine and she'd already used two rounds on Gloria and Swindley. The thirteen shots she had left would be plenty. Thirteen. Unlucky for some. She gave a wheezy laugh. Wasn't that the truth on a stick. Even if she had to take out that Watts bitch and all her little brats, there'd be more than enough to take care of Sam Riley and Brando once and for all.

Monica locked the car, shouldered her rucksack and headed off, her body quivering with chemically charged anticipation as she made her way through the woods towards the farmhouse. Her heart was racing as a rush of euphoria hammered its way through her veins. She felt invincible. She'd show them. She'd run the scenario over and over in her fevered imagination all night long. She'd make sure they knew exactly what was happening to them. Monica Cohen would destroy them as they had tried to destroy her. She'd fantasised about the look on Brando's face when he was told who'd had his father murdered. How would he feel about his new 'mummy' then? He'd hate her, no doubt, and Sam Riley would be devastated. This was going to be Monica's moment of triumph. She'd make them both despair and shatter their cosy relationship, leave them with no comfort, nothing to cling on to in their final moments. Then she'd kill them and walk away laughing.

As she approached the farmhouse, she could see Brando in the garden playing with two puppies. She hated dogs, yapping and shitting all over the pavements. Trust Brando to like those flea-bitten mutts. Maybe she could shoot them in front of him, watch his vile little face crumple into tears, an added moment of retribution before she did away with him. But then Sam Riley and the Watts woman would be inside, so maybe topping the dogs wasn't such a good idea. Unless she could kill all of them one at a time when they ran into the garden to see what all the noise was about – or maybe not. They could have weapons in there, though she doubted it, what with kids in the house. But you never knew. Benny had always been meticulous about hiding guns. 'You can't be too careful with a youngster around,' he'd say. 'They don't appreciate the danger.'

Well, this little shitbag was about to find out. Wasn't he just.

Monica opened the rucksack and retrieved the gun. 'Show time!' as they repeated *ad nauseam* in those cheesy nineties thrillers Benny had insisted she watch with him. With the Glock held down by her side, she walked out of the woods and into the sunlit garden. To her left was the converted barn and, as she approached it, the door opened. A man stood there, stretching and yawning. Who was this? Who gives a fuck! He saw her and instantly hurtled towards her, shielding Brando from her sightline with his body and reaching for a gun in his shoulder holster. She fired at him, three shots. One went wide but the other two hit him in the chest. He fell and she ran towards him. Standing over him, she shot him in the forehead.

Nine bullets left.

Brando dropped the puppy he was cuddling and stared at her, open-mouthed. Monica headed towards him before he could gather his wits and run. She tackled him, held him in a neck lock with her left arm and pressed the gun to his head. 'Mummy's home!'

'Fuck you!' Brando spat.

Sam Riley suddenly appeared at the French windows. There was a horror-stricken look on her face. Monica felt a surge of pure, unadulterated pleasure. All done up now, eh! But she was still a bloody ugly dyke.

'Let him go, Monica. Please don't hurt him.'

'Get back inside,' Monica snarled. 'Or I'll blow his fucking brains out.'

I walked ahead of Monica with my mind racing. I had never seen her so wired. She was twitchy and revved-up with a look in her eyes that was disturbingly close to madness. There was no knowing what she might do at this point. I had to get Brando away from her, had to distract her somehow. Mac was standing by the kitchen table. I nodded to him. He moved slowly backwards, towards the window and the front door.

'Mr Macdonald, what an unexpected pleasure,' Monica sneered.

'Murder the mother and come back for the boy. What a delight you are,' Mac muttered.

I stood by the other end of the table, keeping as great a distance as possible between Mac and myself. Monica was a good shot up-close but she'd have to move her arm in a much wider arc to hit us both. That would give at least one of us a chance to disarm her. I watched Brando's face. It was set. I couldn't detect any sign of fear. That's right, kid, keep it together.

'Speaking of murder.' Monica's mouth twitched into a manic smile and she pressed the gun harder against Brando's temple. He didn't so much as flinch. 'Shall we let this young man in on our little secret, Sam? Tell him who hired that piece of shit to do for his daddy?'

Brando stiffened and Monica tightened her grip on his neck. 'Got your interest now, haven't I, sonny boy?' She glared at me, her eyes filled with loathing. 'Tell him, or I pull the fucking trigger, now.'

I walked slowly away from the table. I was preparing to go for the door, to draw her fire to me so Brando could wriggle free of her grasp. If I took the bullet, then maybe Mac would be able to tackle her and Brando might get a chance to run.

'Stay put, or the kid gets it.' Monica laughed hysterically. 'I've always wanted to say that.'

I edged further out of her sightline. Ready to make my move.

Monica was getting twitchy. 'You fucking tell the brat who got Benny knocked off.'

'Sam hired him.' Brando's voice was steady. His left hand slid into his pocket on her blind side.

'I told him ages ago, you mad fucking bitch.' I followed Brando's lead. 'That's what mothers do. They're honest with their kids. Not that you'd know anything about that, you soulless piece of crap.' Aim the gun at me, Monica. Do it now.

'You fucking evil cunt!' Monica's full attention was back on me, her eyes ablaze with hatred.

The open penknife was in Brando's fist. His arm drew back and before Monica realised what was happening, he stabbed it into her thigh, just above her kneecap. She screamed with pain, and loosened her grip on him. Brando ducked out of the way and the gun fired, hitting the ceiling light. Shards of glass and plaster cascaded down over the kitchen. Monica's face was twisted with agony and she instinctively reached down with both hands to where the knife was up to the hilt in her leg. She dropped the gun and it skittered across the tiled floor.

Brando, having broken free, ran to Mac. I hurled myself at Monica. My shoulder connected with her chest and she went down, the penknife still protruding from her leg. I was on top of her, wanting to crush her, to wring the life out of her. She was like a wildcat, clawing and scratching at my face. I held one of her arms down with my left and punched her with my right. She was momentarily stunned. I hit her again and again in the face, oblivious to the pain in my fist as it connected with bone.

'Enough!' Mac shouted at me. 'Let the police deal with her.'

Monica appeared to be unconscious. I got off her, bent down and yanked the knife out of her thigh. A fountain of blood pulsed out.

'Let the bitch bleed to death.'

'We can't do that, Sam.' Mac was already on the phone. 'Emergency services? We need an ambulance and police—'

'No!' Brando yelled. I turned to see Monica on the floor crawling towards the gun that had landed under the table. I reached for it but her hand found it first. I got a grip on the barrel and twisted it inwards in her grasp but she already had her finger on the trigger. Her eyes were wide with terror as the muzzle dug into the skin beneath her jaw.

Bang!

Chapter Seventy-Nine
11 a.m., Tuesday, 22 July

'Died instantly,' the paramedic told the police just before the ambulance took away what remained of Monica Cohen.

The bodyguard hadn't fared well either; he too was dead. Apparently he and his partner had tossed a coin for who should catch some sleep and who would drive Lenka and the kids to the golf club. The dead guy had won.

I sat with Brando while he gave his statement to the police; he was polite and calmly in control, despite everything. I had lied to Monica. I hadn't breathed a word to Brando about my connections to Joe Murphy. I'd lived in constant fear of Brando finding out and now he knew. Had he figured it out for himself or had Monica's taunting alerted him to the truth? Not that it mattered very much. My emotions were in turmoil. I would have to talk to him about his dad's murder and the very thought of it had me all twisted up inside. And Mac? He was sitting alone in the corner of the gold record room, deep in thought, and I was too fearful of his rejection to approach him.

I recalled something that Lenka had said to me just a few days before: 'Some people have clean hands but dirty soul. You have dirty hands but clean soul, I think.' I only hoped that Mac would see it that way too.

⌣

After the police had gone, Brando raided the fruit bowl and was getting stuck into an apple when I found him back in the garden with the pups. He turned towards me.

'Can we get a dog when we move to the house in Norwich?'

'If that's what you want.'

'Dogs are the best.'

Yeah, they love you for who you are and they don't plot to murder your father. 'I need to talk to you about your dad.'

'He had cancer.' Brando had a pup in his arms and was stroking her.

'How did you find out?'

He gave me a knowing look.

'Listening at doors?' I suggested.

Brando nodded. 'Dad was scared of the cancer. I heard him tell *her* that he didn't want to waste away.'

I had a lump in my throat and felt my eyes welling up. Adults are supposed to know what to say in circumstances like this, but I didn't have a clue. I just stood there with salty tears pouring down my face.

'I used to watch Western movies with Dad,' Brando continued. 'When someone got killed he'd say "they died with their boots on". He was like that, wasn't he? He died with his boots on.'

He remained silent for a moment then put the puppy down gently. He took three steps forward and hugged me tight. 'Don't cry, Sam. You and Mac are my family now.'

'You've got that right, son.' Mac's voice came from inside the French windows and moments later he stepped out into the sunshine. I looked up at him and he gave me a weary smile.

'Even after all that's happened?' Now that all my secrets are out in the open, you can see me for what I really am.

Mac came over to us and wrapped his arms around Brando and me.

'Nobody's perfect,' he whispered.

Acknowledgements

I'd like to say thank you to all the fine folk who have helped me
along the way.

Let's start with those who supplied technical info on everything
from gunshot wounds and medical aid to the legal system, prisons,
police procedure, guns, ballistics and specialist knowledge on how
to deal with close physical danger. I am so lucky to have such valuable friends as Janet Read, Mary Bernardi Edelson, Chris Duffin,
Liz and John Yardley, Ken Walters and Brian Thompson. I took on
board all you taught me and if I've made any glaring mistakes then
that is all down to me.

Then there are those who believed in this story enough for
it to be published, so thank you to my lovely agent, Caroline
Montgomery, Jane Snelgrove at Amazon Publishing and Sarah
Odedina; it has been a pleasure to work with you all.

Special thanks also go to Les Edgerton for all his encourage-
ment and never, ever forgetting my partner and first editor, Ian
Jackson. I could never have done this without you.

About the Author

Lesley Welsh was born in Strawberry Field children's home and raised on a notorious Liverpool council estate. Later she moved to London, where she studied English and drama and worked as a freelance writer specialising in alternative lifestyles. Her articles appeared in *Cosmopolitan*, *Marie Claire*, *Red*, *Bite*, *Forum*, *Time Out* and many others before she established Moondance Media, a magazine publishing company. Her dark and compelling short story *Mrs Webster's Obsession* was turned into a film. She now lives and works in Spain.

March 27 2018
mmY.
CT

Lun
mar 11 8